Number one internationally bestselling author Dervla McTiernan is the critically acclaimed author of five novels, including *The Murder Rule*, which was a *New York Times* thriller of the year. Dervla has won multiple prizes, including a Ned Kelly Award, Davitt Awards, a Barry Award, and an International Thriller Writers Award. Dervla is also the author of four novellas, and her audio novella, *The Sisters*, was a four-week number one bestseller in the United States. She lives in Australia with her family.

Also by Dervla McTiernan

Novels
The Rúin
The Scholar
The Good Turn
The Murder Rule

And the Novellas
The Roommate
The Sisters
The Wrong One
The Fireground

WHAT HAPPENED TO NINA?

DERVLA McTIERNAN

HarperCollins*Publishers*

HarperCollins*Publishers*
Australia • Brazil • Canada • France • Germany • Holland • India
Italy • Japan • Mexico • New Zealand • Poland • Spain • Sweden
Switzerland • United Kingdom • United States of America

HarperCollins acknowledges the Traditional Custodians
of the land upon which we live and work, and pays respect
to Elders past and present.

First published on Gadigal Country in Australia in 2024
by HarperCollins*Publishers* Australia Pty Limited
ABN 36 009 913 517
harpercollins.com.au

A catalogue record for this book is available from the National Library of Australia

ISBN 978 1 4607 6014 7 (paperback)
ISBN 978 1 4607 1355 6 (ebook)
ISBN 978 1 4607 4712 4 (audiobook)

Cover design by HarperCollins Design Studio, based on jacket design by Brian Moore
Cover images © Joelynne Johnson/Getty Images
Author photograph by Julia Dunin Photography
Internal design by Michele Cameron
Printed and bound in Australia by McPherson's Printing Group

MIX
Paper | Supporting
responsible forestry
FSC® C001695

For Kenny, Freya, and Oisín. Always.

"A mother's love for her child is like nothing else in the world. It knows no law, no pity. It dares all things and crushes down remorselessly all that stands in its path."

—Agatha Christie, "The Last Séance"

PROLOGUE

My name is Nina Fraser. There's a good chance that you know who I am. You've probably seen my picture online, and heard my story, and if you have I guess you've already judged me. I mean, not in public, because victim-blaming is a bad look, but in the privacy of your own head, some quiet part of you probably thinks I was stupid or weak or both. Maybe you think that if I'd just stood up for myself, if I'd just walked away, everything would have been okay. I'm not going to argue with you or try to convince you that you're wrong. I just want to say, a thing can be crystal clear with hindsight, but just about as clear as mud when you're actually living it. Also, sometimes it's the walking away that gets you in trouble.

So. Like I said, I'm Nina. I'm twenty years old. I have a sister, Grace, and two parents. And I'm a climber. You know all of that already if you've read my story online. Here's some stuff people don't know. I have calluses on my fingertips, a scar on my knee, and another on my elbow, both from falls. I love to climb. When I am on the mountain, I can't think about anything except my fingers wedged into a crevasse and my feet balanced just so and the route ahead. I never think about what lies beneath me. When I reach the top I sit and I breathe and I look out over the valley. I look back over the route and I work out how I could have climbed it better.

If you know anything, you know that I have a boyfriend named Simon Jordan. Simon and I met in school when we were five years old.

In middle school we became friends. When we were sixteen we fell in love. It's important to me that you know that it was really good between us. I won't say that Simon was perfect, because no one on this earth is perfect, but if there were such a thing as a perfect first boyfriend for an awkward girl who did not know who she was, then he was that. He laughed at my jokes. He was always interested in what I had to say, even when his friends were around. He never played games, never made me feel like some other girl was better. With him I felt pretty, which matters, way too much, when you're sixteen. We slept together for the first time on his eighteen birthday, and it was awkward and a little painful but also funny and beautiful and I was sure, down to my bones, that I would never love anyone the way I loved him. After things started to go wrong, I spent a lot of time thinking about the way we used to be. I looked at our old photos and spent time with friends who had known us from the beginning. I needed to believe that I hadn't imagined everything. That I was holding on for something real.

When we finished high school, Simon went to Northwestern and I stayed at home in Waitsfield and went to UVM. Simon and I didn't think the long-distance thing would be a problem for us. We were solid. And the first year was okay. We came home a lot, and we Face-Timed every day, sometimes two or three times a day, and we emailed. My friend Allie told me that it couldn't last. She said Simon was too good looking, plus his parents were loaded. He'd meet a hundred girls who wanted him, a hundred girls who were more sophisticated, more experienced, and more exciting than the girl next door. Allie can be a bitch like that. I didn't want Simon to dump me, but I'm the kind of person who likes to prepare for the worst, so I put a lot of mental energy into getting ready for the inevitable. I studied hard, and tried to make new friends, and went climbing pretty much every weekend, and I kept waiting for the ax to fall.

But instead of dumping me, Simon just seemed to get more intense. Instead of calling me a couple of times a day, he started calling four or five times. Sometimes he wanted me to "carry him around in my pocket." Which meant FaceTiming him and then muting my phone and taking him with me to lectures or just propping the phone beside me on my desk while I was studying. Simon came home every other weekend, and he wanted to pay so that I could fly out to Illinois to see him too, but I couldn't do that. I had to work in my mom's inn on the weekends. Also, taking his money and spending it like it was mine would have felt weird. He didn't understand. He was really angry and really upset.

Looking back, I can see that that was when our relationship started to change. After I said no to coming to Illinois, Simon had a permanent attitude. Like he had the moral high ground. Like he was the perfect boyfriend and I was the bad, unreliable girlfriend. He made jokes about it, but I could see that behind the jokes his feelings were hurt, so I did everything I could to reassure him. Nothing seemed to be enough. He was rougher with me, in bed and out of it. He would grip my shoulders or hips so hard that I had bruises—purple finger marks on my skin. He bit me, a few times. It really hurt, but I didn't tell him to stop. This is going to sound insane, but I was worried about embarrassing him. I figured that he thought it was sexy or something (it so wasn't), and because everything was weird between us I was afraid that if I told him I hated the biting, that would hurt his feelings too. I told myself that Simon was just going through an insecure stage, that I knew the real him and that we'd get back there again if I could just make him understand how much I loved him. I was stupid, but then, I was a lobster in a pot. The water warmed up so gradually that I didn't realize I was boiling until it was too late.

Simon came home for the October vacation during our sophomore year. He'd wanted to go to Hawaii with friends, and I had to stay home to work, so he came home too, but he was really angry about it. Nothing I did seemed to make him happy, until I finally agreed to blow off work at my mom's inn and take off for the whole week with him. I called my mom and of course she was upset and angry, but Simon seemed to finally be himself again and the relief of that was so intense.

I hadn't realized how much I was stressing about us until I thought I could stop.

Simon's parents had just bought a new house near Stowe. It came with four hundred acres, a small lake, unmarked trails, and climbing routes. He wanted us to go there, just the two of us, to really focus on our relationship. So we went. We hiked and climbed and walked and talked and things really weren't any better. I felt like we were faking things. Pretending to be close but not really. I wanted to talk to him about the bruises and the hurting, but every time I tried my throat closed up. On Friday, Simon wanted to go climbing again. My body was complaining. My fingers were sore, and my right shoulder was hot. I felt like I needed a rest day, but I said yes anyway.

"Let's climb that crag we saw on Wednesday," Simon said. We were eating breakfast. He reached over and smoothed my hair back, tucking it behind my ear. He cupped his hand around the back of my neck. His hand was warm and dry and gentle. For some reason I wanted to cry.

"Sure," I said. "That looked good."

We ate, we dressed, and we hiked out. It was a short hike to the crag. Simon chatted the whole way there, and I smiled and answered and took his hand when he offered it, but I had tears just under the surface the whole way. I hated feeling like that, and I tried to shake it off. I started to cheer up when we got to the crag. It really did look like an awesome climb, maybe eighty feet of granite, with some nice holds at the beginning to get us started. And the weather was good. It was chilly but sunny, and there was no real wind. I dropped my pack and started to take out my gear.

"This was such a great idea," I said. "I'm so glad we're here."

"Better than cleaning another bathroom?" He gave me a little jokey shove that set me off balance.

"Understatement," I said. He picked me up, put his hands on my butt, and pulled me in close. He kissed me. I kissed him back. The messed-up thing is that the kiss felt good. Simon let me go, and we both did our prep and started our climb. I didn't think about us as I climbed. I just zoned out and thought about my holds and my route and I started to feel like me again. I felt stronger.

We got to the top, sat on the edge, and took in the view.

"You okay?" Simon asked.

"Sure. Yes. A little tired. Hungry too." I searched in my pack for the sandwiches I'd made that morning. They were chicken salad, which was his favorite. He unwrapped the sandwich, took a couple of bites, made a face, and handed it back to me.

"Think the chicken might be off, babe. Got any chocolate?"

I had chocolate. I handed him a bar, silently. He ate it. There was nothing wrong with the chicken salad. I'd cooked the chicken myself the day before and made up the salad with all fresh ingredients. I started to feel pissed. A small ball of fuck-you showed up at the bottom of my stomach. I kept eating my sandwich.

"You can't eat that," he said. "You need to throw it away."

"It's fine."

He stared at me. "Okay, but when you're puking tonight don't call me to hold your hair."

I shrugged. His shoulders stiffened, and he turned away from me. Which was my cue to pack up the sandwich, to say sorry and kiss him and thank him for looking out for me. But no. The fuck-you wasn't going anywhere. In fact, it was starting to grow.

"It tastes good, actually. Mmm." I thought he might lose it. Maybe I wanted him to. But he just stood up.

"I need to take a piss." He walked away and took a leak up against a tree. I finished my sandwich and packed everything up in my bag again. Simon started to prepare for the rappel down.

"Let's simul-rap," he said. He had a gleam in his eyes. A challenge. Simultaneous rappelling is when two climbers use one rope to rappel, relying on each other's body weight, with the single rope rigged through a central rappel anchor. It can be dangerous if one climber loses focus or control, but people do it sometimes if they want to get down quickly. We weren't in any rush. We had the whole afternoon to make our descent, and I could have just said that, but I saw that challenge in his eyes and I didn't feel like backing down.

"Fine." I tied on, then tied my stopper knot, which would make sure that my end of the rope couldn't slip through my gear, always the worst-case scenario with this kind of rappelling. If the rope slipped through my gear it would also slip through the rappel anchor, which would mean that Simon would fall. I watched him prep.

"Did you tie your stopper knot?" I asked.

"Of course," Simon said mildly. He showed it to me.

We started down. It wasn't fun. Simon's progress was jerky and unpredictable, which meant that, on the other end of the rope, mine was too. He was doing it on purpose. I gritted my teeth. Decided that I was done pretending that things were okay. When we got to the bottom we were going to get everything out in the open. The rappel didn't take that long. Half an hour, maybe, including the time we needed to detach our gear as we progressed. Simon reached the bottom first. I had about twenty-five feet left to descend. I kicked off, landed, and bounced lightly off the wall, letting the rope slip through my gear. I pushed off again, the rope slipped through, and then it happened. The rope went slack. Completely slack. I had nothing to hold on to. I was falling.

It's the most sickening thing in the world, losing the support of your rope. It had happened to me only once before, in a rock-climbing center in Boston, when an auto-belay apparatus failed. But that was indoors, and I'd only been about five feet up, and there'd been foam mats below me. This was different. I just . . . fell. There was no scrambling, no grabbing for a tree branch or an outcropping. There was nothing to reach out for but air. I fell, I think, maybe ten feet. Not far, but far enough. I landed on my back, on dirt. There were rocks either side of me. Any one of them would have broken my back if I'd landed a foot to my left or right. My head hit the ground hard. I was wearing a helmet, which saved me, I guess, but I still blacked out for a minute. When I woke up, I couldn't feel my body, which must have been shock, and then the pain came flooding in and with it the need to vomit. I couldn't roll to my side. My body wouldn't obey me. I was sure that I was going to choke, and then Simon was there.

"Oh my God! Nina. Jesus."

He turned me onto my side, one hand supporting my neck the whole way. I vomited up my chicken sandwich. When I was done, he rolled me back and ran his hands down my shoulders and arms, and my legs down to my feet.

"Are you okay? Is anything broken?"

I tried to take a mental inventory. Everything hurt. Had I broken anything? Maybe some ribs. My ribs were on fire. I tried to move my legs. They responded. I clenched my fists. That worked too.

"I think I'm okay."

"Don't get up," he said. "Don't even think about it. My God. What the hell were you thinking? You just let go. Did you think you were down already?"

I hadn't let go. Had I let go?

"Can I roll you back on your side again? I want to check your back, that you didn't land on anything."

I said okay, and Simon rolled me. His hands were very gentle, but everywhere he touched hurt.

"Jesus, the back of your helmet is completely fucked. It's cracked right across. Good thing you were wearing it."

I started to cry, though it was a weak sort of noise, a kind of whimper. I was too sore for howling. Simon rolled me over again and took off my shoes and my helmet. He gave me orders—wriggle my toes, my fingers, touch my nose, follow his finger. He was completely confident, like he knew exactly what he was doing, and I did everything he told me to do. At last, he sat back.

"I think you're going to be all right. You got so lucky. You scared me. You really did." He asked me to sit up, and I did. He packed away my climbing shoes and put my boots back on my feet and laced them up tightly. He picked me up off the ground and asked me to try standing. I was sore and shaky, but I could do it. He picked up both packs, took my hand, and led me away from the crag. I think I was still in shock. The pain in my ribs and head was pretty bad, but I just held on to Simon's hand and kept limping along while he chatted and made soothing noises. His mood had changed completely. He was . . . cheery. At the house he brought me upstairs, helped me undress, and tucked me into bed. He brought me painkillers and water and kissed my forehead and told me we would have to go to the doctor the next day but for now it would be better to rest.

"Thank you," I said. "I'm really sorry."

"I'm just glad you're okay." He leaned down to kiss me and then he left the room. And left me with something to think about. When he'd leaned down, I'd caught his eye, and in it I'd seen not concern, but . . . pleasure? Just a tiny hint of joy? Or triumph? I couldn't nail it down.

I rubbed at my forehead with my left hand. With my right I cradled my sore ribs. What had happened on the mountain? I hadn't let go of the rope. For sure, I hadn't. Could the rappel anchor have given? Yes, a possibility, but hadn't I seen the rope, hanging slack but still suspended, from my place on the ground? So the anchor couldn't have given. The only other explanation was that Simon had completed his rappel, then let the rope go from his end. He would have had to untie his stopper knot first. It couldn't have been a mistake. Could he have done it on purpose? Had he wanted me to fall? I told myself that was ridiculous. I told myself that I was being crazy and *of course* Simon hadn't done that, would never do that, would have no *reason* to do that. But it was like I was going through the motions in the privacy of my own head, for no one's benefit. Because I knew, for sure, that he had.

I got out of bed and went to the bathroom. I took off my top and looked in the mirror. There were marks on my body, old and new. A lot of them. Bruises on my shoulders. A bite mark on my left breast. I pushed my pants down. The bruise on my hip was yellowing. I turned, twisting to look over my shoulder. My back was a mess of black and blue. There was blood too, from a new cut on my shoulder blade that I hadn't even felt.

I put my top back on and walked back to the bed. I sat there for a long time, looking down at my toes. I thought I had a decision to make, but when I sat down I realized the decision had already been made. All that remained was to decide how to do it. I searched for the fuck-you deep in my stomach, found it, and fed it. I wanted to be angry. For months, for half a year, he'd made me dance around, trying so hard to please him, trying so hard not to upset him. He'd *wanted* me to be afraid, and I was done with that. I started to get dressed. I put on my jeans and my boots and my sweater. I tied my hair back. I took my clothes from the wardrobe and my toiletries from the bathroom. I packed my bag. And then I went downstairs to tell Simon that we were over and that I never wanted to see him again.

CHAPTER ONE

Leanne

On Sunday afternoon, I went to find Andy in the barn. He's not supposed to work on Sunday. We'd made an agreement that we would take at least one day of the week for family, but since I hadn't even come close to sticking to that promise, I couldn't really give him a hard time about it. I could hear the chain saw going as I crossed the courtyard. There are two doors to the barn. The double doors at the far end, which Andy uses to drive in his mini excavator and dump truck to get them out of the weather, and a small side door that Andy put in a couple of years ago. I went to the side door and pushed it open. Andy was hard at work, cutting a log down into firewood. He was wearing ear protectors, and his back was to me. I decided to wait, rather than tap him on the shoulder while he was operating the saw. I sat on a stool, breathed in the smell of sawdust, which I love, and waited.

Five years ago I applied for a barn-preservation grant from the State of Vermont. The frame of the building is red oak, and that's always been pretty solid, but the roof and sidings and floor were all in bad shape. Andy used the grant money to replace the roof and the sidings and to put down a brick floor. I love the barn. I love that it's open right up to the rafters and I love the way the light comes in through the small windows. I love the smells of machine oil and cut timber, and the way everything in it is so neatly lined up and organized, from the bags of fertilizer and peat moss to the pallets with landscaping stone and the stack of railroad ties in the corner.

Eventually, Andy turned off the saw. He pushed back his ear protectors and started stacking the wood.

"You need some help with that?" I asked. I'd startled him, and he jumped a little. "Nina still hasn't called me back," I said. I had my phone in my hand. I looked down at the screen, as if it might show something new. "I called her twice this morning. Both times it went through to voice mail. I sent her a text and nada."

Andy returned his ear protectors and the chain saw to his tool bench. He checked his watch, took off his work gloves, and leaned against the wall opposite me.

"Well, Lee, she's probably pissed. And I guess, maybe, she's returning the favor."

He was referring to the fact that Nina had called me three times that past week, and I'd been so mad at her that I hadn't answered or returned any of her calls.

"Seriously?"

He shook his head.

"Andy, come on. She was completely out of line."

"Not saying she wasn't."

"It sounds like that's exactly what you're saying."

He smiled. One of those slow smiles that tug right at the center of my stomach. He crossed over to me, took my hand, and pulled me up to standing.

"She was supposed to be back yesterday," I said. "She said she'd be here by nine A.M. at the latest."

"College don't start until Tuesday. My guess is she'll come home tomorrow."

Andy had a stronger accent than I had. He still flattened some of his vowels and swallowed his *t*'s in the Vermont way. "Until" became "Un-ill" in his mouth. I used to have the same accent, but a little more than a year in college in Boston had been enough time for me to shed my heritage like it was a bad smell, and I'd never been able to get it back. I liked Andy's accent. It was a sign of his character, that he didn't feel the need to change for anyone.

"You want me to pick up Grace?" he asked.

I'd completely forgotten about picking up Grace. Our younger daughter. Fifteen years old and horse crazy. After eight years of regular begging and pleading, we'd finally given in and bought her a seven-year-old quarter horse named Charlie. The plan was that we would build a stable at one end of the barn and clear some trees for a paddock. In the meantime, Charlie was stabled at Grace's friend Molly's house, which meant that Grace now spent all her time there and the only time we saw her was when we were picking her up or dropping her off.

"I forgot," I said. Andy wrapped his hand around the back of my neck. His hand was warm and comforting. He stroked the back of my head with his thumb.

"Don't worry about it. Stop worrying, period. Nina's fine. Simon would have called us if she wasn't."

He took his jacket from a hook on the wall. I followed him out of the barn, across the courtyard, and into the kitchen. Our dog, Rufus, was half-asleep on his bed near the stove. He looked up hopefully when we came in. Rufus is nearly ten now, and slowing down, but he loves a walk.

"Andy?"

"Hmm?"

"Do you think I've been too hard on her? I mean, generally speaking. Do you think I expect too much of her?"

Andy thought about it. "Maybe, a little. She's a good girl. She deserves to have some fun."

"Okay, but she left me completely high and dry. It's not like I can call around and get someone else at the last minute. It doesn't work like that, and she knows it. So I had to do my work and Nina's work too, while she's off having fun with her boyfriend."

"That's true."

"Andy . . ." He turned to look at me. "Which is it?"

"It's both. Nina was out of line to blow off her work, and maybe, sometimes, you're a little hard on her." He kissed me briefly on the mouth, found his keys, and left.

I made coffee and took a mug into the living room. The fire had burned a little low, so I added some wood, then I sat on the couch with Rufus curled up at my feet. I opened Instagram and went to Nina's account. She hadn't posted anything new since Thursday. Her last post was a close-up of a red-bellied woodpecker sitting on a branch, head turned to the camera. The one before that was a picture of Nina and Simon together, in climbing gear, on the top of a cliff with deep green forest in the background. They had their arms wrapped around each other and they were grinning.

I put my phone away, picked up the TV remote, and found a season of *Love Is Blind* that I hadn't seen yet. I turned on the first episode, then spaced out completely during the intro. I took out my phone again, opened Nina's Instagram, and liked two of her recent posts. There. She'd see that and know that I wanted to be friends, and she'd call me. The thing about Nina is that she doesn't hold grudges. Also, she's a hard worker. It really wasn't like her to blow off work.

The thought had been nagging at me. Nina had been two years old when I bought the inn. Back then, the only reason I was able to afford the place was because the roof had a huge hole in it, and because the plumbing didn't work. Also because the previous occupant had been a hoarder and the realtor had been so grossed out by the place that he'd taken the first, lowball offer, which had happened to be mine. Even at two years old, Nina had been a tough little girl. It had taken me months of hard work to clean the place out, scrub it, paint it, and make it habitable. I didn't have the money to pay for childcare, and I didn't have family to help, so Nina came with me, every single day. Every day I'd give her some little task to do, to keep her occupied, and she took it all so seriously. She wore her overalls and her little headscarf, and she ran around the place with her small broom or scrubbed at the stone steps with her scrubber. She was always so proud of herself for helping me. When she finished, she'd lean back and press her hands into her lower back and survey her work, like she was a tiny grown-up. And that attitude had never changed. Grace hated working in the inn. She did everything she could to wriggle out of even the small commitments she made. Whereas when Nina said yes, she showed up and followed through.

Andy was right. I must have pushed her way too hard. She was a sophomore now. Maybe she needed more time to study. Maybe we could make some changes. We could look at hiring someone to lighten the load. Not full time, but a few hours would make a difference. I'd talk to Nina about it.

After she apologized.

By the time Andy and Grace got in, I was half-asleep. It used to be that Grace came straight to me for a hug if we'd been apart for any length of time. Sometime in the last couple of years that had stopped. I knew that new distance was a necessary part of Grace's growing up, and mostly I respected that, but sometimes you just need a hug. I got up from the couch and went to her. I kissed her head; her hair smelled like sweat and horses.

"Did you have a good time?" I said.

"The best." She pulled away. "I'm so tired I might die. And I'm starving. What's for dinner?"

"Leftovers." Her answering groan was predictable. I started to follow her to the kitchen. There was plenty of food in the fridge, but if I didn't put something together for her she'd eat cereal and chips. Andy was leaning in the living room doorway. He put out his hand to stop me before I could leave the room.

"Got a minute?"

His tone was serious.

"Sure." I called after Grace, "No cereal, okay? There's lasagna in the fridge. Warm it up."

Grace waved a hand at me over her shoulder. She took out her phone and started to play music through the kitchen speaker. Dua Lipa. "Levitating."

Andy pulled me back into the living room and closed the door quietly.

"What's up?" I asked.

"I had to go down there to the gas station to fill up before I picked up Grace. I got talking to Patrick."

Patrick worked at the gas station, and he was a talker. He saw it as his duty to gather up every bit of information about everyone who lived nearby, from Waitsfield to Warren, and pass it on.

"Patrick says that Simon came back from Stowe on Friday night. He's been home for two days. Patrick says that Simon came home alone."

"Simon came home alone. What does that mean?"

Andy shook his head.

"What are you thinking? That she's gone off somewhere else? With friends?" My anger, which had pretty much dissipated, bloomed again. My phone was on the coffee table. Andy leaned down, picked it up, and offered it to me.

"Call her," he said.

"I've called her twice already. And messaged her."

"Try her again."

I dialed the number. It went straight to voice mail. I held the phone up so that Andy could hear Nina's bright, breezy voice telling me to leave a message, then I brought the phone back to my ear.

"Nina, call me." My voice was sharp. I tried to think of something else to say but everything that came to mind was angry. Andy was leaning against the wall, his arms crossed, watching me with serious eyes. I ended the call.

"What?" I said.

"I don't like this."

"I'm hardly ecstatic about it myself. You've got to be kidding me. Where did she go now? New York City, for a shopping trip? Or no, Paris, perhaps."

"Leanne."

"What?"

"Maybe we should go over there, to the Jordans' place," Andy said. "Drop by and make sure she's okay."

The tone of his voice slowed me down. It was calm, steady, and sensible, because that was Andy. But there was something else that was less normal for him—a small hint of worry.

"Don't you think that's a little over the top?"

He shrugged. "Maybe. Maybe not. They're only ten minutes away."

"I could just call her. Jamie, I mean." I didn't want to call her. Jamie Jordan didn't like me, and she seemed to enjoy making that very clear. I didn't care what other people thought about me. I wasn't a particularly social person. I had my home, my family, and my business, and I didn't need anything else. But Jamie had finely honed the art of making people feel off balance, and I wasn't completely immune. I called her number. It went through to voice mail.

"Jamie. Hi. It's . . . uh . . . It's Leanne Fraser here. I'm just calling because we haven't heard from Nina." I laughed, and hated that I sounded nervous. Ingratiating. "I just wondered if she's with you, by any chance. Or if you've heard from Simon. I'm sure everything's fine, but if you could give me a call and fill me in, I'd feel a lot better. Thanks, Jamie. I owe you one!" I finished brightly, like she and I were just the best of buddies. I ended the call and looked at Andy.

"Let's go over there," he said.

We left Grace at home. Andy drove, and we didn't talk much. I wasn't worried about Nina, not really, but I could feel his tension, and it bothered me. I shifted in my seat. The Jordans' house was on Sharpshooter Road. Simon's father, Rory, owned a precision-tool-machining company that supplied pharmaceutical companies and other high-tech businesses. He'd had help getting started. His own father had had a small custom-tool-machining business. Then Rory had gone to college to study industrial engineering, and he'd come home with ideas. Brilliant ideas, which he'd turned into profit-churning machines. These days the company was worth fifty or sixty million, if you believed the rumors. I'd met Rory many times over the years, at school events, but I'd never warmed to him. He was clever but cold. He could also be ostentatious. The Jordans' house was very large, easily four times the size of the inn. It was set well back from the road and protected by a wall and a cast-iron gate, neither of which are remotely necessary in this part of Vermont, where most people still leave their doors unlocked and wouldn't think twice about leaving their keys in their car.

Andy pressed the intercom button on the gatepost. After a moment, the gate swung open. We drove slowly up to the house. It was a modern building, low slung and vast, with contemporary timber and concrete sidings and minimalist landscaping. From the front, it was like a fortress. The entrance door was solid timber and oversized, and the windows to the front were slim, almost like arrow slits in an old castle. I'd been in the house only once, for a party the Jordans threw for Simon's high school graduation. I knew that inside the house the fortress feeling fell away quickly and the low-slung look was misleading. From the front door you stepped down into the building, through a series of terrace-like entrance spaces. The ceilings in the main living areas were so high that the house felt light and airy, and there were vast floor-to-ceiling windows overlooking the rear of the property, offering incredible views of Camel's Hump. A lot of wealthy people build second homes in this part of Vermont, so we have more than our share of luxury properties, but the Jordans' place was on another level.

When we pulled up in front of the house there were no cars parked out front, but the house has a six-car garage, so that didn't tell me much of anything. Andy hung back a little as we approached the door. I rang the doorbell. We heard footsteps coming from inside and saw a shadow approaching on the other side of the glass. Jamie opened the door. She was barefoot, dressed in blue jeans and a pink blouse, open at the throat to display a light tan and a gold necklace with a round medallion. She looked, as she always did, very pretty. Jamie had the kind of body that no woman over forty has without obsessive focus and absolute discipline. Very thin, and toned to perfection. Her toenails were painted neon yellow, and her hair and makeup were perfect. She looked like she'd just walked off the set of *Selling Sunset*. She looked at *me* like she'd never seen me before. Suddenly I felt like we'd overreacted.

"I'm sorry to bother you, Jamie. I hope we haven't interrupted your dinner?"

She raised one perfectly groomed eyebrow, folded her arms, and said nothing. Even by Jamie's standards, this was rude.

"I'm looking for Nina," I said, a little more abruptly. "Is she here?"

"Why would Nina be here?"

"She told me that she and Simon would be home on Saturday. Yesterday. And I haven't heard from her. I've been calling, but . . ." I let my voice trail off. "Look, Patrick at the gas station said that Simon came home from Stowe already. Is that right? Is he home?"

Jamie let out an impatient sigh. "Simon and Nina broke up. She's not here."

My mouth fell open. I searched for words.

"If she's not with Simon, where is she?" said Andy.

"I don't know. Probably with her other boyfriend. Now, if you don't mind, we're eating dinner. I'm going to have to say good night."

Before either of us could react, Jamie Jordan closed the door in our faces.

I looked at Andy. I could feel my cheeks flushing with anger. "Other boyfriend?"

Andy shook his head. I stepped forward and rang the doorbell again. I leaned on it hard and long. A minute passed, and the door opened again. This time it was Rory Jordan. Six foot three. Handsome despite his broken nose. He didn't look angry. He looked sympathetic.

"Folks," he said. He held his hand out to Andy. It sat there for a second, until Andy took it and shook. "Jamie tells me you're worried about your girl?"

"She was due home yesterday," I said. "We've been calling, but—"

"I'm sorry to hear that," Rory cut across me, shaking his head. "Sorry we can't be more help. But like Jamie told you, the kids broke up. Bound to happen, they're so young. Simon's all cut up about it, to tell you the truth. I'm not sure it was his idea, you understand? But he hasn't spoken to Nina since Friday. They broke up, so he came home. Wish I could be more help, but that's all we know."

I felt so stupid in the face of his confidence. I was a terrible mother. Nina and Simon had broken up and I hadn't even known about it. She hadn't called me. *She'd* broken up with *him*? But she loved him. Talked about him all the time. Structured her whole life around him. This didn't make sense.

"It's not like Nina not to call her mother," Andy said. "You sure Simon don't know where she is?"

"I'm sorry," Rory said, firmly. Then he waited for us to leave.

"Thank you," I said, mechanically. "We'll call her again."

"Tell her we wish her all the best," Rory said. And he closed the door.

CHAPTER TWO

Jamie

I didn't see Simon on Saturday, because I was in Boston. I drove down on Friday night and I stayed over. Every three months I go to see Dr. Jason Marque, who is a genius with a needle. Botox and fillers are an absolute gift, but only in the hands of a true artist, so I'm very careful about who I let touch my face. My husband is fifty-seven years old. He doesn't want a wife with frozen, puffy-lipped Instagram face. He wants natural beauty, and natural beauty takes tiny, careful, regular tweaks by exactly the right person. I had a little Botox and the teeniest bit of lip filler on Saturday morning, did some clothes shopping, and drove home. I got in late.

On Sunday morning, I was up before Simon and Rory. I did my yoga practice, had breakfast, and then went to my walk-in closet. I had to plan my outfit for a gala dinner we were attending in Washington. The dinner was a fundraiser for David Garvey, a Vermonter who was running for Senate, and our table had cost Rory twenty thousand dollars. He was happy to pay the money. Rory could be generous with political and charitable donations, as long as they delivered a return that he thought was worthwhile. Political fundraisers qualified because they offered access. Charitable causes qualified if they delivered column inches in the right newspaper. Rory's philosophy was that the best way to succeed in business was to produce something of real value, something that couldn't be easily copied or replicated.

He said that to survive in business you needed to be smart and capable and willing to work hard. But to thrive, you also needed status, reputation, and connections. Events like the dinner mattered to my husband, so I would choose my clothes with extra care. He would expect me to get it exactly right. I couldn't be too sexy, or I'd look like a twenty-something on the hunt for a man, but if I turned up looking like Claire Underwood from *House of Cards*, that wouldn't cut it either. Robin Wright is a beautiful woman, but in that show she was all about power, and that is not Rory's thing. He likes a woman to be feminine.

Getting clothes right is harder than it seems. I have to look pretty, but not girly. Sexy, but not obvious. Sophisticated, but not boring. And I can't wear anything twice, because the pictures will be on social media at least, and possibly in some online publication. Rory's not tight with money, but he *is* careful, and I used to worry about the cost of my clothes, until I realized that clothing and grooming was the one area of my spending that Rory didn't monitor at all. He wanted me to look good. He liked it if we were at a party or a weekend away and the other women made a fuss about my Valentino minidress or my Tom Ford bomber jacket. So I stopped worrying and started spending more. A lot more.

What Rory doesn't know is that I sell my clothes after I've worn them. He also doesn't know that I replace my most expensive handbags with very good knockoffs, made to order by a guy I know in New York, and that I sell the originals. I've gotten pretty good at it, actually. I use two different apps, and I take beautiful photographs, and I've built up quite a following online. Most of my stuff is snapped up in days. Obviously, I make sure to stay anonymous. Just that morning I'd accepted an offer on my Celine glitter jacket for twelve thousand dollars, and an offer of five for my Prada leather lace-ups. I set myself a target of thirty thousand dollars a month, but most months I do better.

I don't sell my clothes out of any sense of frugality, by the way. I do it to save my own ass. I started my little project just over five years ago, when Rory's friend Tony Webster exchanged his second wife, Sally, for a newer model. Literally, a newer model. Before she'd married Tony, Sally had been on the cover of *Vogue*, and post-babies she was still willowy and gorgeous, but willowy and gorgeous can't compete with *young*. Not if your husband is Tony Webster, an insecure little tooth-pick of a man who has to surround himself with trophies to make up for his lack of personality. Sally was very sweet and completely clue-less and never saw it coming. They had a prenup, of course, and their kids were grown, and she got nothing from the divorce. Last I heard she was back living with her parents in Wyoming.

Sally's wasn't the first divorce in our set, but she started the warn-ing bells off in my head. Six months after the Webster divorce, Marco Perez got engaged to a twenty-six-year-old catwalk model with hair down to her ass, a girl who hung on his every word and anticipated his every need (I heard she did a six-month massage course just so she could properly massage his shoulders after tennis); and I felt a shift in my relationship with Rory. For the first time, I felt that he was comparing me with the other wives and girlfriends, and that he wasn't sure he had the best deal.

I was twenty-two when we got married, so not exactly a *baby*, but I was very out of my depth. Rory was thirty-five, and he'd never been married. He'd never had a relationship that lasted more than a few months, I think because women didn't really interest him. He gets more worked up about machines and technology and ideas and busi-ness wins. The night I met him, I was working behind the bar and he was out celebrating the closing of some big deal, and I guess he'd had a few drinks, because his eyes lit up when he saw me, and he asked me out. He told me afterward that he could see that every guy in the bar wanted me, which was clearly the beer talking because that wasn't what it was like at all. I'm not going to pretend that I don't know I look good. I've worked too hard at it not to know exactly where I stand in the prettiness rankings, which is pretty damn high. But at twenty-two, I was bleaching my own hair and wearing thrift-store jeans. I wasn't some beauty that every guy wanted. I had no money. I was sleeping on a friend's couch because I'd just split up with my boyfriend, a musician who never got gigs anywhere more than once. My ex had been arrested for weed possession, mostly because he pissed off a cop. I'd bailed him out with tip money I'd been saving for six months, and the next day he got drunk and slept with my best friend. So the night I met Rory I was basically homeless, broke, and not exactly full of confidence.

The truth is that I was intimidated by him. He was—still is—a good-looking man. When I met him he was scary smart and extremely confident and completely different from anyone I'd ever met before. I remember feeling like I was so damn lucky he'd even looked at me, and by the time I realized that he didn't love me, things had gone too far. I was already living with him in his glorious apartment overlooking Lake Champlain. He painted a picture for me of the life we would live together. I would never have to worry about money, or where I would live. I wouldn't have to go back to the bar, with my horrible manager and the horrible customers. Rory would look after me, and I wanted that. Maybe I loved him, in the beginning. It's all so long ago now that I can't really be sure how I felt. Maybe I loved him, or maybe I just wanted everything he was offering. Security and comfort are very, very attractive when you've never had either. So he asked me to marry him, and I understood what he wanted—children, and a pretty wife who wouldn't complain when he worked constantly. Someone who would look good on his arm and who would never, ever ask awkward questions. I thought that was a fair deal, and when he sent me to a lawyer who put an ironclad prenup in front of me, I didn't hesitate to sign it. I never really grasped how precarious my position was until Rory's friends started hitting fifty and started divesting themselves of their wives. That was when

I realized I was living on borrowed time. I could come home from yoga some morning to find that my stuff had been packed, the locks had been changed, and a process server was waiting for me.

There was no point in crying about my situation, or in looking to Rory for reassurance. That's a mistake a lot of women make. They feel like they're losing their man and they get clingy and insecure, and that, of course, just makes the end come faster. I went the other way. I kept busy, busy, busy, and I made sure I was useful. At parties, I always knew who everyone was, who the important people were in the room. I kept my calorie intake under fifteen hundred a day, watched my macros, got my little tweaks from the best cosmetic surgeon in Boston, and worked out like a demon. And I sold my clothes. Five years into my little project, I had $1.9 million in an offshore account in my name. Not enough to retire on, but not nothing. I'd get *something* in the divorce. Not a house, because Rory was too smart for that, but *something*.

I took photographs of an absolutely gorgeous Oscar de la Renta embroidered tulle minidress, and then couldn't decide whether I should list it or give it a second outing to the gala. I gave up in the end and packed it away, then put on my workout gear and went downstairs to the gym. Simon found me there half an hour later.

"Hey, baby." I was running on the treadmill. He hadn't come to work out. He was wearing jeans and a green long-sleeved T-shirt. He must have been just out of the shower because his hair was styled, in that casual messy look he likes that I know takes him twenty minutes minimum with a hair dryer and styling wax. He sat on the weight bench and leaned forward, resting his arms on his thighs. "Everything okay?"

"Yes. Sure. It's just that something's happened, and I figured I'd better tell you before you hear it through the grapevine."

I was still running, but something about the set of his jaw told me I should pay attention. I pressed a button, slowed my pace to a walk, and waited.

"Nina and I broke up."

"Oh, Simon!" I was genuinely surprised. Simon was crazy about Nina. They'd started going out when they were only sixteen, and if I secretly wished that he'd picked someone other than Leanne Fraser's daughter to be his first love, I didn't really have an issue with the relationship, at least at first. They were cute together, I thought. A year later, they were still together, and I was over it. Simon had so much going for him. I didn't think it was healthy for him to be so fixated on one girl. By the time they finished high school, I was desperate for him to dump her, but Simon was still talking like they were forever. If anything, he seemed to think that Nina was too good for him, that he was lucky to have her, which drove me nuts. Admittedly the girl was very pretty, but there are any number of pretty girls out there. If anyone understands that, it's me. And Nina was book smart, but I'd always found her insipid. Not that I'd ever been stupid enough to criticize the girl to Simon. No, I'd been nice as pie and crossed my fingers and waited for it to pass. Which, apparently, it just had. I suppressed a little thrill of happiness. "I'm sure you guys will work it out."

"I don't think so, Mom."

"All couples argue."

"She was sleeping around," Simon said bluntly. "Other guys, when I was away at college."

It's surprising how quickly happiness can turn to fury.

"You can't be serious."

He gave me a wry smile. "I wish I wasn't." He was upset. He covered it very well, but I could see the tiredness in his eyes and the unhappiness in the set of his shoulders. "It's okay. Really. I'd suspected for a while, but I kept telling myself that I was imagining things. Then I guess she met someone she liked better than me. She dumped me on Friday night. I asked her if she'd been seeing someone behind my back and she didn't deny it. I asked her if he was the first and she basically admitted that he wasn't."

"That little bitch." I was past pretending. If Nina Fraser had been standing in front of me, I would have slapped her.

Simon shrugged and stood up. He gave me that half smile again. He was trying hard to pretend that he was fine. It made me feel sorry for him, and proud of him at the same time.

"It happens, right? I mean, how many high school relationships survive college anyway?"

"Very few. And the ones that do probably shouldn't."

"Right."

He turned to leave.

"Simon? I can make dinner. Something special for you and your dad."

"Cody's coming to pick me up."

"You're going out?"

"Uh-huh. The guys think I need to drown my sorrows or something. We're going to a bar." Legally, Simon wouldn't be old enough to drink for another couple of months, but he and his friends had been going to one of the bars in town since they were nineteen.

"You won't overdo it?"

"Cody thinks I need to get wrecked. He said it's a necessary stage in the grieving process. Step two is to pick up girls."

"Simon—"

He laughed at me. "I'm kidding. We'll have a few beers and we'll probably end up back at Cody's playing Gears online or something."

"When are you going back to school?" I asked. "Is it tomorrow?"

"Wednesday morning," Simon said. "I don't have classes until Thursday. I've already booked the flight."

He left the room with a final wave, and I started running again. I bumped up the incline and the pace until I was red faced and sweating. I had to do something with all of my energy. I was seriously pissed.

I'd never liked Leanne Fraser. She'd been years ahead of me in school, and probably I wouldn't have known her well, except that she was in the same year as my best friend's older sister, who *hated* her.

Leanne got good grades and she acted like that made her special. Better than everyone else. She got into a good college, and her mother, who was a hard-nosed bitch, went around town boasting about her brilliant daughter. Which made it almost funny when Leanne got knocked up in her second year and dropped out. She did buy that inn and build up her business, which I might have respected if it were someone else, but she's so goddamned humorless and disapproving.

Take her clothes. Leanne lives in the same outfit—basically dumpy jeans with battered sneakers. A fleece jacket over a long-sleeved T. I swear she wore the exact same outfit when she was in high school. She's the kind of woman who pretends she doesn't think about clothes or looks because she's above all that, but of course that's bullshit. Everyone gets up in the morning and makes a choice about the clothes they wear. Whether you choose a pastel twin set, or knee boots and a black leather jacket, or a ratty pair of jeans that are too baggy around the ass, it's still a *choice.* You're still deciding what message to send the world. Leanne's choice was to wear a badly applied smear of lipstick and a smudge of mascara to the school fundraiser and call it virtue. She's been trying to pull off that innocent-girl-next-door look for the last thirty years. Given that she got knocked up and had to come back to Waitsfield with her tail between her legs, you would think she would have called it quits by now, but nope. She keeps on keeping on with her shy smiles and her sideways looks and her butter-wouldn't-melt bullshit. I don't know who she thinks she's fooling, because everyone in town knows she's hard as nails. She runs her inn like a drill sergeant.

I hate that kind of hypocrisy.

And now it was turning out that her daughter was exactly the same way. All fake butter-wouldn't-melt on the outside, while she goes after exactly what she wants. It made me so mad. Simon was good looking, smart, popular, and athletic. Everyone loved him. He was worth ten of her, and it pissed me off that she'd been the one to dump him, rather than the other way around.

After my workout I went to the laundry room to look for Rita. Rita's our housekeeper. She comes three days a week and does the heavy cleaning and all the laundry. Usually I avoid her. Rita likes to talk, and it's always the most boring shit imaginable. Celebrity gossip, which, fine, but she's always at least three weeks behind whatever's going on, and she always seems to expect me to be amazed at whatever random story she's picked up from some friend on Facebook and usually mangled. So I try to avoid her, but I pay her well and I'm friendly when I do see her. It's a good idea to stay on good terms with your staff. You'd be surprised how many secrets they pick up, just from being in the house.

"Hi, Rita," I said brightly. She was standing with her back to me, examining something in her hands. She jumped when she heard me, and turned around, pushing the something—it looked like a cream sweater—behind her.

"Oh, hi," she said. She was a little flushed.

"Everything okay?"

"Everything's great!" She said it with too much enthusiasm. Something was off, but really, whatever small drama she was caught up in, did I want to know about it? I did not. If she'd screwed up and ruined a piece of clothing—I was suspicious about that cream sweater—did I care? I did not. Rita was very good, usually. Everyone made mistakes, and really, I'd rather pay for another sweater than listen to a long, drawn-out explanation as to what had gone wrong.

"I just wanted to pop in to let you know that Simon's going back to college on Wednesday morning. If you could have his clothes ready and packed for him by Tuesday night, that would be great."

"Of course. No problem," Rita said. But there was something about her expression that made me feel awkward, suddenly.

"He should do it himself, of course." I laughed a stupid kind of laugh. "I'm sure he'll get there eventually."

"I'm sure he will," said Rita. She didn't smile, and I was mad at myself. I didn't owe her an explanation.

"Okay, well. His bags will be in his room. You know where to find everything." I got out of there and went to the shower. I got dressed in a pair of jeans so soft they felt like leggings, and a pink shirt with a half tuck, and three buttons open at the neck. I left my hair loose and went back downstairs to prepare dinner. That night, Rory was in a talkative mood.

"There's a great deal of potential right now," he said, over our glazed roast salmon and greens. "After Covid and Ukraine, suddenly everyone's looking at their supply chain, trying to get key suppliers onshore. We've had more inquiries in the last six months than we had for the three years prior. We've started a waiting list." He took a bite and looked at me, waiting for a response.

"Are you thinking about expansion?" I asked.

"We're examining some options. It's pretty obvious that we can grow here. The challenge is going to be getting the pace of that expansion exactly right. Grow too quickly and we'll overleverage or overcommit and burn out. Grow too slowly and we'll miss opportunities and allow our competitors an opportunity to take over our space."

"Sounds challenging." I can do that kind of thing with less than half my brain engaged. Ask questions he obviously wants to be asked. Give him little encouraging responses. I should be grateful that it's so easy, but the truth is, I resent the fact that he doesn't even notice that I'm going through the motions.

Rory opened his mouth to answer me, but before he could say anything the intercom buzzed. Rory frowned at me at little, as if the interruption was my fault. I checked the panel and saw a car I didn't recognize. The camera zoomed in on the driver and I saw Leanne Fraser. I frowned, but I pushed the button that opened the gate. The doorbell rang before I could get to the front door. I opened it to find Leanne and her husband standing there. I couldn't remember his first name . . . Aaron, Andrew? Something like that. Leanne launched straight into a series of questions about Nina. I told her that Simon and Nina had broken up. I didn't explicitly say that Nina was probably off in the sack somewhere with her new guy, though I was tempted. People say that I'm not considerate. They have no idea.

"If she's not here, then where is she?" Leanne said, with attitude. I felt a surge of irritation that they were here, interrupting our dinner, like we'd done something wrong, when it was their girl who'd broken our boy's heart. I told her I couldn't help, and then I shut the door on them.

"Who was that?" Rory asked. He'd come to the kitchen door, his napkin still in his left hand. Before I could answer, the doorbell rang again, longer and harder than the first time.

"Jesus," I said.

"Who is it?" Rory said.

"It's Leanne Fraser and her lunk of a husband. They're looking for Nina. They say she hasn't come home. Surprise, surprise. She probably doesn't want to face the music."

Rory looked at me blankly.

"Simon and Nina broke up. She cheated on him and then dumped him. They broke up at the Stowe house and Simon came home early. And now her parents are here, looking for her."

Rory raised an eyebrow. "I'll go," he said. He went to the door. I retreated back to the kitchen. I was glad that Simon wasn't at home. He shouldn't have to deal with this. After a minute, I heard the front door shut, and Rory came back into the room. He made a comical gesture, as if he was wiping sweat from his brow.

"Phew," he said. "Those two are a little worked up." He sat down again and gestured for me to do the same.

"I've never liked Leanne Fraser. She's a priss. She's boring. And she thinks she's better than everyone else."

Rory nodded absently but didn't answer me. I could tell from his eyes that he was already thinking of something else. He refilled his wineglass and took another bite. He was losing interest in the conversation, but I wasn't ready to let it go.

"I wonder why Nina hasn't come home yet."

"Probably the girl's just upset. Maybe she went to a friend's place to lick her wounds for a few days. You know, if she's hurting, she might be avoiding her mother because she doesn't want to talk about it all yet."

"I guess that's possible." Though not at all likely, given that she'd dumped Simon. But I didn't feel like educating Rory. If he paid any attention to anything other than his business, he'd know what was going on without my filling him in.

Rory started talking again about work. About how he was going to be busy doing site visits to factories over the next two months, checking out possible opportunities for acquisition. I nodded and made all the right sounds in all the right places, and with the part of my mind that wasn't occupied, which was most of it, I thought about where and how I would live when he divorced me. Boston was a leading contender, but there were other places, other cities. Or maybe I should look for somewhere on the coast. That might be nice, I could walk on the beach every day. Maybe I'd get a dog or something. Or a cat. I could be a cat lady. The idea was oddly appealing.

CHAPTER THREE

Matthew

O n Monday afternoon at 2:00 P.M., Detective Matthew Wright arrived at the Black Friar Inn. He drove up the gravel driveway and parked his car in a pretty courtyard at the back of the inn. The small parking lot was half-full. Presumably the cars belonged to guests. That would be better than the alternative, which was that concerned family members had gathered to provide support. In Matthew's experience, when large numbers of distressed family members got together without anyone to reassure them or direct their energies in a useful way, you could quickly find yourself knee deep in problems that distracted from the investigation. Fragmented search efforts at best, and vigilantism at worst.

Matthew walked around to the front door of the inn and pushed it open. Inside he found a quiet, pretty entrance hall, warmed by a fire burning in the grate and smelling faintly of jasmine. There was a reception desk. Behind it sat a small, dark-haired woman. She wore a navy sweater and jeans, and her hair was tied back in a low ponytail. No makeup. She stood up when he came in.

"Mrs. Fraser?"

"Yes, I'm Leanne Fraser."

He offered his hand. "Detective Matthew Wright."

"Yes, of course. Thank you." She hesitated for a moment, as if she wasn't quite sure what to do, then said, "Could you follow me?"

She led the way into the inn's drawing room. The room had dark wood paneling and cobalt-blue walls. The furniture was antique. There was a leather sofa, worn enough that it looked soft and inviting, and a large coffee table with books on Vermont history and geography. Leanne continued through the drawing room to a small hall where there was a door marked PRIVATE. She opened the door, and he followed her through, down narrow stairs, into a basement living room. This part of the house was obviously for the family, and the design style was very different from the main inn. Here the floors were some kind of blond wood—oak, he thought—and the walls were painted white. The living room was cozy and lived in, with a green fabric sofa that had seen a few years, and overstuffed bookshelves. The windows were small, and maybe the room was a little dark, but with the fire burning in the grate, it felt like a welcoming place. There was a man sitting on the sofa.

"This is my husband, Andy," said Leanne. "Could I offer you coffee?" Andy Fraser stood and offered Matthew his hand. Matthew Wright was a big man, at six foot two and almost two hundred pounds, but Andy Fraser had a couple of inches and at least twenty pounds on him, all of it muscle. He had broad shoulders and big hands and the weather-beaten face of someone who works outside.

"No, thank you. Perhaps we could sit?"

Andy and Leanne took a seat beside each other on the sofa. They didn't touch.

"I'm sorry," Leanne said. "We don't know how this works."

"There are no rules, Mrs. Fraser. I'm here to listen to you. I want to know everything you can tell me about your daughter. About why you think she may be missing. And to hear anything you think might help me to find her."

"Okay, well, I guess you know that Nina's a sophomore at UVM. Last week she went away with her boyfriend for a vacation. She was due to come home on Saturday morning, and she didn't, and we can't reach her."

"Have you been able to reach her boyfriend?"

Leanne and Andy glanced at each other. It was Andy who answered.

"We went up there to the Jordans' house last night. We talked to his parents."

Leanne cut across her husband. "They claimed not to know where she was. They said Simon didn't know either. Simon told them that Nina broke up with him. He said something about Nina going off with friends, but she hasn't called us and we can't reach her."

"Is it unusual? For Nina to be out of touch for a few days?"

"It is," Andy said firmly. "She's a good girl. She's never done anything like this before."

That had the ring of truth to it, but at twenty years old, the girl had a lot of firsts ahead of her.

"Has Nina ever suffered from depression? Has she ever had an issue with self-harm?"

"No," Leanne said. She looked shocked by the suggestion. "Never."

"Okay." Matthew nodded. "And what about her friends?"

"We called them," Leanne said. "No one's heard from her. And she hasn't posted to any of her social media since Thursday."

Leanne took out her phone and showed Matthew Nina's Instagram page. She showed him Nina's last two posts, but she didn't stop there. She scrolled through, lingering over photographs and short videos, explaining where and when they would have been taken. It went on too long, but Matthew didn't stop her. He understood what she was doing. She wanted him to know her daughter, to see her as a human being and not just another case. Matthew studied the photos and videos. Nina was very pretty. She was small—in the photographs she barely came up to Simon's shoulders. She had a light tan and brown eyes fringed with long, thick lashes. Her smile was quick, easy, and warm. In some of the photos she wore a tank top, and you could see how slight she was, but also that she had a climber's strength. The muscles in her shoulders and arms were lean and toned. Leanne stopped at a short video that played on a loop. She pointed at the screen.

"That's Simon," she said.

"He's a good kid," Andy said, quickly.

In the video, Nina was standing poolside in a green bikini. There were other kids in the background, some in the pool, a couple sitting on the edge with their legs in the water. Nina looked at the camera with exaggerated innocence, before sidling up to Simon. He was wearing board shorts, aviators, and an expression of I'm-too-cool-for-school on his face. Nina pointed out the camera and they both slipped, as naturally as breathing, into perfect, side-by-side Instagram poses. Bodies stretched and tilted at just the right angles, easy smiles, goofy peace signs. Then Nina slid her arm around his waist and tipped them both into the pool. She came back up for air, laughing so hard it seemed like she couldn't breathe, just as the camera zoomed in. Her hair was a mess, Instagram perfection nowhere to be seen. She looked very young, very pretty, and very alive. Leanne let the video play through three times, then a fourth. She couldn't seem to look away. Andy reached out gently and took the phone away from his wife.

"Do you have any tracking software on her phone? Find My Friend, that kind of thing?"

"We don't do that," Leanne said. "Should we be doing that?"

Matthew shook his head. "I'll need to take Simon's full name, number, and address, please. Also the names and numbers of Nina's friends." They gave him the list.

"Where did Nina and Simon go on vacation?"

"Stowe," Leanne said.

"I'm sorry?" Matthew said. He thought he must have misheard. Stowe was only forty minutes north of Waitsfield.

"Simon's family bought a second property there recently," Andy said evenly. "Big place. A house. Acres. Simon and Nina wanted to explore, maybe climb some, if they found good routes."

"Okay." Matthew stood up. "We'll make some preliminary inquiries and get back to you. Please don't worry. In cases like these, most of the time we find that the young person is with friends."

Leanne and Andy both nodded, but only Andy did it with conviction. Leanne walked Matthew out.

He made a phone call as he drove north to his wife, Naomi, to tell her that he would be late. It took twenty minutes to reach Waterbury, where state police headquarters was located, in a modern, red-brick building in the state office complex. When he got to the squad room, it was quiet, which wasn't unusual. Mostly because they'd been understaffed for years, and investigations took detectives all over the state. There were a couple of senior detectives in the room, Kim Allen and David Beecham, working on their own cases. Also a few keyboard warriors who were good with paperwork but not a whole lot else. Matthew had a full case load already. A new missing persons case always required a lot of work that he was not going to have time for. He needed help. He looked around the room for possible candidates.

Sarah Jane Reid was at her desk. Sarah Jane had joined Major Crimes a couple of months prior. She was staring intently at her screen, her fingers poised on her keyboard. She looked up when he came in and flushed a little. Matthew had noticed that he seemed to make her nervous. He made a mental note to observe her with other members of the squad, to see if it was just him or if she was jumpy around the others too. It was too soon for him to form a view about her competence or lack of it, but he knew that she came with complications. Her uncle, Major John Reid, oversaw the Major Crime Unit. John Reid would be Sarah Jane's boss's boss's boss. She was working in her uncle's direct line of supervision, and there'd been grumblings about nepotism. With that kind of baggage, Reid couldn't afford to be a blushing, nervous rookie. She'd have to be tough to rise above the gossip and the takedowns.

"Morning," Matthew said.

"Oh, hi," Sarah Jane said.

"Early start?"

"Paperwork. I like to get it out of the way early." She said it with a certain dryness, which made him wonder if she'd been getting more than her fair share of scut work. It might be happening. A kind of hazing, maybe. A test to see if she'd take it, to see if she'd play along or call her uncle for help.

"I've got a case," Matthew said. "I'm at very early stages. It might not be anything. I'd like you to work it with me." To Matthew's way of thinking, sitting her at a desk all day was a waste of an officer. She was inexperienced, but the only way to address that was to get her out in the field, let her observe and do the work and learn on the job.

"Thank you," Sarah Jane said. "That would be great."

He gave her the background. "Call Nina Fraser's phone company," he said. "It will take time to get detailed messages and phone calls, but we should be able to get location and use data pretty quickly. Call her bank too. Find out when she last used her cards."

Sarah Jane made the calls while he caught up on other work. Half an hour later, she came to his desk.

"Cell phone tower data puts Nina in Stowe on Friday night, but the last ping was just after midnight. No pings since. No activity on her credit card since Wednesday of last week, when she paid for . . . uh . . ." Sarah Jane checked her notes. "She spent thirty-two dollars in the Green Goddess café."

Matthew grimaced. "That's not what I was hoping to hear."

Sarah Jane looked down at her notes. She didn't ask him what he was thinking. She seemed to be figuring that out all by herself. Matthew stood up and picked up his jacket.

"I'm going to interview the boyfriend," he said.

"Right." She nodded and retreated.

"You too, Sarah Jane."

Her head came up like he'd awarded her a prize.

CHAPTER FOUR

Jamie

The cops showed up at our house on Monday evening at five o'clock. When I came back from yoga their green all-wheel drive was at the gate. I recognized the car as a state police vehicle right away, and I guess I figured maybe Rory was inside the house, meeting with a politician senior enough that they'd had an escort. Not that that was a regular thing, at our house, but that's how far away I was from thinking that the visit was about Simon and Nina. I pulled in behind the police car and pressed my buzzer for the electronic gate. It opened, they drove in and parked, and I followed. They met me at the front door and introduced themselves. Matthew Wright, who was a detective and a senior sergeant, and Sarah Jane Reid, a blond girl who looked too young to be much of anything. Her nose was too much for her face. She would have been pretty if she'd done something about it. Neither of them was in uniform, but even if I hadn't seen them drive in, I would have known he was a cop. Or maybe I would have guessed military. There was something about the way he held himself. He had authority, baked in.

"Okay, well, how can I help you?"

"We'd like to speak with your son. Is Simon here?" Matthew Wright looked past me toward the garage. The garage door was just coming down, but you could clearly see my car and Simon's car and the truck we use to get around in heavy snow. My first instinct was to lie and say that Simon wasn't home, for no reason other than that I felt out of my depth. I shook off the urge.

"He's probably inside," I said. I opened the front door. "What's this about?"

Wright waited for a moment before answering, just long enough, I figured, to let me know that he didn't have to talk to me, that he didn't have to answer my questions.

"Nina Fraser's family have reported her missing. She was expected home on Saturday morning, and she didn't show, and she hasn't been in touch. Her family say that Simon might have been the last person to see her."

"Seriously?" I turned my head and raised an eyebrow at him.

"Afraid so."

He followed me into the house, and I led the way to the kitchen.

"Did Leanne tell you that Nina broke up with Simon on Friday night? She's probably off with her friends. Partying. I told Leanne this last night. Nina's not a child. Leanne's totally overreacting."

He didn't answer. Just followed me as I led the way into the kitchen and put my bag on the counter. There was a cereal bowl with some Cheerios rapidly drying and congealing on the bottom of the bowl. A half-empty coffee cup sat beside it. I gathered them up and put them in the sink while he stood there, watching me.

"I'll get Simon," I said.

"Thank you."

I went downstairs, to the back of the house, and knocked on Simon's door. There was no answer. I knocked again and then pushed the door open. He was lying on his back on his bed, staring at the ceiling. His hands were crossed on his stomach, and his phone was balanced on his chest. He was wearing headphones. Not the little earbuds I wear when I run, but big, over-the-ear cans. There was a smell of stale beer in the room. I hadn't seen him since Cody had picked him up on Sunday. Had he come home last night, or this morning?

"Simon."

He didn't hear me. I waved my hand in the air and the movement caught his eye. He saw me and slid his headphones off.

"There's a detective upstairs," I said. "He wants to talk to you."

"A detective?" He scrubbed at his hair with two hands, like he was trying to wake himself up.

"He says his name is Matthew Wright. He's state police. He wants to talk to you about Nina."

"About Nina?"

I felt a surge of irritation and anxiety. My voice came out sounding sharp and worried. "Yes, Simon. About Nina. Can you get up and come upstairs, please?"

He pushed himself up until he was sitting on the side of the bed. He was wearing boxer shorts and a T-shirt. Just a few years ago he'd been a gangly, clumsy teenager. Before that he'd been a little boy, with hands and feet that seemed too big for his body, but still all smiles and hugs and sudden enthusiasm. In my mind's eye, in my heart, I still saw Simon as that little boy. Every time I turned to look at him and saw the young man he had become, it was like stubbing my toe.

"Be careful when you talk to them, okay?"

He looked at me like he didn't understand me.

"I'm sure Nina's fine, and she'll be home whenever. But . . . just in case . . . be careful what you say."

"Nina hasn't come home? So where is she?"

"That's the point, Simon. Her parents don't know. They called the police. I'm sure she's fine. Really."

"Okay, but if the police are here . . ." He seemed to be waking up, finally. He rubbed his hand across his face. "What if something happened to her, Mom?"

I felt a small sliver of fear at the base of my stomach. Not for Nina, but for Simon. For my son. If something had happened to her, he would be devastated. He might blame himself for leaving her.

"I guess we can ask them what they know." I hesitated in the doorway. "I wonder if I should call a lawyer?" I thought about calling

Rory. He didn't like to be disturbed in the office, but he'd want to know about this.

"Mom. Come on." Simon looked at me like I'd just said something crazy. He left the room before I could say anything else, and I had to hurry after him to keep up. We found Matthew Wright and his side-kick in the living room, standing by the windows and taking in the view. They'd obviously taken advantage of my absence and snooped around. I wondered what conclusions they'd drawn. They wouldn't have seen anything personal, not unless they'd gone so far as to open drawers and cupboards. We aren't the kind of family that leaves clut-ter around.

Simon went straight to Matthew Wright and offered his hand. "I'm Simon Jordan," he said. "My mother tells me you're here about Nina?"

Wright took Simon's outstretched hand and shook it briefly.

"Let's sit," he said, like we were in his home instead of ours. Si-mon sat on the sofa, and Wright took the armchair opposite him. The blond woman—Reid—stood for a moment, as if she was waiting for permission, then sat in the other armchair. Wright looked at me and waited, as if I were intruding. I should have brazened it out, but the awkwardness of the moment got to me.

"Can I get anyone coffee?" I asked, too brightly.

"Thank you," said Wright. "Coffee would be good."

"Not for me, Mom."

"Thank you, no."

I went back up the steps to the kitchen and turned on the coffee-pot. I was still able to see everyone across the open floor plan. I could hear their voices and every word they said, but from the kitchen I suddenly felt like I'd lost control.

"Simon, Mr. and Mrs. Fraser tell me that Nina was supposed to come home on Saturday morning from your trip, and she didn't show. She also hasn't called them, and her cell phone goes straight to voice mail. Do you know where Nina is right now?"

Simon shook his head slowly. "I'm sorry. No." He was leaning forward in the seat, his forearms balanced on his thighs and his hands together. The expression on his face was serious and concerned.

"Can you tell me when you last saw her?"

"That would have been Friday night."

"Okay. And where was this?"

"It was at our house—I mean my parents' house—at Stowe."

Wright nodded. "Who else was there?"

"No one. We went there alone, just the two of us, for all of last week. It was a vacation."

"Stowe seems a little close to home for a getaway. It's too early for skiing. You didn't want to go somewhere else? Somewhere a bit farther afield?"

"Sure. I'd have loved to. But it was a spur-of-the-moment thing."

"Any particular reason why you hadn't planned anything earlier?"

Simon was slow to answer. "Nina was planning to work over the break. She was going to help her mom out at the inn. But she'd had enough, and she decided she wanted to take some time off. It was too late to book anywhere, so we decided to go to my folks' place. It didn't really matter where we went. We just wanted to be together."

"Nina's parents were okay with her blowing off work?"

"Yeah, not really. At least, her dad didn't mind, I don't think. He doesn't really get involved in that stuff."

"Nina's mom wasn't happy?"

Simon's brow creased. "I don't want to say anything bad about anyone."

"I promise I won't judge," Wright said. "But it's better not to hold anything back right now."

"Okay," Simon said, nodding. "I get that. The truth is, Nina's mom is pretty demanding. She expects Nina to work at the inn all the time, not just during vacations, but during school too and weekends. There's not a lot of room left for Nina to have a life. So she finally decided she'd had enough and she told her mom she wasn't going to work."

"Nina had an argument with her mother?"

"I guess. At least, Nina said she was taking the time off, and when her mother started to blow up at her, Nina just ended the call. So it wasn't much of an argument, but I'm sure Leanne wasn't happy. Maybe that's why Nina hasn't gone home."

Wright nodded slowly. "Makes sense."

His response was so easygoing, so outwardly relaxed, that it felt like a trap. I was stuck in the kitchen, waiting for the coffee. I overrode the settings and water started to spill into the filter. I grabbed a mug and sloshed lukewarm coffee into it, then hurried back into the living room. Wright took the cup from me, nodded his thanks, and put it down on the coffee table without drinking. Reid was just sitting there with her ankles crossed and her notebook out, saying nothing and watching everything. I sat down beside Simon on the couch and hoped that Wright wouldn't ask me to leave. I didn't know the rules. Could I insist on staying? Could I ask *him* to leave?

"Tell me what happened on Friday night. Your mom said you guys broke up?"

Simon nodded. "Yeah, that's right."

"Can you tell me why?"

Simon raised his left hand and rubbed the back of his neck. He looked down, like he was giving the question serious consideration, and my heart sank. That was Simon's tell. When he was a little boy, maybe ten or eleven years old, he'd started making that exact gesture every time he told a big lie. When he told me he was going fishing with Lee Donovan, but really they were planning to ride their bikes over to Jack Squire's house to try to blow up tin cans using fireworks. When I asked him about his math teacher's house getting egged in the ninth grade. When he blew off homework to take Nina Fraser to a party. Every time—hand to the back of the neck, eyes down and to the left. I'd never told him how I could tell that he was lying. Most of the time I didn't even call him on the lie, because part of being a good parent is giving your kid space to screw up a little, so that they learn from their mistakes. And, if I'm honest, part of me didn't want him to change. I liked that I knew him just a bit better than anyone else.

"We just grew apart," Simon said. "It was okay last year. But when we went back to college this year the long-distance thing wasn't really working."

"Where do you go to school?" Wright asked.

"Northwestern."

"That's a good school."

"Sure." Simon gave a half shrug that was meant to be self-deprecating.

"And Nina. Where does she go?"

"UVM."

"Right. Her mom mentioned that. So that's why you broke up? You decided that long distance was too hard?"

"That's right."

"There was no argument? No falling out? Because I have to tell you, that's rare in my experience. For most people, there are a lot of feelings when a relationship comes to an end. Tends to result in some fireworks."

"I guess we both knew it was coming. Neither of us wanted to admit it, but when the conversation started, we realized that it hadn't been working. So it was amicable."

Matthew Wright nodded slowly. His face didn't show much, but it didn't have to. It was obvious he didn't believe a word Simon had just said. I didn't either, obviously, because Simon had already told me the truth. Clearly he was trying to put a good face on things for the detective, but it was just making him look like he had something to hide. I shifted in my seat. Simon's eyes flicked to my face. He looked away, cleared his throat, and sighed.

"Look, sorry. The truth is that Nina had met someone else. She was the one who wanted to break up."

"That must have been hard to hear."

"I mean, yeah. Look, I wasn't trying to lie to you guys, or leave stuff out. It's just difficult to talk about. And I don't want to say anything bad about Nina. But she'd been seeing this guy casually behind my back for a while, I don't know how long, and things got to the point where she wanted to end things with me and get serious with him."

"What's his name?"

"Excuse me?"

"This other guy Nina wanted to get serious with. What's his name?"

"I . . . uh . . . I asked, but she wouldn't tell me. I think she was afraid that I'd pick a fight or something, even though that really isn't my style."

Wright's expression didn't change. "Why do you think she was afraid that you'd confront the guy?"

Simon looked uncomfortable. "I don't know. I mean, it's hard to know why people think anything, right?"

"Except that you guys were very close. You know Nina well, I'd guess."

Simon couldn't help himself. "Better than anyone else does."

"Right. So . . ." Wright let his voice trail away and waited. The silence went on too long, until it was obvious that Simon didn't have an answer. Wright nodded, as if he was taking a mental note, then continued. "What happened, after she told you?"

"We argued. I mean, I was upset. She was a little drunk. She'd had maybe three glasses of wine, which wasn't like her, but I guess maybe she needed the courage. The conversation wasn't going anywhere. So I left."

"You left," Wright said.

"Yeah."

"It was your parents' house, but you were the one to leave?"

"I had my car, and she didn't. And she'd been drinking. I didn't want to be there anymore, so I went home. Nina said she was going to call a friend and get a ride in the morning."

"What time did you leave?"

"I'm not sure, exactly. I think around eleven P.M.?"

"And that was the last time you saw her?"

Simon nodded. "Yes. That's right." He looked Wright in the eye. The expression on his face was open and frank. He wasn't hiding anything anymore.

"And you haven't heard from her since? No phone calls? No text messages? No likes or comments on social media?"

Simon shook his head. His eyes lost focus, like he'd gone somewhere else.

"Do you have any idea where Nina might be, Simon?" Wright's voice was gentle, almost hypnotic. Simon blinked and stared back at him.

"No. I don't know."

"Do you have security cameras at your house in Stowe?"

"I think so?" Simon looked uncertain, suddenly. He looked at me.

"I'm not sure," I said. "We can check. I'll get back to you."

Rory's voice came from behind me.

"What's all this?"

All four of us jumped. I turned. Rory was standing in the kitchen, smiling slightly. It was a Monday, but he was wearing his weekend uniform of slacks and a Jordan Precision Tools polo shirt, under a sweater. I'd never been more relieved to see him in my life.

I stood up. "This is Detective Matthew Wright. And Officer Reid. They came by to talk to Simon. About Nina."

Rory stepped forward and offered his hand. "Good to meet you."

Wright shook Rory's hand. "It's good to meet you, Mr. Jordan."

"So, Nina's still missing? She hasn't shown up?" Rory said. He put his hands in his pockets and leaned back on his heels, a look of concern on his face.

"Afraid that's the case," Wright said.

Rory grimaced. "I'm very sorry to hear that."

"I was just asking Simon here if he knew where Nina might have gone."

"I don't," Simon put in quickly. "I don't know where she went."

"Right. I was about to ask Simon to put me in touch with Nina's friends. Presumably, Simon, you know who they are."

"Sure." Simon's head had come up again, as if having Rory there had given him confidence. "Alison. Alison Miller. And Olivia Darlington. They're Nina's friends at UVM. Olivia's parents live in Boston." His brow furrowed. "Now that I think about it, I think maybe Nina said something about visiting Olivia."

Officer Reid took a note. Wright raised an eyebrow.

"When did Nina say this?"

Simon grimaced, like he was trying to remember. "I don't know. It might have been during the breakup conversation, or maybe it was earlier in the day. Sorry. I can't be sure. I just remember that she said something about it." Reid was still busily taking notes. Wright kept his eyes on Simon's face. Rory frowned and took his hands out of his pockets.

"I'm sorry, Detective, but I'm going to have to stop you there. I'm sure you mean well. And I know you have a job to do, but I have to think of my son. I'm sure you understand."

Wright put his head to one side. "Well, not really. A young woman is missing. Your son's very recently ex-girlfriend. Right now it seems like he was the last one to see her. I'm asking some basic questions here, Mr. Jordan. Of Simon. Who is an adult."

"And Simon will be happy to answer them. But not without our lawyer."

There was silence for a long moment. It felt to me like the entire world had just shifted an inch in the wrong direction. Like everything was suddenly a lot more serious. Like Simon really was in danger.

"Look," Rory said. "I'm sure Nina's going to show up. The kids broke up, and she probably didn't want to come home straight after. That's very understandable. I'm sure, in a day or so, she'll come home with her tail between her legs and that will be that."

"Mr. Jordan—"

Rory held up a hand, cutting Matthew off. "But if the worst-case scenario happened, if something happened to Nina, I don't want you guys pointing the finger at Simon, because, and I don't mean any offense here, but you guys don't exactly have a perfect track record. We all know that innocent people can be targeted. I'm not trying to offend you, Detective. And I'm not accusing you of anything. I'm just saying. Our priority is always going to be our son. We just need to make sure that we take care."

Wright's face was a mask. "I'm not sure who you mean by 'you guys,' Mr. Jordan."

"Well, I just mean generally. You know. You hear about these things."

"I feel like it's always better to be specific. 'The police' is a pretty large grouping. I'm not sure that Vermont State Police has ever been accused of targeting innocent persons."

Rory's expression didn't change. Wright did not know my husband. He was not someone you could embarrass or intimidate into rolling over.

"I'm not accusing you or your colleagues of anything, Detective Wright. I'm just saying that we'd like to do things by the book. I'm sure you understand."

There was a pause during which no one moved.

"So, if you don't mind . . . ?" Rory took a step back, clearing the path for Wright to stand and leave the room. Wright took the hint.

"Thank you for your time, Simon, Mrs. Jordan. We'll be in touch if I need anything further."

"I'll have our lawyer call the department," Rory said. "Just so you have his details."

Rory walked them to the door. Simon and I sat in silence, listening to the footsteps cross the hall, the door opening and closing, and Rory's heavy tread returning.

"Simon, can you give us the room for a few minutes? I want to talk to your mom."

I expected Simon to object. He hated being treated like a kid. Always wanted to be part of everything. And I didn't want him to go. I wanted to talk to him, to reassure him that everything would be okay. But Simon didn't object. If anything, he seemed glad of the opportunity to make his escape. Rory waited for the door to close behind him before turning to me.

"Jesus, Jamie."

"I know."

"You should have called me. You shouldn't have let that guy in here. You can't trust cops."

"What was I supposed to do? Just turn him away at the door?"

"That girl is missing. Maybe she's partying with friends, but if something really did happen to her, do you want them to try to pin it on our son?" Rory didn't wait for an answer from me. He took his phone out and placed a call. I listened to him talk to his attorney, Alistair Reynolds, the same man who'd drafted our prenup. Rory explained the situation quickly, asked Alistair to call Matthew Wright, and hung up. He seemed calmer after the call. More confident. He patted my shoulder briefly.

"I'm not trying to give you a hard time. I'm sure you did your best. But you can't trust these people."

I nodded. I hadn't exactly rolled out the red carpet for the cops, but it wasn't the time to argue.

"From now on, let's just set some ground rules, okay? No one talks to Simon unless Alistair is present."

"Yes. Sure."

"Everything's going to be okay, Jamie. We just need to be smart about how we deal with this, so things don't get out of control."

I hadn't planned on confiding my worries to Rory. I wasn't in the habit of turning to him when I ran into trouble, but the words just came out.

"What if she's doing this on purpose?" I said. "To punish him for the breakup."

"Didn't you tell me that she dumped him?"

"That doesn't mean she doesn't resent him for being okay with things ending. People can be . . . complicated, when relationships end."

Rory thought about it for a moment, then he shook his head. "I don't understand that. But whatever is happening here, we have to stay focused. Our job, as parents, is to protect our son."

He was standing and I was still sitting. He reached out and caressed the back of my head. I flinched. I didn't mean to, but Rory didn't usually touch me, outside of bed. He noticed and started to take his hand away, but I caught it and held on.

"You're right," I said. "We need to stick together."

CHAPTER FIVE

Leanne

After the detective left on Monday afternoon, Andy and I had an argument.

"I don't want to tell Grace," he said. "I think it's too soon."

I stood up and went to the kitchen. My body felt weak and shaky, like I was coming down with a cold. I went to the fridge and stared inside and saw nothing. It took much more effort than it should have to focus. I found some of the expensive sausages we buy for the inn's cooked breakfast and took out the frying pan. I would fry the sausages and microwave some potatoes. That would have to do. Rufus lay in his bed in the corner of the kitchen near the radiator. He whined as he watched me but didn't get up.

"Don't you think?" Andy said. He'd followed me from the living room and was leaning in the doorway. "We don't know what's going on with Nina. We don't have any answers for Grace. If we tell her, she's going to be scared, and there's nothing she can do."

I sprayed oil into the pan, dropped the sausages in, put the paper wrapping in the trash, and washed my hands.

"You said he was a good kid," I said.

"What's that?"

"You said that Simon is a good kid. I don't know how you can say that." I shook the frying pan to make the sausages roll. The handle was loose. I'd been meaning to tighten the screw that attached it for ages. I went to the pantry to look for potatoes. There weren't many left, and the few that were there were small and aging. I gathered them anyway.

"Lee, we've known Simon since he was a boy. You can't really think . . . you can't really think . . ."

"You say we've known him, but we don't know him at all. We've seen him at the school, at sports days and graduations."

"He's been here to the house a bunch of times."

I threw the potatoes in the sink and turned on the tap. "Sure. And how much time have we actually spent with him? He says hello, and he disappears with Nina. He's had dinner here a handful of times over the last five years. He's watched a movie with us, what, twice?" I started scrubbing, hard. The weak feeling left me, replaced by a simmering rage. "He's rich and he's entitled." I dropped the potatoes on the draining board, took out my sharp knife, and started piercing them roughly.

"Lee," Andy said.

I ignored him.

"Leanne." He came to me and put his arms around me from behind. He took my hands in his and made me put the knife down, then he turned me around to face him. "You gotta slow down. I know this is tough, but we don't know that Nina's in trouble. I know you're pissed right now, but we do know Simon."

"I never liked him. He was always too smooth. Too pleased with himself."

"They broke up. They had a fight. She was probably upset. Maybe she didn't want to come home. You know what Nina's like when she's hurting. She don't go to anyone for help. She curls up in a corner, licks her wounds, and when she feels better she comes out like a fighter." Andy rested his chin on the top of my head. "Remember middle school? We heard nothing about that from her. Julie's mother told us, weeks after it all started."

They'd been in the seventh grade. Nina and her friend Julie had been targeted by some mean girls. One of them wanted to copy Julie's math test, and when Julie said no, that kicked everything off. The girls had their lunches stolen and thrown in the trash, dirt smeared on their backpacks, nasty notes written about them and passed around class. Nina could have dropped Julie and those girls would have left her alone, but that was never going to happen. The whole thing came to a head on the playground, when one of those girls—a twelve-year-old girl—called Julie a slut, and Nina pushed her over. Then of course the principal found out and we were called in and we didn't have any of the background because Nina hadn't said a word. We had to hear it all from Julie's mom.

"She was a little kid, Andy. It's not the same."

"I know. I get it. But she's caught up in the breakup. She's a kid. I bet you a hundred dollars she's back in that corner, licking those wounds, and we'll hear from her when she's good and ready."

I could smell burning. The pan was too hot under the sausages. I turned away from Andy and lifted it off the ring with my left hand, and as I did so the handle, which had been loose for a while, finally gave way. The pan started to fall, and out of instinct I caught it and held it with my right hand. For some reason, instead of letting it drop straight to the floor, I held on to it long enough to drop it into the sink.

"Jesus, Lee." Andy turned on the tap and grabbed my hand, putting it under cold running water. There were livid red marks on my palm and fingertips. I didn't feel pain, just a bit sick and shaky. "Keep it there," Andy said. He went to the long cupboard and took out the plastic box where we keep a first aid kit that we've never used. "There's burn spray here somewhere."

"I can't. I need a minute." I couldn't wait for him. I couldn't stay in the room for another moment. I took my hand out of the water and dried it on a dish towel. I took my jacket from the back of a chair and went outside. Rufus slipped out just ahead of me, and I let the door slam closed behind us. It was very cold outside, and it was already getting dark. No snow, or I would have picked some up and held it in my hand, which was throbbing. I walked in the garden and I thought about Nina. I knew my daughter, and she didn't have a cruel bone in her body. That's not how she was made. She could be impulsive, and she had a temper, but even as a little girl she'd been quick to forgive. She didn't hold a grudge. So why hadn't she returned any of my calls? Could she have been in an accident? She could be in a hospital bed somewhere, where no one knew her. Or . . . worse. There were worse things. There were predators in this world. My mind started to present me with scenarios. Terrible things. I shook my head hard, and then shook it again. I tried to tell myself that I was letting my imagination run away with me. That there was no need and no reason to think the worst, but fear welled up inside me, and it refused to be pushed back down.

I felt the hairs rising at the back of my neck, like someone was approaching, or watching me. I spun on my heel. There was no one there. I looked to the distant trees, the mountains, and paranoia gripped me. Anyone could be out there watching me. Suddenly I felt like I was in a closed room, under observation. I couldn't get enough air. My throat felt like it was closing in, and my heart felt like it was beating faster and faster. I tried again to breathe and couldn't. I'd never had asthma, but I felt like how I'd always imagined an asthmatic must feel in the middle of an attack. I could draw air into my lungs, but the air didn't seem to do anything. I sank down onto my knees and sank my right hand into the gravel to keep my balance. The stones were sharp and pressed into my hand, and with that small pain came a burst of clarity.

Nina could still be in the house. If Simon had left her there, like he said he did, she could have fallen down the stairs. She could have hit her head or fractured her pelvis. She might have an injury that would make it impossible for her to get to a phone.

Jesus. How had this not been the very first thing we'd checked?

I was still kneeling on the driveway. Rufus tried to push his nose under my arm. He whined.

"It's okay, boy. I'm okay."

I stood and walked on shaky legs as fast as I could back to the kitchen. I called for Andy, but he wasn't there. The pan of sausages was still in the sink. I didn't have time to look for him. It felt like delaying for even five minutes could ruin everything. I got my car keys and jacket and left. I was certain that I would find her, if I could just get to Stowe without any interruption. Certain in a way that made everything around me brighter and sharper.

I drove out of town and turned left on Route 100, in the direction of Stowe. I'd never been to the Jordans' chalet, but I knew from Nina, and from town gossip, that they'd bought some four hundred acres just five minutes from Stowe. I knew that there was a house on the property, and a small lake and a caretaker's cottage, and miles of cut trails, and springs and ponds. I knew enough that finding the house wasn't hard. When I got closer to Stowe, I pulled off on the side of the road and used my phone to look up properties sold near the village over the past year. Then I filtered the search results, weeding out anything that had sold for less than five million dollars, figuring that four hundred acres in that location would be in that ballpark, at least. The filter left me with a list of six properties. I clicked on the links and flicked through the descriptions and the photographs. Bingo. Or, at least, a partial bingo. From the description I thought I'd found the right property, but when I entered the address on Google Maps, the little red pin appeared right in the middle of a forest. It took a little more adjusting and fiddling before I could figure out that access to the property was off Tansey Hill Road. I pinned the access point, turned on directions, and started driving. It started to rain. Ten minutes later I pulled up outside a six-foot solid timber gate. There was no number on the gateposts, nothing to confirm the address of the house, but I knew I was in the right place.

I got out of the car. Given how obsessive the Jordans were about security at their home in Waitsfield, I thought perhaps the gate would be locked, but it wasn't. I was able to push both sides open and drive right in. It was full dark now, and the only light came from my headlights. The house was some two hundred yards back from the road. I don't know what I had expected. Something monolithic, maybe, like the house in Waitsfield. But this house was different. It was a long, slim pavilion, designed, or so it appeared to me, to look almost like one of Vermont's covered bridges. Unlike the Jordans' home, this house was settled into the landscape. It had a quieter presence, the trees and shrubs that surrounded it were mature, and there was moss growing on the roof tiles. No doubt Jamie and Rory would bulldoze it the first chance they got and build something enormous and ridiculous in its place.

I got out of the car and walked to the house through the rain. It was eerily silent; there wasn't even birdsong. The lawn to the right of the house fell away in a gentle slope to a jetty on a small lake. The water was still, dark, and uninviting. The windows of the house were dark too, and there were no cars parked outside. I went to the door and rang the doorbell. There was no response. The front door was enormous, easily nine feet high, and there was a full-length glass panel to the left of it. I tried to open the door, without much hope. It was locked. I could see into a wide hallway with pale timber floors, looking almost gray in the dim light of the late afternoon. There were no lights on inside, no sign that anyone was at home. I rang the doorbell again, then a third time.

"Nina? Nina, can you hear me?"

I had to get into the house. I could feel her, in there, needing me.

I jogged around the side of the house, trying to see in the windows. I got a peek into the kitchen and another into the laundry room, but the drapes were closed on most of the rooms, and I got increasingly panicked and frustrated as I made my way around the back. I thought maybe the back door might be open. In Waitsfield people sometimes left their doors unlocked. But I wasn't that lucky. I tried the door more than once, put my shoulder to it and shoved, but the effort was pointless and I knew it.

I stepped back and searched around for a rock. I found a solid chunk of granite, a stone that had been dug out of the mountain and used with others to form the edging for a garden bed. I hefted it in two hands and crashed it as hard as I could into the closest window. The glass shattered. The noise of it, the shock of it, gave me energy, and I worked faster. I removed a few of the big shards that I thought might come down, then put my hand through the break and opened the window. I climbed inside, avoiding the broken glass as best I could. Soon I was tracking my way through a long corridor, making my way back to the front of the house.

"Nina?" I called. My voice echoed. It was getting late, and the house was dark. I found a light switch, flipped it, and blinked in the sudden light that flooded the hallway. I opened a door and on the other side found a great room. It felt cold and unwelcoming, like a room that had been long abandoned and resented that abandonment. The floors were bare timber. Three large couches had been set out in a U shape, facing an empty fireplace, but there were no rugs for comfort, no coffee table or lamps. There were large windows overlooking the valley, and on another day the view might have been wonderful, but with the clouds and the rain and the sun going down, all I could see was gray. I left the room and found the stairs and took them two at a time.

"Nina?" I called her name as I climbed the stairs. I hurried from bedroom to bedroom, but there was no sign of her, and no sign she'd ever been there.

I stood very still and pressed my hands to my face. I made sounds I was barely conscious of. I whimpered. The certainty in my head was leaving me, and I didn't want it to go. I wanted to be in the world where I found my girl and I held her and kissed her warm head and called an ambulance and I was her mother and she was hurt but the kind of hurt that I could make better. The house was too cold and hard and empty. The house was a rock with sharp edges.

I knew I should leave. Nina wasn't there. Any justification I may have had for breaking in was gone. But I wasn't ready. This was the last place she'd been for sure. I needed to be certain that I hadn't missed anything, any clue about where she'd gone next. I started searching more carefully, going through the wardrobes and checking under the beds. The bedrooms were like hotel rooms; every bed was made, all the surfaces clean and polished, and nothing personal was left out. The master suite had a dressing room full of clothes; presumably belonging to Jamie and Rory. The closets in the first bedroom were empty, but in the second I found clothes that I was pretty sure were Simon's. Some slacks and sweats, long-sleeved T-shirts, underpants, socks, and sweaters. But there was nothing of Nina's.

Where had she gone when she'd left this place? And who had she gone with?

I went back downstairs. I would have to call the Jordans. Confess that I'd broken into their house. Pay for the broken window. I stood in the middle of the great room and closed my eyes. Tried to imagine Nina here. Nina, who was so warm, in this place that was so cold. The room smelled clean, not like floor cleaner or surface spray, but like someone had just done a fresh load of laundry. I went to the kitchen and opened the fridge. I'd expected it to be empty, but there was food inside. A wilting bag of lettuce, an open pack of bacon, butter, and some grapes. And finally something that suggested Nina had been here. Her favorite brand of yogurt, with two gone from a container of six. I moved aside the wilting lettuce and found a bottle of prescription eye drops with Nina's name on the label. Nina had trouble with dry eyes.

I clutched the little bottle in my hand. There was a large door to the left of the fridge. I opened it, expecting to find a walk-in pantry. Instead I found a small hallway and stairs that led down, into a basement and darkness. I flipped on the light switch and hurried down. The door swung shut behind me. In the basement I found a well-stocked boot room, with skis and snowboards and jackets and hats. Everything neatly put away, ready for the snow that was only weeks away now. I nearly turned around and went straight back upstairs, but a flash of red caught my eye. Nina's hiking jacket, peeking out from behind a bigger, navy jacket that I thought I recognized as Simon's. I searched around and found her day pack and a pair of rain pants. I looked inside the bag and found her climbing shoes and chalk, a fleece pullover, and a plastic sandwich bag with crumbs inside. There was a laundry basket in the corner of the room, half-full, with discarded socks and thermals, some of which I recognized as Nina's. I scrabbled through the laundry, pulling out everything I knew to be hers. Thermals, socks, and underwear . . . I shoved it into her day bag, then hugged her bag and jacket to me as if I was holding her. Then I heard the door at the top of the stairs open and a deep voice say:

"Police. Get on the floor. On the floor." I heard heavy footsteps on the stairs and a moment later a very young man, a police officer in full uniform, came into the room, with his gun raised and pointed straight at me. "Get on the floor. Get on the floor right now."

I looked at him stupidly. I was still clutching Nina's things. He gestured with his gun, and I started to kneel, awkwardly. He didn't want to wait. He grabbed me and shoved me to the floor, then wrenched my arms behind my back, handcuffing me. It hurt, and I let out a sound that was something like a yelp.

"I'm just looking for my daughter." I don't know if he even heard the words I said, if he processed them. He was breathing hard, worked up. He pulled me up by my handcuffed arms, like I didn't weigh a thing, and propelled me toward the stairs.

"Please. I need to take my daughter's things."

"Ma'am. I need to you climb the stairs right now."

I did what he asked. He sat me down on a stool in the kitchen, my hands still secured behind my back. There was another officer upstairs, this one a woman. Young, and attractive, with blond hair tied in a low ponytail. I tried to get her to listen to me.

"I'm Nina Fraser's mother. Nina's been missing since last weekend. If you call Detective Matthew Wright at the state police he'll confirm that I'm telling the truth. I came here because this house was where Nina was last seen. I shouldn't have broken in. I know that. I'll pay for the window. I know the owners of the house. Okay? I'm a friend of the family." A lie. Maybe an obvious one. The blond officer exchanged glances with the man who'd handcuffed me. He was the one who spoke.

"Ma'am, we know about your daughter. But you broke into this house. You've just admitted that. So you're under arrest for breaking and entering right now. I'm going to read you your rights, and then I'm going to take you to the station."

"I'm just trying to explain—"

"Ma'am," he cut me off with a warning tone.

I closed my mouth and listened as he read me my rights.

CHAPTER SIX

Matthew

Matthew was halfway to the Stowe house when he got a call from Sarah Jane, telling him that Leanne Fraser had just been arrested for breaking and entering. He swore, turned the car around, and drove back to the station. The arresting officer was waiting for him. He was defensive, as if he expected Matthew to give him a hard time for taking Leanne in.

"If you think I should have done differently, with her daughter being missing and all, I get that, but I couldn't just let her go."

Matthew settled him down and took all the details, and then he made a call and had a difficult conversation with Rory Jordan. When all of that was done, he went to find Leanne. They'd stowed her in an interview room, rather than a cell. The interview room was a lot more attractive than a cell, but that didn't mean it was a welcoming place. The windows were small and opaque and nailed permanently closed. The linoleum on the floor was peeling, and the room smelled strongly of bleach. They'd given her coffee, but they'd also handcuffed her right hand to the table. She looked pale and shaken. Matthew crossed the room and unlocked the cuffs. What idiot had decided that was necessary? He sat opposite her, taking his phone from his pocket and putting it on the table.

"I'm pretty sure I asked you to stay home and wait to hear from me," he said.

Leanne rubbed at her wrist where the handcuff had been. "I should have gone there yesterday. Nina might have had an accident. She could have been in that house, not able to get to a phone, needing me."

"Uh-huh. She wasn't, though, was she?" Matthew took a seat opposite her.

"You weren't doing anything to find her. I'm her mother. You can't expect me to sit at home and just wait."

"Leanne, we met for the first time this afternoon. And almost the first thing I did was have an officer go out to check the house."

That threw her. "You already searched the house?"

"No. We don't search without a warrant, not unless we have the owners' permission. But after I left you and Andy today, I called the local station and an officer came out to do a wellness check. She rang the doorbell and knocked on the doors. No one answered."

Leanne made a face. "She knocked on the doors. That's not enough. Are you kidding me?"

"I had also planned to visit the house this evening myself. You got there at most an hour before me."

"An hour is a long time if someone is injured. What if she had fallen down the stairs?"

Matthew leaned forward. "Leanne, you broke into the house. Presumably you'd already been upstairs before the officers found you?" He waited for her nod, then continued. "You've been all over, then. You've touched surfaces, maybe you shed some hair. If something did happen to Nina there, you've just completely contaminated those rooms. If they were a crime scene, and I'm not saying they were, then you've just destroyed them as a source of evidence."

Leanne flinched. "You think something happened to Nina? While she was in that house?"

"I'm not saying that. What I *am* saying is, you tramping around the place, going off on your own initiative, that won't help the investigation and it won't help Nina. I understand that it's hard to see

progress from the outside looking in, but we really do know our jobs."
Matthew tapped his phone screen. "The warrant just landed in my
inbox. It allows us to search the Stowe house legally, which I would
have done without your intervention. So I hope you can see that you
didn't achieve anything by breaking in. And you might have done a lot
of damage."

"Why didn't you just ask the Jordans' permission to come into
the house and look for her? Why did you wait for a warrant?"

Matthew didn't answer. She was a smart woman, and she was
drawing conclusions he didn't want her to reach.

"Did they say no? Did you *think* they would say no?"

He said nothing. If he denied it, she wouldn't believe him.

"What about Nina's phone? Did you check it? Has she made any
phone calls?"

"We've confirmed that Nina has not made any calls or sent any
messages since Friday. The last ping sent from her phone was on Friday night, to one of the towers near Stowe."

Leanne went very still. What little color there was in her face
faded away.

"I also talked to Simon," Matthew said, carefully. "He said that
Nina broke up with him to be with another guy. Someone she'd been
seeing secretly for some time. He said that after the breakup, he left
the house, and Nina stayed behind. She said that she'd arrange for a
friend to pick her up the next day."

"Bullshit," Leanne said. Her voice was a hoarse whisper. "Nina
wasn't seeing anyone else. She's in love with him."

"She never mentioned anyone else to you?"

"I'm telling you. Nina isn't a cheater. That's just not in her character. And she talks about Simon all the time. Arranges her whole life
around him. Between school and work and Simon, Nina wouldn't
have had time to cheat, even if she wanted to."

Matthew opened his mouth to speak, but she cut across him.

"He said she stayed in the house after he left? That doesn't even make any sense. She would have called me or Andy and we would have picked her up right away."

"And she definitely didn't call you? You had no missed calls?"

Leanne flushed, a sudden dash of pink to her otherwise pale cheeks.

"Last week, yes. I was angry with her for blowing off work at the inn, and I didn't answer. But nothing on Friday night." She took a breath, and her eyes met his. "Look, I found her stuff at the house. That officer took it. Her eye drops, and her hiking jacket and her day pack and some of her laundry. It was all there. Her gear was expensive. She saved up to pay for it. Nina wouldn't leave it behind."

"She might have forgotten it. If she was upset, or in a hurry."

"No. She wouldn't forget her jacket. It's cold out. She would have worn it."

"I'm told that the eye drops were in the fridge. And the jacket was downstairs. So out of sight, out of mind. If Nina had a breakup, if she was upset, it's possible that she forgot her meds, that she forgot that she'd left her gear downstairs. Or maybe she didn't think she'd be needing it anytime soon. Or maybe she thought she'd patch things up with Simon and she'd be back. There are a lot of possible explanations."

She hesitated, seemingly torn between an urge to accept the comfort his words offered and her instinct, which was telling her that something was very wrong. Instinct won.

"You don't believe any of that."

She was right. He didn't believe it. There was something about Simon Jordan he didn't like. Simon had been convincing when he'd delivered his story—in their postmortem after the interview, Sarah Jane had admitted that she'd believed him—but to Matthew, something had jarred. And good detectives do not rely on instinct alone. The complete lack of activity on Nina's phone and credit card was a major problem, but it didn't tell him anything that helped. He needed facts. He needed evidence. He needed not to jump to conclusions.

"I called the Jordans," Matthew said. "They've confirmed that they won't press charges for the breaking and entering. Given the circumstances, I don't think it's in anyone's interest to try to take this further."

"I . . . thank you." She rubbed at her forehead like she was trying to ease a headache.

Matthew tapped on the desk. It was a nervous habit he had.

"We're arranging a press conference for tomorrow," he said. "It would be very helpful if you could talk to the media. You and Andy."

"A press conference. You want me to talk to the press." She looked horrified at the idea.

"You don't need to be nervous. I'll be there. And Andy, I hope. We don't need you to answer questions, if that's too difficult. Just to give a statement."

"It's not that." She passed her hand in front of her mouth, like she'd just tasted something sour. "But you said . . . you said that Nina is an adult. You said that she's probably with friends. That she'll be home in a few days. It's too soon to do this, right?"

It was a complete reversal. A moment ago she'd been pressing for him to take things more seriously.

"Nina was due home on Saturday. Tomorrow's Tuesday. If we don't hear from her in the morning she'll have been missing for three days." Not to mention the fact that her phone was dead and her credit cards hadn't been used. "It's time. We need to get the word out. Get Nina's image out there. Maybe it's not necessary. Maybe she is at a friend's house. Maybe she'll see the interview and she'll come home. It happens, and if it does, great. But just in case, let's get the word out, okay? The department will organize everything. Tomorrow afternoon, in Waitsfield."

"Will you go back to Stowe and search for her? Not just the house. They have all that land."

"We don't have a reason to. Not yet, in any case." His words hung in the air. "Can you send me some photographs of Nina? We need some for the press conference tomorrow." Nina was a pretty girl. Pictures of her would get the media interested. They would have to use that. They'd have to use whatever would help.

"Okay. Yes. I can do that."

Matthew had an officer drive her back to her car. He went back to his desk, where Sarah Jane was waiting.

"How did it go?"

"As well as it could, I guess. She's going to do the press conference. She'll send over some pictures."

"That's good."

"Yes."

"I talked to the officer who arrested Leanne Fraser. He said there are definitely cameras at the house in Stowe. He saw some out front. Can you call Rory Jordan and ask him to send along the footage?"

Sarah Jane took a note. "Of course. Not a problem. And if he says no?"

"We'll get a warrant." He paused. "Leanne Fraser says Nina wasn't cheating. That her whole life revolved around Simon. We need to know if there was someone else in Nina's life. Let's find out who's telling the truth here."

CHAPTER SEVEN

Andy

When Lee burned her hand on the pan and went outside, I let her go. I figured she needed time to herself. She's more like Nina than she realizes, in that way. They both prefer to be alone when they're hurting. I went upstairs to change my clothes, and when I came back down I finished the cooking and put the sausages and potatoes in the oven to keep warm. I saw her jacket was gone. I figured she'd gone for a walk, so I went to the barn to stack the firewood I'd cut on Sunday. When Grace got in from school it was after 6:00 P.M. She came to find me in the barn. She'd had soccer practice and afterward she'd gone to Molly's house to study. Molly's mom had given her a ride home.

"What's for dinner?"

"Hello to you too, Gracey." My tone of voice was stupidly jolly. She rolled her eyes at me.

"Hi, Dad."

"Is Mom inside?"

She shook her head. "Nope. And I'm starving. Like, actually starving."

We went inside. The kitchen was empty and dark. The fire was out in the living room. I checked upstairs, and when Leanne wasn't there, I called her phone. There was no answer. I gave Grace her dinner. Afterward she disappeared up to her room, officially to finish her homework, unofficially to mess around on her phone. I let her go. I set the fire in the living room again, got myself a beer, and tried Leanne's phone for a second time. There was no answer. She finally got in just after eight o'clock.

"Where were you?" I tried to keep the edge from my voice.

She sat down opposite me, still wearing her jacket. "I went to the Stowe house. I thought that Nina might have fallen or something, and that she could still be there."

The idea hadn't occurred to me, but as soon as Lee said it the possibility seemed so obvious. I felt stupid that I hadn't thought of it.

"I woulda gone with you if you'd asked me."

"I broke in, Andy. There was no one there and I couldn't wait. I kept thinking about Nina lying inside in the dark, unconscious. So I broke a glass panel on the back door."

I hadn't seen that coming. "Lee . . ."

"I know, but what was I supposed to do? What if she'd been in there, needing a doctor or the hospital, and I'd just walked away to wait for permission?"

"I get it. I'm just . . . I'm catching up here, okay?" I knew my wife. For most of her life she'd had no one to rely on but herself. We'd been together for nearly seventeen years, and still she didn't know how to ask me for help. So Lee running off to Stowe by herself, maybe that was not a complete surprise. If she'd called the Jordans and asked them to meet her there and let her in, I would have thought, Yeah, sure. Breaking in was . . . it was a little crazy.

She stood up and took off her jacket. She hung it over the back of her chair and then just stood there, like she wasn't sure what to do next. I finished my beer and put the can on the coffee table.

"Nina wasn't there, I guess."

"Andy, Simon told the cops that Nina was cheating on him."

"What?"

"He said she's been secretly seeing some guy for a while, and she dumped Simon to be with him."

I didn't say anything. I was busy trying to make sense of what she'd just told me. Nina wouldn't cheat. She was crazy about Simon, and she was honest as hell. And if she'd had that kind of mess going on in her life I would have seen it. We spend time together. On weekends, she comes and hangs out in the barn sometimes. She helps me clean up or stack wood. Sometimes she comes out on a job with me, does a little planting, helps me fix up a fence. She's capable like that. She bosses me around and plays her music and laughs at me when I don't know the bands.

"He said he left her in the house and came back to Waitsfield on Friday night," Lee was saying. "He claims that she was going to arrange for a friend to pick her up the next day. But why wouldn't she just have called us to pick her up right away? And I found her stuff in the house. Eye drops. Her jacket. She wouldn't have left that stuff behind, Andy."

"What did Wright say?"

Lee took my hand. Her eyes were full of tears. "He said they checked with the phone company. She hasn't made any phone calls or sent any messages. Her phone hasn't even pinged a tower since Friday night."

I tried to get Leanne to eat, but she wouldn't. She wouldn't even talk. We cleaned the kitchen together in silence. Afterward I handed her a beer, took one for myself, and we went back to the living room. Rufus followed us in and out of the kitchen, whining. In the living room, he settled by the fire but looked at us like he knew something was wrong.

"Did Grace eat?"

"Yeah. But I didn't tell her about Nina. I don't know how to do that."

Lee took a sip from her beer. "We'll have to tell her in the morning. The police are having a press conference. Over in a hotel in Waterbury. Matthew Wright wants us to come and talk to the press about Nina."

I flinched. Leanne's eyes met mine.

"I know," she said.

I thought about all the press conferences I'd seen over the years, with broken parents turning their broken faces to the cameras, begging some evil bastard to return their missing children. How many had ever come back? How many bodies had been found? How many were still out there somewhere? I finished my beer. I went back to the kitchen for another one. Rufus followed me out and back, his nose so close to my calves that he must have bumped into me half a dozen times. When I came back, he settled beside Leanne, and she rested her hand on his neck.

"What do you think happened?" she asked. "What's the most likely explanation, in your view?"

"I was thinking, what if she woke up early on Saturday morning? You know, she didn't have her car. She might have considered calling us for a ride home, but maybe it was too early. And maybe she was a little heartbroken. She might have gone for a walk or a hike to clear her mind." I was warming up to my theory as I spoke. "What if she fell or something? She could be out there still. And Nina's really good in the backwoods. She always takes plenty of water and everything she needs to stay warm. You were dead right to search the house, Lee, but I think we should go and search the hiking trails."

Leanne shook her head. "Her jacket, Andy. I found her jacket and her boots and her pack. She couldn't have gone out without them."

"Maybe she borrowed someone else's gear? Or she could have bought something new when she was in Stowe. We could ask Simon." But my hope and belief in my theory sank just as fast as it had risen. I felt stupid. And Leanne looked frustrated.

"You're right, we should search the hiking trails," she said. "We should gather as many people together as we can. Anyone who's willing to help organize a search party."

"That's a great idea. Craig will want to help, and Sofia." Craig was my brother and Sofia was Craig's Danish wife. Craig and Sofia were a classic case of opposites attracting. Craig was book smart, but flaky; Sofia was a kind of New Age hippie. He worked as an accountant, and she believed in living off the land and homeschooling their kids. She made some money fixing up secondhand furniture and had a pretty big following online, according to Craig. They lived in Burlington, which wasn't far, but we didn't spend a whole lot of time together, just because they had twin six-year-old boys and we were all too busy.

"We'll need the Jordans' permission to go onto their land."

"You don't think they'll give it?" I was pissed. "No one's going to stop me from looking for my daughter, I'm telling you that right now."

She gave me a small smile. That made me feel better, but then Grace came into the room. It was just after ten o'clock. Leanne and I both tensed up.

"You're not in bed yet?" Leanne said, in the face of the obvious.

Grace made a face. "I can't finish my math assignment. Do you know what time Nina's coming home? I called her three times and I keep getting voice mail." Grace looked at her phone with dissatisfaction.

I started to get up. "I'll help you, honey."

Grace looked alarmed. "Uh, no offense, Dad. But I don't think so." It had been a couple of years since either Lee or I could help her with her math homework. It had never been a problem, because Nina had always been there.

"I don't mind, really," I said.

"That's okay," Grace said, backing out of the room. She looked at Lee from the door. "Did Nina tell you when she'd be home?"

I could see that Lee was struggling to speak. She shrugged and shook her head.

"It's fine. I'll use Khan Academy or something." Grace disappeared quickly, for fear, I guess, that one of us would follow and try to help. We were quiet for a moment, and then I had an idea.

"We should use the press conference. Shame them into it."

"Shame who into what?"

"We should say in front of the cameras that we want to search the Jordans' land. I don't mean point the finger at anyone. We just say we're worried that Nina went hiking by herself and, you know, we ask for volunteers to search for her."

Leanne thought about it. "That's a really good idea."

"Rory Jordan's not going to say no in front of the cameras, is he?"

We went to bed. Lee looked in on Grace.

"She's asleep," she said. She climbed under our comforter. The lights were out. I closed my eyes. Outside I heard a barn owl screech.

"The couple in the blue suite asked for a gluten-free breakfast," I said into the darkness. The words hung there between us for a moment, ridiculous. Leanne shuddered.

"I want them out," she said.

"The blue suite couple?" I asked.

"All of them." I turned over in the bed. I pulled her closer until her head was resting on my shoulder and my arm was around her.

"You want to close the inn?"

"It sounds so final when you put it like that. But yes. We have to. I can't do it right now."

"I can't either. I mean, I know it's your business. You do all the work. But I don't want anyone in the house until Nina's back home."

"I'll tell them in the morning."

CHAPTER EIGHT

Leanne

got up early on Tuesday morning and went to the kitchen to wait for Grace to wake. She appeared at seven thirty, looking for food, in her pajamas and one of Andy's sweaters, with her phone in one hand and her headphones around her neck.

"My room is freezing, Mom. I mean, like, icicle levels of cold. It's actually child abuse."

It was a teenage exaggeration and not a new complaint. In the inn, the heating came on automatically in all the bedrooms when the temperature dropped below seventy degrees, but in our part of the house it had to be turned on manually. Mostly I didn't. When the girls said they were cold I just told them to put on a sweater or come to the kitchen, where the stove always kept things warm. Why? Because I didn't want my girls to be weak. My childhood had been hard. We'd never had enough money. I was hungry, often, and cold, always. I'd had my brief, glorious escape to college, before everything fell apart again, but for most of my life I'd scrapped and fought and built a life for myself. There's a confidence that comes from making it on your own. I didn't want the girls to experience the loneliness or the despair I'd felt as a girl sometimes, but I did want them to have that confidence. I wanted them to be survivors.

When I made the inn into a success, I worried that if I removed every small obstacle from their lives, they would never develop the strength they needed to take on the world outside our door. But as I watched Grace warm her hands by the stove, I realized how stupid I'd been. I couldn't possibly give them the childhood I'd had. So what was the point of picking out small discomforts and imposing them artificially? My whole philosophy assumed that they had no challenges of their own. That their world outside our house was smooth and simple, and because of that I had made our home a place where they could expect to be pushed and challenged and questioned, instead of loved and cared for and reassured. Nina hadn't trusted me. That was the truth. She didn't come to me with her problems. She didn't ask me for help. And that was my fault.

"I'll fix it," I said. "I'll put your room and Nina's on the same thermostat as the inn, okay? It won't be cold anymore."

She looked confused. "Okay. I mean, it's not *that* bad."

"I'll fix it as soon as you go to school. Now, what do you want for breakfast? Waffles and fruit? Pancakes? You name it, I'll make it."

My tone was too upbeat. I was talking to her like she was seven years old. She looked around the kitchen. Usually, by this time, I'd be elbow deep in breakfast preparations for the inn, and Grace would be pouring herself a bowl of cereal. Today the kitchen was clean and quiet.

"Uh, I was thinking toast. And maybe eggs?"

"Coming up."

Her eyes narrowed as she looked at me. I couldn't put it off any longer.

"Grace, I have something to tell you," I began, just as Andy arrived in the kitchen. He was already dressed, not in his work clothes, but in his new jeans and a pale-blue button-down that suited him. His hair was damp from the shower. He cast me a swift look when he came into the room, then leaned down to kiss Grace on the head before moving to the other side of the kitchen and pouring himself a cup of coffee.

"What?" Grace said. "What's going on?"

I sat beside her at the table. "You know that Nina was supposed to come home last weekend, after her vacation with Simon?"

"Yeah." Her eyes went from me to Andy and back again.

"Well, Nina hasn't come home, obviously. And she's not with Simon, because he came home on Friday night."

"Nina's missing?"

"Well, it's more that she hasn't come home," Andy said, from behind me. "She broke up with Simon and he thinks she was upset. He thinks she went away to stay with friends for a while, but she hasn't called us or messaged us, and your mom and I are worried."

"That's not good."

Grace wasn't scared, yet. Her thumbs flicked across her phone screen. She raised the phone to her ear. I was close enough that I heard Nina's voice mail message. The same message I'd listened to maybe twenty times since Saturday. Grace hung up.

"Do you have Simon's number? We should call him. I think there's been a mix-up or something. Nina and Simon wouldn't break up. There's no way."

Of all times, this was the time that I needed to stay calm and controlled. But despite my best efforts, my voice was sharp when I replied.

"Well, that's what Simon says happened."

"I don't understand. You don't believe him?"

I said nothing. It was so goddamn hard to know how to handle this. I didn't want her to be afraid. But we were about to go to a police press conference about her missing sister. There was only so much patting down we could do here.

"That's not it," Andy said. "And there's no need for you to be upsetting yourself. You know Nina. Probably she went to Boston to stay with friends. But your mom and I don't want to just wait around for Nina to come home. We want to find her."

I turned away and cracked some eggs into a bowl. This wasn't right. We were going to have to do a better job than this. I tried to find the right words, but my brain wasn't working as it should. My thinking felt jerky, like a film that had been badly edited, with abrupt cuts and no transitions.

"Okay, but we should just call her friends in Boston, right?"

"We've tried, Grace," I said.

"What about email?"

"She's not answering right now," I said. "But then she doesn't have her laptop, and if her phone's not working . . ."

"We don't want you to worry," Andy said again, but his voice was less reassuring than desperate.

"That's right," I said. I turned to face her. I gripped the kitchen counter with my left hand. I felt nauseous. "But we do want you to know that some things might be happening that might seem really intense for a couple of days. Your dad and I have called the police to help us to find Nina."

Grace looked from me to Andy and back again. She was paler than usual.

"What the fuck?" she said.

"*Grace,*" said Andy. She ignored him completely. Her eyes were on me.

"There's a detective. His name is Matthew Wright, and he's going to help us to find Nina." I didn't look at Andy. I knew he'd be staring straight at me, willing me to stop talking, trying to let me know that we'd already said enough. But we couldn't hold back. Grace had to go to school. If they weren't already talking about it when she went in today, they sure as hell would be talking about it tomorrow.

"Matthew thinks it's a good idea for us to go on TV and ask people to let us know if they've seen Nina." Using his first name with her was a weak attempt to make everything seem less frightening. "Your dad and I have said yes. We'll be doing that this morning."

Grace's eyes filled with tears. She wiped them away roughly with the back of her hand.

"You're lying," she said. "The police don't hold press conferences because they're, like, mildly worried about someone. They must think that someone kidnapped Nina, or . . ." She wasn't able to finish the sentence.

I went to her. I wrapped my arms around her and hugged her tight. Hugging Grace was so different from hugging Nina. Grace was taller. She leaned into the hug. Even when she was mad at you, Grace sought comfort.

"I don't believe you, Mom."

"We're not lying to you, baby. We're telling you everything. This is scary. Of course it is. But Nina could walk in the door any minute." For a moment I saw it. I saw Nina walking in the back door, hair a little wild, mud on her pants and color in her cheeks. A little embarrassed, a little sorry, but mostly eager to tell us about the adventure that had kept her away. The picture was clean and clear, and I wanted to hold on to it. And then Andy spoke, and it slipped through my fingers and was gone.

"That's what we think will happen," he said. "But we don't want to wait, so we're just going to get help from everyone we can to find her. And if that means the police and the TV, then that's what we're going to do, okay? I don't want you to make too much of these things."

Grace leaned out of my hug.

"But do you think, you must think that someone, like, *hurt* her, or something," Grace said. She wiped her nose again with the back of her hand.

"We have no reason to think that," I said. "Really, Grace. We don't." I sounded convincing, and maybe because it was me who was saying it, rather than Andy, she seemed to believe me. Because I was the tougher one, maybe she didn't expect me to lie to comfort her. I let her go. I took out plates and filled glasses with orange juice from the fridge.

"So we're going to have a weird couple of days. And if you have any questions, you can ask your dad and me, but your job is to just get on with everything you usually do, and not to think too much about it."

I made her breakfast. She ate a few bites and left the room, claiming that she was going to shower, but I think really she wanted privacy. Maybe to think. Maybe to call a friend. Andy drove her to school a little early. I thought she would fight it, but she seemed relieved to be going. I wanted her there. I wanted her safely in class and nowhere near a screen when Andy and I were interviewed. Though she'd almost certainly see it as soon as school let out. She'd go online and search for it.

I shook off the thought and started knocking on bedroom doors in the inn, to tell our guests that there would be no breakfast that morning and that we needed them to vacate. I told everyone a short version of the truth. Our daughter was missing, there was a police investigation ongoing, and we needed our space and privacy at this difficult time. I got almost exactly the response I expected to get. Most people were at least outwardly polite and understanding, though a few made a very limited effort to hide their disappointment and frustration. One man tried to convince me that he and his wife would be no trouble to us, that we'd barely know they were there. It was their anniversary, he told me, and it was really important for their marriage that they stay. I cut him off and moved on. I cut every conversation short because I didn't care about any of them. Only one woman seemed to actually take in what I was saying. An older woman, in her sixties, staying alone in the green suite. She reached out and took my hand and held it in hers.

"Is there anything at all we can do?" She had an accent. Scottish, I thought, though it might have been Irish. I'm not great with accents. I shook my head.

"I'm not a believer. If I was, I'd offer prayers. But I'll be thinking of you and your daughter. And hoping." She gave me a card. "Call me, anytime. Day or night." The card told me that she was a florist in Boston. An image flashed into my mind—white lilies draped over a mahogany coffin. I went straight to the kitchen and threw the card in the garbage. I felt like I was going to vomit, so I went and leaned over the toilet in the small bathroom for a couple of minutes, but nothing came up. I sat at the kitchen table, opened my laptop, and went on-line and canceled all my bookings for the next two weeks. The explanation I gave was short and to the point.

> The proprietors of the Black Friar Inn are dealing with a family emergency and as a result will not be able to honor your booking. They sincerely regret any inconvenience and will refund your booking deposit immediately.

The message wouldn't save me. There would be a flurry of one-star reviews for the inn on all the booking websites. My ranking would plummet. Bookings would go down. It would take months of work to undo the damage, if the damage could be undone. I couldn't bring myself to care. I was torpedoing a reputation that had taken me twenty years to build and I felt nothing at all. I started the process of refunding the deposits, but it was too involved, and I couldn't focus. So I closed my laptop and left the house, taking Rufus with me. We left through the back gate and went for a walk through the woods. By the time I came back, the parking lot at the front of the inn was empty.

CHAPTER NINE

Matthew

M atthew Wright and Sarah Jane Reid were driving on I-89, on their way to Burlington. Matthew had picked Sarah Jane up at the station. The press conference was scheduled for 11:00 A.M., which didn't give them a lot of time, but Matthew was determined to get as much done as possible before he saw the Frasers again.

"Who are we interviewing?" Sarah Jane asked.

"Olivia Darlington. The friend that Simon Jordan said Nina might have been planning on visiting in Boston. I called her mother last night. She said Olivia's gone back to school. I thought we could meet her there."

"You think it's important to talk to her in person?"

Matthew inclined his head. "I do. And I want to speak to someone who saw Nina and Simon together recently."

Sarah Jane nodded. After that, conversation between them was limited. She asked questions about the case and he answered them, but they didn't know each other well, and at this early stage in the investigation, there wasn't much to discuss. If she'd been a man, it would have been easier. He could have talked sports. Was it sexist of him to assume that she wouldn't be interested?

"Do you follow hockey at all? You catch the game last night?"

She looked at him blankly.

"Not a sports fan?"

Sarah Jane smiled a little. "Not really." She opened her hands. Her palms and fingers had thick calluses.

"A rower?" asked Matthew, hazarding a guess.

"That's right," she said. "Used to be pretty good. These days I just row for fun."

Matthew gave her a sidelong look. He didn't know much about rowing, but what little he did know made him think that it wasn't something people did for fun. It was a sport for masochists. Sarah Jane pulled out her phone and started to scroll, and Matthew abandoned his attempts at conversation.

They pulled into the parking lot outside a student residence hall. They got out of the car, took their jackets out of the back seat, and put them on. It was still early, and cold enough that they needed them.

"Is she expecting us?" Sarah Jane asked.

"Her phone was turned off when I called her last night. Maybe she was still flying in. But I'm guessing her mother's called her by now."

THEY HAD TO BUZZ the door at the dorm entrance three times before a sleepy student answered and listened to Matthew's brief explanation before buzzing them in without further question or comment. They climbed the stairs to the third floor.

"Her mother told me she's in 303," Matthew said. They found the right room and Matthew knocked on the door.

"Hold on. I'm coming." The door was opened by a young woman. She was wearing sweats and a T-shirt, and her wet hair was wrapped in a towel. She was about five foot seven, Matthew figured, a little taller than Sarah Jane. Her hair, where it could be seen around the edges of the towel, was dark. She had big blue eyes and a nose that turned up a little at the end. "Sorry, I was in the shower."

Matthew took out his ID and showed it to her. "Sergeant Matthew Wright. I'm a detective with the state police. And this is my colleague, Officer Reid."

Olivia didn't look at the ID. She put out her hand and shook theirs in an oddly formal gesture. "My mom said you'd be coming over. I guess I just didn't expect you this early."

"Sorry about that," said Matthew.

"No, no. It's not a problem. I mean, this is important, right? It's just I'm not really . . ." She let her voice trail away and gestured to her towel-wrapped hair. "Can you give me a minute?"

"Of course."

Olivia shut the door. She didn't take long. A couple of minutes later she was back, fully dressed, with socks and sneakers on her previously bare feet, and her hair tied back in a messy bun. The ends of her hair had pink streaks. She was carrying her jacket in one hand.

"Sorry. My roommate's still in bed. Is it okay if we talk outside?"

"How about we buy you a coffee?" Matthew said.

She took them to a dining hall in the basement of the dorm. There were some students already there—early risers on their way back from the gym or a run, still in their workout clothes—but there were plenty of free tables. Matthew paid for coffee and muffins and they carried them to a table in the corner.

"Thanks," said Olivia. Now that they were sitting and facing each other, she seemed less sure of herself. She picked at her blueberry muffin and looked anxiously at Matthew. "I didn't know that Nina was missing. I would have called if I'd known. Or maybe I wouldn't. I mean, I don't think I can be much help or anything. I don't know where she is. I've been trying to think of places that she might go, but . . . I mean, obviously there are plenty of places she could go if she wanted to get away, but I'm not personally aware of anyplace that she might have a special connection to, do you know what I mean? And if she changed her mind and decided to go see another friend, I mean, everyone's on campus now because classes start again today. But she could have decided to visit a friend from high school, right? But I guess you guys have already thought of that." Olivia slumped a little.

"What do you mean, changed her mind?" Matthew asked.

Olivia's phone was on the table, beside her coffee cup. Sarah Jane was sitting very quietly. She was watching and listening to everything, but she'd made no effort to interject, to add anything or to try to develop a connection with Olivia. That was fine. She was new to this case and new to the job in general. In a few months he would expect her to get more involved, but for now he'd rather have a junior who knew what they didn't know than one who plunged forward in an effort to impress. Olivia's hand strayed to the phone, and she tapped the screen absently.

"Well, she never came, you know? I did call her, but it went to voice mail and then she didn't call back, and then, you know, school started again, so that was that."

"You were expecting Nina to visit?" Matthew said.

"I thought you knew," Olivia said. "I thought that's why you wanted to speak to me." She picked up her phone, and swiped and tapped to bring up a message. She handed the phone to Matthew so that he could read it.

> Hey babes, are you in Boston? I'm heading your way in the morning. Can we meet up? Could use some fun. Simon and I are over (boo hoo). Always going to happen (who stays with their high school boyfriend??)

Matthew swiped upward and saw a second message, and then a third, both from Nina to Olivia.

> If you're awake, call me! Need to talk and Simon already left.

> Phone about to die. See you tomorrow! Want to introduce you to someone kind of special. Don't ask me about Simon overlap! 😳 😵 😬

That was it. There were no other messages. Matthew handed the phone to Sarah Jane so that she could read them.

"You didn't message her back?" he asked Olivia. She shook her head.

"I was asleep. I mean, she sent them at like, midnight. I called her as soon as I woke up, which was just after eight A.M. on Saturday. I called her a bunch of times over the weekend, but my calls just went to voice mail and she never called me back."

"Were you surprised?" Matthew asked.

"What, that they'd broken up?" She waited for his nod, then grimaced. "I mean, yes, but also, not really? Like Nina says in the text message, everyone who stays with their high school boyfriend or girlfriend thinks that they're going to be different. That they're the ones who'll make it. But pretty much everyone breaks up sooner or later. I guess I was surprised that she was so chill about it."

Matthew nodded. "Did you see Simon when he came to visit Nina on campus?"

"Sure. We hung out a few times."

"What did you think of him? Of them, as a couple?"

Olivia widened her eyes. She'd been midway through taking a sip of her coffee, and she put it down hurriedly.

"1 mean, they were great together. Simon's a good guy. He was completely crazy about Nina, and he was really interested in her life here. He's really funny too." Olivia's smile lit up her face, briefly, before she remembered the seriousness of the situation and let the smile drop. "I know I said I wasn't that surprised that they'd broken up, but there weren't any signs that that was coming. It seemed like everything was great between them."

"No arguments?"

She shook her head. "Not that I saw, no. They weren't into drama. Their vibe was more joking around."

"Are there any other guys in Nina's life? Any other boyfriends or guys she was interested in?"

"Nope. Not that I know of anyway. But we aren't, like, *super* close."

"Simon said you guys are good friends."

"We are. I mean, we're friendly. We hang out."

"So Nina didn't mention any guys who'd shown particular interest in her?"

Olivia shook her head again, her eyes serious. She understood what he was asking and why he was asking it.

"I'm sorry. No."

"Okay. Well, thank you for your time."

"I'm sorry I wasn't more help."

"You've been very helpful, Olivia. One thing—can you put together a list of Nina's friends at UVM?" He handed her a card with his number and email address. "If you could do that, and include cell numbers, and send it to that email address, I'd appreciate it."

She took the card. "Sure. Of course. No problem."

Matthew stood. Sarah Jane did too, but something in the expression on her face told him she didn't think the interview was over. He paused, and there was a moment of wordless communication between them. Sarah Jane obviously wanted to ask a question, and she was checking with him to see that it was okay. Matthew nodded. Sarah Jane turned to Olivia.

"Did Nina often call you babes?"

Olivia looked blank. "I don't know. No. Maybe?"

Sarah Jane hesitated. "You said you weren't super close. Were you surprised when she said she wanted to meet up in Boston?"

Olivia shrugged. "Not really. I mean, like I said, we might not be the kind of friends who tell each other everything, but we hang out."

Sarah Jane subsided. "Okay. Thank you."

They left Olivia in the dining hall, picking at her blueberry muffin and scrolling through her phone. They walked back to the car. Campus was much busier now, with students out and about and on the way to classes.

"What made you ask if Nina—"

Sarah Jane cut him off in a rush. She seemed embarrassed, like she felt she'd overstepped. "It's just I was looking at Nina Fraser's social media in the car, and the tone of her text messages to Olivia seemed off. She didn't strike me as that type. You know, bubbly or gushy. Her posts are mostly about climbing. She seems kind of serious."

"You're thinking that she didn't send the messages." Matthew said.

Sarah Jane gave him a quick glance. "I guess I just wondered. It seems so convenient. And that second message saying that Simon had left."

Matthew nodded. "You think he sent the messages himself to create an alibi, and then sent us to Olivia Darlington so that we'd find it."

"I do," she said. She gave him a sideways glance.

"It has that feel about it."

"You think he killed her?"

Matthew wanted to say no. He wanted to meet Nina Fraser one day. He wanted to discover that she'd walked away safely from Simon Jordan and that she was, right now, hanging out with some unknown friend or love interest, oblivious to the worries of her family and friends.

"What I think is that one way or the other, we have to find Nina." Matthew looked at the clock on the dashboard. He had to be in Waitsfield by ten thirty to pick up the Frasers and take them to the press conference. "If we hustle, we should have just enough time for one more interview."

Sarah Jane had her phone out, open to her notes. She scrolled through a list of names and numbers. "Who do you want to talk to next?"

"Let's start with Julie Bradley. She's on the list Nina's mother gave us. A friend from high school." It would be good to talk to someone who had known Nina and Simon from the beginning. Olivia Darlington had been too new to Nina's life to have any real insight into her friend. "Give Julie a call. See if she's free to meet."

Sarah Jane made the call while Matthew drove. Julie was available. She was at work, cleaning up and restocking at her mother's bar in Waitsfield, and she'd be happy to meet them there if that was convenient. Matthew drove on, satisfied. Driving gave him time to think.

Time to sift through the impressions he had formed and the facts he had gathered in the eighteen hours or so since he'd taken the case.

There were three possible explanations for Nina's disappearance. The first was that she had chosen to leave of her own accord, possibly to visit Boston, and there she'd either gotten into some kind of trouble that had prevented her from contacting her family, or she'd chosen not to contact family or friends for her own reasons. The second was that an unknown third person had taken her from the Stowe house after Simon Jordan left on Friday night. So far there was no evidence to suggest that that might have happened, but he couldn't definitively rule it out, not yet. The third possibility was that Simon had killed her, either on purpose or by accident, and had disposed of her body before returning to his parents' house on Friday night.

Matthew had a bad feeling about the case. Simon was slick. He'd handled himself well enough in his interview. The Olivia Darlington alibi was thin and obvious, but it was the kind of thing that could create a lot of noise in the hands of the right attorney. Matthew needed to get back to basics. To look at Simon's movements. Sarah Jane was still scrolling through her phone, checking her email.

"The warrants have been signed off," she said. "That was quick."

They'd both worked late on Monday night to fill in warrant applications for Nina and Simon's detailed phone call and message history.

"Judge Warwick likes to start early. Let's get those sent off right away."

Sarah Jane was still scrolling. "We haven't heard back from Rory Jordan about the security cameras at the Stowe house. I called last night, like you asked, and left a message. I emailed too. Nothing yet."

"Follow up again. Let me know if he hasn't gotten back to you by this evening."

They hit unexpected traffic. A minor rear-ending had caused a traffic jam that took them thirty minutes to get through. Matthew didn't want to put off the Julie Bradley interview. They had too many people to speak to, and not enough time. He glanced at Sarah Jane.

"Do you think you could talk to Julie?"

"By myself?" She was surprised.

"I could drop you at her mom's bar in Waitsfield, then pick up the Frasers and take them to the press conference. We can meet for lunch afterward and you can fill me in."

"Yes. I can do that. Definitely." She sat up straighter in her seat.

Matthew nodded, pleased with the decision. Running the interview by herself would be good experience for Sarah Jane. If he needed to, he could always speak to Julie himself later in the day, but there was every chance that Sarah Jane would do better with her than he would. Julie Bradley might be more inclined to be forthcoming about her friend to another young woman rather than an older man. And Sarah Jane was sharp. She had good instincts. It was time to give her the opportunity to put those instincts to the test. In the meantime, he would focus on Nina's family and the difficult task that lay ahead of them.

CHAPTER TEN

Andy

Matthew Wright was late. He'd messaged Leanne to say that he'd pick us up at ten thirty, and he showed up at ten forty-five. He didn't fall over himself apologizing either. I don't know how I feel about that guy. He keeps his distance. Talks to us like we're not on the same team. Like we can't be trusted enough to be let inside.

"I wanted to talk to you before the press conference," Wright said. "As I explained to you, Leanne, we need you to make a statement about Nina. Just words from the heart, about how worried you are about her, how much you need her to come home. Don't go into any details about where she was or that she was with Simon. You can leave that part of it to me, and I'll be choosing my words carefully."

"You going to make that public?" I asked. "That Nina was last seen with Simon?" We were standing in our kitchen. Leanne and I had our jackets on. We were ready to go.

"Yes. It's not going to be possible to avoid that fact entirely. But we're not going to dwell on it. The point of the press conference is not to point fingers or suggest that anyone has done anything wrong. It's to get Nina's face out there, so that if anyone has seen her, they can get in touch."

Leanne crossed her arms. "I don't like that."

Wright's face was impassive. "Which part?"

"I mean, obviously someone did something wrong. Nina's not here, is she? She's missing. And Simon was the last person to see her. And his story doesn't even make sense. I told you, if they broke up she wouldn't have stayed in that house. She would have called us, and we would have picked her up."

I cleared my throat.

"We've known Simon since he was a little kid. We're not trying to say he did anything to Nina. But right now his story don't make a lot of sense."

Matthew Wright leaned forward, resting his forearms on the table. "Mrs. Fraser. Leanne—" he began. Leanne cut him off straight away.

"Please," she said. "Don't placate me."

"There's nothing to be gained by using this press conference to paint a target on Simon Jordan's back. Whether or not he is a suspect in your daughter's disappearance is something for the police to deal with. I'm going to have to ask you both to trust us. Believe me, I know how hard this is, but if we don't work together as a team, we're going to be in trouble from the get-go."

"We'll trust you," I said. "As long as you don't give us reason not to."

WE FOLLOWED MATTHEW WRIGHT to a hotel just outside Waterbury, where the press conference was going to be held. In the parking lot there were two TV vans, the kind with the antennae on their roofs. Wright waited for us at the door. We got out of the car, and he led the way inside. He pushed open the glass doors. He seemed to know exactly where to go. The receptionist watched us pass, curiosity all over her face. But when I looked right at her, she looked away and got real busy moving papers around her desk. Wright led the way across the foyer and stopped outside a set of double doors. There was a timber plaque marked CONFERENCE SUITE in curly letters. I could hear a hum of voices coming from inside the room. Suddenly I felt like everything was happening way too fast. I wanted to stop and check that Lee was okay. I wanted to talk through our plan. But there was no time.

"Take a deep breath," Matthew said. "Just be yourselves. Say exactly what I asked you to say and you won't go wrong. Remember, you're doing this for Nina."

He pushed open the door. The room was a good size, with seats enough for about forty people, and it was half-full. Heads turned to stare as we came into the room. There was a podium set up at the front of the room, with four chairs, along with bottled water and microphones. There was a projector screen behind our chairs displaying a big photograph of Nina. As we walked to the podium, the photo transitioned to a video. It was the same video Lee had shown Wright on Nina's Instagram, the one of her in a bikini, pushing Simon into a swimming pool, then laughing into the camera. Lee stopped walking. Her eyes were fixed on the screen. The screen flicked again, to a photograph of Nina standing on the edge of a cliff wearing climbing gear, then to another of her eating ice cream. Another and another and another. It was too much. Leanne stopped in her tracks. I put my arm under hers to steady her. I don't think Wright even noticed. He just kept on walking.

"Are you all right?" I asked in her ear. I could feel all the eyes on us.

Leanne gave me a short, sharp nod. She dragged her eyes away from the screen, focused them on the carpet, and started walking again. We took our seats, and Matthew cleared his throat and leaned into the microphone.

"Thank you all for coming here today. I'm Detective Sergeant Matthew Wright, with the Major Crimes Unit of the Vermont State Police. I've been tasked with leading this investigation. You've each been provided with a packet that includes some of what we know so far, as well as information about Nina and the police personnel tasked with finding her. Digital copies of the packet are also available."

I looked around the room, trying to find someone I recognized.

Oscar Milligan was here, standing off to the side, leaning against the wall like he owned the place. I guess maybe he felt he had more claim to it than anyone else in the room. He'd run the *Waitsfield Bugle*, our local paper, cobbling together a budget out of subscriptions from the few retirees who held on to them out of a sense of duty, or maybe just forgetfulness. He'd given up a few years before and moved on from Waitsfield. I'd never heard where, but it looked like he'd stayed in the game, at least. The other journalists I didn't know. There were two blond women with the kind of makeup that looks like a mask in real life, but I guess looks right on TV. There were two guys operating cameras.

"This is Leanne and Andrew Fraser, Nina's parents. They'd like to say a few words."

Lee and I hadn't talked about which one of us should speak. I froze up. For a moment, I couldn't say anything, and then Lee jumped in, speaking fast, the way she always does when she's nervous.

"Yes. I'm Nina's mother. We love her very much and we want her to come home." The words came out sounding like something she'd practiced. Like something she'd been told to say. Lee took a deep breath and tried to slow down. "We don't know what happened. We hope Nina is okay, but it's not like her not to be in touch with us. If anyone out there knows where she is, please get in touch with the police or with us."

One of the blond women put up her hand. She didn't wait for Matthew Wright to call on her.

"Can you tell us a little more about Nina, Mrs. Fraser?"

It was my turn. I wasn't going to leave everything up to my wife. "Nina loves animals. Loves the outdoors. She's very generous and kind. Everyone loves Nina." I felt stupid. I was trying to be honest, to say the important things, but the words didn't sound right. They didn't sound like her.

"And she was with her boyfriend up until the night she disappeared. Have you talked to him?"

Matthew Wright spoke up. "We've talked to Nina's boyfriend. He's given us an account of everything that happened the last time he saw Nina. Nina was planning to stay overnight at Stowe. A friend was going to collect her the following morning, but we don't know who that friend was, or if they showed up."

Another journalist put his hand in the air. "Can we get Nina's boyfriend's name, please? How long were they seeing each other?"

"Simon Jordan," Matthew said. "They've been dating for four years. As I said, Simon has been fully cooperating with the police investigation and has given us a full account of their last evening together."

That was my cue. I leaned closer to the microphone and spoke slowly.

"Simon says they broke up on Friday night. After the breakup, he left, he says, and Nina stayed behind in the house. That's something we don't really understand. The house belongs to Simon's parents. Nina could have called us for a ride. We'd have gone right over there."

The atmosphere in the room changed, sharpened. Everyone leaned forward. Lee took my hand under the table and held on tight.

"We're really worried about Nina," she said. "The house she was last seen in was the Jordans' house, which is obviously on private land. We would like to carry out a search for our daughter, with the help of friends, but we will need permission from the Jordans to access their land. I'd like to ask the Jordan family if they would agree to a search party coming onto the land to search for Nina."

Immediately there were a bunch of hands in the air. A few people shouted questions. Matthew Wright put his hand to our microphones, pushing them away.

"I'm afraid that's all we have time for right now." His voice was very calm. "The family has released photographs of Nina, and some video. They're all accessible from your digital packet. Any further questions should be addressed to the state police. Thank you all very much for your time."

He stood abruptly. We followed. Lee was still holding my hand, and she held on tight all the way outside. Flashes went off. The sudden noise and the bursts of light coming from different angles were disorienting. More than that, they felt dangerous. Like we were hens inside a chicken run and they were all hungry dogs just outside it. The shouted questions, the pushing and shoving in the pack as they jockeyed for a better position, it was a lot. Lee was pale as a ghost and shaking. I put my arm around her until we got to the car.

"My god," she said.

"Yeah," I said. It was real now. It was actually happening.

CHAPTER ELEVEN

Jamie

t was Rory's decision not to press charges against Leanne Fraser for breaking into our house in Stowe. He didn't ask me for my opinion. He said something about Wright putting him under a lot of pressure, and also that we had to consider the court of public opinion. It wouldn't look good, he said, if we pressed charges against a worried mother looking for her daughter. I could see his point, but I wasn't exactly thrilled about his decision. Breaking into our home was the behavior of a crazy woman. A normal person would have asked the police to check the house, if they were that worried. Or called us and asked if we had been there since Friday. If there was any chance Nina could still be at the house. In itself, that wasn't an unreasonable question. But just driving up there and taking a great big rock and heaving it through a window . . . I mean. Honestly, it worried me. If she was willing to break into the Stowe house, what was to stop her breaking into our home in Waitsfield? Clearly, she was blaming Simon for Nina's disappearance. What if she took it into her head to go after him?

Of course, Leanne didn't find Nina, just some bits and pieces of clothing she'd left behind in the laundry. That was Monday. On Tuesday, Simon went out first thing in the morning and stayed gone all day. When he came back at five o'clock he told me he'd been to Burnt Rock Mountain, and he acted like it was the most natural thing in the world, to go for a hike when the girl you'd very recently been in love with was missing, when the police were asking questions. And maybe it was natural. What else was he supposed to do? Sit around at home, reading a book or playing video games? Rory went to work. I tried calling him a couple of times during the day, but he never answered.

All of which meant that I was alone with the whole thing. I had no one to talk it over with. I couldn't call anyone, because I couldn't trust anyone not to repeat every word I said to three other people the moment we hung up the phone. I knew enough about human nature to know that the story of Nina going missing would be like catnip. People would not be able to resist talking about it, speculating about what might have happened and what it all meant. For most of the day I stayed off social media. I busied myself with photographing clothes—this time a Dolce dress and a Prada skirt and jacket. It takes time to photograph clothes well. You need to steam the garment, then hang it so that it flows perfectly, and you need to light it and frame it just right. The work was a good distraction, but just after lunch my phone buzzed with a message from Georgia White. She'd seen Leanne Fraser at a press conference on local news, and *thought I'd like to know*. I switched on the TV, but the conference was already over, and I had to wait for an hour before the edited news report was uploaded on the channel's Facebook feed. By then I'd finished one glass of wine and started on my second. When the post finally came up, I clicked play and watched as Leanne and Andrew Fraser took to the podium. There was a poster-sized still of Nina on a screen behind them. She was laughing and looked extremely pretty. Leanne looked like hell. Like she hadn't slept in a week, like she'd never been introduced to a hairdresser or the concept of makeup. They talked about Nina. It was hard to watch. Leanne came across badly. She was robotic and unnatural. I think I was actually starting to feel sorry for her, until right before the end, when she all but said straight out that our family was hiding something. That we were preventing a search of our land, which was utter bullshit but was exactly the kind of thing that would supercharge the gossip engine. She also made it clear that she thought Simon was lying. When I finished watching the clip I stayed online and watched the comments as they came flooding in.

The first person to comment was someone I knew. That bitch Bianca Glasier—she's my second cousin, and she's always been a jealous cow—posted, saying that it was *clearly* suspicious that Simon had left Nina alone after a breakup that night, and that she'd never been seen again. Bianca said that the police had been holding back information at the press conference, probably because Simon was under investigation. I mean, are you kidding me? She had no clue what she was talking about, no clue. But that wouldn't stop her from spreading that shit around on the internet. Her post got plenty of likes too. Plenty of supportive comments. Only one or two people said it was too soon to know exactly what had happened, and that hopefully Nina would come home under her own steam.

I finished my glass of wine. What really worried me was the people who weren't posting. My WhatsApp groups were silent. Other than Georgia's gloat-text, my phone was quiet. There were no calls or concerned messages. The women I knew, our wider circle, they weren't posting online, but there was no way they weren't talking about this. Of course they were. Right at that moment, private groups were being set up, excluding me. Oh, they would couch my exclusion in sensitivity or politeness. *Poor Jamie*, they would say. *She must be so worried right now. I don't want to bother her. I'm sure she needs a break from thinking about this.* What they really wanted, of course, was the freedom to say anything and everything. To speculate about Simon and Nina and me and Rory and our lives and our parenting and exactly what had happened at our house in Stowe.

I put my tablet away and poured another glass of wine and took it to my bathtub. I sat there and worried until the water cooled. I was dressed again by the time Simon came home. I said nothing to him about the press conference and I didn't ask him any questions. I just offered him something to eat and plastered on a fake smile, and he retreated to his bedroom as soon as he could. I went to the living room with yet another glass of wine and turned on the television. I can't remember what was on. Reality TV, I think. A *Survivor* rerun, maybe. Simon used to love that show when he was a kid. It was one of the only shows we watched together. He loved the drama of the plotting and the planning and the blindsiding. I stared at the show mindlessly and worried. I was sure that when Rory came home, he'd have spoken to our attorney in detail, and he'd be confident that everything was going to be fine. And maybe he would have been right if this had been happening twenty years ago, but these days everything is trial by internet. If this story got national attention (and I thought it would, if only because Nina was so goddamn photogenic), then Simon's future, and ours, was going to be decided on Facebook, Reddit, and YouTube. Opening arguments were already being made in the court of public opinion and there were no attorneys involved.

Rory got home late. I was half asleep on the couch when I heard the front door open and shut. I went to the kitchen, poured two glasses of wine, and then went to find him. He was in his study, hunched over his computer. I stood in the doorway.

"Baby," I said. He jumped a little and turned in his seat like I'd caught him watching porn. Maybe I had. I kept my eyes off his screen.

"Can I talk to you?"

He gave me his focused look. His you've-got-my-attention look. "Something on your mind?"

I sat in the chair opposite his desk. "I'm worried, Rory. People are talking online. They're going after Simon. Leanne Fraser said something really stupid at their press conference today, something about searching our land. She basically said she thought Simon was lying. So now people are just jumping to wild conclusions."

"I saw it."

I took a breath, kept my voice soft and low, just the way he likes it. "I'm worried because this stuff has a way of getting out of control. There are people out there who love a story like this. They want to be part of it. They're going to pore over Simon's social media and Nina's too, and they're going to be looking for clues to this or that or whatever they want to believe, and they're going to find them and blow them up and analyze it all to death."

Rory was looking at me with a weird half smile on his face.

"Maybe I'm overreacting," I said. "Maybe I'm getting ahead of myself here, but I—"

"You're not overreacting." He studied me for a moment, like he was debating whether or not to confide in me, then he pushed his chair back and gestured to his computer screen. "I agree with your analysis. If anything, I think the situation is worse than you've said. There's already been enormous interest in the story. The press conference video has been shared twenty-eight thousand times so far across all major platforms. I'm told by people who know about these things that that's likely to increase exponentially over the next few days."

The number horrified me.

"Who told you that?"

"Alistair referred me to a PR firm. I guess you'd call them pretty niche. They specialize in reputation management. They work for politicians and celebrities, but also companies that have a reputation to protect. I had a meeting with them this afternoon. They'd already started tracking everything."

I bit the corner of my thumbnail until it cracked.

"These guys said that you can't stop this kind of thing when it starts. It's like playing Whac-A-Mole. They said the only real option is to flood the field with moles of our own."

Rory turned his computer screen so that I could see it. I leaned forward. He was logged into YouTube, into a channel called *Justice for Simon*. There were two video posts up on the channel so far. One from the press conference, a video of Leanne Fraser talking about her daughter, but this video had new audio, one of those voice overlays like the one teenagers use on TikTok videos.

Why does Leanne Fraser sound like a robot when she talks about loving her daughter? What's up with her body language?

The second video was a bunch of photographs and video of Simon and Nina, culled from their social media and edited together. In the photos they were smiling, laughing with friends, kissing. In one of them, Nina, dressed in a bikini, pushed Simon into the pool and then laughed into the camera. She looked beautiful. They both did. A young couple in love. But the video ended with a still from the press conference. A close up of Leanne's face, twisted and distorted in the midst of some painful expression. Her hair looked greasy, her face gray. And across the screen, written in bloodred letters, were the words:

Why did Nina run away from home? What aren't they telling us?

"What is this?" I asked.

Rory's eyes were still on the screen. "The PR firm got these to me within an hour of our meeting. They set up the channel and posted the videos, and they're using bots to amplify them. The theory is that the noise over this kind of thing will confuse the narrative. People will be less likely to paint Simon as the bad guy because things won't be clear cut."

I shook my head. I'd been worried that Rory wouldn't get it, I'd wanted him to take the situation seriously, but I didn't know what to do with what was in front of me.

He looked up and his eyes met mine. "Are you okay?"

"I don't know." I tried to read him. He looked so sure of himself. "This is just . . . it's a lot."

"I had to do something, Jamie. You saw the press conference. You saw yourself what it was going to do. It was a dog whistle to every true crime fanatic out there. If I hadn't done something, Simon would have been convicted in everyone's minds before the week was over. This is our son. We can't just sit and wait while everything happens around us. We have to take action."

"Yes." I couldn't argue with him. He was just repeating back what I'd said to him, in different words. "But what are we trying to say with this? We don't think Leanne . . . I mean, this is clearly suggesting that she . . ." I let my voice trail off, and I gestured at the screen.

His hand reached out and gripped mine. It made me jump. I tried to cover that up. I softened my hand and allowed him to hold me, but maybe he was more perceptive than usual. He squeezed my hand briefly, then released it.

"No, I don't think Leanne is responsible for Nina disappearing, but she created the problem. She pointed her finger straight at Simon at that press conference. We can't just stand back and let her do that. We need to get ahead of things, to remind people that there are other people in Nina's life. And my guys aren't going to paint a target on Leanne. They're going to blast a range of different theories and possibilities into the online world. Sow as much confusion as possible. Think of it as noise. The more noise, the better. But we have to do this, and we have to do it now. My PR firm tells me this story is already getting national traction. It's because of the photos and video. Nina and Simon look good on camera, and there's so much footage of them that the networks are going to have a field day. Every day that girl stays away from home, this story gets bigger. As things stand, even if she came home next week, there'd always be a cloud over Simon. Every time someone googles his name, years from now, this story will come up and all the rumors with it. And what if she doesn't come home, Jamie?"

I let out an ugly, involuntary sound, like the beginning of a moan, and cut it off abruptly.

"They'll say he's a murderer. And they'll come after us. You think all this surmising and talking and examination will stop at our boy? If the world decides that Simon did something to Nina, you and I will be picked apart. They always blame the parents. What kind of horror-story parents raise a boy who's capable of killing his girlfriend?"

I felt a sudden strong urge to vomit. I pressed my fingers to my mouth, and Rory continued, more placatingly.

"I still think Nina will come home. I don't know where that girl got to; maybe disappearing like this is her way of punishing Simon for some imagined injury. Like you said before. And when she thinks he's suffered enough she'll come home. But by then, if we don't do something, it might be too late. Simon's reputation will be trash. And if she doesn't come home . . ." Rory shook his head. "Police feel the pressure from public opinion, maybe they charge him. And a jury is chosen from the kind of numbskulls who read this online crap and think it's the truth. I'm going to do whatever it takes to make sure that that doesn't happen."

"You'll be caught," I said. "Someone will trace the IP address and they'll figure out who you are, and then everything will be so much worse."

His face took on that expression he wears when he thinks I'm being stupid.

"Jamie, these guys have been doing this for a long time. They know what they're doing. They use incredibly sophisticated methods to make sure that the trail is as confused as possible. They have overseas bot farms that will feed the algorithms in exactly the way we need them to, to make sure that it's our content that comes out on top. And you know what? Maybe the FBI could figure out who's doing this, if they took the time to look, though I doubt it. But why would they bother? There are millions of internet trolls out there every day doing exactly this shit for nothing but kicks and clicks. No one's going to pay particular attention to one more." Rory reached back to the desk and picked up the glass of wine I'd brought for him. He took a long sip and narrowed his eyes. 'Besides," he said, "you watch. We won't have to do much. All we have to do is get these people started, and then it will run itself. They're going to take over."

He was so sure of himself, and I couldn't find it in me to argue with him. I didn't want to, because he was absolutely right. He was defending our son, even if he was doing it by throwing Leanne Fraser under a bus. His screen still showed that twisted still of Leanne's face. He—or his PR company—had gotten this so right, framing the narrative as Simon and Nina, gorgeous and in love, versus gray-faced, middle-aged, tense Leanne. There were people who would run with this, who would *love* to run with it. Men who hated women, and there were plenty of them. Women who hated women; there were enough of them too. They would see a young man under attack and they would be *eager* to flip the script. They would go into Leanne's life and they would rip it apart. What would that do to her, with her daughter already missing? And did I care enough about that to try to stop him? If I had to decide between giving Simon a chance at a normal life and protecting Leanne Fraser from emotional distress, was there even an argument?

Rory was reading my mind, it seemed.

"You owe her nothing, Jamie. You've never been close. And she and her daughter are going to destroy our son. Our boy, who's done nothing wrong. His life might be over, right here. And when Nina comes home, none of this will matter. Nina will move back in with her parents and the chatter will fade away."

A hundred images flashed through my brain in what felt like a fraction of a second. Simon, his soft baby hand holding tight to my hand. Toddler Simon, trying so seriously to stack his blocks. Simon at eight (or was it older?) flushed with pride when he won a race at school and trying not to show how much it mattered to him. Simon following Rory around like a lost puppy, wanting his attention and never getting enough of it. I was his mother. I really didn't have a choice.

"I can help," I said.

"How?"

I took a deep breath and a deeper swallow from my wineglass. "We should have some sock puppet accounts set up that I can run. I can respond to and boost the video posts. I know social media. You don't. I know how people talk to each other."

He smiled at me fiercely, like we'd just won something. Maybe we had. Everything was going to hell, but at least we were a team.

"I should go and check on Simon," I said.

"Leave Simon to me," Rory said. "I'll talk to him as soon as I've finished here. And I'll call the PR firm. Get those accounts set up."

We looked at each other for the longest moment, and in other circumstances I might have smiled. I felt closer to him than I had in a very long time. I had to remind myself that the crisis with Simon might make us a team for a while, but it wouldn't change anything else. And I was fine with that.

CHAPTER TWELVE

Leanne

After the press conference Andy and I went straight home to the inn. I was tired. My legs were weak, like I'd been hiking all day. Andy was being careful around me, like he expected me to fall apart at any moment. That was far enough from our usual dynamic that it made me realize, again, that I needed to pull myself together. It was beginning to hit me just how much work we had to do. The first thing I did when we got home was to call Lucy Palmer's mother, Selena, and ask her if she could pick Grace up after school and take her to basketball practice and then to their home for a couple of hours. Lucy was Grace's best friend, and her mother was a nice woman. I figured Grace would be better off with them while we were trying to get things organized for the search. The phone call was more difficult than I expected. Selena was kind and supportive, but of course she asked questions, and it was hard to keep it together. I learned what I'm sure many frightened parents had learned before me. Explaining things to other people and dealing with their reactions forces you to deal with the enormity of the situation. I got off the phone and started making toasted sandwiches for me and for Andy. It was a relief to realize again that we didn't have any strangers in the house upstairs, that I wouldn't have to get up in the morning and deal with breakfasts or changeovers or any of the rest of it.

Andy was sitting at the kitchen table with his laptop open.

"There's a website that could be helpful," he said. "I was searching earlier and I found it. Look—it's a kind of guide for the families of missing persons, put together by an advocacy group. It has some information about how to organize physical searches, as well as other steps you can take."

I came over to stand beside him, and we started reading through some of the suggested steps. The guide was big on cooperation with the police. It emphasized the importance of not stepping on toes, being careful not to do anything that would jeopardize an investigation, which made me feel guilty and impatient at the same time. Maybe I shouldn't have broken into Stowe. Maybe we should have given a heads-up to Matthew Wright about what we were going to say at the press conference. On the other hand, Nina was our daughter. We couldn't just sit around and wait for things to happen. We needed to take action. We were smart, capable people, and it was too much to ask that we switch off our brains and put away our abilities and do nothing while our daughter was missing. Andy scrolled down the page and we read more. The guide had suggestions about how to get information out to the public, including localized options like posters and billboards, and also social media.

"We need to get on all of this," I said. "As soon as possible. We need posters, and to get on local radio, and we need to start posting to social media. The press conference was a start, but not enough. If there's anyone in the world who knows something or saw something, we need to make sure they know that Nina is missing."

Andy was nodding. "We're going to need help. I'll call Craig and Sofia, and you should call any other family or friends you think will help. We should break down all of this work into chunks that we can parcel out."

Andy's parents were dead, and Craig was his only brother. I had no siblings, my mother had been dead for a long time, and my father was still living in New Jersey. We hadn't been in touch in years. Not since Nina was a little girl. There was no point in calling him. Would he come to Vermont if he knew his granddaughter was missing? I doubted it. He'd come up with some excuse. Claim that Claire, his wife, was in the hospital, or some other equally serious reason why he couldn't make it. And I'd have to make the right noises back and pretend I believed him. I didn't have time for all that. I had no other family, so I started by calling Nina's friends from school: Beth Ann Corbett and Julie Bradley. Beth Ann started crying when I told her. She was away, vacationing with college friends, and hadn't heard anything about Nina going missing. She and Nina hadn't seen much of each other since high school. I ended that call as soon as I could. Julie Bradley was much more helpful. She said she'd come over, and that she'd take her mom, Delores, and her brother, Isaac. Andy called Craig and Sofia, and they promised they'd be over as soon as they could. I called Alice Marsden too. She used to be a teacher at the school. She taught both my girls, and though we're not friends, exactly, we're friendly, and she's smart and sensible and I thought she would be helpful. Andy thought we should hold off on calling anyone else until we were a bit more organized, and I realized I didn't really have friends I wanted to call. I've never thought of myself as a lonely person, but I'm not particularly social either. The situation was forcing me to realize that maybe I'd been more isolated than I realized. I hadn't gone for coffee with other parents after school drop-off for years. I'd never joined a book club. We weren't the kind of family that invited people over for dinner, or a barbeque in the summer. I'd never felt like that was a bad thing. We were happy in our own company. But Nina's disappearance and our need for help made me realize just how cut off from other people we had become. That was mostly my fault, I think. Andy had had lots of friends when we'd gotten married, but slowly he'd stopped seeing most of them. Was that because I had never wanted to go along? Or was it something that would have happened anyway?

While we waited, Andy and I prepared. He lit a fire in the inn's living room. I made coffee and sandwiches. Delores and Julie arrived first. Delores had dyed her hair since I had last seen her. It was platinum blond, and she wore navy eyeliner that had smudged. She gave me a one-armed hug like she meant it and pressed a frozen casserole into my hands.

"I don't know why I brought this," she said. "Except that's what people do in a crisis, don't they?"

"Isaac is at work," Julie said, "but he wants to help. He said to just think of jobs for him to do and he'll do them. No problem."

I thanked Julie. She avoided eye contact, which surprised and disappointed me a little. Julie was a strong girl. I guess I just expected more of her than that she'd be afraid to look at me. I told myself I was being unfair, and forced myself to smile at her, which only made her more awkward. She flushed and found a seat beside her mother. Soon after Julie and Delores were settled, Craig and Sofia arrived, followed by Alice Marsden, and then Patrick from the gas station.

"I called him," Andy murmured. "I thought he might have some useful information."

There was small talk, but it was a strained beginning. Craig had gone into what I thought of as shutdown mode, which nearly always happened when there was a lot of emotion in a room. He asked and answered questions stiffly, like he was at some kind of formal enquiry, and avoided all eye contact. Sofia tried to make up for that by being more effusive, and the imbalance made everyone a little uncertain.

"Thank you all very much for coming," I said. "As you all know, Nina's been missing since Saturday. Today is Tuesday, so she's been gone for three days. As far as we know, Simon Jordan was the last person to see her, and that was at his family's home in Stowe. We want to organize a search for her, and we're hoping that you can help." I stopped talking, but no one responded. They just looked at me with expectant faces. "Uh . . . I guess we need to figure out how many people we can get out to help. And then we can figure out the best process." I thought that was pretty weak. I wished I'd had more time to think everything through, to make a plan, but Alice Marsden gave a firm nod.

"Sounds sensible to me," she said. "Why don't we each make a list of everyone we think would be willing to help? Then we can cross-check our lists to make sure we don't double up, and then start calling everyone. When are you thinking for the search, Leanne? I'd imagine as soon as possible."

It occurred to me that I still didn't have the Jordans' permission. "I guess I'd better go and make a call." I went to the kitchen. It wasn't a conversation I wanted to have in front of anyone else. I found Jamie Jordan's number. The call rang out and went to voice mail. I thought I would wait fifteen minutes or so and then try again, but my phone buzzed in my hand almost immediately.

"Jamie."

"Hi, Leanne. How are you holding up?" Her tone was formal. Polite.

"I'm okay, thank you." I hesitated. I'd been so focused on finding Nina that I hadn't considered how I would actually present the search request. I wasn't going to mention the press conference, even though I expected she'd have heard about it. We lived in a small town. Someone would have mentioned it. "Look, Jamie, the reason I'm calling is that I want . . . I would like to search your land. For Nina. I'm afraid that she might have gone for a hike and gotten lost, or maybe injured. It's the only thing we can think of."

"Of course," Jamie said briskly. "That's not a problem. We should have thought of that ourselves. It's dark now. Is it too late to go today? First thing in the morning? Rory and I will help. And Simon."

Her voice was firm on Simon's name.

"I . . . yes. First thing in the morning." I didn't want them there, but I couldn't stop them.

"At first light? Dawn is at six thirty A.M. right now. Should we meet at our house at six A.M.? I don't think I need to give you the address." Her voice had an edge to it. She knew I'd been inside, obviously.

"No." There was silence on the line for a long moment. "Thank you, Jamie." I forced the words out.

"You're so welcome, Leanne." She was saccharine sweet.

We ended the call. I went back to the drawing room. Things had moved on in my absence. Julie Bradley had brought her laptop. She'd already started a contact list with everyone's name, number, and email address. Her awkwardness seemed to have passed. She'd started a task list too, in a table format, and she was busy assigning names across the grid.

"This is going to sound weird, but the missing-persons' guide says that we should choose a brand for our campaign," she said. "We should choose a short name to represent what we're doing, something we can use across all social media, as a hashtag, you know?" Julie looked at me, anxious that she might have offended. "I know it sounds messed up, but it really is necessary. We need people to share our stuff, to talk about Nina, to ask questions. The guide suggests using something like 'Nina come home,' but that doesn't seem right to me. '#NinaComeHome.'"

"No," I said, sharply. "That's not right. It makes it sound like she made a choice. Like she's out there somewhere, just deciding to stay away."

Everyone went quiet. They all looked down or away or at their phones or at Julie's laptop. Anywhere but at me.

"What happened to Nina?" I said, loudly. Julie looked up. "That should be our hashtag. Our campaign name. Whatever. That's what we're searching for. For the truth."

"I think that will work," Julie said slowly. "It will draw people in. Make them feel like they're part of something. A quest for the truth."

"Okay," I said. "Let's go with that."

Andy started explaining to me the plan they'd begun to develop when I was out of the room. Julie wanted to set up a Facebook group. Something she could use to invite people to join the search and then keep them informed about future campaign plans. Alice was already working her way through her contacts by phone, asking everyone she knew to join the search party.

"A lot of people are working tomorrow," she said apologetically. "But I have eight yeses so far, and all of them are going to invite two more people each."

"We need posters," Andy said.

"I know a graphic designer who can design a poster for us," Sofia said. Sofia had a very slight accent. She'd moved to the US from Denmark with her family in her late teens. Her English was perfect, but she still pronounced her words precisely, in that Danish way. "If you are okay with it, Leanne, I'll make a call. Printing can be expensive, but I think I can call in a few favors."

I felt a sudden wave of gratitude wash over me, so powerful that it left me dizzy and blinking back tears. But before I had a chance to thank her, a voice came from behind me.

"Am I interrupting something?"

I turned around and saw Matthew Wright standing in the doorway. He was back in what I was fast coming to recognize as his personal version of a uniform. Navy pants, navy hiking boots, navy jacket. I hadn't heard him arrive. He must have let himself in through the front door.

"You didn't ring the bell," I said.

"I saw the cars. Figured there was a group meeting. Do you have a moment? Could we talk privately?" He looked from me to Andy. Andy was frowning, not happy. I figured it was because Wright had come in without knocking. It wasn't until we were in the kitchen and Andy closed the door behind us that it suddenly occurred to me that Wright might have come with bad news. I held on to the back of one of the chairs.

"Have you found her?"

"I'm afraid not."

I let out a breath and closed my eyes.

"We're getting up a search," Andy said, firmly. "First thing tomorrow morning we're going to the Jordans' place, and we're searching those hiking trails."

"You got their permission," Wright said.

"We did," Andy said.

"They couldn't say no, not when you asked them through the media." He was looking at me, with something that might have been approval.

"Jamie Jordan says they'll join the search. Simon included."

"And how do you feel about that?"

"I don't want him there."

"I think it's better if he comes," Matthew said.

"Why?"

He hesitated. It was obvious that he didn't want to answer me. After a moment I figured it out for myself.

"It's because you think he might find her, isn't it?"

"No. It's because if they spent the last week hiking together in the area, he'll have a better idea than anyone else about where she might have gone if she went back out alone."

"That's not the only reason though, is it? You think if he hurt her, if he ... killed her, he might just go out with the search party and 'discover' her." Where had I come across that idea? It felt like something I'd seen in a TV show, the idea that killers sometimes come back. That they can't leave things alone. It surprised me that I was able to ask the question without choking on my words.

"I don't think that." His voice was low and firm, and I couldn't tell whether he was lying to reassure me or telling the truth. "Right now we don't have any evidence that Nina has been hurt by anyone, okay? It's only been a few days. She could turn up here tomorrow."

"Most missing people show up within the first forty-eight hours, right? We're already past that point."

"It's better to stay off the internet. I know it's not easy, but searching for information about missing persons, looking up statistics and trying to apply them to your situation, that's not going to be helpful. Every situation is different."

The coffee cups and plate from our lunch were still sitting on the kitchen table. I picked them up and took them to the sink. Andy sat on the end of the bench. His hands were clenched so tightly that his knuckles had whitened.

"You said you wanted to build trust with us," I said. "You said that was important."

"Yes."

"Trust doesn't just go one way. If you want us to believe in you, you have to trust us too. I'm telling you that Simon Jordan's story doesn't make sense. There's something he's not telling you."

There was a long pause. Then he said, "I know."

I turned to look at him. He held my gaze. He seemed different from the man who'd lectured me in the interview room at the police station. There was something in his eyes.

"Something's changed," Andy said, suddenly. "What did you find out?"

"Nothing's changed."

I was sure he was lying. I don't know why, because he had a rock-solid poker face. There was nothing in his face to give him away, and nothing in his body language, but I was certain he wasn't telling us something. I tried to push him. He was polite, but he slid away from my questions easily and left a few minutes later, after first promising to help with the search. I watched him go, and my body felt like it was just one ache, in need of answers. I thought it might help if I could cry, but the tears seemed a long way away. For a while, shame kept me sitting there at the kitchen table. This was my fault. This disappearance hadn't come out of nowhere. Something, *something* must have been going on in Nina's life that I had missed. She'd called me and I hadn't taken her calls, hadn't bothered to call her back, for the stupidest, *stupidest* reasons. Andy waited with me until I could pull myself together, and then we went back to the living room, where the plans for the next day's search, and for Nina's campaign, had advanced.

CHAPTER THIRTEEN

Rory

On Tuesday evening we had dinner together—Jamie, Simon, and I. Jamie was making a special effort. She'd made gnocchi with slow-roasted lamb, which she knows I like. Simon was in a good mood, at least to begin with.

"My flight's at ten in the morning," he said. "Are you driving me to the airport, Mom? No biggie if not. I can book a car."

Jamie looked at me. I put down my fork.

"I think you're going to have to postpone that flight," I said. Simon looked at me quizzically. "The Frasers want to search the house at Stowe. I mean, not the house, but the trails. They have some theory that maybe Nina went for a hike on Saturday morning, after you'd left, and that she got into some kind of trouble. They think maybe she's still out there."

Simon's expression changed. There was a flicker of dismay. It came and went so fast that if I hadn't been looking right at him I would have missed it entirely.

"No. No way. She'd had enough of hiking by Friday. She said to me that she couldn't see herself going again until after snow season. Also, she had an injury. She'd twisted her ankle. So she couldn't have gone hiking even if she'd suddenly wanted to."

I studied his face. "Well, that's all useful information, and we'll pass that on."

"You think they'll cancel the search?"

"I doubt it. Maybe they're clutching at straws, but I think they need to feel like they're doing something right now."

"And you're going to let them do it? You're going to let them in?"

"I don't think I have much choice in the matter. Now that Leanne's gone so public with it."

Simon pushed his chair back from the table. "That's bullshit."

Jamie put down her knife and fork. "Simon . . ." she said, in a warning tone of voice. He ignored her completely.

"Dad, they don't think that Nina went for a hike and got into an accident. They think that I hurt her. That I killed her or something, right?"

I didn't answer him. I didn't move.

"Yeah, exactly," he said, as if I had agreed with him. "And you're letting them search our land? That's like letting them put up a big fucking sign that says 'Simon Jordan, Girlfriend Killer.' You're letting them say that about me, okay?"

"Simon—" Jamie tried again, but he shot her a look so angry, so *vicious*, that she closed her mouth.

"You need to stop them. You need to pick up the phone to your lawyers, or whoever you need to talk to, and you need to just fucking stop them, get a restraining order or something, and you need to make sure—"

"Sit. Down," I said, enunciating each word, cutting across him. He stopped talking, but he didn't sit. I took a breath. "Simon, you're being ridiculous. If you used your head for a second, you'd realize that refusing our permission would do exactly what you don't want us to do—it would send out a signal that we've got something to hide. Is that what you want?"

Simon didn't say anything. He stood there, looking trapped.

"You can also be assured that if we were stupid enough to refuse to allow the Frasers to search for Nina, the police would get a warrant the very next day."

Still, Simon said nothing. The silence went on too long.

"You didn't do anything wrong," I said, as gently as I could manage. "There's nothing to worry about here. We'll allow the search. Hell, we'll do better than that. We'll go along and help. We'll be the most cooperative hosts the police have ever seen. And the signal we'll send to the world is that you are completely innocent. That you are just as worried about Nina as her parents are. Okay?"

Simon nodded.

"Yes. Sorry. I . . . I guess I wasn't thinking."

"Well, it's a difficult situation." I glanced at Jamie. Usually she'd be the one to jump in about now, with a comment or a joke that would take the sting out of the conversation, but she said nothing. "Sit down, Simon. Finish your food."

Simon looked at his plate and curled his lip. "I'm sorry. I'm not hungry."

"They'll be at Stowe by six A.M. tomorrow morning." I said. He was irritating me now. His refusal of the food was childish. "And we'll be there to greet them, and to help with the search. All three of us. Understood?"

He looked at me like he was thinking of challenging me, and then he subsided.

"Sure, Dad. Whatever you want."

Simon left the room, leaving me alone with Jamie. She was very quiet. She just stared down at what was left of her food. Her brow was furrowed.

"What?" I said. "You think I could have handled that better?"

She shook her head like I was missing the point, then started to clear away the dishes. I hadn't finished eating.

I WENT AND TOOK a shower. The shower is, in my experience, a good place to think, and I couldn't get that look on Simon's face out of my mind. That momentary look of dismay when I'd said that the Frasers were going to search our land. The more I thought about it, the more that bothered me. Simon didn't want the search, and not just because he thought it might make him look bad. He was afraid of something bigger than that.

I dried off and got dressed and went to my home office. The night before the police had called and asked me for any camera footage we had from the Stowe house. I'd put in a call to Ronnie Garcia. Ronnie was CEO of the security firm I used for all my personal and business matters. Ronnie has an admirable loyalty to the people who pay him, and he understands the importance of discretion. When I bought the Stowe property I'd asked him to install cameras, because our insurers had required them, but I'd never followed up to check if they were in place. Ronnie had called me back later in the afternoon to confirm that yes, the cameras had been installed and they were working fine. He said that he arranged for all the recordings to be available at the same link I use for all of my other properties. He also told me that he'd had a brief look at the recordings from Friday night and that there was nothing untoward. As a result, I had been in no great rush to review the recordings myself. I'd planned on taking a look at some point that evening, before sending them over to the police as requested, but I couldn't get that look on Simon's face out of my mind, and now I was afraid that Ronnie had missed something.

I clicked on the link to the security system and entered my password. The system was complicated, with a lot of features, but I'd used it before and it wasn't difficult to navigate. There was a separate icon for each of the properties I owned. I clicked the newly added icon for the Stowe house, which brought me to the live footage. There was a button at the bottom of that page that linked to prior recordings. I clicked it, and my page filled with a calendar view. Every day where a recording was available was shaded green. Every day without a recording was red. The dates for the Stowe house were green every day from the second of October, which was the day after we'd closed on the property. Ronnie had been as efficient as always.

I clicked on Friday's date. My screen immediately split into eight rectangles, each showing a different black-and-white view of the grounds around the house. I knew from prior experience that the views were only black and white because it was nighttime. During the day the cameras recorded in full color. It seemed we had external cameras only, nothing inside the house. That made sense. It was consistent with our setup at our home in Waitsfield. The quality of the recording was excellent. Every view was crystal clear. One camera appeared to be at the end of the driveway, pointing at the entrance. One was above the front door. That one showed the steps up to the door, most of the gravel parking area, and some of the driveway. The other six cameras were set around the perimeter of the house, facing outward, completing a ring of security with no gaps in coverage. As I played the video back, I could see footage from all eight cameras playing simultaneously. I hit the fast forward button. All was quiet. The first action came well after dawn.

In the center rectangle, I watched Simon and Nina leave the house. The time stamp on the video told me that it was just after 9:00 A.M. on Friday. They were carrying backpacks with climbing ropes and helmets attached. They went out the front door and walked around to the back of the house. I watched them cross from one camera view to another. They walked across the lawn. When they reached the trees they disappeared from view, down a trailhead that I could just make out at the very limits of the camera's view. Nothing happened after that for hours. I fast-forwarded through the footage again until it was near dark, and slowed it again as I saw Simon and Nina re-emerge from the same trailhead. I checked the time stamp. It was five minutes past six in the evening. This time Simon was carrying both backpacks. Nina was limping. As they approached the house, Simon put his arm around her. They went inside and the cameras were quiet again. I hit the fast-forward button. Nothing happened. I watched right up till midnight, when the video came to an end.

I clicked back out of Friday and clicked on Saturday's video. The same grid appeared on my screen. Once again, the recording started a second after midnight, so it was in black and white. I fast-forwarded and saw Simon come out of the house. The time stamp said 1:36 A.M. He was carrying his small backpack and he was alone. He went to his car and drove away, and I let out a long, slow breath of relief.

I have a bar in my office, built into some cabinetry. Jamie had it put in—it's not really my thing. I rarely drink, and I think having a bar in your office is a little cheesy. Not that I'd say that to my wife. I went to the bar, possibly for the first time since we'd moved into the house, looked for a beer, and found one. I opened it at my desk, took a long drink, then sat down and watched the footage again. I replayed the video. I took a certain pleasure in watching Simon leave the house, just as he'd said he'd done. Entirely innocently. I looked forward to handing the video over to the cops. My email would be polite, up to a point, but I would make it clear that they could shove their suspicions up their collective asses. I clicked the fast-forward button twice and sped through the early hours of Saturday morning, until the sun came up, and beyond. Trees swayed in the breeze. Occasionally a bird or a squirrel appeared in the camera view, but there was no sign of human activity. There was no movement at the house. I kept playing, kept expecting to see a car drive up to pick up Nina, but it didn't happen. I played the video all the way through to the end, to midnight on Saturday. Nothing. There was no movement at the house. No new arrivals, no departures. I clicked on Sunday's video and did the same thing. Still nothing. I clicked on Monday's video and fast forwarded through until finally I saw someone. Leanne Fraser. I slowed the footage down and watched her drive up to the house, walk around back, pick up a rock, and break in. It was all there and there was no pleasure in watching it. There was a look of such naked desperation on her face as she heaved the rock at the window. It left me feeling unsettled. I watched the cops arrive. Watched them take her from the house in handcuffs, put her in the back seat, and drive away.

I sat back. I didn't understand. Where was Nina? She couldn't possibly be in the house. Leanne had searched it. The police had searched it. But if she wasn't inside the house, how had she left without the cameras capturing her departure? It didn't make sense. I went back over the footage again and saw nothing new. I finished my beer, opened another, and went back over the footage again, slower this time. Still nothing. I stared at the screen. I had to be missing something obvious.

It was another hour before I saw it.

Each video started from one second after midnight, where the previous day's video left off. I was starting the Saturday video for the fourth or fifth time when I realized that something wasn't right. The view from one of the cameras had changed from the previous day. The camera view in the middle of my grid still showed lawn and trees, but the trailhead that Simon and Nina had used in the Friday video was now nowhere to be seen. I squinted, zoomed in, fast-forwarded again through the footage until the sun came up. Still, there was no trailhead.

I went back to the Friday night video and flipped back and forth between them until I was a hundred percent sure. I wasn't imagining it. Someone had shifted the camera's view at exactly midnight on Friday night. Up to midnight you could see the trailhead. After midnight you couldn't. Someone had shifted the camera to the left.

Someone.

There could only be one someone.

The system did not allow you to move the cameras remotely. You would have had to have physical access to the camera to adjust its positioning, and whoever had done it made the change at exactly midnight, when the file changed over and it was least likely to be noticed. It had to have been Simon. He was at the house. He must have leaned out of an upper window, maybe, waited until midnight, and then just . . . moved it.

There was only one reason he would have done that. Something had happened in that house, and Simon had tried to hide it. Christ.

My mouth felt dry and tacky and I reached for my beer, but all that was left was a single warm sip at the bottom of the bottle. My hand was shaking when I put the bottle down. Logic told me that Simon could be hiding only one thing, but I had to be missing something. I knew my son, and I knew that what I was thinking, what I was afraid of, simply wasn't possible.

I checked my watch. It was nearly midnight. I must have been looking at the recordings for hours. And in six hours the Frasers and their extended family and friends, not to mention some cops, would be tramping all over our land. I stood up and paced the room. I had to be sure. Maybe Simon had screwed up, maybe he was covering for someone, or maybe I was putting two and two together and getting a hundred, but I had to run this thing to ground and find out what the hell was going on. Before I left, I used the system to switch off all the cameras at the Stowe house.

Jamie was asleep and the house was quiet. I went to my dressing room and changed into black jeans and a black hoodie, then I went to the garage. Out of habit, I buzzed my car and then realized I couldn't take it. We had GPS security trackers on our cars. If anyone checked the log later, they'd be able to see that I took my car to Stowe. I swore to myself.

We had one other vehicle. An old four-wheel-drive truck we used to tow the trailer for our snowmobiles during the winter. It wasn't worth much, and I'd never bothered to have it tagged. The keys were on a hook under a bench at the back of the garage. I found them and unlocked the truck. I found a flashlight and got into the car, hesitated, and went back for a shovel. I put it in the back seat. I took my phone from my back pocket, muted it, and left it on a shelf in the garage.

The roads were dark and quiet. I was pumped up and agitated and driving too fast. I forced myself to slow down. The moon was out, full and bright. When I got to the house, the moon was reflected in the dark water of the lake. The little wooden boat that Jamie had thought was so picturesque bobbed in the water beside the jetty.

I parked in front of the house, got out, taking the shovel with me, and walked around back. I didn't know the grounds well. I'd inspected the house, of course, before buying it, and Jamie and I had spent a weekend there after we'd settled. I'd read my agent's report on the land carefully, and I'd seen photographs, but I hadn't hiked the trails or taken the boat out on the water. I hadn't bought the place for leisure, but as an investment. I turned on the flashlight and walked across the grass to the trailhead. The grass was long, and soon my sneakers and the bottom of my jeans were wet. Twice I stopped walking. I was filled with doubt. What I was thinking was crazy, wasn't it? There must be some other explanation. Except that I couldn't think of one, no matter how hard I tried.

I walked down the trail. The ground underfoot was covered in leaves. We hadn't had any rain for a week, and it was cold, so the earth was relatively dry and hard underfoot. I walked up the trail for two or three minutes and saw no sign of anything suspicious. I came to a deer track. It led off to the left, uphill, while the main trail continued straight on. I hesitated, shining my flashlight up the deer track, then the main trail, then back again. I chose the deer track. If Simon had come down here needing to hide something, he would have had to go off the main trail. The deer track was harder to navigate. It was narrow and slippery. Branches snagged at my face and clothing. I thought about turning back, but I hadn't been climbing long when I came to a small clearing. It was hidden under the tree canopy, and very little moonlight made it through the branches overhead, but my flashlight was perfectly effective. It showed me a large patch of dirt. Dirt that had recently been dug up.

It took me some time to decide to take the next step. I stood there in the darkness until I started to shiver. Then I decided that I had to get my shit together. Time was going by. My options were to walk away or to keep going.

I started to dig. The ground was near frozen, but it had been recently broken up, and I had the shovel. I made progress. I hit something soft less than a foot beneath the surface. I cleared more dirt with my hands until I could see what I'd found. A rug, rolled up. It was wrapped around something. Something that was almost certainly human shaped. I sat back in the dirt and pressed my hands to my eyes until I saw stars. The cold damp started to seep through my pants.

"Stop it," I said. "Fucking stop it."

I forced myself to open my eyes, to dig away the dirt, to pull the rug-wrapped bundle from the ground. I unwrapped the bundle. I saw her. Nina. Her small body, her little face. She was in jeans and a long-sleeved T-shirt. Her eyes were open and cloudy. Her skin was mottled. The left side of her face was a mass of bruises, and there was blood at the corner of her mouth. I closed up the rug again, carefully. I rested my hand on top of it and then found I was patting it.

"I'm sorry," I said. I said it once and then I couldn't stop saying it. *I'm sorry. I'm sorry. I'm sorry.* I clenched my teeth and forced myself to stop. I sat there, in the dirt. I started to feel the cold, started to shiver. I stood up and paced the small clearing. What was I going to do? What were my options?

I could leave, find a phone, and call the cops. I could go home, talk to Simon, figure out what to do depending on what he told me. What time was it? I had no way to tell. No phone with me, and I didn't wear a watch, and the Frasers were due at the house at 6:00 A.M. I could put her back, exactly where I found her, but I must have left my DNA all over the place. Jesus. *Fuck.* I didn't have a choice. I picked Nina up, still wrapped in her rug, and placed her a little off to the side. Then I filled in the grave, as best I could, and smoothed over the dirt. Working faster, I gathered leaves from farther up the trail and from the woods around me to try to disguise the disturbed ground. It worked better than I'd expected. I picked up a fallen branch, so heavy I could barely lift it. I dropped it where the grave had been, and then I heaped and scattered more leaves in as random a pattern as I could manage. If only it had been snowing. Snow would have covered everything.

I left the grave and returned to Nina. I told myself she was the rug and only the rug. I balanced the shovel on top and picked her up. I carried her down the trail. It was difficult. Wrapped in the rug, she was heavy, and I had to keep shifting the weight in my arms. Her body started to slip through the rug and soon I could see her hair, then a little of her forehead. I clenched the rug tighter to me and looked straight ahead. The moon was full and bright when I walked back out from the shelter of the trees. I took her all the way to the lake, to the jetty. I had to put her in the boat, and that wasn't easy. I was tired and clumsy. The boat tipped dangerously, and I dropped her. The rug came loose. Her head was completely exposed in the moonlight. I heard myself groan, as if the sound had come from someone else. She was dead, but she was still Nina. She was wearing her small gold hoop earrings. Jamie had bought them for Simon to give to Nina for her birthday back in May. She'd come over for dinner. Nina had been so happy. She'd kissed him and thanked him and insisted on putting them on right away. Jamie had been pleased, even though she didn't like the girl. I couldn't look away from those earrings. And the bruise. It was large and unmistakable, around her left jaw and cheek. I looked closer. Her lip was split.

I reached out and flipped a corner of the rug back to cover her face. At the same time a barn own screeched nearby and scared the shit out of me. My hands were shaking. I forced myself to move. I went back to the house. I took off my shoes before I went inside. There was a gym downstairs with dumbbells. I took a set with me. There were ropes in the back of my truck. I took the dumbbells and the ropes to the boat. I tied the ropes around the rug at the top and the bottom, knotting them tightly so that they wouldn't unravel. Then I tied the dumbbells on too. I tied knots upon knots, checking everything to make sure it was tight and secure. I found that I was checking the knots again and again, checking each one until I got to the end and then starting from the beginning and doing it over and over in a loop. My breath was coming faster. I had an image in my mind of the lake the way I had first seen it, shimmering blue under a sun-soaked sky. I imagined children playing on the shoreline, Simon's children, our grandchildren. I heard their laughter. And then, in the background, I saw Nina's body floating to the surface in pieces and bobbing there in the water, horrors waiting to be discovered. I had to force my hands away from the knots, force myself to finish my work.

When everything was done, I rowed out to the center of the lake, and I slipped her body into the dark water. For one awful moment I thought she was going to float, but the weights did their job, and her body disappeared in moments, sinking fast. I dropped the shovel in after her. The weight of the metal was enough to sink it.

I rowed back to the jetty. I checked the boat to make sure I hadn't left traces. There was dirt in the bottom of the boat, but there had been when I'd arrived. My hands and nails and clothes were filthy. I couldn't stand it. I walked into the freezing water until I was submerged. I scrubbed at my hands, my face, my hair, until my whole body was shaking from the cold. I staggered back to the truck. The house that Jamie had fallen in love with looked like a house of horrors to me now, lying low and dark under the moonlight. We would never be able to sell the place. We'd be stuck with it for the rest of our lives.

For one awful moment I thought I'd lost the keys to the truck, that they were buried at the bottom of that grave in the woods, or that they'd fallen into the water along with Nina's body, then my fingers found them at the bottom of my pocket. I stripped off my wet clothes and threw them on the floor of the passenger seat. There was an old sweatshirt in the back seat. I pulled it on, started the car and turned up the heater. My hands were shaking so much that I could barely drive, but I couldn't wait until I had warmed up. It was nearly 4:00 A.M., according to the truck's display. I had just enough time to get home and shower and dress before I had to come back with my family and pretend to search for this dead girl. I tried to tell myself that it was over. That it was done. I wanted to put the memory of that night into a box, to seal it with lead, and to drop it deep into the recesses of my mind, never to be taken out again. I tried hard, but I couldn't do it. All I could think about as I drove away was Nina's face.

A mile down the road I pulled off to the side, opened the door, and dry retched. Afterward I drove on. My fingers were clenched around the steering wheel. The car warmed up. I stopped shaking. I knew my son. I knew him. He was not a murderer.

CHAPTER FOURTEEN

Leanne

On Wednesday morning I put on my hiking gear—old hiking pants and boots, and a light wool long-sleeved shirt with my fleece over it. I would put my jacket on as another layer before leaving the house. I packed a day pack with water, my rain gear, food, and my compass. I'd use my phone where I could, but it was better not to rely on phones because service would likely be patchy, and offline trail maps only worked as long as your battery lasted. Besides, I'd searched online for trail maps of the area and had found nothing. I wondered if the Jordans had some. I wondered if they would meet us, as promised.

When I got downstairs, Grace was waiting. She was dressed in thermal leggings and boots and a fleece sweater. Her jacket was hanging on the back of a kitchen chair, and she was tying her hair back into a ponytail when I came in. She turned to face me.

"I'm coming," she said.

Andy made a helpless gesture in my direction. He'd obviously already tried to talk her out of the idea and failed.

"I don't know, Gracey," I said.

"I'm not staying at home, or worse, going to *school*, while you guys are out searching for Nina. How could I ever explain to her that I sat on my ass when she needed me? And the other thing is, the Jordans' place has a lot of land. We're going to need to cover a lot of ground. Every person counts today."

She was right. I couldn't argue with her, so I put my arms around her and hugged her tight. Andy drove, I sat in the passenger seat, and Grace sat in the back. We didn't talk, and Andy turned off the radio. Everything felt heavy and quiet. I reached out and took his hand, and we drove like that for a while. His skin was warm and dry. He had calluses on his fingers, from his work and from playing guitar. He squeezed my hand.

"I think . . . maybe we're not going to find her today," Andy said. "This idea. It's a real long shot."

I looked out the window. Andy was doing what he always did. Getting ahead of the problem. Trying to prepare Grace and me for bad news, or no news. He hated to see us upset, which was not a bad thing, except that it so often resulted in him avoiding conflict, avoiding *reality*, when it was ugly. If Nina was with friends in Boston, she would have called us.

"Dad?" Grace said, in a very quiet voice.

"Hmm?"

"Do you think . . . you don't think that Nina might have hurt herself or something? If she was really upset about breaking up with Simon?"

"No," I said. I turned around in my seat so that I could look Grace right in the eye. "You know your sister, Grace. She's a strong girl. She loves you, she loves her family, and she loves her life. Nina would never do that. Okay?"

"Okay, Mom."

We weren't the first to arrive at the Jordan house. Alice was there, and Julie Bradley and her brother, along with seven or eight others. Alice and Julie greeted me with hugs. Grace hung back a little.

"You remember my brother?" Julie said. She was less awkward than she'd been at the house. More willing to look me in the eye.

I said hello. Isaac Bradley was tall, almost as tall as Andy, with dark hair and brown eyes. When I'd seen him last, he'd been going through that awkward, pimply stage, but he seemed to have grown out of that. He looked very young, but he and Julie were twins, so he must be twenty, Nina's age. I asked myself why she couldn't have fallen for this boy instead of Simon. I'd never liked Simon, not really, but because Nina was crazy about him and because they were so young, I'd trained myself to ignore his bad points. His self-obsession. His arrogance.

"I asked Isaac to record some video today, if that's all right," Julie said. "I think we should make some videos for social media. If people can see what we're doing, if they can see us actively searching and asking questions, then I think they'll be more likely to want to get involved."

"I won't get in the way," Isaac said. He held up his phone. "I'll just be using this. It's just a boots-on-the-ground kind of thing."

I thanked him. I couldn't remember if he was in college. When she was younger, Julie used to talk about him all the time, but then she'd stopped coming around the house.

"I meant to tell you, Julie, I gave the police your number. There's a detective—Matthew Wright—he might be in touch."

Right away, Julie looked uncomfortable. "Actually, he's already spoken to me," she said. She looked at the ground.

"The Jordans are here," said Alice.

"And there's the great detective," said Andy, with a hint of sarcasm that surprised me. We all turned to watch as a black BMW X7 approached, followed by Wright's police car. The mood in the little crowd shifted as the Jordans got out of the BMW X7. Jamie came straight to me.

"Leanne. How are you holding up?" She hugged me as I stood there stiffly.

I could smell her perfume. Her hair was up and her makeup was immaculate. She looked very pretty. Over her shoulder, I could see Simon. I stepped away from her.

"Simon," I said.

He looked me straight in the eye. His chin came up. "How are you, Mrs. Fraser?"

"I'd be better if I had my daughter."

He took a step closer. "I can't stop thinking about it," he said. "I can't sleep. Not that that matters. But I should never have left her alone that night. I'm so sorry. She was mad at me. She wanted me to go. But I shouldn't have listened."

"But then you had no reason to think that she wouldn't be safe," I said. My eyes were on his face. Reading him.

"That's exactly it," he said, eagerly. "Of course if I'd thought anything could have happened to her I wouldn't have left."

Andy put his arm around my shoulders. "What *do* you think happened to Nina, Simon?" he said. I was conscious that Jamie was standing just to our right. That Grace was there, and that somewhere behind me were Alice and Julie and Isaac and all the rest. That the tall, shadowy figure in my peripheral vision, standing behind Simon and off to the side, was probably Matthew Wright. But I was focused on Simon Jordan's face. On every forced facial expression. On his widened eyes and his sincere directness.

"I don't know." Simon looked thoughtful. "She was upset, and I think she probably didn't want to come home, because she might just bump into me in town, or whatever. I get that, because, honestly, I felt the same way. So maybe she just took off for a while. To put some distance between us. But then . . . it's weird that she hasn't been in touch with you guys. That's not like her."

I resented him so much in that moment. That he felt qualified or entitled to say what she would or wouldn't do.

"Do you think she might have gone hiking?" Grace said. She was guileless. Completely sincere. "I mean the morning after you left?"

Simon looked past us, off toward the forest, and narrowed his eyes, like he was really thinking about Grace's question.

"I doubt it," he said at last. His eyes were damp, I realized in shock. Tears were gathering as he looked at Grace. "I'm so sorry. I wish I knew what happened. And maybe she did go out. I hope that she did and that we're going to find her today and that she's going to be okay. But we'd hiked a lot. By Friday she was tired. She'd pulled a muscle too, in her back, so she was ready for a break. I just don't think she'd have gone out again by herself on Saturday morning." He took a breath and steadied himself. "But I can't say for sure."

"It's okay," said Grace, in a wobbly voice. "It's not your fault. And we're going to find her."

I looked away. I didn't want to see him cry and I didn't want to see Grace reassure him. I was confused. Maybe I had been wrong about Simon. Maybe I'd rushed to conclusions. Without meaning to, I caught Rory's eye. He looked like he knew exactly what I was thinking. It made for an uncomfortable moment.

"Do you have maps of the trails?" I asked.

"Just of the trails that Nina and I hiked," he said. "We'd started mapping them on our phones. I can share those routes with you, if you want. But there are more trails out there than we've covered, a lot more."

"Maybe the previous owners have trail maps," Jamie said, in a clear voice that carried in the still morning. She turned and spoke to her husband. "What do you think, baby?"

"I'll make a call and find out," Rory said. He was dressed from head to toe in black. Black Canada Goose jacket and beanie, black pants, black boots. Black wool gloves. Everything looked brand new. He glanced at his watch. "Might be a little early to get the real estate agent, but I'll try." He walked away a few steps and made his call. More people had arrived and continued to arrive as we stood about. After a minute Rory rejoined us and told us that his call had gone to voice mail, but that he'd left a message and would continue to try.

Alice approached me. "Do you want to say a few words?"

I shook my head, and she squeezed my arm in quick understanding.

"Well, then, if you're okay with it, I'll get things started."

If I hadn't known she was a teacher, I'd have guessed it from the way she managed to draw everyone's attention and quiet them down. She explained briefly what we were doing there, though obviously everyone present already knew. She told us that we'd be breaking into groups of a minimum of two people, a maximum of four or five, depending on experience and ability, and that we'd each be assigned a suggested route. As the routes weren't all mapped, we were asked to track where we went using a mobile phone app. We should call Nina's name regularly and look out for anything unusual. If we saw something, anything at all, we should not touch it, but should take a photo and drop a pin on the location using our phone app. Everyone was to be back before dark and should plan their return accordingly. If anyone there was not an experienced hiker, they had to make sure they joined a group with someone who had experience. Alice had Simon email her the file with the routes that he and Nina had mapped, and she distributed it through the Facebook group to everyone else.

Quickly people broke into groups and chose routes. The Jordans made it clear that they wanted to walk alone. I took a step toward them, and a voice spoke in my ear.

"I wouldn't." I turned and looked up into Matthew Wright's impassive face. "You're about to suggest that you join them. Don't do it."

I searched his eyes. "You want them to be alone. So that if they're going to find anything, they won't be . . . inhibited."

He didn't say anything.

"Are you coming?" I asked.

"I have work to do here," he said.

ALICE STAYED BEHIND TO greet and organize late arrivals. I went out with Andy, Grace, and the Bradleys. We planned to hike the first couple of miles together until we got farther out, and possibly break into subgroups to tackle separate side routes. Everyone knew what they were doing in the backcountry, and we made good time, though the trails were not in good condition. It must have been years since

anyone cleared them. Once we got off the main trail, the trails de-
teriorated until they weren't much more than animal tracks. Very
quickly I lost whatever small hope I'd had that we might find Nina.
The undergrowth was thick and seemed undisturbed. More than
once we broke through spiderwebs that seemed like they must have
been untouched for weeks. We saw no footprints but our own. We'd
deliberately chosen a route that would lead us to a small lake that
was marked on the map, a route that Nina and Simon had not previously taken, but that might be attractive to her. After a couple of
hours, I stopped.

"Should we go back?" I said. "I don't think she came this way."

Julie looked at the map on her phone and considered. "Maybe. If
we go back, there's a shorter route closer to the house that Simon
and Nina walked before. If she was going out by herself, maybe she'd
choose a route she already knew. Something she felt confident she
could do in a half day."

"None of the other groups chose that route?" Andy asked.

Julie shook her head. "Everyone's pinned the routes they chose.
There's no pin on that one."

We started back down the trail. By lunchtime we were effectively
back where we had started, on the main trail. Our phones had service
again, but there were no messages from any of the other searchers.
We sat on a couple of downed logs and ate the food we had brought.
Grace didn't eat much. She was very pale. Isaac tried to get her to
talk. He asked her about her horse and about school and teachers
he'd once had that she had now, but she answered him in monosylla-
bles, and after a while he left her to her thoughts. I could see that she
was fighting back tears. We finished our food and set off on the new
route. I walked beside Grace at the back of the group. I took her hand
in mine and held it tight.

"I love you, bunny."

She nodded and wiped her nose with the back of her sleeve. She kept her eyes on the ground ahead, lifted her chin, and picked up her pace. This time we could see that someone had hiked the route recently, but other than disturbed undergrowth and a few broken twigs, we found nothing. We turned back.

"We need to call for her," said Grace.

At the beginning of the day we'd taken turns calling Nina's name regularly, but now we walked almost in silence. A sense of hopelessness was settling over all of us. Grace called her sister's name. Her voice cracked on the first attempt, but she cleared her throat and tried again.

"Nina!"

Andy and Grace took the lead. They took turns calling out Nina's name into the silent trees that surrounded us. Julie and Isaac Bradley fell back a little. In between the calls of Nina's name, I overheard snatches of quiet conversation. I dropped back to walk with them. Isaac had been showing Julie something on his phone, but when he saw me, he flushed and shoved his phone into his back pocket.

"Everything okay?" I asked.

"Uh-huh. Sure."

I looked at Julie. She didn't exactly avoid my gaze, but she glanced at me and then her eyes slid away. Something wasn't right.

"Julie?" I said.

"It's nothing," she said.

I raised an eyebrow at Isaac. He was still flushed and obviously uncomfortable. He looked to check where Grace was and lowered his voice.

"Sorry," he said. "It's just, my friend Sally Ann's mom came to help with the search today. Did you see her, earlier? She had a dog with her. A German shepherd."

I shook my head. I'd been aware of other people milling about, had recognized a few faces, but most of my focus and attention had been on the Jordans.

"Well, it's just that the dog—her name's Trudy—she used to work for search and rescue. Sally Ann's mom brought her along in case she could help out."

"That's good," I said. "A dog would be really useful."

"Yep," Isaac said, but his flush didn't fade. It occurred to me that the dog would need something with Nina's scent if it was going to try to find her. No one had asked me for anything.

"What aren't you telling me, Isaac?"

Isaac threw a desperate glance in Julie's direction. Julie was the one who explained.

"The dog—Trudy. She did work for search and rescue, but she was . . . she was a cadaver dog. She searched for human remains, until she got too old. And Sally Ann just messaged Isaac. She says that earlier today her mom was out searching on a trail and Trudy alerted like crazy. They didn't find anything. I mean, they didn't find a body. So maybe it's nothing. Trudy's old now. She's retired. And Sally Ann's mom isn't a professional dog handler or anything. Trudy could have been confused or maybe someone had butchered a deer or something."

I nodded at Isaac and Julie as if I was just fine, as if what Julie had just told me hadn't made me feel suddenly sick or made sweat break out on my forehead and lower back. I kept walking. I couldn't be sick here, in front of everyone. In front of Grace. I concentrated on walking. One foot in front of the other. I counted my steps until I got to one hundred, then started again. I pushed the fear down. It wouldn't help me.

We got back to the Jordan house just as the sun was going down. We broke out from the trailhead into the lawn, and even from a distance we could see that the house was a hive of activity. There were more vehicles, lots of them, and more people. Returning searchers, but others too. Two officers passed us as we crossed the lawn. I thought they were coming to talk to us, but they just nodded as they passed and kept on going. One of them was carrying a large roll of police tape.

"Why are they going out so late?" I asked Andy.

He shook his head. His eyes were narrowed and fixed on the house. As we got closer, I saw Jamie Jordan standing off to the side, directing caterers who had set up a barbecue station. The caterers were grilling hot dogs and handing out food to returning searchers.

"Jesus Christ," Andy said. "They're treating this like a fucking PR exercise." He stalked ahead of me, over to the barbecue area.

"Mom," Grace said, alarmed, but I was distracted by the other activity at the house. There were two white vans, unmarked, pulled up right outside. I saw men in white plastic overalls leaving the house. Matthew Wright was there, standing with his back to us, his arms crossed. One of the men in overalls approached Matthew, removing a mask and head covering as he did so. The man in overalls was in his sixties, maybe. He was thin and balding, and what was left of his hair was cut very close. He wore round, wire-framed glasses, and he had a set expression on his face.

"Stay here, Grace," I said. I walked toward the house, leaving her behind me.

"Anything?" Matthew was saying to the balding man. I got closer, trying not to be too obvious about it. Matthew had his back to me, and the other man was very focused on their conversation. There were other people about, not quite as close as I was. I took out my phone, turned so that I was facing away from Matthew and the balding man, and held my phone as if I was fascinated by whatever was on my screen. At the same time, I strained my ears to listen. Matthew kept his voice low, but the balding man spoke loudly, like someone who was hard of hearing.

"Nothing. No blood, no indication that anything happened in the house."

"Right. Okay."

"There's just one thing. The whole house smells strongly of detergent."

"You mean, like, bleach?"

The balding man shook his head. "More like the kind of floral scent you get from fabric cleaners. We ran some tests. The living room floor has been cleaned with a detergent that contains sodium percarbonate."

"What exactly does that mean?" Matthew said.

"Sodium percarbonate is a chemical that some manufacturers have started putting in their fabric cleaners. They market it as active oxygen. They say it kills viruses and bacteria and so, you know, there's a lot of demand. The problem for us is that active oxygen interferes with luminol. It stops our tests from working. You could have blood all over the floor, you clean it with a detergent with sodium percarbonate and that's it. We could spray luminol all day and still see nothing."

"Did you search the house for cleaning products?"

"Sure. There's nothing in the house with active oxygen in it. Maybe whoever used the product finished the bottle. But like I said, it's not something they put in floor cleaners, as a rule. So, to me, that's suspicious."

As I listened to them talk, my breathing started to come faster. My lungs tightened. I turned around. I saw Simon Jordan near the barbecue stand with his mother. Andy was there too, shoulders back, chest up, looking antagonistic. I felt like everything was shifting and spinning around me. Grace was standing by herself, her hands stuffed in her pockets, her face still so pale. I tried to slow my breathing. I drew in one long breath, and then another one. I was conscious only of the air entering and leaving my lungs, and a kind of roaring in my ears. I turned away and started walking toward the barbecue. Behind me, I heard Matthew say my name, but I had broken into a run. Simon saw me at the last minute. His mouth dropped open in disbelief, just before I reached him and punched him with everything I had.

CHAPTER FIFTEEN

Matthew

Leanne Fraser's fist connected with Simon Jordan's face like she'd been training for the moment all her life. His head snapped back and he staggered backward, but she kept coming, kept reaching for him. Matthew had seen the hit coming, a moment too late to stop it. He got there in time to stop it from going any further. He caught up with Leanne, grabbed her around the waist, and pulled her backward, while everyone else was still frozen in shock. Leanne was stronger than she looked. He had to lift her off the ground and carry her backward, and she fought him all the way, struggling and twisting. Matthew carried her back toward his police car, aware all the time of all the eyes watching. It would be a miracle if the whole thing wasn't being recorded on someone's cell phone.

Matthew bundled her into the back of his car and shut the door. Leanne tried immediately to open it, but it didn't open from the inside. She banged at the windows with her forearms, and when that didn't work she leaned back on the back seat and kicked at the window with her booted feet. The windows were reinforced, and her feet bounced off. There were other voices by now. Jamie Jordan's voice rose above the clamor, shouting something about pressing charges. Matthew got into the car and drove away. He didn't really have a choice. The alternative was to sit there while Leanne Fraser lost her mind in front of fifty people and their cameras.

"He killed her. He killed her. And you know it."

"That was stupid," Matthew said. She kicked at the back of his seat.

"Shut up! Shut the fuck up."

"You need to calm down."

"Shut the fuck up!" She screamed the words at him. There was a security partition between them. If there hadn't been he figured she would have reached through and hit him. She bashed at the partition with her hand. It barely moved. She tried again to break the window to her left, this time with her elbow, and using all her strength. Her elbow bounced off the reinforced glass. Leanne groaned and bent forward at the waist and cradled her arm. She took deep breaths, like she was trying to breathe through pain, or maybe nausea. Or both.

"You need to stop," Matthew said. But Leanne was past hearing him or anyone else. She turned sideways on the seat until she was half lying down, and she started kicking the partition. She kicked it and kicked it, screaming at him to let her out, to take her back. Matthew kept driving, slow and steady. Eventually, the kicking and screaming stopped. She straightened up in the seat. She grew quiet. Matthew checked on her through the rearview mirror. She was staring out the window of the car, and the expression on her face was completely blank.

"Leanne?"

She didn't respond. She didn't so much as twitch. It was like she hadn't heard him.

"Leanne!" Matthew said her name again, louder. It took three times before she finally reacted. She blinked like she was waking up, and turned her face toward him.

"Do you need a doctor?" Matthew said.

"I'm fine."

Shit. She needed help, and he had no choice but to charge her. The Jordans weren't going to let this one go.

Matthew drove her to the station. She was calm when he opened the back door and made no objection when he escorted her inside.

He put her in an interview room and had someone take her a cup of coffee, which she didn't touch. He read her her rights, took her fingerprints himself, gently, and explained the charges. She sat quietly through all of it. She said nothing at all. In the end, Matthew sat in the chair opposite hers and tried hard to reach her.

"I get that this is an impossible situation. But you need to keep it together. You've got to let your brain run this show, not your emotions, if you want to find Nina."

Her eyes finally met his. She looked broken. Years older than she had just that morning. "No one's going to find her. Nina's gone. She's dead. He killed her, and he buried her body somewhere on that mountain."

"You don't know that."

Anger sparked in her eyes. "Don't you lie to me. I heard what the forensics guy said to you. Someone cleaned up the house so that you couldn't find bloodstains."

"I'm sorry you overheard that. It's just a theory. There could be any number of explanations. It's possible that someone just cleaned the floor using a new brand of cleaner. We need to ask and answer these questions before we start trying to draw conclusions."

She looked at him with obvious disgust. "Julie Bradley told me everything. Would you have told us if she didn't? I don't think so. Nina's our daughter, but you hoard information as if it doesn't impact us. Like we're just spectators on the sideline. When your investigation is over you'll just move on with your life, but this *is* our life. Why don't you get that?"

Damn. When Sarah Jane had interviewed Julie, she'd had the sense to ask the girl not to tell Nina's parents what they'd discussed. Julie had, under pressure, agreed to keep it to herself. It looked like she'd broken that promise.

"We asked Julie not to tell you about the bruises for a lot of reasons. The main one being that her personal theory about what happened isn't proof. She asked Nina straight out if Simon had hurt her, and Nina denied it, so her theory doesn't actually move us forward right now."

Leanne looked confused. Matthew tried again, talking a little slower.

"Proof is everything. If Simon Jordan is responsible for what happened to Nina, whatever that might be, I will do everything possible to prove it. But there may be another explanation here. Leanne, I'm not keeping things from you for any reason other than that I'm trying to do my job, the best way I know how."

Matthew waited for her to reply. When she did, she spoke slowly and deliberately.

"When I said Julie told me everything, I was talking about the dog."

"Oh," Matthew said. *Shit.* They looked at each other for a long moment. He waited for her to ask him about the bruises, but she didn't. She just sat there with eyes that looked right through him. He swallowed.

"Leanne, I'm asking you to trust me to do my job."

Leanne said nothing.

"You need to stay away from the Jordans. When your case is heard and you have to defend yourself for assaulting Simon, the court's going to have a lot of sympathy for you, under the circumstances, but not if you keep going down this route."

Still she said nothing.

"Please, I want you to listen to me carefully. You think you know what happened, but you don't. I've been a detective for a long time. I've worked a lot of cases. The most dangerous thing you can do is jump to a conclusion. You do that at the beginning of the case and you stop looking for the truth. You start seeing only the evidence that supports your theory. We don't know for sure that Simon did anything to hurt Nina. We don't know that he had anything to do with her disappearance. So stay away from him. Trust me. And give me time to get to the truth."

He arranged for a junior officer to drive her home, though that turned out not to be necessary. When he walked her out, they found Andy and Grace waiting for her. Matthew excused himself quickly and retreated back into the station. Sarah Jane was waiting for him when he came back. She'd watched the interview through the one-way glass.

"Do you think she listened to you?" Sarah Jane asked.

"I don't think she's hearing anyone right now."

"I'm not sure I blame her."

He shook his head. He didn't either. "I screwed up. About Julie." He'd added fuel to an already volatile situation. Sarah Jane obviously knew it too. There was a moment of awkward silence.

"I thought you'd like to know that we had more calls," she said. "Three more sightings of Nina."

Three more meant five in total, in response to the press conference and their request for help from the public. The first two had come in within a few hours, but they'd been from regular callers, the kind of people who reported seeing Elvis in their local diner, and easily dismissed.

"Anything worth paying attention to?"

"One of the callers said they saw Nina in California in the company of a 'creepy cult dude.' That one sounded flaky. But the other two were both from Boston. One caller said they saw Nina in a bar on Boylston Street on Saturday night. That person gave their name and sounded credible. Another caller—this one was anonymous—said they saw a girl who looked just like Nina buying drugs on a street corner one block over from Boylston Street. Also on Saturday night." Sarah Jane sounded excited.

"Can you call the bar and ask if they have security footage? Also, call Boston PD and see what they've got for the street corner and any of the surrounding blocks."

"I already called the bar. They've got the whole night on tape. They've got three cameras that capture the whole bar, and everything gets backed up to the cloud. I asked them to send it over, and they'll do it without a warrant, but we won't get it until the morning. They've got a private security company that manages the backup, and they're not available until nine A.M. tomorrow."

"Good work. That's very good work."

"I'll call Boston PD now and get back to you." She sounded pleased.

"Let me know if you run into any resistance."

"I'll do that." There was a pause. "Do you think it could be her? That we might find her?"

It sounded positive, two sightings in the same location at around the same time, but Matthew did not feel hopeful. He'd received too many calls in the past that had led to nothing, calls from members of the public with poor eyesight or overactive imaginations. And despite what he'd said to Leanne Fraser, everything was pointing him right at Simon Jordan. Boston just felt like a distraction.

"There's one more thing," Sarah Jane said. "While you were at the search, we got two calls from a guy complaining about the Fraser family. Well, about Andrew Fraser mostly. The caller gave his name as Dick Cheney, and he said he lived at the White House, so . . . you know. He said that Andrew was a convicted pedophile and that he murdered Nina to stop her coming forward. I mean, obviously the guy is, you know, delusional, but then we got a call from another lady asking if we knew that Andrew had abused girls in the past and wanting to confirm that we're looking into him."

"Shit."

"I checked to see if Andrew Fraser has a record, and he doesn't."

"No, I know that. And all high-profile cases attract this kind of thing. Conspiracy theories and fixated individuals. It's tough on the family, but it happens. I just . . . I'm surprised it's happening this fast."

"Maybe that's the nature of the internet these days. Everything happens bigger and faster."

"I guess that's it," Matthew said. They walked back to the squad room together. "I want to look into this theory about the floor cleaner.

Can you follow up with forensics? Ask them for a list of all the cleaning products available locally that would produce this active oxygen effect. And let's ask the Jordans who their cleaners are. Let's talk to them."

Sarah Jane took a note. "I did some research. Active oxygen cleaners are pretty new, but the information about how they interfere with luminol is online. Still, I can't imagine most people would know that information unless they deliberately went looking for it."

"If Simon killed her, he could have just looked up how to clean a crime scene and then found the right detergent in the house somewhere. In their laundry room."

"Yes. In which case that search would show up on his phone data, right?"

They exchanged glances.

"Anything yet from the warrants?" he asked.

She shook her head. "I've called and emailed, but you know, it could be months before they get back to us."

"Sometimes they're slow, sometimes they're fast. Let's hope we fall into the latter category. Try calling them again. If you speak to a human and not a messaging service, remind them that the case is getting a lot of airtime." Maybe it would help that the case was getting so much publicity. Maybe some data wonk over in Mountain View or Cupertino would read about Nina Fraser and get curious.

"Okay. Of course. I'll get right on it. Also, I still haven't heard from Rory Jordan about the security cameras."

"He came to me at the search and told me that the cameras hadn't been commissioned yet. They were installed two weeks ago, but the security company was waiting on a router."

"Damn. That's bad luck." She paused. "Do we believe him?"

"He gave me the number of his security firm. I'll call them, see what they have to say."

Matthew let her go. What he really wanted now was a warrant to search the Jordans' house in Waitsfield, for cleaning products and anything else they might find. Unfortunately, he didn't think a warrant would be granted. Rory Jordan was a powerful man, and generous with his political donations. Judges would be slow to sign off on a warrant without something solid. Matthew needed more evidence. The alert from the cadaver dog was interesting. Matthew had gone out himself to inspect the disturbed ground where she had alerted. He'd had men dig, but they'd found nothing. It was highly suspicious. Unfortunately, the dog alert could not be used as evidence. She was an older dog, retired, and she hadn't been with a professional handler when she'd alerted. But there was nothing to stop them from sending out another dog, this time following all the required procedures. Matthew picked up the phone, called a friend at the K-9 unit, and called in a favor.

CHAPTER SIXTEEN

Leanne

Matthew Wright offered to arrange for me to be driven home, after our little interview and his warning to me in that shitty room in the police station. Andy looked grim. Matthew Wright didn't wait around to explain anything. He just disappeared back into the police station. Maybe he thought he was being discreet, or sensitive, giving us time to talk as a family.

Andy hugged me briefly, and we left. I tried to take Grace's hand as we walked to the car, but she put her hand in her pocket and kept walking. Andy started the engine, reversed, and drove out of the parking lot without saying a word.

"Are you guys okay?" I asked.

"We're fine," Andy said. Grace didn't answer.

"I'm sorry if you were worried." I was searching for words. Not for the first time in our married life, I wished that Andy could read my mind. There was so much I had to tell him, and I couldn't say any of it in front of Grace.

"Whatever," said Grace, with perfect teenage disdain.

"Grace." Andy said her name with a warning note.

"What?"

"Really, I'm sorry if you were worried. Matthew Wright says that it's not too serious. That, given the circumstances, I'll probably just get a slap on the wrist." Which was not what he had said, of course, but I had an overwhelming urge to reassure them both, and I was willing to lie to do it.

"They charged you?" Andy said. He was genuinely shocked. I could hear it in his voice.

"I guess they didn't have a choice."

"Well, you *punched* Simon Jordan in the *face*. In front of like, a hundred people, so I don't know what you expected."

"Grace!" Andy's warning note had moved up to a reprimand.

"What, Dad? She's acting like a crazy person."

Andy was red faced and angry. He opened his mouth to say something, but I reached out and squeezed his hand. I turned in my seat to look at Grace.

"I'm sorry," I said. "It's a difficult situation."

The words were completely inadequate. Grace shifted in her seat and subsided into silence. We drove on. When we got home, we parked in the courtyard and went through the back door into the kitchen. Rufus gave Grace an ecstatic greeting. She gave him the briefest pat on the head, then pushed him off. She turned to face us. She looked exhausted, and pale, and very young.

"I'm sorry, Mom."

"It's okay, Grace. I get it."

"I just think you need to remember that Simon loves her too. I mean, maybe they broke up, whatever, but they were together for a really long time. And he's really, really upset. You guys saw that."

I tried to answer her. I just couldn't find the words. Andy turned away and went to the fridge.

"I'll make us something to eat," he said.

"I have to go out," I said. They both stared at me. "I'm sorry. Just for a few minutes."

"That's a bad idea," Andy said. He was looking at me like I was losing my mind. I tried to convey with my eyes that I had a lot to tell him, that I had a very good reason to leave the house at this delicate, delicate moment. I tried to ask him to trust me. I don't think the message got through. He turned away, shaking his head, and opened the fridge door.

"Go," he said. "If that's what you want to do. Grace, what do you feel like eating? We've got bacon. I could do something with pasta."

I could feel the anger coming off him. That hurt me. I wished he trusted me more than he did, but it was something I would have to deal with when I got back. I had a brutal, relentless urgency inside me. I went to Grace and gave her a quick hug. She stood stiff and unresponsive in my arms. I got my keys and jacket and left the house.

Julie Bradley's mother, Delores, managed a bar just off Main Street in Waterbury. By the time I got to the bar it was almost 7:00 P.M. and the place was busy. Not ski-season busy, but busier than I would have expected, given that the college-aged kids had gone back to school. There were a few regulars, faces I recognized from around, enough so that there was a hum of conversation over the music. The booths that lined the walls of the bar were mostly empty. The previous week they would have been full of college kids who'd come to Vermont for their week's vacation, to hike and climb and kayak and hang out. We saw them around town every year. They wore hiking pants and T-shirts and had flushed, laughing faces and endless, twenty-something-year-old energy. Nina energy. You could feel their absence in the bar, almost like a hollowing out of the air.

The kitchen was still serving buffalo wings and popcorn chicken, and the beer was still flowing. Nathan Lowery was the barman. I'd known Nathan for years. He had a reputation as a bit of a bore, but he wasn't a bad guy. He kept an eye on the young girls in the bar and made sure that when they left, they left with friends. Nathan was shooting the shit with a small group of college-aged guys at the other end of the bar. I waved to him. He saw me, I thought, but didn't wave back. He just stayed where he was and kept chatting. I sat on an empty stool at the bar and waited to order, but all his attention was on the guys.

"Nathan," I said. He didn't hear me. I raised my voice and tried again. Still no reaction. I was about to walk down the bar and stand in front of him when I felt a hand on my shoulder.

"Mrs. Fraser. Looking for me?" It was Julie. She'd changed since the search. She was wearing clean jeans and a T-shirt with the bar's logo on it—a kicking mule. Her hair was wet from the shower.

"You got home okay?" I asked.

"Everyone left. Mr. Fraser—Andy—was going to go to the police station. He didn't find you?"

"He found me," I said. There were two empty booths in a dark corner over at the back of the bar. I nodded in their direction. "Can we talk?"

Julie said she'd get some food. I went and sat in one of the booths. She emerged from the kitchen a few minutes later with a couple of baskets of popcorn chicken and two Cokes.

"Do you mind? I haven't eaten since lunch, and I'm working tonight." She offered me the second basket, and I shook my head.

"I'm okay."

Julie nodded. She picked up a piece of chicken and popped it in her mouth.

"Your mom around?"

"Not tonight. She was tired. She went home."

"Thank you for your help," I said. "For searching today, and for last night." I was trying to move slowly. I didn't want to scare her off. But Julie was smart and perceptive. She could tell that I had something to say, and she was waiting for me to start. I took a breath.

"Julie, I think Nina is dead, and I think Simon killed her. Not just because of what happened with the dog today."

Julie's elbows were on the table. She folded her arms across her chest and compressed her lips.

"I think Simon killed Nina," I said. "I think he buried her body somewhere on the property and then cleaned up after himself. Maybe his parents know about it, maybe they don't, but either way they're going to protect him. If we don't find Nina, I think it's going to be very hard to prove what happened. And I don't think I can live with that."

"You shouldn't give up hope," she said, but her eyes filled with tears. I didn't say anything. A minute passed. The bar was noisy with music and laughter, but all of it felt unreal, like it was a movie soundtrack that had been overlayed on the wrong scene.

"Can you tell me more about the dog? What happened, exactly?"

Julie wiped her eyes and nose. "Trudy picked up a scent and followed it down a deer track, and then she alerted. Sally Ann says she sits when she smells human remains."

"Do you think she could have gotten confused? Someone might have shot a deer, or some other creature might have died there."

"Isaac asked that question after you left, and Sally Ann says no. Cadaver dogs are trained only to react to human remains. And . . . well, the ground in the area had been dug up and then sort of covered over, Sally Ann says."

"But they didn't find Nina."

"No."

I thought about it. Neither of us was eating. The chicken was cooling in the basket.

"You said I should still hope, and I get why you'd say that. But I keep thinking about all the families who lost daughters or sons and who waited for years, waited their whole lives, and never learned the truth. I can't live like that, Julie."

"Yeah." She wiped her nose again.

"Matthew Wright told me that you had a theory about Nina. He said that you asked Nina straight out if Simon hurt her and she denied it. What was he talking about?"

I think Julie had known that the question was coming, maybe as soon as she saw me enter the bar. She turned her glass slowly on the table. Her hand was tanned, and her fingernails were short. She had blue eyes, very different from Nina's, which were dark brown. Nina had been the better student in school, but Julie had been a better athlete. In many ways they hadn't been the most likely of friends.

"I never saw a couple as in love as they were," Julie said. "Simon always acted like he couldn't believe he'd gotten so lucky. Because Nina's so beautiful." Julie's eyes met mine briefly, before sliding away. "And she's nice too. Kind. Every guy in school was crazy about her. Whereas Simon wasn't that popular."

That surprised me. "I thought he had a lot of friends. He always seemed to have a crowd around him."

Julie frowned. "People didn't hate him, but he wasn't top of the heap either. He made jokes that didn't quite land. He was good at sports, good enough to make ski squad, but only just. He was never a star. He's really smart, but he was never going to be valedictorian or anything because we had Brit and Anne in our year and they were super smart too and they worked way harder." She paused. "Some people liked Simon, or looked up to him, but those kids were the ones who were, you know, easily impressed. Or they were sort of insecure themselves. A little on the outside. The cooler kids could take him or leave him. I think all that was a problem for Simon. It's like he felt he should be number one, and he was pissed when he wasn't." She paused. "But then when he and Nina started going out, suddenly everyone noticed him. Together, they had a kind of glow."

"You said they were in love."

"Sure."

"Nina too?"

"Oh, yeah. She was crazy about him. I mean, really. He made all these grand gestures, like he sent her a dozen roses at school when he asked her to prom. That kind of thing. Which wasn't really her style, and she was embarrassed, but . . . I think it made her feel good too. He made her feel secure."

I didn't answer. I didn't know what to say. I wanted to know why my daughter had needed those gestures to feel secure in herself, but I didn't think Julie would be able to answer that question. I wanted to prompt her, to bring her back to the point, but I also felt like she needed to tell me in her own way. After a long moment, Julie grimaced and continued.

"Nina and I barely saw each other after high school. She had to work at the inn, and she had to study, and she had Simon, and she really didn't have any time left for anything else."

"Oh." That hit me. Nina had complained, more than once, about having no time for a social life, but I hadn't taken her seriously. It felt different hearing it from Julie. By making Nina work at the inn so much, I had narrowed her world. Julie picked up a piece of chicken and turned it in her hands. She kept her eyes down, not looking at me as she spoke.

"Nina never talked to you about Simon?" Julie said. "She never said they were having problems?"

I shook my head.

She moistened her lips, a nervous habit I remembered from when she was a girl. "I don't know anything for sure. That female cop, Sarah Jane Reid, she came here on Tuesday morning, and I told her what I'm about to tell you. Sarah Jane made me promise not to tell anyone, including you. I shouldn't have listened to her. I'm sorry about that."

I shook my head. "It doesn't matter. None of this is your fault."

"I told Sarah Jane that the last time Nina and I saw each other, she asked me some questions that bothered me." Julie looked away, across the bar, fixing her gaze in the distance. "My mom had a boyfriend, when I was a kid, who liked to hit when he got drunk. Nina knew about it because I told her. I told her how scared I was, for me and for my mom. Eventually my mom dumped him, and we all moved on. It's ancient history. But a few weeks ago, Nina came to the bar. We had a couple of drinks together. When it got late she asked me about that guy. She wanted to know what kind of thing had set him off. I know it doesn't sound like anything. But it was weird. We hadn't talked about that guy in years, and it wasn't like he came up naturally in conversation or anything. Also, Nina had bruises on her wrist."

"What kind of bruises?"

Julie gave me a look. "Smudges. Four oval, blue-green smudges on her wrist. Three almost in a straight line and one on top. They were fingerprint marks. Someone had grabbed her and held her."

An ache passed through my whole body. I closed my eyes.

"She never said it was Simon."

"Did you ask her?"

"Of course I asked her. She was my friend. She *is* my friend."

"What did she say?"

"She was very calm. She said everything was fine. I freaked out. I told her every battered woman in the history of time thought she could change her man, or that he would change by himself. I told her that guys who hit don't stop once they start."

"She didn't listen?" I had a pain in my heart. That boy had hurt my girl, and she hadn't loved herself enough to walk away. And she hadn't trusted me enough to come to me.

"She hugged me and she said she was sorry she had brought the subject up, that it truly had just been a random thought and that she'd hurt her wrist climbing. She was so completely calm that, in the moment, I believed her. It was only afterward, when I had time to think, that I remembered all the bullshit excuses my mom came up with back in the day. She could be pretty calm too. Until it happened again."

Under the table, I clenched my hands into fists. All I could see was Simon's stupid, false sympathy at the search. His bullshit tears. Julie looked worried.

"We don't know for sure that he did anything. And Nina never said that it was Simon who hurt her."

"Of course it was Simon."

"I'm sorry I didn't tell you before."

Someone turned the music in the bar up louder. I didn't recognize the song, but some of the other customers did. They started singing along.

"I have to go," I said.

"Sure."

I hesitated, but in the end, there wasn't much left to say, other than thank you. "Thanks, Julie. Thanks for everything." I passed Nathan Lowery on my way to the door. He was collecting glasses. I nodded an absent hello and moved to pass by, but his lip curled as he looked down at me.

"You should be ashamed of yourself," he said.

I looked at him, completely uncomprehending.

"You know exactly what I'm talking about. It's disgusting, what you're doing."

He walked away and went behind the bar. For a moment I didn't know what to do. I turned and saw Julie standing and frowning in Nathan's direction. I couldn't deal with it, so I walked away. Whatever was going on with him was a problem for another day. The information that Julie had just given me about Simon was still reverberating in my head, bouncing around, getting louder and louder and making me feel like I might lose my mind. I walked out of the bar into the night air, turned to the side, and vomited. That earned me a mocking cheer from a group of guys on the other side of the parking lot. I wiped my mouth and kept walking to my car. I climbed in and rested my face on the steering wheel, and I wept. I thought that I might be broken in a way that would never, ever heal. I thought about Nina. About her face, her hair, her hands. The small freckle on her index finger that had appeared when she was four years old and was still there today. The birthmark on her left knee. Her brown eyes. She was all alone somewhere, and I needed to be with her. To hold her and let her know that she was loved, that even in death, if that was where she was, she was loved.

CHAPTER SEVENTEEN

Andy

I don't get angry easily, and I don't like to fight. I know some guys who do, or did when we was younger, but fighting don't do anything for me. When some guy comes into the bar, full of piss and vinegar, I'm not going to go out of my way to catch his eye. There's a guy that works for me by the name of Billy Pearson. Now, Billy has a volatile temper. I've known him for some thirty years, and I've seen him walk himself into one problem after another because he can't control himself, and there are times when I feel sorry for him, but yeah, I judge him for it. Losing your temper seems to me to be a teenage kind of thing to do. It's something you should grow out of, and if you don't, it's because you aren't trying hard enough or because you have a weak character. Looking back, I can see that I was smug about my own cool head. They say that you can't be considered brave unless you've had to overcome fear. In the same way, I don't think you can take credit for a cool head unless you've felt rage enough to kill a man, and you've walked away.

When I saw the Jordans handing out hot dogs to searchers, like they was the hosts at some kind of fucking Fourth of July party, I got angry fast. People had been out looking for Nina all day. They was tired and hungry and, I'm sure, grateful to be handed something hot to eat. If it had been anyone else standing beside that barbecue, I would have been grateful too, but coming from the Jordans, it was such a fucking *move* that I lost it. They wasn't even doing the cooking—they'd brought in a guy for that. A guy in a white chef's hat—who wears a fucking chef's hat to a barbecue? They was just standing to the side, in spotless white aprons, handing out hot dogs and burgers and sodas with smiles plastered across their faces, thanking people for coming out. I left Leanne and our small group behind and stalked over there. I could feel the heat rushing to my face. Jamie Jordan pretended not to see me. Rory turned a slick smile in my direction. If he'd offered me a burger I would have shoved it down his throat.

"You running for office, Rory?"

"Excuse me?"

"Your setup. It's all pretty polished." I glanced around. "I don't see any babies."

He looked at me blankly. He hadn't shaved. His jacket and his boots looked brand new, but he hadn't shaved, because why? He thought a little five o'clock shadow made him look like a guy who cared?

"I figured that you'd have some babies lined up and ready to kiss. Get some photos out there. Rory Jordan and family. Fine, upstanding citizens."

Rory's smile disappeared. I wasn't making any effort to keep my voice down, and people were tuning in. I guess he didn't like that.

"We're just trying to help," Jamie said. She took hold of Rory's arm, gently. Not like she was trying to hold him back. It was more of a gesture of support. "It's been a tough day for everyone. You and Leanne most of all, of course. We thought that this was the right thing to do."

"Oh, sure." I said. "Out of the goodness of your hearts."

"You should go on home now, Andrew," Rory said. "Better that you focus on your own family, rather than ours."

"Focus on my family? Maybe if you'd spent some time with your son we wouldn't be in this situation."

"What the hell is that supposed to mean?" Rory said.

"You want me to say it again slower?"

I didn't see it happen. I was so goddamn angry, and all I could see was Rory Jordan's stupid smug face. My back was to Simon, so I missed it when Leanne hit the kid right in the face. Rory Jordan didn't miss it. His attention was fixed on me right up until the last second, and then his focus shifted to something behind me, his mouth dropped open, and his eyes widened, and I heard the smack of fist hitting flesh. I turned on time to see Simon staggering backward, holding his face. Lee was still going after him, until Matthew Wright picked her up and started carrying her to the closest police car. I went after them, but Rory Jordan grabbed me by the shoulder and yanked me around to face him, and I lost it. I grabbed him by the wrists, pulled his hands off me, and shoved him backward. He fell, landing on his ass in the dirt. He scrambled backward, trying to get up, his boots slipping on the grass. He got to his feet and waved a finger in my face. He was scared. It didn't give me any pleasure to see it, but it didn't make me respect him any either.

"You need to stay away from my family. You and your wife. Go home now. Get the hell out of here. And you tell Leanne that if she trespasses on our property again, if any of you set so much as a *foot* on our land, we will press charges."

I walked away, but I was already too late. Wright was bundling Leanne into the back of his car. He saw me coming—he looked right at me as he pushed Lee into the back seat of his car and closed the door on her. I started running, but he climbed into the car and drove away. I stumbled to a stop and stood there in the driveway with my fists clenched. A hand landed on my shoulder. I was so fucking furious that I just about threw it off me, and turned, ready to swing, but it was my brother, Craig. He had the remains of a hot dog in one hand.

"What's going on?"

"Lee punched Simon Jordan. Matthew Wright took her away."

"Jesus. Why would she do that?"

"Why do you think?"

Craig had a sorry look on his face that was intensely aggravating. Everyone else was standing around in small groups, pretending they weren't watching. Behind Craig, I saw the Jordans, standing together in a huddle. Simon was holding his face and Jamie was fussing over him. Rory was talking to a police officer and looking my way. I saw Grace. I'd forgotten about Grace. The Bradleys were trying to talk to her—Julie was patting her on the shoulder—but Grace wasn't responding. She looked scared. Frozen in place.

"I guess Wright must be taking her to the station," Craig was saying. "Do you want me to drive you?"

"No. Thanks, Craig." I was already walking away, fishing my keys out of my pocket.

"Andy." I heard Craig calling my name, but I didn't stop. I was past the point of being able to tolerate anyone's company, including my brother's. Craig's not a bad guy, but he's not easy to be around at the best of times, and though I'd always denied it to Leanne, I was pretty sure he didn't like her that much. I went to Grace and put my hand on her shoulder.

"It's okay, honey."

"It's not. It's really not."

I took Grace to the car. When we passed Simon and his mother, Grace paused.

"I'm really sorry," she said.

"Grace, Jesus." I tried to hurry her past, but she resisted me. Simon's eye was already swelling.

"S'okay," he said. "Not your fault."

"My mom's just really upset," Grace said. She would have said more, but I grabbed her upper arm and propelled her forward.

"Leave it alone," I said.

We got to the car and climbed in. There were people watching. Too many people. I drove away, drove south in the direction of state police headquarters at Waterbury.

"Why did she do it?" Grace said. "That was completely nuts."

I did not feel qualified to deal with the conversation. "She's upset, Grace. And she's angry."

"Yeah. We all are. But why did she go after Simon? He's just as worried as we are. And she *hit* him. In front of everyone."

The same question was going around in a loop inside my head.

"Dad?"

"I don't know, Grace. You can ask her that yourself, okay?"

She got real quiet. I drove on until we reached Waterbury. We didn't talk again until I pulled up outside state police headquarters.

"Are they going to let her come home with us?"

"Sure they will," I said, with confidence I didn't feel.

We had to wait for forty minutes at the police station. It felt like hours, with Grace sitting beside me, chewing on her fingernails. When Leanne finally came out, with Wright by her side, she looked like she'd been through hell and back. Her hair was falling out of its tie, her eyes were wild, and she had smudges of fingerprint ink on her hand and on her cheek. We drove home, mostly in silence. Then in the kitchen, before we had a chance to talk or settle Grace down or do anything else, Leanne said she had to leave. She was gone for over an hour. I fed Grace and myself, and Rufus. I cleaned the kitchen, drank a beer, and then another. I lit the fire, got another beer, and sat and stared into the flames, waiting. Stewing. I was pissed. I was so goddamn tired of Lee thinking she knew best.

When I met Lee, she was twenty-three years old, and I was turning twenty-seven. I already had my landscaping business, and she was trying to turn the crumbling dump she'd bought into an inn. She knocked me out the first time I met her. I'm not going to say that it was love at first sight, but I know I couldn't stop looking at her. I'd listed some limestone pavers, left over from a job, for sale at half price. Lee showed up at my place with Nina on her hip, looked over what I had to sell with a that-don't-impress-me-much look on her face, and started bargaining. I was already selling the stuff at a knock-down price, but she took that price as a jumping-off point for negotiation. She was so serious. There was no flirting, no playing around. She haggled with me like it mattered. I can't remember what discount I gave her in the end. I know it was huge. I mean, I was basically giving the stuff away, and then she asked if I'd throw in delivery. I did it too. I wanted to see her again.

That was nearly seventeen years ago. We didn't take as many photographs back then. We didn't video everything. I wish we had. I wish I had a hundred photographs of the way Lee looked in those days, in jean shorts and a shirt, her hair tucked under a scarf. She worked so goddamn hard. If you look at the inn today, you would think it had always been this pretty, antique-looking thing, but you'd be so wrong. About the only original things in that house are the walls. By the time I met Lee she'd already ripped out the old kitchen, which was rotting, and put in a new one. Well, I say new, but it was actually secondhand—she bought it from someone who was renovating a cabin over near the ski resort. By the time Lee was finished with it, painting it and all that, it looked like something you'd see in a magazine. Some of the floors are original, but Lee had to replace a lot of them. That stone mantel in the drawing room came from a teardown over in Waterbury. Lee bought it for practically nothing and cleaned it up, and I helped her to install it.

I didn't ask her out or anything like that. I just started showing up at the inn sometimes. I'd take her some plants and say they were left over from a job, and then I'd dig them in for her and try to help out with whatever project she had going on. Nina liked to be in the garden, so I got her a little kids' spade and rake, and she would poke around in the dirt when I was planting and make her mud cakes. But Lee didn't let me help anywhere near as much as I wanted. She didn't let me in. The inn was always her project, her business. I figured she didn't want to accept too much help because she didn't want there to be any confusion about that. And I got it. Lee had fought like hell to give herself and Nina a chance. It made sense that she would want to be careful.

I kissed her one evening. I'd brought a tree for her. I told her it was a left over from a job, but it was a beautiful ten-foot Canadian maple, and I guess Lee figured out I'd paid for it myself. One thing you can never accuse Lee of is being slow on the uptake. She came outside and watched me plant the tree. She was holding two beers, one for herself and one, I figured, for me, for when I finished. After the job was done, I went to her. She handed me the beer. We both looked at the tree. The sun was going down.

"In ten years, that tree will be a knockout," I said.

She took my hand and held it. Like it was as natural as breathing. Like she'd been doing it all her life. Even I couldn't miss that signal. I kissed her. She kissed me back, and everything was different. I'd been with other women. Once I'd even thought I was in love. But being with Leanne made all that seem like high school stuff. I knew then that I wanted to marry her, but I waited for nearly a year before I asked her. I thought she might say no if I asked her too soon.

Lee had a hard time growing up. Her dad left when she was a little kid, and her mom was an angry woman. She treated Leanne like she was a competition that could be won. Pushed her all the way through high school. Lots of expectations, not a lot of love. Lee's mother was a religious woman, but when Lee got pregnant with Nina and dropped out of college, her response was anything but Christian. She felt humiliated, and she thought that gave her the right to be abusive. Lee got up to insults at the breakfast table and came home to the same at dinner. Lee's mother hit her too, not a whole lot, but some. I wasn't around when that was happening. By the time I met Lee her mother was already dead from cancer. Lee had taken her tiny inheritance, gotten a fat mortgage (with the help of a crooked broker who lied about Lee's income on the application form), and bought the inn.

I thought I understood why Lee was the way she was. I was sure that with time, she'd trust me enough that she would let me in. I wanted her to lean on me, but seventeen years have passed, and she never truly has. She loves me, I've never had to doubt it, and I don't have to worry about her cheating on me or playing around, but it don't feel good to know that she has never come to truly trust me. She don't consult me on the important things. She makes up her mind what needs to be done, she does it, and then she fills me in later. I've been angry about that, sometimes, but mostly I'm just sorry about it. I watch her trying so goddamn hard, throwing herself at a problem like a trapped bee at a glass window, and I wish she'd just ask me if I could open that window for her. I think, when she's in trouble, Lee don't even see me standing there.

She was gone for nearly an hour and a half. She came in through the back door and came to find me in the living room, still wearing her jacket and her outdoor boots. I said nothing. I just waited for her to tell me.

She sat on the chair opposite mine.

"I went to the bar. To Delores Bradley's bar. I had to speak to Julie."

I didn't understand. She'd just spent the day in Julie's company. There was no good reason I could think of that she'd have had to leave me and Grace to rush off and see Julie again. But then Lee told me everything. About the dog. About what she'd overheard at the Jordans'. About Nina's bruises.

"You think Simon hurt her?" I asked. My mouth tasted sour.

"I know he did," Lee said.

She went upstairs to check on Grace, leaving me alone downstairs. I crushed my beer can in my hand and a few drops of beer spilled on the rug. I wanted to punch someone. I thought of Leanne hitting Simon and wished it had been me. Wished I had that kid right there in front of me so I could beat the hell out of him, if that was what it took, to find out the truth. I went out into the cold night air and walked around the house, my feet crunching on the gravel. It was too dark to see the irises and crocuses that had started to bloom, but I got the scent of winter honeysuckle at the front of the house. Nina had helped me to plant that honeysuckle. She loved scented plants. Loves. *Jesus.*

I went back inside, got some soup from the freezer, and put it in the microwave for Lee. When she came back down she was carrying Grace's laptop. I was opening a bottle of wine.

"Do you think that's a good idea?" she asked.

"I do." I poured two glasses and handed her one. "Is Grace okay?"

"Not really." Lee brought her laptop to the table and opened it. "Someone sent her this video today." She turned the screen so that I could see.

The first minute of the video was a bunch of clips from Nina's and Simon's social media. Pretty pictures of them kissing in a forest. The two of them standing in the snow, arms wrapped around each other. That video of Nina pushing Simon into the pool and laughing, the one from the press conference. The audio track started out something I didn't recognize, something pretty and romantic, but that didn't last. The image on the screen changed abruptly to a still of Leanne, taken from the press conference. The image had been frozen at a hard moment. Her mouth was open and twisted, her eyes a little wild. She was wearing her black, long-sleeved T-shirt, but there was a stain on the shoulder that I didn't remember noticing on the day and her hair looked like she hadn't washed it in a while. She didn't look like herself. She looked more than a little crazy. In case that point had been missed, the video doubled down by adding *Jaws*-style music and some overlayed text in blood red. The image stayed the same as the *Jaws* music played, but the captions changed every few seconds:

HER GIRLS HAVE TWO DIFFERENT FATHERS

WHAT HAPPENED TO NINA'S FATHER?

NO ONE'S HEARD FROM HIM IN YEARS!

NOW NINA'S MISSING

WHAT IS HER MOTHER HIDING?

"Look at the comments," Leanne said.
I pulled the laptop closer and scrolled down.

Bit harsh (also misogynistic overtones much??). But . . . I did think
there was something off about her at the press conference. Like a
robot.
[674 ♥]

Totally!!
[32♥]

Robotic. Like someone had told her what to say.
[521 ♥]

Gorgeous couple. It's so, so sad that she's missing.
[1089 ♥]

Oh, come on. It's ALWAYS the boyfriend.
[387 ♥]

What crap. I'm so tired of this #believewomen. What did we
learn from Amber Heard??!! Guess what? Women make shit
up too.
[69 ♥]

Go back to your momma's basement you woman hating fuck.
[22 ♥]

Sophisticated argument. Is this what they teach you at your women's studies classes?

There is SO much more to this story. What about Nina's stepfather?? I've heard all kinds of rumors about him . . . Nina was a little girl when he got together with her mom. I mean . . . what was the attraction there?
[823 ♥]

I hate a tease. If you have info . . . spill!!
[13 ♥]

If there were any REAL journalists left in the mainstream media they'd be looking into the stepfather, that's all I'm saying because I don't want to get SUED.
[461 ♥]

What did happen to Nina's father? Why wasn't there an investigation when he disappeared? That's fucked up.
[1041 ♥]

I think it's weird that she didn't at least put on a clean shirt before coming to beg for her daughter's life. I mean. I know she had a lot on her mind but it seems to me that's just something you'd do.
[21 ♥]

SO NOW WE'RE POLICING WOMEN'S LOOKS AT GODDAMN PRESS CONFERENCES ABOUT THEIR MISSING DAUGHTERS? IS THIS FOR REAL??
[363 ♥]

It's not about policing looks, okay? I'm just asking a question.

This whole story is a red flag. They want to distract you from what's really going on and make you beleeve that all men are not to be trusted. Look deeper and DO YOUR OWN RESEARCH! Nina Fraser is an actress. She's not a real person. Ask yourself whose behind this story? Why is it all over the internet? Whose pushing this thing?

[16 ♥]

😑😑????

It went on and on. Hate, hot takes, and nonsense. Very little of it was about Nina. Most of it seemed to be about Leanne or me.

"It's getting worse," Lee said. "I looked around before I came back downstairs. This is just one video, but there are others. And Julie Bradley's campaign on Facebook is really taking off. That page has twenty-two thousand followers and it's growing really fast, but most of the comments are . . . not supportive. They're like this. Horrible."

I looked down at her screen again. "People aren't going to believe this, are they?" That shit about Nina being a little girl when Lee and I got together. I felt sick.

Leanne took a sip of wine. "Grace got some horrible messages today. I told her to turn off her phone."

"What kind of messages?"

"Some of them were from 'friends.'" She used her fingers to make quote marks in the air. "Girls who said how sorry they were about Nina, and that they were worried about Grace. One girl came right out and asked Grace if she felt safe at home. With you."

I stared at her.

She shook her head. "I don't know. People are messed up."

For a minute I couldn't speak. I drank more wine. "Maybe we shouldn't have let Julie go online with everything. Do you think that was a mistake?"

Lee looked exhausted. "I think there's nothing wrong with asking people's help to find out the truth." She paused. "You know we can't just sit here and wait, Andy. We're her parents. She's our daughter."

We were talking about everything except what really mattered. I took her hand.

"Everything you said. About the dog, and the cleaning, and Simon. You're telling me that you think he killed her. You think that Nina's dead."

Leanne sat very still for a long time, and then she slowly shook her head.

"We have to have hope," she said.

CHAPTER EIGHTEEN

Rory

As soon as Andy Fraser left Stowe, I wanted to go too. Simon was still holding on to his face and resisting Jamie, who was trying to pull his hand away to get a closer look.

"We're out of here," I said. Jamie turned to look back at the barbecue set up. "Leave it," I said. The caterers could clean it all up. They were being paid enough. The cops were still walking in and out of the house. I went to our car and started the engine. Jamie and Simon were too slow to follow. I wanted to roll down the window and scream at them to hurry up. I couldn't be there anymore. Couldn't look at the lake, at the boat bobbing gently at the jetty. It was like a goddamn horror movie. Finally, Jamie and Simon climbed in. Simon's door was still closing when I accelerated away.

"Rory!" Jamie said.

"Sorry." I didn't slow down.

"I don't blame you for being upset. Jesus. That woman is crazy. She's lost her mind. I mean, completely lost her mind."

I kept driving. I wanted to get home and shower again. I needed to talk to Simon.

"I'm going to call Matthew Wright as soon as we get in. He better not think we're going to let this one go."

I didn't respond. At that exact moment, I didn't give a shit about anything except getting home and getting back into the shower. All day, all I'd been smelling was lake water, from my hands, my clothes, my whole body. It felt like the water had soaked into my skin. Like I was sweating the stuff, which wasn't possible. I'd gotten home from Stowe just before 5:00 A.M. I'd parked the truck in the garage. I stripped there and threw my clothes and boots straight into the trash can, then walked naked to the bathroom in the gym downstairs. I'd been in there for less than five minutes when Jamie came looking for me. She assumed I'd been working out, and I didn't correct her. I'd just had time to dry off and dress and then I'd had to drive straight back to where I'd just come from.

"Don't you think we should call Wright and make sure he's going to charge her? What if she turns up at our house? I honestly think anything's possible at this point."

"Let it go, Jamie."

Her whole body stiffened. She gave me a look that I didn't like.

"Just give me a minute, okay? It's been a long day. I need time to think."

She acted then like she was fine with whatever, but that meant nothing. Jamie is very good at hiding what she really feels. We got home. I went upstairs and straight to the shower. I turned the water up as hot as it would go and washed with shampoo, twice, then body soap, three times. When I got out and dried off, I could smell only eucalyptus. I dressed and went looking for Simon. I found him in his bedroom. He was lying on his bed, with his shoes still on, headphones over his ears, scrolling through his phone. He looked up when he saw me, slid his headphones back, and gave me a sunny smile. He looked like a kid. Like a boy.

"Hey, Dad."

"Shoes off the bed." I said it automatically. How fucking stupid.

Simon slipped his shoes off, let them drop onto the floor, and sat up straighter on the bed.

"You were right about the search. It was the right thing for me to go. Sorry I was kind of an asshole last night. It's just a lot, you know?"

He was upbeat. Almost giddy. Because he thought he'd gotten away with something.

There was an armchair in the corner of Simon's room that I'd never noticed before. It was oversized, tan leather, and the cushion was firm. It was masculine and stylish. Designer. I could tell by looking at it that the cost of the chair was probably more than my first car. Simon hadn't picked it. He sure as hell hadn't paid for it. Jamie must have put it here, but when? Was it a recent purchase, or had it been there since we moved in? I didn't know. How much else had I missed?

I sat in the chair and looked at my son.

"They're not going to find her, Simon." I watched his face. The smile didn't drop. "They're not going to find her, because I already did."

I saw the shock of it hit him. The smile disappeared. His mouth fell open. His body stiffened. He tried to pull himself together, to bullshit his way past it.

"You found Nina? But that's so great. Is she okay? Where was she?"

"Stop. Stop it."

I closed my eyes. I couldn't look at his face. I couldn't watch him try to figure out how best to lie to me. But I couldn't sit there with my eyes closed either. I turned my head and looked outside. Night had fallen. The pool lights had come on and the water was an eerie blue in the darkness.

"Why did you do it?"

There was the longest silence. His response, when it came, was a whisper. "It was an accident."

I saw everything start to slip away. His future. The life we'd lived together as a family, the life I'd wanted for him, all of it started to slip away. I swallowed.

"Tell me."

The words came out in a rush.

"We'd been drinking. And we'd been hiking all day. We were both tired. We started arguing about stupid stuff. Whose turn it was to make dinner, you know. And so I made dinner, but I was pissed at her and she knew it and she didn't want me to be angry. Like, she wanted me to make dinner but also say that it was my turn and that I was fine with it, but it wasn't, and I wasn't, and it all seems so fucking stupid now." He was crying. The words kept spilling out of him. "She wouldn't leave me alone. I went upstairs and she followed me up. So I went back down to the living room and she followed me there too. She kept asking me to apologize and I wouldn't and she wouldn't let it go. She kept at me and at me and pulling at me and the more I shook her off the more she got worked up. And then she grabbed my arm and I just . . . sort of . . . pushed her off me. That's all, Dad. I swear it. But she stumbled backward and her boots were on the floor and she fell over them. She hit the back of her head, really hard, on the stone hearth. And she just . . . she just died."

I said nothing.

"Dad, I swear. I swear. It was an accident."

I tried to remember the last time I'd seen Nina alive. Could it have been in the summer? I tried to picture it, but the only image that came into my mind was of her messing around by our pool, pushing Simon into the water and laughing, but that had been a video clip the police had shown at the press conference. Had I even been at the house when that happened? She'd had a sweet laugh. Joyful. It started like a giggle and grew.

"She was such a beautiful girl."

"I'm sorry," Simon choked out.

I walked to the other side of the room and stared out through the glass doors. The moon was up. There was enough light that I could see the pool patio clearly. The chairs were stacked over to the side, covered for winter. Nina and Simon had spent a lot of time in that pool in the summer. Nina had spent a lot of time in this house. Had they been happy together? I tried to remember how many times I'd actually spoken to the girl, other than to say hello or goodbye. Twice or three times, maybe, and even then it had been nothing more than the smallest of small talk. I turned back and looked at my son. He was sitting on the edge of the bed, hunched over. Simon was six foot three. He was taller than me by two inches, and bigger too. He had the body of a man, but wasn't he still just a boy?

"Why didn't you call an ambulance? Why didn't you call me or your mother?"

"You don't understand. You don't know what it was like. One minute we were fighting, and then she was just . . . gone. I held her . . ." He made a kind of cradling gesture with his hands. "There was blood from the back of her head. It went everywhere. On my shirt. On the floor. Her eyes were open and staring. I didn't even try to do CPR in the beginning. I should have, but I don't know how much time went by before I even thought of trying. And then it was like . . ." His face crumpled and he started to cry again. "It felt like I was defiling her. Pushing and shoving at her dead body. I knew she was dead. She was dead the moment her head hit the stone."

"You're not a fucking doctor, Simon!"

"You don't need to be a doctor to know when someone is dead! She wasn't breathing. She didn't have a pulse. Her eyes were open and fixed, and I just knew, okay?"

"So you took her to the woods and you put her in a shallow grave?"

"I was in shock. I must have been, because time went by and then it was like I just woke up. If you'd been there, Dad . . . There was blood everywhere. All over the rug, all over me. If I'd called the police, *no one* would have believed that it was an accident. I mean, you have to understand that. Like, the whole world's all 'me too' and 'believe women' and that's all great, okay? I am all for that, in principle. But people have gotten crazy with this stuff. We're always, always the bad guys, even when we're not." He reached out a hand toward me, his face pleading. "Dad, if I called the cops, how was I going to explain it? Here's my dead girlfriend. Yes, we were fighting but she just happened to fall, nothing to do with me. Except that there's blood everywhere and I look like a fucking homicidal maniac."

"So you decided not to try. You decided to bury her." I hated him for it. For what he'd made me do. But there was no undoing what I'd done. If I went to the cops, how could I explain away my decision to dig that girl up and put her into the water?

Simon stood up. He clenched his fists.

"Yes, all right! I fucking buried her. I put her in the ground. I covered her with dirt. I did that."

I looked at the floor. I was sick with guilt. My hands were shaking again. My hands had never shaken before Nina. No matter the problem. Once I'd bitten off more than we could chew at the company. I spent millions on a patent for a tool that was obsolete six weeks after we closed the deal. In the six weeks before the patent was superseded, I spent millions more on a facility and on supplies, all of which were suddenly useless. I took on debt that we wouldn't have the revenue to service. For months, I was staring down the barrel of losing everything, and in all that time my hands didn't shake once. I was cold as fucking ice.

"Dad," Simon said. His voice was ragged. He took a step closer to me. I didn't move. He took another step, and then another, until he was so close that we were almost touching. "Please, Dad." His voice cracked. And I reached out with my right arm and pulled him to me. He wrapped his arms around me and held on tight, like I might just be able to save him.

"My life is over," he said. "My life is over. I'm so sorry. I'm so sorry."

We stood there like that for a long time. It felt like that moment should be the end of it all, but it wasn't. Time passed, and we had to deal with what came next. I let him go. I sat on the bed, and he sat beside me. Sooner or later, Jamie would come looking for us.

"I don't want to go to prison," Simon said. "I mean, what's the point? My whole life in a concrete box. Mom would insist on coming to see me. You know? And that would mess her up. Having to come and see me in some hole of a place and pretend that things were going to work out. We'd all be better off if I just took your gun and ended it."

"You're not going to prison."

The words sat between us. Simon didn't look at me. He kept his head down and spoke in a voice that was not much more than a whisper.

"Dad, what did you do when you found her?"

I swallowed. "I moved her. To a place where no one will ever find her again."

He nodded slowly. I did not have a choice about what we did next. If Simon had called me the moment Nina had fallen, we would have had options, but once he put her into the ground those options were narrowed to exactly two. I could choose to help my son, or I could send him to prison for the rest of his life. Because no one was going to believe that it hadn't been murder.

"Nothing we do now can bring Nina back. What happened was an accident. You screwed up. You didn't mean to hurt her, and you're going to have to carry what happened with you for the rest of your life. But you didn't mean to hurt her. And we need to focus now on keeping you safe. Listen to me, Simon. Once we leave this room, we are never going to talk about this again. You are not to tell your mother. You are not to tell anyone. And if anyone comes after you, we are going to take them down."

He looked at me with eyes wide and teary. "You can't do that. I can't drag you into this, Dad."

As if I wasn't already in it. As if I hadn't sunk her body in the middle of our fucking lake. I saw myself sitting in the dock of a courtroom, trying to explain my actions. I saw the look on Jamie's face when she found out what her son had done. What I had done.

"You're not dragging me into anything, because Nina didn't die in that house," I said firmly. "You understand? What you just told me tonight stays between us. You are never going to tell another living soul what happened between you. You just stick to your story, no matter what. Even between us, Simon, we don't say anything else, okay? Because you never know who might be listening."

Slowly, he nodded. His tears dried up. Hope dawned in his eyes. I gripped his shoulders.

"This was an accident, Simon. A terrible, horrible accident. You screwed up, and you're going to have to carry that for the rest of your life. But you didn't mean to hurt her."

He stood up and we hugged for a second time, and I tried to remember the last time, before that night, that I had touched my son. It had certainly been months. Had it been years? Maybe, if I'd been a different kind of father, his first instinct would have been to call me for help instead of trying to cover things up. I shoved the thought away. Simon wasn't a *murderer*. He was no more responsible for her death than he would have been if Nina had died in a car accident where he had been driving carelessly. In that situation he'd get a slap on the wrist, and some people would blame him but just as many would feel sorry for him. They'd want him to have a second chance.

Simon wasn't a murderer. He was a kid who'd made a mistake. That was it. I told myself I believed it. I *did* believe it. I just couldn't stop thinking about that bruise on the left side of Nina's face. The thoughts rolled around and around in my head. Andy Fraser had said that if I'd spent more time with my son, none of this would have happened, but that was bullshit. No amount of parenting could prevent an accident. And that's what this was. An accident. An accident. An accident.

CHAPTER NINETEEN

Jamie

After the search for Nina at Stowe, we went home. In bed that night, I couldn't sleep. I gave up on it and wandered the house. I went to the living room and sat in the dark and looked out at the trees. We'd installed lighting in the backyard, beams of white light that pointed upward from the base of some of the bigger trees. The beams caught the branches as they swayed in the wind, and the swirls of rain caught in the gusts. The lighting looked great at parties—dramatic—but to sleep-deprived me, it just looked like a perfect setup scene for a horror movie, and I wondered what the hell we'd been thinking. I went to use the bathroom, washed my hands, and stared at myself in the mirror. I was a mess, with dark shadows under my eyes, lank hair, and a zit coming up on my forehead. I had to pull myself together. Falling apart would help no one.

At 6:00 A.M. I got in the shower. I used the hair dryer and took my time drying my hair with lots of volume, then tied it back in a messy, casual high ponytail that always makes me look five years younger. I put on my new Alo Yoga leggings and tank top and my red jacket with the lightning stripe down the right sleeve. Then I put on makeup, with a heavier-than-usual layer of foundation to try to deal with the worst of the ravages. I looked in the mirror at 7:00 A.M. and I still looked like shit. The zit was angry, and no amount of concealer was going to deal with that. The shadows under my eyes had turned into bags, and the makeup was just sitting on my skin. I closed my eyes, took a deep breath, and grabbed my sunglasses and a baseball hat.

I checked on Simon before I left the house. I opened his bedroom door as quietly as I could, pushed it ajar enough so that I could see into the room. It was a pigsty. There were clothes on the floor, a few dirty dishes, books. The room smelled of body odor. All of which was not normal for Simon, who liked things to be clean. He was asleep on his stomach, his head turned away from me, his body sprawled in a way that made it look like he'd been fighting his covers in his sleep. I wanted to go to him, to adjust his gangly limbs and tuck him in safely, but he was too old for that, so instead I closed the door very quietly and left the house.

The press had been outside the house the day before. Not many. Just a couple of shady-looking guys with cameras sitting on the hoods of cars parked across the street. But Nina's story must not have been hot enough to justify an early-morning start, because when I drove out of the gate, there was no one there. I was the first to yoga. Misha, our instructor, was there, setting up, but she prefers not to talk before class, which suited me perfectly. I put my shoes and jacket away in a cubby, laid out my mat, and did some deep breathing while I waited. By seven twenty-five, people started to trickle in. David Armstrong arrived first. David is sixty-two. He started yoga in his forties after a back injury. He comes for coffee with us occasionally, but he's no fun. He doesn't join in the gossip, just sits back and listens with this supercilious look on his face that says, *Silly women.* Which would be annoying at the best of times, but it's all the more annoying because he so clearly doesn't want to miss a single word. Predictably, when he saw me that morning he worked very hard not to react, to pretend he had no idea that anything unusual was going on in my life. Georgia White took the opposite approach. Georgia must have seen my car in the parking lot, which gave her plenty of time to plan out her perfectly delivered little theatrical gasp of surprise when she saw me in the studio. She rushed over, hands out as if she was going to embrace me, or catch me, or push me.

"Oh my God, Jamie. You are. So. Brave. Amazing woman. What can I do to help? Of course you were right to come. Don't listen to anyone who tells you different. You're among friends here. But you look so tired. Are you sleeping?"

I gave her my very best don't-fuck-with-me smile and brushed her off. I turned to the front.

"Let's get started, Mish."

Behind me, Georgia turned and spoke to Anne Wellington in a faux whisper.

"We have to be kind. It must be awful for her. What people are saying about Simon. Of course, it looks terrible."

I kept my back straight, pretended I hadn't heard, though everyone was looking at me, even Misha, who has never really liked me, in a kind of frozen sympathy. Misha started the class, and I tried so hard to focus, but I fell out of Vasisthasana and I couldn't hold my Astavakrasana, and out of the corner of my eye I could see Georgia's head popping up as she tried, so hard, not to show her triumph. I could have cut and run, but that would just have given them more to talk about. I got through the class, took extra time with Savasana, and chatted lightly to Misha about a new book I'd heard about that I thought she might like, as I put on my shoes. And then I walked out with my yoga mat under my arm, as casually as you like, as if I hadn't noticed that everyone had already left for coffee without me.

It must have been a hard call for them. Without me there they had the freedom to get really nasty, of course, but if I'd gone with them they could have indulged in all that fake sympathy, and they might have had a small chance at an inside detail or—jackpot—some tears from me. I guess they'd decided I wasn't a good candidate for tears and confessions. I told myself that that should make me feel better, and I got into my car, but I couldn't face going home. Not yet. I turned back and drove to the bakery on Bridge Street, where I bought a cappuccino with two sugars, three chocolate muffins, two cinnamon Danishes, and a giant chocolate croissant that I told myself was for Simon but that I demolished in the car. By the time I was driving back down our road at 8:30 A.M., I was feeling almost human. Except that I couldn't stop thinking about the look on Leanne's face when she'd hit Simon—the twisted fury on her face and the fear in her eyes—and the fact that Nina had now been missing for five days. And then I saw the scrum at our gates.

At first I couldn't make sense of it. Instead of the two shady guys with cameras, we had, what . . . fourteen? Sixteen people? And there was a TV camera crew, right in the middle of the gang. They were all huddled at the gate, as if they were waiting for something. I drove up slowly behind them and buzzed the electric gate. They parted to let me through, and camera flashes went off as I drove past. Our garage door rolled open automatically, and I drove in and parked beside Rory's car. I pressed the button again to close the roller door and the outer gate, but the door and gate had barely started to close when they stopped and froze in place. I got out of the car. Rory was waiting for me by the front door, his car keys in his right hand. He'd used his own buzzer to stop the gate from closing. He smiled at me; it was an attempt at his usual everything's-under-control smile, but he looked like hell. He looked like he hadn't slept at all. He was nicely dressed in slacks and a button-down with the sleeves pushed up, but he was jittery. Full of nervous energy.

"Are you going out?" I said. I was so aware of the cameras flashing from the gate and the shouted questions. I tried to look natural, like all this was completely normal. Like I was having a casual morning chat with my husband.

"I think we're going to have to talk to them sooner or later. Let's just get it over with."

Before I had a chance to respond, Rory took my hand and turned me back in the direction of the press. I almost tripped as I turned, stumbling over my own feet. I wasn't ready for this. I was sweaty after yoga, and probably covered with croissant crumbs. I wanted to grab my baseball cap to cover the zit on my forehead. I wanted to tug Rory back toward the safety of the house. The gate was open, but it was as if there was an invisible line keeping people back. The press stayed just outside the gate, but the questions came immediately, shouted at us. It was just like it was on TV, but it felt very different in real life. Much more aggressive. I shrank back.

"How's Simon doing?"

"Do you know where Nina is?"

"Why did Simon leave her alone?"

Rory held his hand up to everyone, gesturing for silence. He drew me close until I was standing right beside him.

"Thank you, everyone. My wife and I would like to make a short statement. This is a very difficult time for our family, so we won't be taking questions right now. We hope you understand." He drew a deep breath, then continued. "Simon and Nina have been together since they were sixteen years old. They've been very much in love, but they are also very young. They broke up on Friday night, and Simon came home. This was not their first breakup. They've broken up a few times in the past. As I said, they are very young. Nina told Simon that she would stay in our vacation property, as she'd been drinking. She asked Simon to leave. She said a friend would pick her up the next day. Simon has not heard from Nina since he left the cabin. He is extremely worried about her, as you would expect."

There was a question from the back of the press pack, something about Nina's phone, but I didn't quite make it out. Rory ignored it.

"As a family we love Nina very much, and we are all very worried about her." Rory turned to the TV camera. "Nina, if you hear this, we ask you please to call us, or call your mom, and let us all know that you're safe. Better yet, just come home. Everyone misses you and wants to see you." Rory squeezed my arm tightly and took a half step forward. He raised his chin and his voice.

"There's one more thing we want to say. We've seen the videos, the terrible things people have been saying about Nina's mother, Leanne, and her stepfather, Andrew. We do not agree with them, and we ask the people out there who are coming up with these theories to stop. It's harassment. The truth is that almost no one has led the kind of completely blameless life that will stand up to internet scrutiny. But making mistakes in your life doesn't mean that you are a . . . that you deserve that. We ask that all those internet sleuths out there, coming up with theories about the Frasers, or indeed about Simon, we ask you to stop, please, and let the police do their jobs. Thank you for your time."

Rory pulled me backward and hit the button on his key fob. The gate started to slide closed. The press pack shouted questions, but no one tried to step inside the gate, and we turned our backs and quickly retreated to the house.

"Rory, what was that?" I hissed.

"Wait until we're inside," he said quietly.

I followed him into the house and shut the door behind me. He leaned back against the wall. He looked exhausted.

"We were going to have to talk to them at some stage," he said.

"Why did you say what you said about Leanne and Andrew? We don't want people to stop asking questions, do we?" He didn't answer me, but he didn't need to, because my brain had finally caught up. He'd denied the story to feed the story. Video clips of his statement would play on all the news channels, on the internet. Of course people wouldn't stop talking about the Frasers and debating and wondering, just because Rory went on TV and asked them to. They'd talk *more*.

"People are going to see through this," I said. "They're not stupid. They're not going to believe that you went out there to try to help the Frasers out."

Rory nodded. "Maybe some people will question my motivation. That doesn't really matter. What matters is that we keep muddying the waters. People are going to be talking either way. What we want is a lot of confusion, we want people to feel like there's more going on here than meets the eye. Like there are secrets they don't know, like there's information that's being kept back."

"Kept back by who?"

"It doesn't matter, Jamie." He pushed himself off the wall and went into the study, and I followed him. He took a seat on the couch and I sat beside him. It was very quiet in the house, and the light in the study was muted. It was hard to believe that I had just been outside, having questions yelled at me by the press. That they were still out there, guarding our gate.

"Look, to build a conspiracy theory, you need to feed two appetites. The first appetite is that people want to feel like they're in the know. Like they're smarter than someone else. They want to have the latest twist or little bit of information that they can pull out when their smart-ass, know-it-all brother or sister or friend or colleague starts to talk. Just to be clear, it doesn't matter if that piece of information is correct or not. Nobody trusts facts anymore; it doesn't matter if the source for the information is an expert in their field or some bottom dweller living in his momma's basement. They'll get equal weighting online." He paused. "Actually, the bottom dweller will probably get more eyes on his content, because it will be more entertaining, and it will attract more argument.

"The second appetite we're feeding is that people want to feel safe. No one out there really wants to believe that Leanne and Andy Fraser are good parents. No one wants to think that they're innocent. Because if they are, and if Nina is equally blameless, then that means that Nina's disappearance is completely random. And people don't really want to believe that, not deep down. Because if bad things happen to good people, and it's all completely unpredictable, what's to stop it from happening to them too? People would much rather believe that the Frasers did something to deserve this."

"But they didn't." I didn't know Andy, and I didn't like Leanne, but she was a good mother. Or at least she had been, until she lost her mind.

"No. They didn't." Something passed over his face. Something dark. "And I don't give a shit. This is war, Jamie. We didn't ask for this to come into our lives, but it has. Something like this could destroy all of our lives, and I'm not going to let that happen. Whatever it takes, I'm going to protect this family. If that means taking down the Frasers . . ." He shrugged. "You saw the way they were in Stowe. They're not thinking about being fair, about understanding both sides. They are only thinking about Nina, and I don't blame them for that because I would be the same. But I'm not going to play nice while they go after our son."

He reached out tentatively and took my hand. He waited, I think to see if I would pull away, and when I didn't, he slid his arm around my shoulders and pulled me to him. My head rested on his chest. I felt awkward. I was leaning into him at an uncomfortable angle, and besides that, this was not how we did things. What did he want from me, exactly? Not sex. I didn't get that vibe. But something. Carefully, I slipped my right arm around his waist to his back. He let out a long breath and sagged back into the couch. His arm tightened around me. Comfort. He wanted comfort. Okay, I could do that. I adjusted my position so that I was more comfortable, and I relaxed into him. If anyone had walked into the room they would have seen the picture of a loving couple, turning to each other after a difficult day. It was just an act, but for some reason I felt tears stinging my eyes. I blinked them back.

"The PR boys have set up an interview with one of the morning shows. They want to come to the house. You don't need to worry about it. Arrangements have been made. The interviewer will be friendly."

"When?" I said.

"Later today, if possible. Tomorrow, if not."

"Okay," I said. I sounded hoarse. I cleared my throat. I tried to think about what clothes we should wear, about where we should sit, but I couldn't focus.

"I know you're scared," he said, "but it's going to be okay."

I felt an unexpected wave of warmth toward him. Of affection.

"Every time I go to sleep I dream about Simon in prison," I said.

"It's not going to happen. We won't let it happen."

"Right. That's right."

I stayed there for a while, for as long as I could, and then I sat up and laughed a little. "Just next time maybe warn me before you drag me in front of the press. I look terrible."

"You look great," Rory said. "You always look great." He sounded almost like he meant something by it. I stood up.

"I should go and check on Simon. See if he's had breakfast."

Rory nodded. If he was disappointed that I was leaving, he didn't show it. "Don't push him to talk right now. Trust me when I say he's not ready. Just be there for him. As his mother."

"I can do that," I said. I went to the kitchen, still feeling off balance. I turned on the coffee machine and went looking for Simon. I found him in the living room. He was sitting on the couch with his back to me. He had his earbuds in, so he didn't hear me coming. I leaned down. I was going to give him a hug, but he was holding his phone with two hands, the screen pointed upward, and my attention was caught by the message he was sending. Without really intending to, I read it. The message said:

Send me a pic

Part of me froze. I decided to look away, to give him his privacy. He was an adult. His relationships were none of my business. I thought all of that but still I didn't move. My eyes were glued to his screen as the picture came in. He clicked on it so that it expanded and took up all of his screen. The picture was. . . . not what I expected. It was a selfie, taken by a young girl. It showed her smiling shyly up at a camera that she was holding at an angle. But she was fully clothed. In fact, she was wearing a jacket and a riding helmet and she was on horseback. I gasped involuntarily. Simon turned quickly, and our eyes met. He flipped his phone upside down. He made the move so smoothly, so naturally, that all my warning bells went off at once.

"Hey," he said, and he smiled at me warmly.

"Who was that?"

"Who was what?"

"That picture. On your phone. Who was the girl?"

He looked at me blankly, the picture of innocence. Something churned at the base of my stomach.

"I know her. It was Nina's sister, wasn't it? It was Grace." There was a sharp edge to my voice.

He hesitated. It was just the merest pause. A fraction of a second. He used that time to think about whether or not he should lie to me. I saw him do it. He decided against it. He went with bruised innocence instead.

"Sure," he said. "We've been in touch."

"Do you really think that's appropriate?" The words "send me a pic" rolled around in my mind, like an unpleasant aftertaste.

"Why not?" Simon said. "She's sad and lonely and her parents are acting like crazy people."

I stared at him. He sighed, like I was being deliberately stupid.

"Mom, she messaged me, okay? She reached out to me. She felt really bad about the way her parents were behaving. She knows that Nina and I were crazy about each other. She knows I'm not the kind of guy who would . . . do what they're saying I did. She wanted to tell me that, and then we got to talking and she's . . . Look, she has no one to talk to."

Send me a pic. Send me a pic. I swallowed.

"Simon. She's fifteen years old."

He rolled his eyes. He was completely unembarrassed.

"I think I know that. I'm just being supportive. Nina wouldn't want me to ghost her little sister."

I stayed very still. The part of me that was his mother said that I believed him. Of course I believed him. Because what was the alternative? That he was flirting with Grace? Playing games with the fifteen-year-old sister of his missing girlfriend? I tried to shake it off. I tried to smile at him. But there was another part of me. It was the part that felt sick when I was fourteen years old and my dad's friend looked at me for a little bit too long. It was the part of me that knew to avoid the skeevy guy who was looking for a roommate at rent that seemed too good to be true. The part of me that saw it coming just a second too late when the bar manager at my old job cornered me in the basement. That part of me was saying that something wasn't right.

"Promise me right now that you'll delete her number."

"Are you kidding me?"

"Promise me, Simon. In fact, I want to see you do it. Right now. In front of me."

He widened his eyes at me, like I was being crazy.

"I mean it."

"Why?"

"Because if people knew, if her parents knew, that you guys were in touch, they'd go batshit crazy. You'd better believe they'd go to the media and make you look like a pervert." I told myself that was the only reason.

Simon made a face. "I don't think so. People see what's really going on here."

"Simon." My voice was sharp and raised. I took a half step forward.

"Oh my God. All right. If it means that much to you." He lifted his phone, went to his contacts, and deleted Grace's number.

"The messages too," I said.

"Fine. Whatever." He deleted them.

I hesitated. He could get her number again, easily. She'd probably message him. Or he could contact her through social media. I couldn't police him. I couldn't take his phone away.

"You should block her number," I said.

He smirked. "I would, Mom, except you just made me delete her number. I don't have it to block it."

"Well, block her if she messages you again."

"If it makes you happy." He sounded like an adult indulging a batty old lady.

"And you won't meet her in person."

"Oh my God."

"Simon, *promise me.*"

He looked at me, his eyes narrowed. "Wow, you're really serious about this, aren't you?" He waited for my nod and shook his head. "Look, I have no intention of meeting Grace. I really do get that that might look weird, to a certain kind of person. I'm not trying to get myself in more trouble."

"Okay."

He stood up and slipped his phone into his back pocket. He came around the couch and gave me a hug. He was so much taller than me. So much broader.

"Thanks for caring, Mom. You're the best." He kissed my cheek and left the room. And I sat on the couch and cried.

CHAPTER TWENTY

Andy

When I woke up on Thursday morning, Leanne was gone from the bed. Used to be I was always the first one up, but by Thursday I think Lee had stopped sleeping entirely. I wasn't sleeping much either, but every time I woke up, she was sitting up in bed, or sitting in the chair near the window, staring out into the darkness, as if she expected Nina to walk up the driveway at any minute.

I got dressed and went downstairs. Lee was in the kitchen. She must have been up for hours, because everything in the room was gleaming. There was a fire burning in the living room fireplace. I could smell coffee and bacon.

"How long have you been awake?" I asked.

She blinked at me, like she didn't understand the question. Grace came into the room, and Leanne looked at her for a moment like she didn't recognize her.

"Mom?" Grace said. She sounded scared. Lee shook herself.

"I made bacon and pancakes," she said.

"Thanks." Grace sat at the table and Lee put a plate in front of her. Grace picked up her fork. "I'm not going to school." She said it like it was a statement, but her body tensed up, to see how that statement landed.

"You are," I said. "You need to go. There's no point sitting at home. We'll come and get you if there's any news."

Grace dropped her fork and stared at me. "You can't be serious."

"I know it's hard," I said. "But you'll be better off at school, with your teachers and classes and your friends, and all the normal high school stuff. If you're at home with us you'll be watching the clock all the time." I looked to Lee for support. She was slow to respond.

"Your dad's right," she said, after a delay.

"You don't get it."

"What don't I get?"

Grace shook her head, her face screwed up in frustration. "I can't concentrate. I'm going to be sitting in class and I'm still going to be watching the clock, only I'll be at school, with everyone *looking* at me and talking."

"People love to talk, Grace," I said. "You know how I feel about that. Talkers are talkers and doers are doers. If people are talking about you, you just let them go right ahead."

Grace rolled her eyes. "People aren't talking about me because I'm a *doer*, Dad. They're talking about me because I'm Nina's sister. And it's horrible."

Lee reached out and took her hand. Her eyes met mine over Grace's shoulder.

"I know it's hard. Dad knows that too. It's really hard for all of us. But school is the best place for you to be at the moment. Any day now, Nina will come home, or we'll find her, and we can all put this behind us. In the meantime, I need to ask you to try to hang in there. Can you do that?"

Grace didn't look at us. She pulled her hand from Lee's and stood up. "I'm not hungry." She left the room, closing the door softly behind her.

Lee got up, went to the sink, and started to wash up. I watched her and waited for her to turn and look at me, but she didn't. Her movements were jerky. Something wasn't right.

"You're off to work?" she said, still not looking at me.

"Not for a half hour or so. My first job canceled. I can take Grace to school." I didn't want Leanne driving on no sleep. "Or . . . Lee, I can stay home today, if that would be better." I felt slow and stupid. Maybe I should have already made plans to stay home. I couldn't just keep on going to work like nothing was wrong, could I?

"No. You go. With the inn closed, we're going to need the money."

I thought maybe Grace would fight us more on the issue of going to school, but half an hour later she showed up at the kitchen fully dressed, with her hair combed and her bag packed. By the time she'd said goodbye to Rufus and loaded her school bag into the car, it felt almost like a normal day. In the car she started grumbling about her math teacher. We didn't see the crowd of press waiting at the end of our driveway until we was almost on top of them—a bunch of journalists and photographers, dressed in winter coats and hats, holding paper coffee cups, standing around at the end of the driveway. We saw cars parked down the road, narrowing it to a single lane. I wanted to turn around and go back to the house, but my instinct was to pretend to Grace that everything was okay. That I knew how to handle the situation.

"Keep your head down," I said. I had to slow as I approached the end of the driveway. Camera flashes started to go off, and all the shouting kicked off. It was a mess of noise and lights and movement. I kept the car moving forward, but we could hear the shouted questions.

"How are you holding up?"

"Grace! Grace! How do you feel about Nina going missing?"

"Who's Nina's real father?"

Someone stood in front of the car, and I hit the brakes, but then someone started shouting Grace's name over and over again and I put my foot back on the gas. I moved slowly enough that anyone who wanted to could get out of the way, but I didn't stop to wait for them.

"Dad . . ." Grace said. Her voice sounded small and frightened. Camera flashes were still going off on either side of the car.

"Keep your head down, Gracey. Don't look at them."

The last of the group parted.

"It'll be all right," I said, and I wasn't sure if I was trying to make her feel better or myself. "I guess the story of Nina going missing is getting a whole lot of attention right now. Try your best to ignore it."

"Jesus, Dad." Grace didn't swear, as a rule, but I guess she thought that that idea was pretty stupid. She wasn't wrong. For a long moment neither of us spoke. I was watching my rearview mirror. There was a car behind us, a black Range Rover, about fifty yards back. I was pretty sure they was following us.

"They won't be at school, will they?" Grace said.

"Definitely not," I said. Fuck. What if they followed us to school and piled out after Grace and started taking pictures in front of all the kids? If that happened, she would get back in the car and that would be the end of school for her. I pressed my foot to the gas. Grace shifted in her seat and said nothing. But the Range Rover stayed right with me, and when we got to the school it was just behind me. The drop-off lane was full. The rules of the lane are strict—you can pull in just long enough to drop your kid and their bags, you wave good-bye, and then you're out of there. There's no parking allowed, and if you make the mistake of hanging on a little too long, more than one person will lean on their horn to hurry you up. The line was moving slowly. There was no way I could join it. We'd be sitting ducks. I drove straight past.

"Dad?"

"It's all right, Gracey."

I drove all the way to the top of the lane and then past it. I drove through the gate and right up to the small parking lot that was near the administration building.

"Dad, you can't. This is for teachers." Grace shrank down in her seat as if she was afraid that someone would see her. I reversed quickly into a space.

"I think today we get a free pass, don't you?"

She shook her head, mutely.

"Well, we're here now, and the sooner you get out of here and go to class, the smaller the chance that someone will see you and start asking questions."

That got her out of the car. She took her bag and lunch money, gave me a quick, one-armed hug and a muttered "I love you," and she disappeared. I went straight to the administration building, asked to see the principal, and waited for twenty minutes before she appeared, looking frazzled, irritated, and vaguely sympathetic, all at once.

"Mr. Fraser. Hello. I'm so glad you came to find me. Come in. Please come in."

I followed her into her office. Cally Gabriel had been principal when Nina had been at the school. I'd had very little reason to ever speak to her. Nina wasn't the kind of kid who won prizes at the end of the year. She'd never captained a team or come first in a race. She'd also never gotten in any fights, sent any bullying emails, vaped behind the bike shed, or cheated on any assignments. She was a good kid who flew beneath the radar.

"I was so very sorry to hear about Nina," Cally said. She crossed to stand behind her desk and indicated with her hand that I should take a seat in front of it. I sat, and then she hovered for a moment, which made me feel on edge. "Of course, all of us here have such fond memories of Nina's time with us. I'm praying to the good Lord that she'll be returned to you any day now."

"Yes," I said. "Thank you." I don't believe, myself. My mother brought me to church and all that, but it just didn't stick. I don't mind religion. I've known some good people who put God at the center of their lives, and that's fine. But when people shout about their prayers it makes me wary. Probably because the people I've known who talk most about God have always been the people with the least humanity.

"I'm aware that there's been a lot of chatter," she said. "It's inevitable, sadly. But I'll do my best to quash it within school grounds. And I'm aware that some parents were hanging around at drop-off this morning, presumably for gossip. I put a stop to that too, let me assure you." She sounded pleased with herself.

"Thank you," I said, because it seemed like what she expected. She gave me a little nod of her head.

"Of course! If there's anything else we can do for you at all, please don't even hesitate to ask."

"Well, now that you say it, there is something I need your help with."

The smile dropped away.

"There were journalists and photographers outside our house this morning, waiting for us. I think some of them may have followed us here. It won't take long for the others to figure out that this is where Grace goes to school. I'm worried they'll come on school grounds. They're going to be real interested in getting pictures of her, for a while."

"I see," said Cally Gabriel. She was frowning, a very little bit. Her forehead didn't move a whole lot, but I think that was because she'd frozen it up with injections. I could tell she wanted to frown by the tightness of her eyes and lips.

"So I was thinking you could arrange for some . . . I guess security, or something, to make sure that no one comes onto school grounds."

"Well, we have Jem, of course."

"Sure." Jem was Jeremiah Lambe, the school's security guard. He was a retired cop with a drinking problem, a gambling problem, and not a whole lot of interest in doing his job. "I was thinking of some-one to . . . uh . . . help Jem out. Just until all of this blows over."

"Of course, of course."

Some of the worry inside me loosened a bit. "That's great."

"Oh, sorry, no. Actually, I mean I understand why you might have been thinking that way, but sadly, the school budget just doesn't stretch to extra security. Every dollar that we spend on security is a dollar taken away from band camp, or the academic decathlon, or our sports teams. I'm sure you understand."

"Well, Mrs. Gabriel, I'm not sure that I do. I mean, I'm sure they wouldn't come on school grounds, but what if they did? The photographers, I mean."

"I'm sure they won't." She smiled at me reassuringly. I did not feel reassured. "We have cameras, of course, and we'll keep a very close eye on those and on Grace. We'll call you if there's any problem at all."

"Okay," I said slowly. "Well, thank you."

"You bet." She moved her chair, obviously expecting me to stand up. I stayed where I was.

"Mrs. Gabriel, I wanted to ask you also about Nina and Simon. They were together for their last years here, at the school. I wanted to ask you if you'd ever heard anything, or noticed anything, that caused you concern."

Immediately, her face took on a serious expression. "Oh, no. Nothing at all. Of course we take our duty to our students very seriously. If any of my staff had seen something concerning, we would have taken action. From everything I saw, they were just a sweet young couple."

I couldn't tell from her face whether or not she was lying. She sure wasn't thinking about Nina when she answered my question. She was thinking about making sure that the school did not get blamed if something had gone very wrong. I had no real reason to think that she knew something. She had no cause to pay particular attention to one teenage couple over another. But if she had seen or heard something that would suggest that the relationship was sour, she would admit it now.

"Thank you for your time, Mrs. Gabriel." I stood up. "If . . . If it's a question of money. For the extra security, I mean. My wife and I could make a donation to the school, to cover the cost."

I'd surprised her. For a moment she looked uncertain, but then the mask came back.

"Thank you. Your offer is appreciated. But I would have to consult the school board before we accepted any funds. And we'd have to consider the impact on the other children of a security presence. Some parents might object."

My fingers tightened on the back of the chair that I'd been sitting on. "Grace is a child, and she's one of your students. Don't she deserve to feel safe? To *be* safe? How can she come to school if she's being harassed?"

The calm assurance was back. "Let's hope it doesn't get to that."

"And if it does?"

"If that happens, I'd suggest a short period of homeschooling for Grace, just until all of the publicity passes over."

"Are you serious?"

"Mr. Fraser, please don't raise your voice."

"I'm not raising my voice." But I was. I tried as best I could to sound calmer. "You're telling me that the solution to these people harassing my daughter is to take her out of school? Her sister's missing. You think she should have to hide at home like some kind of fugitive?"

If she was bothered by my temper, she didn't show it. "What I'm saying is that you should consider the wisdom of running a gauntlet of press and photographers every morning with Grace, just to get her to school. She's a bright girl. It won't hurt her to have a few weeks away from class. Her teachers can provide her with work. Better that than the alternative."

There was some sense in what she was saying, even in my worked-up state I could see that. But I could see that Cally Gabriel cared only about herself, and that made it hard to hear her. She wanted Grace gone, so that the scandal and the gossip and the inconvenient journalists and photographers would all go away.

I left her there and went to the parking lot, where one of the teachers, Mrs. Fortescue, who was pushing seventy and who should have retired years ago, shouted at me for parking in the teachers' parking lot. On another day I would have joked with her, cheered her up, and talked her around, but I didn't have the patience. I got in my car. The school was much quieter now. The bell had rung and the kids had gone inside. Other than Mrs. Fortescue, who was still standing there, staring daggers at me as I pulled away, there was no one around. The Range Rover was gone. But at the school gates there was a man dressed in jeans, boots, a heavy jacket, and a green beanie, hovering and staring at his cell phone. He looked up as I approached and waved at me to stop. I thought he was looking for directions. I stopped the car and rolled down my window.

"Can I help you, sir?"

He came real close to me, leaned down, and put his two hands on my doorframe, so that I couldn't put my window up. Up close you could tell immediately that something weren't right about him. Physically, he looked okay. He had a reddish beard and pale blue eyes set a little too far apart. But he had a little crazy in his eyes, like a TV evangelist.

"I know what you are," he said. "You're a pervert. You're a piece of shit." His mouth was wet. Spittle flew from him every time he pronounced a *p. Pervert. Piece.* I jerked backward, and he came forward, putting his head inside my car. "You should be arrested. Locked up."

"Get out of my car." I started to put my window up. He reached in and tried to pull my hand off the switch. I hit the gas, too hard, and the car jumped forward. He fell backward, but not fast enough to avoid whacking his head, hard, on the side of the window frame. The car lurched forward and then stopped as I immediately lifted my foot from the gas. I saw him in my side mirror, standing there, clutching his head, and staring after me. He was angry. Angrier. I put my foot down again and drove away, fast, all the way home, where the journalists were waiting.

CHAPTER TWENTY-ONE

Leanne

When Andy came home from dropping Nina at school, I was still sitting at the kitchen table. The sound of the back door opening made me start. I hadn't moved since he'd left, hadn't even realized that I was staring at the wall, seeing nothing, thinking of nothing. I stood up when he came in and started to gather the breakfast dishes from the table.

"Lee."

Something in his voice made me turn to him right away. He pulled off his baseball cap and ran a hand through his hair.

"What is it?"

"Have you been outside?"

I shook my head.

"There are journalists and photographers at the end of our drive-way. Some of them followed us to school."

It took me a minute to understand what he was saying. I went to the living room and looked out the window.

"Are they still out there?" I couldn't see the gate clearly from the window. Andy had planted a hedge of honeysuckle in spring, and it had grown enough that the view was obscured.

"They're still there."

"Should we go talk to them?"

The expression on Andy's face told me that I wasn't getting it.

"They're not a friendly crowd, Lee. When I came back a couple of them yelled questions. Nasty stuff."

"What kind of nasty stuff?"

Andy shook his head and looked away. After a minute he said, "I tried to talk to the school about keeping Grace safe. Making sure no one gets into the school. I offered Cally Gabriel money to pay for temporary security. She said no."

I frowned. The Jordans gave a lot of money to the school. Was this Cally taking sides?

"No one knows which classes she's in," I said. "And there's no reason for anyone to try to talk to her. Plus, she's surrounded by other kids, and the school does have some security."

"She can't stay there, Lee. We need to take her out. Take her somewhere safe."

"Take her home, you mean."

"Lee . . ."

"What?"

He came to me and put his arms around me. He held me close and rested his chin on my head. "Baby, I don't think Grace can be at home right now. I think we should take her to Craig's place. To the farm."

I went still. I didn't want that. I wanted her home.

"She can be with her cousins. Homeschool for a week or two. It might be fun."

What he didn't say was that the farm was two miles from the main road, and Craig and Sofia had a guard dog, a great big bullmastiff who was a gentle giant in the house, but scary as hell if you arrived uninvited. It made sense. It was the right thing to do, but I hated the idea.

"I don't know."

"I can go and get her right now. She'll be at Craig's before lunch. You can video call her there."

I leaned back and looked up into his face. "What aren't you telling me? It can't just be the journalists. You were fine just an hour ago with Grace being at home."

He hesitated. "There was a guy at the school. Some weird guy. I don't know, I just think with all this attention it's possible that we could attract some crazies."

I turned around so that I could see him properly. "What did he say?"

Andy couldn't look at me. "That I'm a pervert. That I should be locked up." He looked sick to his stomach. It hurt me to see him like that. I rested my head against his chest.

"Take her," I said. "Take her to Craig and Sofia."

IT WAS THE RIGHT decision, but as soon as Andy left I felt lost. I found my laptop and brought it back to the kitchen table. I made myself coffee and added a large shot of whiskey to my cup, and sugar, and cream. I sat down and opened the laptop. I know my way around social media. I run a Facebook page and Instagram profile for the inn, I prompt guests to leave Tripadvisor and Google reviews, and I log in every few days to post and manage any comments. On Instagram I like to watch baking content, and I follow some of the really good DIY renovation accounts. It's the kind of thing that Nina and Grace quietly roll their eyes at, but I like it. I'm not on Twitter or Reddit or TikTok, but I live in the world, and I'd have had to completely shut myself off not to be aware of just how toxic some of the online stuff had gotten. Still, what I found that day was on another level.

I started with Julie Bradley's campaign Facebook page, and I branched out from there. It wasn't hard to find content. People had embraced our campaign name. All I had to do was enter the hashtag "#WhatHappenedToNina" and I found thousands of videos and comments and reels and shorts and hot takes. The more I looked at the videos and the comments, the more obvious it became that the vast majority of these people, even the ones who posted sad or concerned comments, saw Nina's disappearance as entertainment. They didn't try to hide it. Some of them just outright made jokes or memes. The sad ones were performatively sad. The kind of posts that said *this story is so tragic, that poor girl and the situation is so trigger-*

ing for me personally because of my anxiety/ptsd/depression and I've really spiraled as a result today but I helped myself by going for a brisk walk and making my favorite matcha smoothie! check out my recipe and follow me on insert-platform-here for more on my mental health journey and like and subscribe! It was sickening. They didn't see Nina or any of us as human beings, just as characters in a story they could use to sell, sell, sell. And that . . . that was the least toxic side of things.

According to the internet, I was a slut who charged for her services, I'd had two children with two different men and I had no idea who the fathers were. Or, alternatively, I was a frigid, lesbian, liberal bitch who hated all men and who'd tried to lock up her two beautiful girls. I hated my girls and I abused them, or I loved them too much and desperately tried to keep them safe from dangers that didn't exist. One anonymous poster claimed to be Nina's best friend, and she said that Nina had told her that I used to starve the girls because I wanted them to be thin. Another poster said it was well known around Waitsfield that I was into devil worship. Another said there had been a rumor that Nina's father had been poisoned. That comment, which had been posted under an edited YouTube video of the press conference, had 2,563 likes. I kept searching and scrolling. Once I'd started it was impossible to stop. I watched all of a three-minute video of a girl putting on her makeup to camera. She gave makeup tips while talking her viewers comprehensively through all the conspiracy theories around Nina's disappearance and ending with a critique of Nina's makeup in her Instagram photos, pointing out how she could do it better.

I went back to the #WhatHappenedToNina page that Julie had set up and trawled through the comments again. There were thousands of them. Some of them were positive, but most of them weren't. I came across a comment with a link to a new page, run by someone who called himself BobSpeaksTheTruth. This page had reposted all the toxic YouTube videos that targeted me. There was also a post where "Bob" claimed to have firsthand knowledge that Andy had been a teacher in New Jersey, that he'd been arrested for child molestation in New Jersey, two years before he'd moved to Vermont and married me. According to "Bob," Andy hadn't been charged because his victim had killed herself. It was all utter bullshit. Andy had never lived in New Jersey. He hadn't gone to college and he'd never worked as a teacher. He'd lived in Vermont all his life.

Andy and I met when I bought some pavers from him for the path at the inn. He was selling them off at a great discount because they were left over from some job or another. And then he started coming by, with leftover bits and pieces. He never asked me out, never seemed like he was all that interested in me as anything but a friend. I wondered if maybe he was gay. Then I figured maybe he wasn't, because he was a great bear of a man and there was nothing polished about him. Then I felt stupid because obviously gay men come in every shape, size, and level of sartorial sophistication. I thought about Andy a lot. I loved him before I knew it. He was always there, gentle, quiet, and supportive. He was the kindest man I'd ever known.

Nina's father and I met in college, and we were together for exactly four and a half months. When I found out I was pregnant, he called his mother, who flew in from New York City. She was very nice to me. She took me out for lunch at a fancy restaurant and offered me money for an abortion, and when I said I didn't want that, she flew back to NYC and took her son with her. The next I heard, he was on a foreign exchange program at a university in Paris. I tried calling him once, but his number was disconnected. We have never spoken since, but I heard through an old friend that he got married and lives in Connecticut with his wife and three children. I've always assumed that just like I know about him, he knows about me and Nina. Nina knows his name and where he lives, and I made it clear that if she wanted to get in touch with him, I'd help her to do it. She never had any interest in reaching out to him. She said she already had a father, and she didn't need another one.

Andy and I met when Nina was three, and we got married when she was four. She loved Andy from the beginning. When we got married she was so happy. She asked if she could call him her dad, and he's always been that to her, always gentle and encouraging and . . . I don't know. It's so hard to find the right words to describe their relationship, how special he was to her in those early years, how his care and love made her bloom. From the beginning Andy always acted like he *liked* Nina. Even before he loved her. Like, he thought she was a cool little kid. He asked her about her day and built her a little obstacle course with logs and scrap lumber, and then cheered her on when she conquered it. He filled her with confidence. The stuff about Andy was the worst of everything I'd read. They were poisoning something that was pure and beautiful, and it made me sick to my stomach. BobSpeaksTheTruth had gotten his tone just right. Serious, concerned, and with every "fact" he dropped he sounded measured. He couched everything with an "allegedly," and he came across as someone who could be trusted. People who didn't know Andy, hell, maybe even people who did know him, some of them would believe this. And once a rumor this ugly started, would we ever be able to set the record straight? Or would this follow us for the rest of our lives? I buried my head in my hands. I hated Bob, whoever he was. I hated all of them. The venal ones and the just plain stupid ones. Everyone who was feeding this crap with their clicks and their attention and their shares.

I stared down at my hands. My nails were short and cracked. My only jewelry was my wedding ring. These hands had built something. A home and a business and a family. We were going to lose the inn. My Tripadvisor and Google reviews were now a cesspool of one-star reviews and links to pornography. Our girls were our life, but the inn was our home. Our safe place. And these bastards, these sad, bored, basement-dwelling bastards with their pathetic conspiracy theories and their desperate need for attention, they were going to destroy it all. But it was worse. Much worse than that. What would this do to Andy? Grace had already seen some of this stuff. What would this do to her?

I stood up and paced the kitchen. I felt like my skin was too small for my body, like I was going to fly apart. My tongue was dry. I poured a straight shot of whiskey, then another. I drank because I wanted to destroy something, and the only thing available was myself. Rufus was watching me. As I looked at him he whined. Not a high-pitched, I-want whine, but a low, worried rumble.

My cell phone rang. It was Andy. I picked it up and answered.

"Hello?"

"She's not here. She's not in school." He sounded panicked. Terrified.

"What?"

"They had me sitting here, outside the *fucking* principal's office, and all the time they knew she was missing and they didn't tell me because they were hoping to magically fucking find her and they knew they wouldn't. Lee, she didn't even make it to her first class."

"Grace?" The world started to shift around me.

"Yes, Grace. Of course. I don't know what to do. What should I do?"

"Grace," I said. I think I dropped the phone. I think I must have sat on the floor, or fallen, because that's where Andy found me later. But I don't know because I can't remember. Everything was black.

CHAPTER TWENTY-TWO

Matthew

B y 9:00 A.M. on Thursday morning, Matthew's friend in the K-9 unit had already delivered up. He called Matthew on his cell phone. Matthew took the call standing in line at the coffee shop down the street from the station.

"Damien. How did it go?"

"As expected. Trudy did not mislead you. I took Drake out and he alerted on the spot. No doubt whatsoever that someone put a body in that dirt and then took it back out."

"Shit."

"Yeah, I guess it must have been your girl."

"Hard to think it could have been anyone else."

"You'll be sending forensics back out?"

"I will."

"Fair warning that they might not find anything helpful," Damien said. That ground is pretty churned up. And it's raining out there right now. You know the dogs can pick up traces that forensics can't?"

"I know it. Thanks, man. I owe you one."

"Well, not really." Damien sounded amused. "But if you'd like to imagine that you do, put in a good word with your sister for me."

Matthew's sister Lucia was a cop with Burlington PD. She was tough, and smart, and when it came to men she knew what she wanted and what she didn't want. What she didn't seem to want was any relationship that lasted more than a couple of months. What she seemed to be very good at was ending things quickly and simply and without leaving any bad feelings in her wake. Unfortunately for Damien, Lucia never went back.

"I can try."

"Nah, man. I was just kidding around. Tell her hi from me though, okay?"

They ended the call. Matthew picked up the coffees he'd ordered and hurried back to headquarters. When he got there Sarah Jane was not at her desk. Kim Allen eyed the extra coffee cup in his hand.

"Looking for your girl? She's in an interview room downstairs."

Matthew was taken aback. Sarah Jane had done a good job interviewing Julie Bradley. A very good job. But that didn't mean she was ready to take on witness interviews by herself. It sure as hell didn't mean that she could choose to do so without his knowledge or permission. His displeasure must have shown on his face.

"Calm down, storm cloud," Kim said. "It's not a witness. Or at least, not a real one. It's a crazy lady who gave the boys on the desk a hard time and wouldn't leave without speaking to someone on your case. They called up. SJ said she'd deal with it. She's doing them—and you—a favor."

Matthew left the coffee on his desk and went downstairs. Only interview room 1 was in use. He thought about going in and decided instead to watch the interview from the side room, through the one-way glass. Sarah Jane was sitting opposite a well-dressed woman in her forties. The stranger had dark hair cut into a sharp bob, large brown eyes, and a small, pointed chin. She was agitated. Sarah Jane was not.

"The point I'm trying to make, if you would only *listen* for one minute, is that this man was alone with my children. Okay? Do. You. Get. That?"

"I do, Mrs. Sugarman." Sarah Jane had a pen in her hand and her notebook open on the table in front of her.

"So what are you going to do about that?"

"You gave your permission for your girls to stay over at the Frasers' house. And according to your girls, nothing untoward happened," Sarah Jane said, in the tone of someone repeating herself.

"That is not the *point*."

"We're talking about a sleepover that happened more than two years ago."

"I told you about the sleepover only so that you would understand my personal connection to this issue, my concern as a mother, okay? I mean, clearly I overestimated your capacity for empathy. I guess you don't have any children. But just forget about that. I'm asking you, as a *citizen*, what you're going to do about this man." There was a certain amount of triumph in her voice.

"As I've explained to you twice now, Mr. Fraser hasn't done anything wrong."

"That's bullcrap." Sugarman pointed right in Sarah Jane's face. "And you know it. He raped a little girl in New Jersey. And now his stepdaughter is missing and you people are doing nothing about it."

"That's simply not true—"

"Why are you protecting him? It's disgusting. It used to be that you could rely on police to go after people like this. The world is going to hell, that's what it is. You people want to sit around and drink coffee and eat snacks and talk like you're all so important, and in the meantime the rapists and the child molesters are everywhere. It's no wonder people are taking things into their own hands. They don't have a choice. Andrew Fraser better watch his back."

Sarah Jane closed her notebook carefully. She placed her pen down on the table.

"Mrs. Sugarman, Andrew Fraser has broken no laws. He did not rape a little girl in New Jersey. You are referring to a lie which has been peddled by an online troll, by someone who gets their kicks getting people like you riled up."

Sugarman flushed. Her pointy chin came up. "People like me!"

"People like you." Sarah Jane was calm, controlled, and very cold. "Mr. Fraser is dealing with a personal horror right now. His daughter is missing. He should be getting support from his community, not accusations and mistrust. And I'm warning you right now, any action taken by any member of the public against Mr. Fraser will be met with the full force of the law." She stood up and picked up her notebook and pen. "It's time for you to leave."

Sugarman stood up. She bristled with outrage. Sarah Jane's speech had not had the intended effect.

"You wait and see, when the truth all comes out, you're going to lose your job. Or maybe you'll go to jail too, for protecting him. See how smart you are when that happens."

They left the interview room. Matthew gave Sarah Jane enough time to escort Mrs. Sugarman back out to the reception area. He waited for her in the hall. She pushed her way through the double doors with force and stalked along the corridor until she saw him and came to an abrupt stop. Her eyes went from his face to the interview room doors behind him, then back to his face again.

"You watched?"

"I did."

Sarah Jane cleared her throat. "I apologize if I overstepped. I told her three times that the New Jersey story was made up. She didn't want to hear it."

Matthew started up the stairs. "You did fine. People like that are difficult to deal with. They see every fact you give them as evidence of some greater conspiracy. Probably there was nothing you could have said to change her mind."

Sarah Jane followed him. He told her about the update from Damien at the K-9 team.

"Damn," she said.

"Yeah."

"It must have been Nina. Right?"

"I think so."

"So he moved her. He found out that the Frasers were going to search for her on Wednesday, and he went back and moved her."

Matthew nodded. "And he would have to have moved her on Tuesday night. The decision to search the grounds came after the Tuesday press conference. That gives him a small window of opportunity."

"We need to trace his movements on Tuesday. Find out where he was. Where he went."

"Anything yet from the phone data warrants?"

"Nothing." She shook her head. "I realized this morning that it's only been two days since we sent them in. It feels a lot longer, somehow."

"I've been thinking that I should call Simon's lawyer and ask him to voluntarily surrender his phone."

"You think he'll do that?"

"I doubt it very much. But it will put him under pressure."

"Great." Sarah Jane sounded thoughtful. "You know, if he did move her, that's a mistake."

"How so?"

"Because if he'd left her where she was and we'd found her, he could have claimed that someone else must have killed her after he'd left the house. They'd spent a week together. Slept together. Even if his DNA was all over her, that wouldn't prove he'd killed her. But to move her he'd have had to go back. He'd have had to drive from Waitsfield to Stowe. Someone might have seen his car. He could have driven past someone's security camera. We will eventually get his phone data and we'll be able to check his location history. We can check his car GPS data."

"Always assuming he was stupid enough to take his phone with him. To drive his own car."

"Murderers aren't known for their stunning intellect."

"Agreed," Matthew said. "Though Simon goes to Northwestern, so he's no dum-dum."

"Fear makes people do stupid things," Sarah Jane said.

"Also true. But it's his parents' house. If we can prove he went back there, so what? It wasn't a crime scene, so far as we knew. It wasn't restricted. He was perfectly entitled to go there."

"You're assuming he'll admit it if we ask him. Maybe he'll lie."

They were quiet for a moment.

"We need a body, don't we?" Sarah Jane asked quietly. "It's going to be impossible to prove he killed her if we don't find her."

Matthew sighed. "Maybe not impossible, but very difficult."

They'd reached the door of the squad room. They paused as the same time, both feeling, perhaps, like the conversation wasn't done.

"Did you always want to be a cop?" Matthew asked.

Her eyes met his briefly and slid away. "Why do you ask?"

"No reason in particular. Except that you're doing good work, and I wondered." He couldn't tell if the pink in her cheeks was a reaction to the compliment or to the cold. For a second he thought she wasn't going to answer him.

"My brother was the one who wanted to be a cop. He talked about it right through high school." Sarah Jane reached out and pushed the door open. He followed her inside. Kim was there, and Dave, and a handful of others. They were busy at work, on the phone, or talking among themselves. There was a hum of quiet conversation.

"He loved the job," Sarah Jane said. "He was killed in a car accident eighteen months ago."

"I'm very sorry," Matthew said.

She nodded.

"So that's when you applied?"

She gave a half shrug, half nod, and it was clear she didn't want to continue the conversation. Matthew wasn't going to push her. She changed the subject.

"What I don't understand is how the dog could smell something that the forensics guys couldn't pick up. I mean, if there was something there for the dog to smell, shouldn't there be traces of blood or tissue left for the forensics guys to find?"

"I'm not going to pretend to understand that either, but I'm assured that that's how it works sometimes."

Matthew's cell phone rang, a call from a number he didn't recognize. He nodded goodbye to Sarah Jane and answered the call on the way back to his desk.

"Detective Wright? This is Ronnie Garcia. You left a message for me."

"Mr. Garcia. Yes. I left a number of urgent messages for you. Yesterday, and again this morning."

"I was traveling, Detective." There was no apology in Garcia's voice. "How can I help you?"

"I understand your firm handles security for Rory Jordan and his companies. I'm calling to confirm—"

"If this is about the cameras at Mr. Jordan's Stowe home, as Mr. Jordan already told you, those cameras have not yet been commissioned. We'll have someone out there to do it this week. It's unfortunate, of course, that it wasn't done sooner, but we can't travel back in time."

Garcia's tone was loud and brash and very confident.

"You checked that yourself, Mr. Garcia?"

"I did."

"And if we were to issue a warrant to your company, for all data regarding the cameras at the Stowe house? And, while we're at it, all cameras at the Jordans' home in Waitsfield?"

"You can do that if you like, Detective. I don't think it would do you much good. The company I work for is based out of Panama, which is also where our servers are located. We don't keep any data in the United States. I guess you could serve your warrant in Panama? I don't know how international law works, so maybe that's possible." This was said in the tone of someone who knew down to the finest detail exactly how the relevant international law worked. "What I do know is that the data-retention laws in Panama are different from our laws here. The company I work for deletes all client data on a very regular basis, as a matter of policy. But, like I said, in the case of the Stowe house, there would be no data at all, as the cameras hadn't been commissioned yet."

Matthew ended the call. He was pissed. Garcia was a fixer, and Rory Jordan was playing games. He was getting ahead of them, cutting off avenues of investigation. This was not the first time Matthew had gone up against a suspect with money. The last time it had been a rapist with a trust fund. Matthew had won that round, mostly because the guy had been dumb as a rock. Simon Jordan was not stupid, and neither was his father. Matthew was feeling more and more like he had a mountain to climb. They couldn't afford to waste time. They needed to get into the Jordans' home in Waitsfield and seize every computer, tablet, and phone before data could be deleted or destroyed. Surely a documented K-9 alert would be enough to convince a judge that they had probable cause to search the house? Matthew picked up his phone. He was about to place a call to a friendly prosecutor to ask for advice on how best to frame the application when something caught his eye. Sarah Jane had stood up at her desk, her phone pressed to her ear. She turned to look in his direction, her face showing her distress. Matthew stood up. She came toward him, finishing her call on the way.

"That was Andy Fraser," she said. "He's at the school. Grace Fraser has gone missing."

CHAPTER TWENTY-THREE

Andy

called the school on the way over there and told them that I was on my way to pick up Grace. That's the procedure. You let the school know and they arrange for your kid to be waiting for you at the office when you get there. Except that when I got there, Grace wasn't waiting for me. Cally Gabriel's assistant asked me to take a seat, and like a fool I did it. I sat there for half an hour like an obedient child, until Cally finally came out of her office, looking defensive.

"Where's Grace?" I said.

"Grace was not in class," Cally said. "She didn't attend any of her classes this morning."

"So where is she?"

"I don't know," Cally said. "But I suggest that calling her cell phone might be the best way to find out."

I've never hit a woman in my life, and I've never wanted to before that moment. I told myself that the only thing that mattered was finding Grace, that I didn't have time to tackle Cally or tell her what I thought of her. Despite all that, I found that my left hand was clenched into a fist, and the index finger of my right hand was in her face.

"I told you. I stood here and I warned you. I begged you to help and you gave me some bullshit, and now we see."

Her lips were tight in anger. "Mr. Fraser—"

"No," I said. "You don't get to talk." I walked away, already pulling out my cell phone. Over my shoulder, I told Cally Gabriel that she'd be hearing from our lawyer. We don't have a lawyer, but maybe it was time we got one. I called Grace's cell phone four times on my way back to my car. It went to voice mail each time. I was about to get in the car, about to call Leanne, when I turned back and looked at the school. The bell had rung and kids were pouring out of classrooms.

I walked fast in the direction of Grace's classmates. I saw kids I knew. All of them looked at me like I was a threat. A scary guy. That made me pause. These kids had grown up knowing that school was not a safe place. I couldn't make them afraid. I couldn't do that. I stopped walking. I was going to go back, but then I saw Molly. I called her and she came over, dragging her feet.

"Hi, Molly."

"Hi, Mr. Fraser." She didn't look at me.

"Do you know where she went?"

She shook her head.

"Molly, you gotta know how serious this is. Nina's missing. Grace is missing now too. She didn't want to go to school this morning. If she's gone off somewhere just to get away and you know it, you need to let me know right now, because my next call is going to be to the police."

She shook her head again, but this time she looked me in the eye. "I thought she was coming to school, but she never came to class. I haven't even seen her today. I would have called her, but I haven't had the chance yet."

"Okay. Thanks. And you'll call me, or ask your parents to call me, if you hear anything?"

"Uh-huh. Sure."

I turned and walked away. There were a lot of eyes watching me. A boy around Grace's age said, "Pervert!" loudly, half covering it with a fake cough. I stopped walking and looked at him, daring him to say it again. He didn't flush and he didn't back down. He looked like he wanted to take me on. I walked away. I called Lee. I told her that Grace was missing. I can see now how stupid that was. I should have known that hearing the news that way might mess her up. I should have gone to her. I should have held her when I told her, been there in person to reassure her. But I was panicking. I didn't know what the hell to do, and Lee is the person I rely on.

I called her. I told her. I heard her drop the phone. I was out in front of the school by then. I felt like I had a hundred pairs of eyes on me, and none of them were friendly. I felt like I was going to fly apart. I went to my car. I called Matthew Wright. The call went to voice mail. I called the main number for headquarters. They put me through to Sarah Jane Reid.

"Mr. Fraser?"

"Grace is missing. I dropped her off at school this morning and I watched her walk in through the doors. She never went to class. I'm at the school right now. They don't know where she is. I spoke to her best friend. She says she hasn't heard from Grace, and I believe her."

"Does Grace have access to a car? Can she drive?"

"No. No car."

"Did she pack a bag this morning? Pack any clothes?"

I tried to think. "She had her school backpack. I don't think she had any clothes."

"What did she wear to school today?"

My mind was blank. I couldn't see it. "I don't know. Jeans, I think. Her jacket is green, so I guess a green jacket?" I sounded like I was making it up. I think she heard that.

"I'm going to hang up the phone now, Andrew," she said. "We'll get people moving on this end. We're going to get cars out looking for her right now, and we'll check the bus station. Go home. We'll meet you there."

"There was a guy at the school gates today. A crazy fucking guy. He had some insane ideas about me being a danger to the girls. Could he have taken her?"

"You say you saw her walk through the doors into the school?"

"Yeah."

"Then it doesn't seem likely, but we'll check it out."

I gave her a description of the guy and then I drove home. I drove past the reporters at the gate and parked in the courtyard. I found Lee on the floor in the kitchen. She was sitting with her back up against the cabinet. Her phone was on the floor beside her, the screen cracked. Rufus had curled up to her, as close as he could get. He'd pressed his head into her lap, but it was like she didn't see him. Like she didn't see me. I picked her up and carried her into the living room. I sat with her on the couch in the living room, and I held her. She rested her head against my chest, but she didn't say a word.

"It's going to be okay, baby. I promise you, it's going to be okay. We're going to get her back. We're going to get them both back."

I kissed her head and I held her close and I cried. That's what I did. Two daughters gone. My wife broken. And I sat on the couch, and I fucking cried.

CHAPTER TWENTY-FOUR

Matthew

The high school was twenty-one miles from headquarters. Matthew asked Sarah Jane to drive. He needed his hands and attention free, so that he could call around with the description Andy had given them of the stranger who'd accosted him at the school gates that morning. Sarah Jane was a good driver. She drove fast, which was required in the circumstances, but she didn't take unnecessary risks. Matthew managed to reach Dr. Karen Sears, a psychiatrist at the UVM Medical Center who specialized in forensics. Sears was part of a task force that regularly assessed high-risk individuals in the Vermont system, and they'd worked together on a previous case. Matthew quickly filled her in on the background and gave her the description Andy Fraser had provided.

"I can't be sure, but that sounds like it might be James Mannion. He'll be in your system. Borderline personality disorder. He has a history of fixating on high-profile individuals."

"Have you treated him?"

"Not personally, no."

"Do you think he might have taken her?"

"I can't answer that question with any confidence. I believe he's been charged in the past with stalking and harassment, but he has no history of violence that I'm aware of. He's only in the system at all because he sent a series of threatening letters to Hillary Clinton.

He believed that she was part of a pedophile ring. He threatened to kill her. But he never took any concrete action. It was all a fantasy."

"Clinton would be a pretty challenging target. The Frasers are local. Easily accessible. Do you think he might have escalated?"

There was a pause. "I don't know. Like I said, I haven't treated him. Let me call his care team. I'll get back to you."

They ended the call. Sarah Jane gave Matthew a quick look of inquiry, and he shook his head.

"Unclear," he said.

They reached the school. Sarah Jane pulled up in front of the administration building and parked. They went inside. The doors opened into an outer office, with a long reception desk and a row of four chairs opposite. There was a bulletin board with posters advertising various extracurricular activities—signup sheets for a ski team, a production of *Guys and Dolls*, and an after-school homework club were the most visible. There was a young blond woman behind the reception desk. She seemed to be expecting them. She pointed them nervously toward a closed door marked PRINCIPAL. That door opened before they could reach it and a woman came out. She was wearing a knee-length navy skirt with a pale pink sweater. Her hair was short and tightly curled, and she wore very pink lipstick and tortoiseshell glasses. She offered her hand to Matthew.

"I'm Cally Gabriel. I'm the principal of this school."

"Detective Matthew Wright. This is Officer Reid. Is Mr. Fraser still here?"

"I don't believe so. I think he left."

"He's looking for Grace?"

"I really couldn't say."

Matthew was picking up a definite attitude. "What time did Grace get to school this morning?"

"Her father dropped her off at eight thirty A.M."

"When did you realize that she was missing?"

"You have to understand, we have hundreds of students in this school. We can't keep tabs on every individual student." Gabriel didn't seem to be aware that she'd raised her voice. She didn't like being questioned. "We have to have a system. Students go to class. The teacher takes a roll call on her tablet and the results of that roll call come back to the office, here. If a student is absent and a parent hasn't called ahead to let us know, or logged their absence through our system online, then the discrepancy is flagged. That's when we call the parents."

"I understand. Which class did Grace miss?"

There was another pause. "Grace didn't attend any of her classes today."

Matthew glanced at his watch. It was almost eleven thirty. Andy Fraser had called headquarters just after eleven. This *system* did not appear to have worked.

"I'm not sure I understand. Grace's first class would have been, what, eight thirty? Eight forty-five?"

"It was my fault," broke in the blond woman who was sitting behind the counter. "I didn't check the alerts. We don't usually do it before recess, because so many kids are late. I usually check the alerts around eleven thirty and then I call all the parents at once, you see?"

"Thank you, Becky," Gabriel said sharply. She gestured for Matthew and Sarah Jane to follow her into her office and shut the door firmly behind them. "Obviously it's less than ideal that we didn't check the alerts earlier in the day, but as I tried to explain to Mr. Fraser this morning, we simply do not have the capacity to provide extra security or supervision for one individual student. This is a public school. We have to think of the needs of all of our students equally."

"Understood." Matthew was not going to take the time to explain to her that in his view, taking three hours to let parents know that their kid hadn't shown up to school was less than adequate supervision for anyone. "Do you have any idea where Grace Fraser may have gone?"

"I'm afraid I don't."

"You have cameras," Sarah Jane said. "I noticed some around the front. Is the footage recorded?"

"I . . . don't know," Gabriel said. "You'd have to speak to our security officer, Mr. Lambe. If you follow me, I'll escort you to his office."

They followed her as she led the way out of the administration building, across a courtyard, and down a flight of stairs into a long, badly lit corridor.

"The whole situation is a tragedy, of course, but I can't help but think that the Frasers need to take a little more responsibility here," she said, in an aggrieved tone.

"I'm not sure what you mean," Matthew said.

"Well. With both girls running away, it does call into question what's happening in the home, doesn't it? Clearly something isn't right there. Not that I lend any credence to any of the wilder rumors that are going around . . ." She let her voice trail off and paused long enough to give Matthew a look that suggested that she was lending credence all over the place. "And I understand why they're casting about, looking for other people to blame, but really, it's very irresponsible to point fingers at young Simon Jordan, which is certainly what they're trying to do. A lovely young man. Very much in love with their daughter too, which makes it all the sadder."

She paused at a door that had once upon a time been painted a bright, cheery blue, but was now stained with years of dirt and grease. She knocked briskly, a schoolteacher's knock, and opened the door.

"Mr. Lambe? These police officers would like to speak to you about any security camera footage you might have from this morning."

The room behind the door was grim. The only window was a small one. The floor was gray linoleum, well worn and a little grubby. There were shelves with old cleaning supplies and, toward the back of the room, a desk with a computer that looked like it might have been obsolete ten years before. A small electric heater in the corner of the room pumped out heat. The man seated behind the desk was overweight and unshaven. There were dark patches of sweat under each armpit and the room smelled strongly of stale alcohol and body odor. Lambe gave them an appraising look from behind the desk.

"I can help you out there. Anything in particular I can help you with?" He moved his mouse and clicked something. The screen was tilted away from the door so that it wasn't possible to see the content unless you crossed the room and looked over his shoulder.

"Grace Fraser," Matthew said. "She's missing. Her father dropped her to school at eight thirty A.M. and she never made it to her first class."

"I can look for her on the cameras, sure, but if she ditched class, she probably went out through the back. No cameras back there. Budget doesn't stretch."

Matthew looked at Cally Gabriel, but she made no attempt to clarify Lambe's casual statement. Gabriel's hand was pressed to her mouth, and she was wrinkling her nose.

"If you'll excuse me, Detective. I have a busy morning. If you need anything further I'll be in my office." She withdrew with an audible sigh of relief. In other circumstances, Matthew might have had some sympathy—the smell combined with the heat made the room an unpleasant place to be—but it seemed to him that Gabriel had completely failed to grasp the seriousness of the situation.

Lambe was smirking at him like he knew exactly what Matthew was thinking.

"I'm Burlington PD, retired," he said. "Grace is Nina Fraser's sister, correct? I understand your concern, but most likely she ditched. All the kids do it, and I guess she has better reason than most." He gestured to them to come closer and pointed at his screen. "The system we have is pretty good. I can play back the cameras from this morning. See if we can spot her."

He did that, quickly and competently. They watched the morning procession unfold, the cars arriving, the kids unloading. Lambe fast-forwarded quickly until he got to 8:27 A.M., then slowed it down. He was the first to spot Andy Fraser's car pull in.

"There," he said, pointing at the screen with a finger stained yellow from cigarette smoke. "That's Grace, right?"

They watched as she disappeared into the school, past the range of the cameras. They watched Andy enter the school administration building, watched him leave twenty minutes later. Lambe let the tapes run. They watched the school clear out. There was no sign of Grace Fraser leaving the campus.

"There was a man at the gate this morning," Matthew said. "Harassing Andrew Fraser. Do you have a camera at the gate?"

Lambe shook his head. "'Fraid not. But if he was out there, he didn't come in here." He gestured at the screens, as if they proved his point. "Cameras would have caught him."

"You said Grace probably ditched and left through the back, where there are no cameras?"

"Sure."

"And all the kids know that that's the way to go out, if you don't want to get caught?"

"That's right."

"So presumably anyone who went to school here also knows that's the way to get in without being seen."

Lambe wagged a finger at Matthew and made a clicking sound, as if you say, "You got me."

"Right. Okay. Thank you for your time." Matthew turned to go. He wanted out of there.

"I think he did it, for what it's worth," Lambe said.

"Excuse me?" Matthew was at the door. Sarah Jane was already outside. Matthew turned back.

"Simon Jordan. She—" Lambe jerked his thumb in the direction of Cally Gabriel's office. "She thinks the sun shines out of his ass. He's good at that. Charming women."

"You don't like Simon," Matthew said.

Lambe leaned back in his chair. He let it swivel from side to side and scratched at his stomach.

"I do not. Let me tell you a story about Simon Jordan. In his last year he didn't make the ski team, okay? Made it every other year, but not his last. We had a new kid. Can't remember his name. Paulo something. Demon skier. He got a spot and Jordan didn't. So Jordan's all smiles and congratulations, right? First one to clap the new guy on the back. What a stand-up guy. What a sweetheart. Except three weeks into term we start getting reports of petty thefts. This and that. Someone's phone, or lunch money, or a new sweater or expensive textbook. That kind of thing. And Jordan quietly tells his friends that he's going to get to the bottom of it. He gets his dad's security guy to give him some little trackers. This was before AirTags were a thing, okay? But they were like that. Little plastic things small enough to be discreetly slipped into personal possessions. And Jordan sticks these little trackers to a bunch of stuff. A pair of sneakers he left in the locker room. A math textbook. A wallet. And guess where they all turn up?"

"Paulo's locker," Sarah Jane said, from behind Matthew. This time she got the wagging finger.

"You got it. Exactly right. And of course Jordan was *devastated*. Could not have been more shocked that his good friend Paulo was the thief. It was all bullshit. That Paulo kid got kicked out of school. Jordan got his spot on the team back and came out of the whole thing smelling like roses."

"So you think Simon set him up. How come you saw it when no one else did?" Matthew asked.

Lambe smiled. He took his time answering.

"Two reasons," he said at last. "Firstly, because I was a cop, once upon a time, and I've seen some shit. Secondly, because Jordan never bothered to put on an act for me. I had nothing he wanted. I saw him play everyone around him, and he knew I saw him do it, and he didn't give a shit. Because what could I do? I couldn't touch the kid, and he knew it."

Matthew and Sarah Jane left Lambe in his small office and made their way back toward the administration building.

"Do you believe him?" Sarah Jane asked.

"I think he believes what he's saying. Whether it's the truth or not, who the hell knows? It might be true. If Simon Jordan killed his girlfriend, he's sure as hell capable of running a number on another kid to take his place on a team. I'm just not inclined to . . . Lambe's been sitting on his ass here for how many years? He knows the security in this place is a joke. He knew Jordan got a kid kicked out of school, probably charged too, for theft. And what does he do? He does nothing. He sits on his ass and feels superior to everyone." Matthew picked up his pace, then stopped abruptly. "See if you can talk to some of Grace's friends. Find out if they know anything. I'm heading back to headquarters. I'll get a location ping for Grace's phone. Let's start from there."

It was all too goddamn sickeningly familiar. He wondered how Leanne and Andy were doing. Not well. Well wasn't an option in circumstances like these.

CHAPTER TWENTY-FIVE

Grace

didn't stay in school. I left Dad in the car and I pushed through the doors and then just kept walking, along the corridor and then downstairs to the gym. The gym was deserted because classes wouldn't start for another fifteen minutes. I went to the girls' bathroom and into the last cubicle on the right. I put the seat down on the toilet, stood on it, and opened the small window high on the wall. All the other windows in the bathroom stalls have a security bar, which means they can't be opened very far, but years ago some kid with a screwdriver rigged this one so that the security bar can be taken off and put back on. I unclipped the bar and pushed the window wide open. I slid my bag out first and waited until I heard it drop onto the ground below. Then I climbed out the window and lowered myself down. The gym backs onto the edge of the school property. There's a fence—with a convenient hole already cut in it—and beyond that, trees. I grabbed my bag, pushed through the hole, and then I was in the trees, where no one would be able to see me.

I felt bad that I had left the window open behind me, and that I hadn't replaced the security bar. Usually, when kids use the gym route to ditch school, they have a buddy come in behind them to cover their tracks. I guess I could have texted a friend and asked them to close up after me, but I didn't want to. I didn't want anyone to know where I was, and I didn't want to have to explain. Everyone wanted to talk to me right now, and I didn't want to talk to anyone, because no one understood. They were all so weirdly fucking *excited*, even my friends. Like Nina going missing was just another scandal. Some really juicy gossip to distract us from the boredom of precalc.

The kids who weren't my friends were so much worse.

I walked into the woods. There isn't a whole lot to do in Waitsfield. Basically, we've got one main street with the stores and the creamery, and if you go there you'll be spotted by about twenty different parents in under five minutes. Not an option. There's no mall you can disappear into. Most kids who ditch end up spending the whole day sitting in a clearing in the woods, which is pretty boring, which is probably why cutting class isn't such a big problem at our school. I wasn't going to spend the whole day just hanging out in the woods. I had a plan. My friend Molly's house was only a mile and a half from school. Her parents both work in Burlington, so they wouldn't be home. We keep my horse, Charlie, at Molly's house, because they have stables and we don't. I was going to hike across to Molly's and pick up Charlie and take him out for the whole day.

It was a nice day, actually. It wasn't raining, and I guess it was cold, but I was wearing my jacket and I was walking, so I had no problem staying warm. I took out my phone and checked my messages, but there was nothing new. Everyone I knew would be in class by now. Or nearly everyone. I'd been messaging with Simon since the night before. I wasn't going to reach out to him, but things just snowballed. I was in bed, on my phone, scrolling through Nina's feed and looking at her photos and hoping that I'd suddenly see something new pop up from her. After I'd gone through all her stuff I went on to Simon's profile and starting looking at his photos, which were mostly of Nina anyway. I guess I liked one of them, and then a few minutes later he liked one of the pictures on my feed, which was just a goofy one of me and Molly at a pool party last summer. I figured that "like" was his way of telling me that he wasn't mad at me, so then I DM'd him. I was so embarrassed about what my mom had done. I'm not mad at her. I think she's kind of going crazy right now and I get it, I really do get it, because since Nina went missing the whole world feels wrong. I don't understand why she's blaming Simon except that maybe she needs someone to blame. Whatever's going on with her, she shouldn't have hit him. She can't seriously think he had anything to do with Nina disappearing. Simon is *crazy* about my sister. Everyone knows that.

Anyway, I messaged him and said that I was sorry and he messaged me back with a picture of his face and saying that he thought his modeling career was on hold. He already has a bruise—a bad one—around his left eye. He was smiling in the picture, but I felt so bad. I messaged him again. I can't even remember what I said exactly. But then he messaged me and said that he was kidding by sending the picture and that he was way too fugly to ever be a model and was I okay and that Nina wouldn't want me to worry. Honestly, that made me cry a bit. It's like, I miss Nina so much and I'm so scared for her, and him saying that she wouldn't want me to worry made me feel like she was close by. Anyway, we messaged for like an hour last night, and I honestly think Simon is the only one who understands how I feel right now.

I've been trying to stay off the internet. Mom only let me have my phone because I absolutely promised her that I wouldn't look at any of the stuff about Nina online. I promised, but I didn't mean it. It's honestly completely unrealistic to expect me not to see that stuff. People send it to me anyway, links to videos and photos and posts. If I stuck to my promise and stayed off the internet, that wouldn't protect me from anything. I'd just be putting myself in a position where I'd only see what other people think I should. You know what I mean? And don't think for a second people only send me "nice" stuff either, if there even is nice stuff in a situation like this. You wouldn't believe the fucked-up shit people have sent me. Things about my dad that made me want to puke. I can't talk to Mom and Dad about that stuff, but I think they know about it. I don't understand how they can expect me to sit in class while all this stuff is going on, while the kid who sent me some of those videos is sitting two seats away from me. It's like they think it won't hurt me if we just don't talk about it.

I put in my earbuds while I walked and listened to a podcast about chaos theory, which might sound like it would be boring but is actually really interesting. I listen to podcasts a lot. I used to listen to some true crime—like *Serial* and all that—but I can't anymore. And I can't listen to music because all my favorite stuff makes me cry.

I got to Molly's house and climbed over their back fence. Molly's dog Simba was there, but he knows me and anyway he's kind of old and more of an official greeter than an actual guard dog. I gave him some love and then I went to find Charlie. He was in the stable and not in the paddock, because I'm riding him a lot right now. He was pretty happy to see me. I found a brush and gave him a rubdown, and I changed my clothes before I saddled him. I can ride in jeans, but on cold days you can end up with raw patches if you ride for a long time. Jodhpurs are more comfortable. Molly's mare Whisper wasn't very happy that we were going out without her. I gave her a rub and told her sorry, and then I led Charlie around the paddock, down to the back gate. I closed the gate behind us before I mounted up, and I took him through a fast walk into a slow trot to give him a chance to warm up before we pushed on into a canter.

I love to ride. I really do. When I'm out on the trail with Charlie I feel like myself. I feel . . . I don't want this to sound cheesy, like a stupid inspiration quote on Instagram . . . but I feel strong, and kind of free. Usually riding makes everything I'm worried about in my real life seem much smaller and like it doesn't matter. Or at least, doesn't matter so much. I wanted that feeling so bad, but it didn't come. Nina being missing is just too huge. Not even Charlie can make that problem go away.

We slowed to a walk and I took out my phone again. I had a new message from Simon, asking me how I was doing. I told him the truth. That I'd ditched school and I was with Charlie and it wasn't making me feel much better. He asked if Charlie was my boyfriend and I sent him a laughing emoji and explained. So then he asked for a picture and I sent it. He went quiet for a while after that, which made me feel more lonely and kind of depressed. I took Charlie down a trail that had some medium jumps. We did those, and then I guess I just rode aimlessly for a while before I started to circle back. It was getting pretty close to lunchtime when my phone buzzed again. Another message from Simon, saying sorry for disappearing, and did I want to meet up. That made me smile. It really did. He said he could drive closer to where I was, and I told him which trail to take, and we agreed to meet for lunch in a clearing between two trails, where I knew there was a clean stream where I could water Charlie.

I got there first. I loosened Charlie's girth so he'd be more comfortable. I watered him, and then I slung his reins low and loose around a tree branch so that he could still nuzzle at the ground if he wanted. Not that there was much grass available, but he likes to explore. After that I sat on a fallen tree and unpacked my lunch, which was just stuff I was able to grab quickly from the kitchen without Mom and Dad noticing. A bread roll and a little pack of cheese and crackers, an apple and a bag of chips. It felt kind of juvenile suddenly, and I didn't want Simon to see it. But I was also really hungry, so instead of packing it away again I started eating really fast. I'd finished the bread roll and the apple by the time he got there.

"Hi," he said, and smiled at me.

I smiled back, and regretted it right away because I was pretty sure that I had bread in my teeth.

"Sorry," I said, and I closed my mouth.

He looked quizzically at me and went over to see Charlie. Simon was wearing black jeans and boots and a black jacket with this bright orange skinny stripe down one arm. It was very cool. He's actually a really good-looking guy, which isn't surprising, because if you ever met my sister you would know that she's completely beautiful.

"So this is your guy?" Simon said. He laid a hand on Charlie's neck, and Charlie kind of skittered sideways. He doesn't always like strangers.

"Uh-huh."

"He's beautiful."

"Do you ride?" I almost offered him a ride on Charlie, even though Charlie doesn't really like anyone riding him but me, but Simon shook his head.

"Not my thing," he said. He came over to sit beside me on the fallen tree. "How are you doing?"

He was so kind. I shrugged, but then I was scared I was going to cry because I could feel the tears wanting to come. I offered him the cheese and crackers to distract myself.

"Want some?"

He took the packet and opened it, and made a cracker-and-cheese mini-sandwich and ate it in two bites. He brushed the crumbs off his hands. "Pretty good," he said. He scratched at one of his teeth with his thumbnail, to dislodge a bit of cracker, I guess. If I did that I'd look like a troll, but he actually made it look cool. He gave me a serious look. "Really, Grace. I mean it. How are you doing?"

I looked down at the dirt and pushed at it with the toe of my boot. "I'm fine, I guess."

"I don't think that's true."

"I'm sorry about my mom," I said. It was probably the tenth time I'd said sorry, but it was easier than talking about my feelings. I expected Simon to just say that it wasn't my fault again, but instead he sighed.

"My parents are pressing charges."

My stomach turned over. "But . . . but they can't do that."

Simon shrugged. "Parents be crazy. I told them to let it go, but my mom's pretty mad. And she thinks . . . sorry, Grace . . . but she thinks your mom's kind of losing it and might be dangerous."

"That's not true. That's not true at all." Except I was scared that maybe it was true. She'd hit Simon. And she kept spacing out. Not like normal spacing out, where you get distracted for a few minutes. It was like she was disappearing into another world.

"Well . . ."

"Mom's not crazy. She's just scared and upset. She shouldn't have done what she did, but you get it, right?" I really, really wanted him to agree with me.

"I hear you. But you know, she broke into the house, and then she hit me . . ." He let his voice trail off.

"She broke into your house?" That was the first I'd heard of that. My skin went hot and cold. Simon looked at me sadly, which made me feel like a little kid. I hate that feeling. Maybe he saw that, because he leaned over and gave me a quick hug.

"I could talk to my mom, if you want. Ask her again to just let things go."

"That would be really good. Please. If you can."

He nodded and looked away across the clearing. "I guess no one else in the world knows exactly how we feel. No one else loved Nina the same way."

The way he said it made me feel weird. Loved Nina. Like she was gone. Like she wasn't coming back. But I got what he meant otherwise. No one else did get it, not in the same way. Mom and Dad loved Nina just as much as I did, but they were the adults and kind of in control of the situation, as much as anyone was. They were doing everything they could to find her and make things better, but they were keeping so much from me, only telling me things when they had no other choice. They were a team, and I was alone. And, I guess, so was Simon.

"Yeah," I said.

"We need to be there for each other, Grace. Until we get to the other side of this thing."

"Yeah," I said again, and I smiled. A small, weird smile, but him saying that made me feel so good. I'd have someone to talk to. My own teammate. And he'd talk to his mom and make her leave my mom alone, and maybe Simon and I could figure out where Nina had gone. No one knew her as well as we did, not really. I was about to say that when he took my hand. He held it in his, and he turned to look at me.

"You look kind of like her, you know. Not the same, because your hair is blond, and you're taller and a little bigger. But you're just like her around your eyes. And your mouth."

He looked at my lips. And his thumb caressed the back of my hand. And it did not feel good. Not at all.

I snatched my hand away and pushed both of my hands between my thighs. My shoulders hunched over. He put his hand on the back of my neck and held me there, gently.

"It's okay, Grace."

I shook my head. I didn't know what to do.

"You don't need to feel guilty, you know. It's natural to feel this way. You miss Nina and so do I. It's natural that we'd be drawn together."

His hand was still on the back of my neck. He rubbed the back of my head and my neck, like a massage, but slower. Everything he was saying was exactly what I had thought, but twisted.

"Nina would want you to feel good."

I stood up. My bag of chips fell on the ground. He picked it up. He smiled at me, like I'd done something cute.

"I have to go," I said. I picked up my backpack from the ground and slung it on my back.

"Stay and finish your lunch."

I shook my head. "I have to get Charlie back."

"You asked me to come here and meet you, you know. I drove all the way over here. It's kind of shitty to just disappear."

Was that right? Had I asked him to meet me? Hadn't he suggested that he come?

"I'm sorry," I said. "I'm just . . . not feeling well."

His brow furrowed. "Did I do something wrong? I thought we were friends." He blinked and rubbed at his eyes. I could see tears, real tears. "You know, Grace, it's been a really shitty week. First Nina dumped me, and then she disappeared, and half the country, or at least half the people online, seem to think I had something to do with it. Do you know how that feels? Your sister is missing, but at least no one thinks you had anything to do with it."

"I'm sorry," I said again. I felt so bad for him. I must have misread things. I took a step toward him, and he stood up, and then he hugged me. I hugged him back. I thought maybe he was going to cry. He didn't cry, but he held on to me like he needed me just to stand up.

"I miss her so much."

"I know," I said. "Me too." And then I was the one who was crying. He rubbed my back and then the back of my head.

"It's okay, Gracey."

Only my mom and dad and Nina call me Gracey. It made me cry harder.

"Shh," he said. "Shh. It'll be all right. We'll make it all right." He slid his right hand to the side of my face until he was cupping my face. He kissed my neck. He kissed my cheek. He tilted my face and kissed the side of my lips. He tried to kiss me open mouthed. I pushed him away, hard, and fell backward, landing on my backside. He put a hand out to help me up.

"Grace. . . ." He looked at me with his head to the side, a sad expression on his face, like I'd just gotten things wrong and really disappointed him. I held up a hand in a back-off gesture.

"No," I said. "No." I scrambled backward, stood up, and kept backing up until I bumped into Charlie. Simon frowned. He came after me, until he was too close. I ducked under Charlie's neck, and Simon looked mad as hell.

"What is your problem? You can't lead me on and then just walk away."

I was scared. Scared enough that my hands were shaking. But fuck him. I hadn't led him on. I hadn't done anything. I lifted Charlie's reins over his head, and I put my hand on his withers and pushed so that he would swivel fast. Simon had to step back to get out of the way, and I had my foot in the stirrup and I was mounted before he could do anything. I only remembered that Charlie's girth was still loose when it was too late and I was halfway up and the saddle shifted on his back. It held, though, and then I was on.

"Jesus, Grace. You're acting crazy. Maybe it runs in the family."

He stepped back and stood in the center of the clearing, his arms spread wide, blocking my way to the trail. We looked at each other. I could tell he wasn't going to move. I said the only thing that came into my mind.

"You're not a nice guy. I thought you were, but you aren't."

He shook his head, half laughing. "Your mom attacks me. You ask me to meet you here, you lead me on, then you act like I'm some kind of pervert and I'm the bad guy."

"Can you just get out of my way please?"

He looked at me and put his head to his side like he was considering it, and then he shook his head slowly, like he regretted the situation but he had no choice.

"You need to say sorry first. Say, 'I'm sorry, Simon, for my crazy mother. And I'm sorry for being a bitch.' And then I'll move and you can go, and maybe someday, when you grow up a little more, we can be friends."

I started to get angry. The anger made the fear a lot smaller. I squeezed my legs and Charlie started to walk forward. I could feel him wanting to walk around Simon, but I signaled him with my legs and my hands to go straight forward. Simon didn't move. He thought he could win a game of chicken with a fifteen-hundred-pound horse. I decided to show him he couldn't. I squeezed my legs firmly and gave Charlie a small kick. He leaped forward. Simon stumbled backward, swearing. I urged Charlie on and he went into a flat run. We left that asshole in our dust.

CHAPTER TWENTY-SIX

Andy

Grace came home. Just like that, she came home. I was still sitting on the couch with Lee when I heard the sound of hooves on the gravel. Rufus lifted his head and whined. I wasn't imagining it.

"Lee? Do you hear that?" She didn't answer me. I moved her to the side so that she was sitting on the couch instead of on me. She curled up into a ball and buried her head in the cushion. I went outside. And there she was, our beautiful girl, with Charlie. Grace had already gotten off the horse. She was standing with her arms around her horse, her forehead resting against his neck.

"Grace?"

She turned to me. Saw the look on my face. Her face crumpled. "I'm sorry, Dad. I'm really sorry."

I went to her and picked her up and hugged her too hard. She was still holding Charlie's reins. He blew out air and shifted his feet uncertainly. I reached out and patted him.

"Good boy," I said. "Good boy."

Grace was half crying, half laughing. "He really is."

"Where were you?" She shook her head, like she wasn't ready to talk about it. "I'm sorry I made you go to school, baby. I went right back to get you."

We tied Charlie up at the back door. I held Grace's hand as we went inside. I didn't know how to warn her about the state her mother was in. When we got to the living room, Grace froze at the door. Lee was still curled up in a ball on the couch, her face like stone.

"Mom?" She sounded scared, and years younger than fifteen. Lee didn't react. Didn't move an inch. Grace went to her mother and sank to her knees by the couch. She caught Lee's arms and pulled them until they were around her in a limp kind of a hug. "I'm here, Mom. I'm here, okay?"

Something sparked. Lee's hands curled into fists, gripping the back of Grace's jacket. She held on tight, then her head came up and she pulled Grace hard against her. She said Grace's name, once, then again and again until it sounded like a mantra.

"I'm okay. I'm here. I'm okay."

Lee's hands went to Grace's face and tilted her face back and looked at her like she needed to really see her. I had tears in my eyes. I walked away. I called Matthew Wright and told him that Grace was okay. Then I went outside and put Charlie away in the barn. For months Grace has been asking me to make a stall for him, and I still haven't done it. I couldn't just let him loose in the barn. It wouldn't be safe for him with the landscaping supplies around, so I had to tie him up, but I let him have a loose rein, and I gave him water. I didn't have any hay. It would have to work until he could be picked up. I called Molly's mother and told her that Charlie was with us. She's a kind woman. She didn't ask a lot of questions, but she did volunteer to drive over that evening with her trailer and take him back. I untacked Charlie and brushed him down. At first I thought I was imagining it when I heard a car engine start. Then I thought maybe one of the journalists had driven up to the house, or maybe Craig had come by. But when I got out of the barn, I saw Lee's car pulling away down the drive. I went inside. Grace was sitting alone on the couch looking very pale.

"Grace?"

"I told Mom that it was Simon. He asked me to meet him in the woods, and I did, and then I got scared. I thought he was a good guy, and he's really not."

My hand was on the doorjamb. I gripped it, hard.

"Did he hurt you?"

She shook her head. She swallowed and looked ashamed. "He tried to kiss me. Charlie got me away."

"Where's your mother?"

"I don't know. I told her about Simon, and then she got her keys and she left."

Jesus. I turned and ran for the kitchen. Grace's voice followed me.

"Dad?"

"Stay here. Stay in the house," I called back to her, and then I was running. I got in my truck. I blasted my horn as I went down the drive and the journalists and photographers got out of my way, fast. There was only one place she could have gone to. How much time did she have on me? Five minutes? Ten?

There were journalists at the Jordans' house too. Not many. Two men, standing together beside a car, cups of coffee in hand. One of them was smoking. There was another car, parked off to the side, where a woman sat in the driver's seat, on her phone. Maybe that's how Lee convinced them to open the gate. Maybe she threatened to cause a scene if they didn't let her in. Or maybe the gate was just open when she got there. However she'd done it, Lee's little Hyundai was pulled up almost at the door to the house. I pulled my truck right in behind her and got out in a hurry. Lee was at the front door, talking to Rory.

"You tell him to stay away from our daughter," Lee was saying. "Do you understand me? He needs to stay away." She kept running her left hand through her hair, again and again.

Rory's eyes met mine. He looked like shit. He hadn't shaved and his eyes had deep black shadows.

"Andrew," he said.

I joined Lee at the door. I took her hand. She didn't look at me.

"Tell him to come up here," she said to Rory. "I need to talk to him."

Rory put his hand out and gripped the doorframe, blocking the way. "I can't allow that. You seem upset. I don't think now's the right time."

"I'm not upset," Lee said. She widened her eyes in an unconvincing attempt to seem sincere. "Not at all." She wasn't well. I needed to get her to a doctor. We needed to get her help.

"Baby," I said. "Come on, baby. Let's go home. We need to go home to Grace." I tried to lead her away from the door, but she didn't move. Rory's jaw clenched and his grip on the doorframe tightened. Jamie emerged from the corridor behind him. She was barefoot, and she walked like she was putting on a performance. Her toenails were painted scarlet. Leanne's shoulders lifted as she took a deep breath.

"Jamie. Please. Please. I need to speak to Simon. He might know something that would help us find Nina, even if he doesn't know it. If I could just speak to him for five minutes."

Jamie came forward. She ducked under Rory's arm, then leaned back so that the arm that had been holding the doorframe was now draped over her shoulders. She wrapped her right arm around his waist. The two of them stood there blocking the doorway like the defending team in Red Rover.

"You shouldn't have come here," Jamie said, flatly. "You need to leave, now, or I'm going to call the police."

I put my hand on Leanne's shoulder. I wanted to lead her away. There was no way they would let us speak to Simon. We weren't going to get anywhere with them. But Lee stepped forward and took hold of Jamie's hand. Jamie looked horrified.

"I'm begging you," Lee said. "Mother to mother. I know you understand that I . . . that we can't survive unless we know what happened to Nina. Your son knows the truth. We . . . we won't survive. Please, Jamie. Please. Please. Please."

Lee swayed, and for a horrible moment I thought she was going to go down on her knees. A look spasmed over Rory Jordan's face.

Disgust and pity, mingled. Jamie shook off Lee's hand. She stepped back into the house. Lee tried to follow her.

"Mother to mother. I'm asking you."

Jamie's face hardened into hostility. "You need to leave us alone. This is harassment. I'm calling the police. Add to the charges against you."

Lee rocked back on her feet. I put my arm around her and pulled her away.

"Come on, baby."

But she couldn't walk. Her body folded in on itself, and she started to cry.

"Take her home," Rory said. There was pity in his voice, and I hated him for it. Lee was leaning on me, weeping. I held her against me and looked at them and hated them.

"Simon hit Nina. Did you know about that? He left bruises on her body. That's the kind of boy you raised. I hope you're proud of yourself. Two hours ago he asked Grace to meet him in the woods. He tried to kiss her. She had to push him off. She's fifteen years old."

Rory didn't react, not really, but Jamie flinched. It didn't matter to me. I didn't give a shit what they thought or felt or anything else.

"If he killed Nina, he'll pay the price," I said.

I didn't know if that was true or not. I wanted to believe it, but we didn't live in a world where bad people paid for what they did. I had to get Lee home. I tried to lead her away, but she was a dead weight. In the end I just picked her up and carried her to my truck. The journalists and photographers had crossed into the property. Camera flashes went off as I put Lee into the passenger seat. A female journalist asked if Lee was okay. I didn't answer. I fastened Lee's seat belt. She buried her head in her hands. We drove home. I parked the truck in the barn, and we sat there for a long time. Lee stopped crying. She leaned back in her seat and looked at me, right in the eye, for the first time since Grace had gone missing.

"I can't live with never knowing," she said. "It's going to kill me."

CHAPTER TWENTY-SEVEN

Matthew

Matthew was back at headquarters when Andy Fraser called to let him know that Grace was safe. Matthew wanted details, but Andy ended the call quickly. He needed to be with his family. Presumably Grace had done exactly as Jeremiah Lambe had predicted and ditched school for a few hours to get away from the pressure. Matthew felt almost weighed down by relief that Grace Fraser was home and safe with her family, where she belonged. Sarah Jane was still at the school. He called her and asked her to come back in. After that he called his prosecutor friend to talk through a possible warrant application for the Jordans' home in Waitsfield.

"You don't have enough," his friend said, bluntly. "Rory Jordan is connected. He has the best law firm in the state on retainer. The K-9 alert is a start, but you need something more."

Matthew went to buy a sandwich. He needed time to cool his head and think things through after the chaos of the day so far. Also, he hadn't eaten since breakfast. He bumped into Kim Allen at the café and they walked back together.

"How's Naomi?" she asked.

"Well, thank you," he said.

"You've got John Reid's girl running around for you on your case. How's she doing?"

"Good work, so far. She's keen and she's smart. No complaints."

Kim nodded. They walked on. It was getting late and the temperature was dropping. The sun went down early at that time of year.

"You've worked with her?" Matthew asked.

"Some," Kim said. She gave him a sideways glance. "Pretty girl, but she's all about the work. Josh Heard, Dave Beecham, and Anna Arlidge all asked her out and got turned down."

"Beecham asked her out?" Matthew shook his head. That sad son of a bitch. Sarah Jane couldn't be much more than twenty-three or twenty-four and Beecham was in his forties. Also, married with three kids.

"Shouldn't be a surprise. Man's a dog."

Inside, Sarah Jane was waiting for him. Her head lifted as soon as he came into the room. She gave him just enough time to get settled, then came over to his desk.

"Uh, the security tapes from the bar in Boston have just arrived."

They watched the recordings in an interview room. The caller who'd reported seeing Nina in the bar had been very clear about the timing. He'd said he'd spotted her at 10:15 P.M. exactly, and he knew that because he'd seen her just before he'd left the bar, and after that he'd called a cab and he had a record of that call on his phone. Matthew and Sarah Jane fast-forwarded to 10:00 P.M. and watched every minute up to 10:30. Matthew paused the recording and sat back.

"I don't see her."

There wasn't any doubt. It wasn't like the bar was packed. There was one possibility. A girl sitting in the corner with friends. She'd come to the bar to order drinks just before 10:00 P.M., and she matched Nina's general description—tall, with long dark hair—but only in the most general terms. The camera caught her very clearly when she came to the bar. She had smaller eyes and a longer nose, not to mention a large shoulder tattoo that peeked out from her tank top. Nina had no tattoos.

"Do you think he got the time wrong?" Sarah Jane asked.

"It's possible."

They rewound the recording and watched it at triple speed from 9:00 P.M. right up until closing.

"She's not there," Sarah Jane said.

"Nope."

"But what about the other caller? The woman who said she saw Nina buying drugs around the corner from this place?"

"We still need to check that out."

"It seems like a weird coincidence."

"Might not be a coincidence."

Sarah Jane turned to look at him, a question in her eyes.

"The guy who called us about seeing Nina at the bar, did he also post about it online? I worked a case once where we got four sightings of a missing girl, all from different callers, all for the same city block in Burlington. We were sure we were onto something. Turned out the first caller had made a genuine mistake. He really thought he saw our girl. But after he called us to tell us, he went online to tell the world. Which brought some crazies out of the woodwork. The other three calls were all copycats. Attention seekers."

"Shit," said Sarah Jane.

"Exactly."

Matthew stood up. "Let's wait and see if Boston PD come back with anything."

She nodded, but he could see her disappointment.

"This is still good work, Sarah Jane. This is what we do. We run things down and rule them out, and that's how we get to answers."

Matthew went back to his desk, sat, and thought. He held his pen between the first two fingers of his right hand and tapped it lightly against his desk. So far he hadn't been able to find out who was responsible for cleaning the Jordans' house. When he'd followed up with Rory Jordan's attorney about the cleaning, he'd received a message back that the Jordans knew nothing about it. They claimed that it must have been something done by the previous owners or their property managers, perhaps in preparation for the property's listing.

As the previous owner of the property was some movie producer who had never visited Vermont, that was proving difficult to confirm. The producer's property manager had hired a cleaning agency that hired casual workers, and they didn't have a record of who had worked the Stowe property. It looked like the cleaning angle was a dead end. They would not be able to prove who had cleaned the property and when.

Matthew ran a search online for the property and found the original sales listing. He clicked slowly through the photographs. Did it look cleaner than the house he'd been in on Wednesday? Dirtier? There was a photograph of the kitchen, and another of the laundry room, but there were no cleaning products conveniently left out. Every surface had been cleared. In the photographs the countertops gleamed sleekly. How much of that was clever lighting, and how much was postproduction? In person the house was undoubtedly beautiful, but real estate photographs always seemed to conjure another world, where every room was vast and borderless, with endless natural light and perfect accents of subtle color. Matthew frowned and clicked back a couple of photographs. Something had caught his eye, but he wasn't sure what. He found himself staring at a photograph of the living room. Something in the room was different. He narrowed his eyes and leaned forward. What was it?

Damn. It was so obvious, he nearly hadn't seen it. There was a cream-colored rug in front of the fireplace. That hadn't been there when he'd visited the house.

"Sarah Jane?"

"Yes, sir?"

"Call the property managers. Ask them if they took anything out of the house after the sale. There's a rug in the living room in one of the photographs. In front of the fireplace. Ask them if they took that."

"Will do."

She picked up the phone. She was on the other side of the room and she spoke quietly. From that distance, Matthew couldn't make out what she was saying, but she ended the call quickly.

"The property managers say they didn't take anything," she said. "The sale contract was for everything, the house and all furnishings, including lighting and soft furnishings. They didn't move the rug."

"Okay."

He made a few more calls. Found out that Simon Jordan had changed lawyers, or rather his father had. Rory had moved on from Alistair Reynolds, who was, after all, a commercial lawyer. He'd retained Arnie Waugh to represent his son. Waugh was a criminal defense lawyer, a specialist. Matthew called him. Waugh took the call straight away.

"Detective."

"Mr. Waugh. I understand you represent Simon Jordan."

"That's right. Nice kid."

Matthew paused. "Okay. I'm calling to ask if Simon would be willing to hand over his phone for examination. Voluntarily."

"Interesting idea. Unfortunately, we're not going to be able to do that." Waugh's tone was relaxed and urbane.

"That *is* unfortunate."

"Obviously I'll put the request to my client, see what he says, but I'll be advising him against it, and I would expect him to take that advice. Phones these days carry too much data. Absolutely no offense meant, Detective, but I'm not going to facilitate a fishing expedition."

"No fishing expedition. In fact, if it would make you feel better, why don't we choose a private lab? A neutral lab. Simon can hand his phone over to them and we'll ask them to answer a few very specific questions. Questions we'll agree with you on in advance."

"Like what?"

"Location and search history for last Friday and Saturday." He paused for a moment, then added, "Tuesday too."

There was silence on the other side of the call. Matthew could picture Arnie, sitting in his expensive suit in his expensive office, frowning.

"I'll get back to you," Arnie said, and ended the call.

"You do that," Matthew said, into the silence.

He went home and took a shower. Naomi was working a late shift, so the house was quiet. Matthew turned on the oven and took a microwave pizza out of the freezer. He opened a beer. The house was cold, and there didn't seem to be much point in lighting a fire just for himself. He took his pizza and his beer into the living room and turned on the TV. He needed distraction. To think about anything other than Nina Fraser and Simon Jordan for a couple of hours.

He was in the kitchen, dumping the last of the pizza in the trash, when Andy Fraser called him. It was after 10:00 P.M. Andy sounded like he'd been drinking.

"Tell me you're going to get him," he said.

Matthew didn't pretend not to know who he was talking about. Nina's father deserved more than that. He also couldn't lie to the other man.

"I'm going to do everything I can. I promise you that."

There was silence on the other end of the line. Then—

"He came on to Grace. He got her to meet him, alone, in the woods, and he came on to her. He tried to kiss her. Grace is fifteen years old. You understand what I'm telling you? Simon's not some innocent kid. He's a goddamn predator."

Christ. For a second, Matthew closed his eyes.

"Would Grace be willing to talk to me? To make a statement?"

"If she did, would it make a difference?"

Matthew paused. He really didn't want to say what he had to say next. "Did anyone else see what happened?"

Andy said nothing.

"Because the risk is that—"

Andy cut him off. "I know what the goddamn risk is. They'll say she's making it up. That we put Grace up to it to make Simon look bad, because we blame him for Nina."

Matthew stared out of his kitchen window into the darkness. The bright lights of the kitchen meant that he couldn't make out a thing outside of the dubious protection of his four walls. Safety was an illusion. The world had too many Simon Jordans. He and Naomi were trying for a baby. Had been for a long time, and now she wanted to talk adoption. Maybe they should forget about it entirely. You put everything into your kid. Your love for each other, your hopes and dreams for the future. And then some predator comes along and destroys not only your precious child, but everything that made you you.

"I have to ask you to trust me. I promise you, I'm good at my job, and I care about this. I care about Nina. I'm not going to give up."

"That's not good enough. Tell me you're going to get him. You need to promise me that you're going to put him in jail."

Matthew was not a fidgeter. Usually he worked hard to school his body into stillness, because he saw outer calm as a necessary precursor to a disciplined mind. But this case was getting to him. He rubbed at his jaw, feeling the rasp of two days' stubble.

"I can't do that," he said. He thought again about what he'd said to Sarah Jane. That without a body it would be an uphill battle. "All I can tell you is that I'm going to do my best."

There was another long silence, then Andy said again, quietly, "Not good enough," and hung up the phone.

Matthew went to bed. He had a bad night's sleep, broken with nightmares of missing girls calling for help. He went to work on Friday morning groggy and bad tempered. The breakthrough, when it came, was unexpected. He was at his desk when a call came in from the front desk.

"Woman here to see you by the name of Rita Gallo. Says she wants to talk to you about the Fraser case."

He very nearly handed the interview off to Sarah Jane. Afterward, he wasn't sure what had prompted him to stand up and go downstairs to talk to the woman himself. Maybe it was just that he was frustrated and needed a change of scene. The woman waiting for him downstairs was older. In her sixties, maybe. She wore jeans and sneakers and an old Patagonia jacket.

"Ms. Gallo. How can I help you?"

She took his hand and shook it. "I don't know. I think maybe I can help you."

He led her into an interview room. He offered her coffee.

"Thank you, no. I try not to drink caffeine. It keeps me up at night."

They sat at opposite sides of the table. She looked around, briefly. It wasn't a very friendly room. It wasn't intended to be. He could see that she was intimidated by her surroundings, but she did a better job than most of hiding it.

"I used to work for Jamie Jordan," she said abruptly. "Well, the whole Jordan family. I was their cleaner, until a few days ago."

"I see," Matthew said. "At the Stowe house?" Was she a Rory Jordan emissary? Had he sent her in to see him, to provide a neat explanation for the floor-cleaning question?

"Oh, no. I've never been to that house. No, I worked for the Jordans at their home in Waitsfield. For nearly twelve years, until this week, in fact."

"What happened this week?"

Her lips tightened. "Nothing at all, according to one way of looking at it. I told my daughter, and she told me I was making mountains out of molehills."

"But that's not how you see it."

She shook her head.

"Why don't you tell me in your own words what happened?"

Rita settled herself in her chair and crossed her arms. The rhythm of her speech changed. In her mind, it seemed, they'd reached the formal part of the interview. The part that mattered.

"I went to the Jordans' house at ten A.M. last Saturday morning. I went in through the downstairs doors, straight to the laundry, like I always do. There were clothes in the washing machine." She leaned forward and held Matthew's gaze. She wanted him to understand that this was important. "I never leave wet clothes in a machine over-night, and definitely not for two nights. Wet clothes left in the ma-chine smell, even if you air them out. It's a very bad idea. When I left the house on Thursday, the machine was empty. You understand?"

Matthew nodded. "I do."

"The clothes that I found in the machine belonged to Simon. A pair of jeans, a blue T-shirt, and a cream wool sweater. Also, some socks." She paused again to make sure that he was paying attention. "Everything had been boiled, virtually. He'd put it through a hot wash, and the sweater was shrunk to nothing."

"Does Simon typically do his own laundry?"

"No!" she said, triumphantly. "That's what I tried to tell my daughter. I worked in that house for twelve years, and not once did anyone but me put so much as a pair of pants in that machine. I said to her, don't you think it's a little too much of a coincidence that the first time in twelve years that boy takes it into his head to wash his own clothes is the morning after his girlfriend disappears? When he was the last one to *see her alive*?"

She drew in a long breath and let it out. Satisfied that she had made her point. Pleased that he was taking her seriously.

"I never liked that boy, you know. Or the husband neither. Jamie, I liked. She has some fight to her. She'd need it too, with that husband. He looks right through you, you know? Like you're not even a person."

"Why didn't you like Simon?"

She thought about it. "Not because I always thought he was a killer. I'd be lying if I said that. But I did think he was dangerous. You know, he looked at his father, at all the stuff his father had, and he thought, that's mine. I don't like Rory Jordan, but I won't deny the man worked for what he has. Simon thought he should have every-thing his father had without lifting a finger. And he had a temper." Rita blew out a breath. "Hoo boy, yes."

"Ms. Gallo—"

"Rita, please."

"Rita, then. Did you notice anything else different in the laundry room that morning?"

She looked at him blankly for a moment. "Nothing. I mean, there were no drops of blood or anything, if that's what you're asking."

"That's okay. Thank you."

"Everything was just the same as usual." She nodded. And then said, as an afterthought, "There was a bottle of detergent that I didn't buy. Not my usual brand. But I don't suppose you'd be interested in that."

CHAPTER TWENTY-EIGHT

Jamie

On Friday Rory went to work. I envied him the option. I've always regretted not having a job of my own, but when we married the only thing I was qualified to do was waitressing, and Rory would not have been okay with his wife serving people. And waitressing was a job I was more than happy to leave behind. If I'd been a different kind of person, maybe I could have tried again after Simon started school. But I'd never been bookish. Going to college wasn't an option for me. What I'd really like now is a little business of my own. I could be a stylist, or a personal shopper. Maybe, when all this is over and Simon moves on with his life, when Rory finally ends things between us, that's exactly what I'll do.

Rory sent over two assistants to pick up Leanne Fraser's car, which was still sitting in our driveway, and deliver it back to their home. I felt better when it was gone. Leanne was falling apart. Andrew had had to pick her up and *carry* her to their car. How much of that was due to what we'd done by setting the trolls on her family? I know she started it, and I know we really had no choice if we were going to protect Simon, but guilt nagged at me. I needed distraction. I thought about going online—I had offers from buyers for my clothes that I needed to respond to—but my heart wasn't in it. If I went online at all I would probably feel the pull to check social media, and I didn't want to see that stuff. Besides, I didn't want to work on my side hustle while Simon was under suspicion. Most of the time, going behind Rory's back and selling my stuff had seemed not only justified, but actually, in a fucked-up way, good for our marriage. The existence of my secret nest egg made me confident. I didn't get needy or clingy. I didn't try to convince Rory to transfer a house into my name, or to give me expensive jewelry, both of which are, in my book, fatal errors. And my side hustle kept my interest in clothes and grooming alive, which meant that I looked good, which he liked. All in all, I felt just fine about what I was doing. But since Nina disappeared, I had no heart for it anymore. It all seemed so petty and pointless, in the face of what was coming for us. Also, Rory was so completely committed, completely focused on keeping Simon safe. It would have been cheap of me to be anything less.

Putting the shop on hiatus meant that I had nothing to do. I worked out in the gym, but that only took an hour. I showered and cleaned rooms that didn't need cleaning, and the minutes ticked by like hours. Simon was buried in his bedroom. I didn't want to talk to him. Andy Fraser said that Simon had tried to kiss Grace. That scared me. I didn't want to think that it could be true, but I believed that Simon had gone to meet Grace when I'd begged him not to. Simon had never liked being told what to do, and it would be like him to do the exact opposite of what I'd asked.

But trying to kiss Grace? If that was true, it was something different from a demonstration of independence. Something bigger and darker. Maybe Grace had misread a hug or some other attempt to comfort her. Which wouldn't have happened if he'd stayed away from her like I'd asked.

Just before lunchtime, Rory called me.

"Can you take Simon to Burlington? His lawyer wants a meeting. Two o'clock."

"Is everything okay?" It was such a stupid question. Of course, nothing was okay. By asking the question, I was asking him to treat me like a child. To reassure me. To make me feel better. "Never mind," I said.

"I hired a criminal defense lawyer for him. Name is Arnie Waugh. He's supposed to be the best. Name of the firm is Dexter, Split and Waugh. They're on St. Paul Street."

"Okay, fine. Does Simon need to dress up, or—"

"Whatever he's wearing is fine."

"Okay."

For a moment his tone softened. "Thanks, Jamie."

"Of course."

"See you at two."

I went downstairs and told Simon. He was sitting on his bed, his legs under the comforter, headphones on and laptop in front of him. He looked up, irritated at the interruption.

"Your dad called. Your lawyer wants a meeting."

I made him get changed, into slacks, a button-down, and a sweater. I wore a black dress to the knee, with a jewel-green cardigan with dramatic bell sleeves so that I didn't look too funereal, and heels. The photographs of Andrew carrying Leanne to the car the day before had already hit the papers. The story was hot again, and as a result we had more photographers and journalists at our gate. When we drove out past them, Simon sat up tall in the seat. He looked confident and relaxed and not at all like someone who'd been accused of the most terrible crime. I was pissed at him for going behind my back to meet Grace, but I was proud of his attitude. It takes guts to stand up under that kind of pressure.

"They'll get bored soon and move on," I said, as reassuringly as I could. He gave me a sideways glance.

"Not if I'm charged."

"That's not going to happen."

"We can't know that for sure, Mom."

For a moment I couldn't speak. He was, of course, right. There was no way of knowing where things would go from here.

"I know that you didn't do anything wrong," I said, firmly. Did I sound like I believed it, or like I wanted to believe it? Andrew had said that Simon had hit Nina. He'd said it like it was a *fact*, like he had evidence, but it was all bullshit, wasn't it? Just his worry and grief talking. I felt a fluttering kind of nervousness. Simon shifted his weight on his seat and turned to look out the window. I wondered why Rory had asked me to drive Simon, when Simon could easily have driven himself. Maybe the lawyer wanted to talk to me too. Or maybe Rory was worried about Simon being out there alone, afraid, and unsupervised. I reached out and took Simon's hand in mine.

"Your dad is a very smart guy, with a lot of resources. He loves you more than anything in the world, and there's nothing he wouldn't do to keep you safe. That's not nothing, Simon. I think maybe that's everything."

Instead of pulling away, Simon let his hand sit in mine for a long moment before squeezing my hand briefly and disconnecting.

"Thanks, Mom," he said. He said it absently, like he was in no way engaged in our conversation. Like I was a child he was patting on the head, a child with no understanding of what was actually going on. I felt afraid. Like there was something coming. I tried to shake the feeling off.

The lawyers' offices were so fancy that I figured they must charge a fortune. The building itself was brand new, but the floors were herringbone parquet, with the dull gleam of a heritage floor. Reclaimed, probably. The lobby was very large, but there were only two sets of chairs, upholstered in fashionable greige bouclé and sitting far apart from each other. There was a single large abstract artwork on the wall. The artwork was a mass of clashing colors, all the more attention grabbing for being installed in such a muted room. There was a long, polished walnut reception desk, and the receptionist was young, attractive, and impeccably groomed. Her hair was dark and tied neatly at the nape of her neck, her eyebrows were perfect, and her nails were short and so dark they were almost black. She knew me on sight, though we'd never met.

"Mrs. Jordan, Mr. Jordan." She stood up to greet us. "Your husband is waiting for you upstairs. Please, let me escort you."

We followed her to the elevator, which took us quickly to the fourth floor. We emerged into a much busier space than the one we'd just left. As she led the way down the corridor, we passed open-plan spaces occupied by slick-looking young people in suits, and glass-walled offices. We found Rory sitting in a large corner office, with views across the city to the water. He stood up and gave me a quick hug and a kiss on the cheek. His eyes met mine, briefly, as I pulled away, and something passed between us. An understanding, I thought, about just how messed up this situation was. A commitment to get through it together. Or maybe I was just reading too much into things.

"Jamie, Simon, this is Arnold Waugh. Arnie has agreed to represent you, Simon."

Arnie Waugh offered his hand, and Simon and I took it in turn and shook gravely. Waugh had blond hair, a little long but styled back from his face. His features were chiseled, and he was lean. His fingernails were trimmed neatly. He looked like the kind of guy who started his day with a 6:00 A.M. row on the river. The kind of guy who spent his summer at his grandmother's home on the Cape. How had he ended up in Burlington?

"It's a pleasure to meet you both," Waugh said. "Please, take a seat, make yourselves comfortable."

We all sat, except for Waugh. He leaned against his desk and faced us. There was a moment of awkward silence.

"Arnie was just telling me that the police have been in touch," Rory said. "They asked if Simon would be willing to give up his phone voluntarily, so that they can review his location and search history."

All three of us turned to look at Simon. He shifted in his seat.

"Is that . . . but isn't that an invasion of privacy? I mean, I want to help, but that seems over the top. My whole life is on my phone."

There was an awkward pause, then Arnie clapped his hands together briskly. "That's exactly my own view, Simon. But let's put a pin in this conversation for a moment. Rory, Mrs. Jordan, if you don't mind, Simon and I will adjourn to another room for our consultation." He turned to me. "I've already explained to your husband, Mrs. Jordan, that my meetings with Simon have to be private, in order that he enjoys the full benefit of attorney-client privilege." He stood up and put out a hand to usher Simon from the room. "Someone will be in momentarily to get you coffee."

The door closed behind them with a gentle whish. Through the glass wall I watched Simon walk away down the corridor. His shoulders were hunched defensively.

"It'll be okay, Jamie. Arnie Waugh's the best. He comes highly recommended."

"Good." My voice sounded small. I cleared my throat. The door opened again, and a young man came in, took our coffee orders, and disappeared again.

"Should Simon give them his phone? It might be good to cooperate. Maybe they'll clear him faster?"

Rory's eyes slid away from mine. "They're asking for a lot. His messages and phone calls. His search history, and any location data."

"Right." Still Rory didn't look at me. "But he should probably give it to them, then, right? Because there'll be nothing on the phone that can get him in trouble, because he didn't do anything wrong. And maybe when they see that they'll rule him out. Move on to finding out what really happened."

"That would be great," Rory said, heavily. "But it doesn't always work like that. Sometimes, if a detective is convinced that they know what happened, they stop actually investigating and start looking for evidence that supports their theories. They could trawl through Simon's phone and pull out little things that make him look like a bad guy. What if he and Nina had a disagreement over text one day, for example? Even the happiest couple argues. Arguments are a sign of a healthy relationship. But out of context it's very easy to make things look like something they're not."

Rory and I never argued. Anyone looking at our phone messages would probably think we were colleagues who barely knew each other.

"Yes. But couldn't he just give them his location data, or something? That way they'd see that he was exactly where he said he was. Wouldn't that help?"

Rory shook his head. "It doesn't work like that."

I caught his gaze and held it. He was lying to me. They were both lying to me.

The door opened again, and we both jumped. Our coffees were delivered. We both managed polite, strained smiles and thank-yous, and waited in tense silence for the door to close again. Rory leaned forward in his chair.

"The problem is that if we give them only location data and hold back messages, they might use that to create a picture that Simon is hiding something. It's all about manipulation of perception. Better to give them a wall of nothing. The less they have to work with, the better."

"Rory, what's really going on?"

He looked away from me. "I don't know what you mean."

"What does Simon think they'll find if they get his phone?"

Rory's eyes met mine again. I thought I saw an answer there, and my stomach turned over. We both jumped as the door whooshed open again. Another assistant, this time with a plate of petits fours. We had to wait for him to leave before we could talk again, and then Rory shut the conversation down.

"This isn't the place to discuss it," he said.

So I had to sit there in silence, turning things over and over in my head and waiting for Simon and Waugh to return. When they came back, Simon looked hunted and Waugh looked energized. He clapped his hand on Simon's shoulder as they entered the room. Simon shrugged the hand off.

"Okay, well, that was a great start," Waugh said. "Great to spend some time talking to Simon. We've agreed that it would be best for him to stay close to home for the next week or two. It's a delicate time, and it's important that all communication goes through my office. Yes?" He looked brightly from me to Rory. I mumbled my agreement, not really knowing what he meant.

"Rory, do you have a few minutes?" Waugh asked.

"Sure."

"Excellent. If you could stay for a bit, perhaps we could iron out the rest of our arrangements. And Mrs. Jordan, you're welcome to take Simon home."

Just like that, he disposed of us all neatly. Rory gave me another kiss on the cheek and told me he'd see me at home. I didn't want to leave without talking to him, but really, I didn't have an option. Simon and I descended in a silent elevator and went back out into a day that felt cold and gray.

CHAPTER TWENTY-NINE

Jamie

drove Simon home. I was tense and nervous, but something had changed since Simon's private meeting with Arnie Waugh, because so was he.

"Are you okay?" I asked.

"I'm fine."

"Are you sure?"

"Come on, Mom."

"What did you guys talk about?"

"Arnie says I shouldn't repeat anything we discussed outside the room. He said it's important. Sorry."

"No, of course." I drove on. After a moment I realized that I was biting my thumbnail, and I forced myself to put my hand back onto the steering wheel and keep it there.

"Are you going to give your phone to the police?"

Simon's fingers were pinching at the crease in his pants. Pinch, release. Pinch, release. "Not right away. Not voluntarily. But Arnie says they'll get it eventually." He fell silent, and so did I. His head was turned away from me, and it took me a few minutes to realize that he was crying.

"Simon?"

"I'm fine. I'm really fine. It's just a lot, you know?"

My heart twisted. My fear ratcheted up another notch. We drove in silence for a long time. I kept thinking about Andrew Fraser saying that Simon had hit Nina. I thought about the fact that Simon was the last person to see Nina alive. About the look on Rory's face when I'd asked him what was really going on. About Simon trying to hide whatever was on his phone. I could keep trying to pretend that all of this meant nothing. I could try.

I reached out my right hand and took Simon's in mine.

"Baby," I said. "You know that Nina's parents came to the house last night. Andrew said that you had hit Nina, that you'd hurt her. Before she disappeared." Simon didn't look at me. "I wanted you to know. I don't want to keep anything from you."

The silence went on too long. Then Simon said, "He doesn't know anything."

"Okay."

He pulled away from me. "And my relationship with Nina was *private*. It was nobody else's business."

"Yes." He still wasn't looking at me. The side of his face that I could see was reddening.

"Everyone's acting like she was the perfect angel, just because she's missing. Just because she was a woman, that didn't make her perfect. She fucked up, like, a lot."

"I know that." Was. *Was* a woman. The words rolled around in my head. They didn't mean anything, except that really we were all beginning to accept that Nina wasn't coming home. Too much time had passed for that.

Eventually, I said, "Nina's father said you met Grace in the woods."

"Jesus." Simon shook his head. "She *begged* me to come. Her parents won't talk to her about anything. They're treating her like a kid, and it's making her more scared. She didn't want to talk to her friends because they're all into all the online stuff and she doesn't trust them. So she asked me to meet her to talk. And now, what, they're trying to make that into something?"

"She said . . . I think she told them that you tried to kiss her."

Simon turned and looked at me as if I'd just slapped him. "She's fifteen, Mom."

"I know. I know." The shock on his face was genuine, and I felt terrible that I'd allowed doubt to creep into my head. I reached out and squeezed his hand again. I wanted him to know that I wasn't accusing him of anything. That I was on his side.

He shook my hand off and went back to looking out the window.

"Simon. Simon. Please talk to me. Please, baby."

He kept his face turned away from me. He brushed stray tears away angrily with the back of his hand, and took a deep breath, but the tears kept coming.

"Tell me what happened. Please tell me what happened."

"I told you everything already. I guess you don't believe me. I guess you think I'm some kind of murderer, right? You say you're on my side, but you're so much worse than everyone else. You're my *mother*."

"I'm on your side, Simon. I'm always on your side." I reached for his hand again, but he pulled it away.

"So you think I murdered Nina and you're on my side? That's fucked up, Mom. That's what that is."

I drove on in silence. I couldn't go home. If I took him home he'd disappear into his bedroom and lock the door and I wouldn't be able to reach him. I took the turn for Stowe. There was no good reason to do it, except that instinct told me that answers lay there.

"Where are we going?" Simon asked sharply.

"I think you know."

"Turn the car around. I don't want to go to Stowe, Mom. Jesus."

I kept driving.

"Mom, I'm not kidding." He raised his voice. He was angry, but around the edges of the anger I could hear panic. When I didn't answer or slow or turn the car, he took out his phone. "I'll call Dad. Okay? If you don't turn around."

I kept driving. He called Rory's number, but the call went straight to voice mail.

"Fuuuck." Simon kicked out hard in the footwell of the passenger seat. Then he turned his body away from me and acted like he didn't care one way or the other. He stared out the window. We drove up to the house. I parked.

"Come on," I said. I got out of the car, and I stood and waited for him. After a minute he joined me. There was yellow police tape fluttering at the door. We couldn't go in, but maybe we didn't need to. It was cold and I pushed my hands deep into my pockets. The forecast was for snow, and you could feel it on the wind. I took a deep breath and tried to put a lid on all my emotions. If I was going to get through to him, I would have to be very calm and steady. Even when he was a little boy, Simon had never liked being pushed into anything.

"You have to tell me what really happened that night with Nina. You can't carry this around with you for the rest of your life. It will be like a poison inside you. You need to tell someone, and I'm that person. Whatever you tell me today will stay here. We will never, ever speak about it again. But at least, after today, you'll know that I know, and that I love you, and that will make things just a little bit easier."

He turned his back and walked away from me. He went to the water, right to the edge of the jetty. I followed him.

"Simon?"

He didn't react. Didn't respond to me at all, and I knew. It was like a doom settling over me, stripping away everything that made me who I was. I was nothing at all, except the mother of a boy who had killed a girl. I turned the idea over in my mind. What did it mean? Had I made him the way he was? Had I formed him with not enough love, or too much? An image of Nina's face, laughing, inserted itself into my mind against my will. I shook my head to try to clear it. I pressed my hands to the sides of my face. Simon turned to me. I didn't see him coming and then he was there, right in front of me.

"It was an accident," Simon said, so quietly that I could barely hear him. So quietly that if I wanted to, I could pretend I hadn't. He put his arms around me and pulled me closer. He hugged me so gently. I rested my head on his shoulder and I cried. We stayed that way for a long time, until snow started to fall silently around us and he started to shiver. We could have gone home, but I don't think either of us was ready to get in the car.

"You don't have to tell me any more if you don't want to," I said. "But if you do, I'm willing to listen."

Whatever had happened, it had been an accident. Of course it had been an accident. Nothing else made sense. He had loved her so much, and he was not a murderer. I wasn't blind to Simon's faults. I knew he could be selfish. That he could be entitled. Maybe that was my fault. We'd raised him with so much, Rory and I, and Simon had watched me build my life around Rory's needs and wants. Maybe Simon had never seen the real me inside the pretend me. So maybe we'd sent him the wrong messages about what a relationship should be, but we had not made a killer. I'd watched my child grow up. I'd seen him gently carry a stray moth or a spider outside, before Rory or I could swat it with the back of a magazine. He'd been given a character award in the sixth grade, for God's sake, for defending some kid against a bully.

Simon was hesitating.

"If you're worried that I'll tell your father, I have no intention of telling him anything." Though from the look on Rory's face in the lawyer's office, he already suspected the truth.

"He knows," Simon said.

I didn't think I'd heard Simon properly. The words didn't make sense. Except that they did. I'd seen it in Rory's eyes, in the lawyer's office.

"Your dad already knows. You've talked about it?"

Simon nodded. His eyes were on my face, worried. I tried to shake off my feelings of betrayal.

"Okay." I took a breath. "I know everything's scary right now, but your dad will take care of things. Everything's going to be okay."

Simon's face tightened. "I don't think so." He took his phone out of his pocket and gestured with it. "The police want my search history. Arnie says they'll get it eventually, whether I agree to hand over my phone or not."

"What's wrong with your search history?"

"I was really stupid. I guess . . . I guess I was in shock. When Nina died, I looked some stuff up. About how to clean up blood." He looked at me anxiously. "She hit her head, Mom, on the fireplace. It was an accident. Nina fell, but I freaked out."

"Okay."

"And I looked up how to clean up blood so that police couldn't find it. I used an incognito search, you know? Because I thought that would be safe, which is so fucking stupid. Arnie says police can easily get around that. All incognito does is block cookies. I thought it made your searches anonymous." He looked miserable. "I'm so scared, Mom. About what's going to happen to me."

We both stared down at the phone in his hand. Such a little thing, to condemn him. I reached out and took it from him, and then I turned and threw it, as hard and far as I could, into the lake.

Simon looked at me with his mouth open. I tried to smile.

"They can swim for it, if they want."

"The police—"

"I'll tell them I did it," I cut across him. "I'll tell them I dropped it in the lake. I'll take a polygraph, if they like. I'm a good liar, Simon. Better than you are."

"It's all on the cloud," Simon said, flatly. "That's why Arnie said that it doesn't matter about the phone, they'll get it all eventually. They'll send warrants to Apple and Google, if they haven't already, and they'll get my search history and pretty much everything else they want."

My heart sank lower. Of course. Of course everything was on the cloud. I knew that. I wasn't an idiot or a Luddite. "Fuck 'em. At least this way, they have to work for it."

We started walking back to the car.

"I love you, baby."

"I love you too, Mom."

I took his hand.

"Mom? If I have to run, will you help me?"

"To the ends of the earth, if that's what it takes."

CHAPTER THIRTY

Andy

Craig came on Thursday night and took Grace home with him. I called him on Friday morning, to talk to her. She wanted to talk to Leanne, but Lee couldn't do it. Things had gotten worse with her, and she couldn't get out of bed, couldn't eat. It was like she just wanted to withdraw from the world, like she didn't have the energy to face it. I lied to Grace. Told her that Lee had had to go to the supermarket, and that she'd call her later. I tried not to think about what would happen when later didn't come. We'd made Grace leave her cell phone at home, so she couldn't call Lee directly. Maybe I could control things for a few days, for long enough to get Lee some help.

After I spoke to Grace, Craig stayed on the line for a while. I told him what was happening with Leanne.

"I've been thinking maybe I should come and take Grace back home after all," I said. "If she was here, I think Lee would do better. She'd force herself to, for Grace's sake."

"That's a lot to put on a teenager," Craig said. "You don't think that maybe Lee needs to see a doctor? Get some help? When she's a little better and things have calmed down, that might be a better time."

"She thinks Nina's dead, Craig. It's going to take more than a couple of days for her to get over this."

Craig sighed. "Yeah."

My stomach clenched. I wanted him to deny it. To tell me that I was crazy. That of course Nina wasn't dead.

"Look, Andy. There's something you need to know. Maybe you already know, but Sofia said I have to talk to you about it, and I guess she's right." Craig paused. "I know you're not online much, but you need to know that there's some disgusting stuff being said. About you. About Nina."

I didn't answer him. I didn't really have anything that I could say to that, other than the obvious. Craig took a deep breath.

"They're saying you're a pedophile."

"Yeah. Okay. I get it. I know about it."

Craig seemed relieved. Like now that he'd said it, the worst was over. "Grace tells me you closed the inn."

"We couldn't have people in the house."

"You guys doing okay for money? Sof and I could help out."

That hit me. "Thank you. We'll be okay. I got projects lined up at work. And savings. Enough that we won't have to worry for a while."

"You don't think . . . you don't think the online stuff will hurt your business?"

For a second I thought he meant the inn, then I realized he meant my landscaping business.

"No. I can't see that happening."

But within a half hour of that call, everything started to go to hell. Some guys from Rory Jordan's company came by with Leanne's car. They didn't say much, just knocked on the door and handed over the keys, but while I was dealing with them I missed a call from Don Roberts. He left a voice mail. Don and his wife were building a weekend house over near Sugarbush. I'd had a meeting with them, and I'd sent them my quote for the work just the week before. They'd called me after and they'd been excited. We'd talked for nearly an hour. But the Don on the voice mail sounded like a different guy. He sounded angry. The message was short; he just said they'd decided to go in a different direction, then he hung up. I tried calling him, twice, but he didn't answer. An hour after Don's message I got an email from the state buildings and general services agency. I've had a contract to maintain the grounds of all public schools in the Waitsfield and Waterbury areas for coming up on six years. My contract was due to be renewed in eight weeks, but the agency wrote to tell me that they weren't going to do it, that they'd be putting the work out for tender. Maybe I might have been able to put that down to coincidence, but the last line of the email said, "Please note that your contract is terminated as of today's date. You will be paid out the remainder of your contract. Please do not attend any school properties. All licenses and authorities granted to you under your contract of service are hereby revoked." I checked my other emails and saw two other cancellations.

So then I knew. Craig, my flaky little brother, had seen this coming, and I'd been kidding myself. Real people, people who knew me, now believed I was some kind of animal. All based on what? Some anonymous posts on the internet? I left my cell on the kitchen table and went outside. Rufus followed me. I walked around the yard, taking deep breaths, thinking about what Lee had said about our lives changing forever. I thought about the guys I worked with. My suppliers and my subcontractors. If they hadn't already heard the rumors, they were going to. Jesus.

It felt like I couldn't get enough air in my lungs. I'd left my jacket inside, and it was a cold day. I went to the barn and started splitting firewood. I had to do something. I couldn't just sit or stand around and think about everything. I split logs until I ran out of blocks. Then I started fixing up the barn. Moving bags of cement and sorting scrap lumber. I lost track of time. When I went back into the house it was two o'clock, but Lee was still in bed.

"Aren't you hungry, baby?"

"Not really." Her voice was listless, and she didn't look at me. I went downstairs and found some soup in the freezer. I defrosted it and warmed it up and brought a bowl to her. I had to help her to sit up, and then she looked at the soup like she didn't even see it. I took the spoon and filled it and raised it to her lips. Her eyes met mine, and some of the blankness left her. She swallowed, and then she took the spoon from me.

"Thank you," she said.

"You're welcome."

I went downstairs, feeling a little more hopeful. But when I came back to check on her, the bowl of soup was on her bedside table, more than half-full, and she was asleep again. I didn't know what to do. I kissed her and took the bowl downstairs. I went looking for beer, but there was none in the fridge. No wine either. I poured myself a whiskey and took the bottle to the living room. I turned on the television. I was looking for sports, but I found a special report on Nina and Simon. The sound on the TV was muted, but I didn't need it to be on to understand what was happening. The channel played a reel of Nina and Simon, culled from their social media and edited. But then the picture shifted, and I saw Simon, at home in his parents' garden, walking with his head down, looking thoughtful and sad. The picture cut to Rory and Jamie, sitting side by side on the sofa in their living room. He was wearing a navy button-down with an open collar. She was wearing a white silk T-shirt. They looked like good people. They looked concerned. Rory held Jamie's hand in his as he leaned forward to say something to the interviewer.

I turned up the sound, but the report moved on. This time the interviewer was talking to Cally Gabriel, the principal. She'd had her hair done for the interview and her makeup too. You could tell by the perfect waves and the red, red lips.

"Of course I know Simon and Nina well. Simon was one of our star pupils. Such a bright boy, from a loving family. Simon was very nearly valedictorian of his year, you know. He was a real presence around the school."

"And Nina?" the interviewer asked.

Cally Gabriel paused. It was a very small hesitation, less than a second, but it was just long enough.

"Nina was very well liked also."

I put my glass down on the table. My hands wanted to clench into fists. I forced them to relax. They played the clip of Nina pushing Simon into the pool. That fucking clip. The way she laughed. I heard it all the time now, inside my head. The interviewer moved on. This time she was talking to a young girl in a dorm room. I'd never seen the girl before in my life, but she claimed to be Nina's best friend.

"I'm sure you've seen the rumors that have been widely discussed on social media," the interviewer said, leaning forward and dropping her voice into a cozy, let's-just-chat register.

"Oh my God, that Simon might have murdered Nina? Everyone's talking about it."

"Of course, those rumors are just allegations," the interviewer said sweetly. "We have no evidence to suggest that they're true."

"Well, I can tell you for sure that they're not true. I know Simon. I saw them together. He *loved* her. And he's not the type, anyway. He's a really gentle guy. That's what I told the police."

"Thank you, Olivia," the interviewer said. "And is it true that you received a message from Nina the night she disappeared, telling you that she was on the way to Boston to see you?"

"That's right," Olivia said, eagerly. "But she never got here. I think something happened to her on the road."

The interviewer turned to the camera. "We spoke to many people in Simon and Nina's hometown of Waitsfield. Everyone we spoke to who knew them as a couple confirms that they seemed very happy together." She drew her eyebrows together. "But there are darker rumors swirling around Waitsfield today."

The picture shifted again. This time the interviewer was outside Mehuron's supermarket. She was dressed for the weather, and she was holding out a microphone to Arlene Sugarman. Arlene had twin girls the same age as Grace. They used to be friendly but had grown apart over the years. Arlene looked nervous and excited.

"My girls used to stay over at that house all the time. When I heard,

I was terrified, of course. What if he'd touched my daughters? It could easily have happened."

"That's a very serious allegation."

"I'm not alleging anything, I'm sure. I don't want to get sued. I'm just saying what I've read. I'm not saying it's *true* because I don't know, do I? But you read something like that online and any responsible parent is going to take action, aren't they?"

The reporter started to turn away, like she was going to bring the interview to an end, but Arlene wasn't finished.

"If there wasn't anything in it, the younger girl wouldn't have run away too, would she?"

"Excuse me?"

"The younger girl. Grace. She ran away today. Everyone at the school is talking about it."

The reporter turned to the camera and raised an eyebrow, as if to say *there you have it, folks. An exclusive.*

They finished the piece with a short interview with Simon. He was talking to someone off camera, telling them what a great climber Nina was. How they'd been each other's best friend. How he couldn't sleep. How he'd never stop thinking about her.

I turned the TV off. I couldn't stand to watch it. Lee was right. Whatever happened between Simon and Nina in Stowe, he was never going to be forced to tell the truth. He was never going to answer for what he did. All this bullshit online wasn't happening in a vacuum. I may not be book smart, but I'm not a fool. Simon's parents were wrapping their boy up in lawyers and money, and when all of this was done he'd just move on with his life. I sank the whiskey and poured another. I changed the channel until I found an old basketball game, and then I stared at the screen. I was like Lee, staring at something and taking in nothing. Was this our future? The two of us broke, like zombies, while Grace . . . what? What would happen to Grace? If we couldn't fix this, she'd be better off staying with Craig and Sophia. At least that way she'd have a chance. The day drifted by. I thought about making dinner and decided there wasn't any point. I thought about everything and nothing. I felt sorry for myself until I just about made myself sick.

It was late when I started to come out of it. I'd poured myself another drink—was it my third, or my fourth? I'd lost track of that, and of time. I got up and went to the kitchen and poured the drink down the sink, and the contents of the bottle too. I went upstairs to check on Lee. She was sleeping. Almost before the plan had taken shape in my mind, I started preparing. I put on an old pair of black work pants, a navy thermal shirt, and a sweater. I took my gun from the safe in our room. I held the box of bullets in my hand, feeling the weight of them. I could leave them in the safe. I had no intention of shooting anyone that night, and if I left the bullets where they were, I could make sure of that. On the other hand . . . if I wanted to get answers from the boy I might have to frighten him into talking. I might have to make a show of strength. I slid the magazine into the gun, double-checked the safety, and put the gun in my pocket.

My jacket was hanging in the mudroom by the kitchen. I rubbed Rufus on the head on my way through, put on my jacket, and opened the door. It was a cold, dark night. There was snow in the air. I could feel it. They were forecasting four inches, and another four the next day. I went to the barn and without turning on any lights, I got out Lee's day pack and put in my headlamp, my binoculars, an extra layer, and my water bottle. I moved the gun to my jacket pocket and zipped it securely, then I set off for the back of our house and the trail that ran from there. I didn't know for sure whether the press were still at our gate, waiting. It was cold and dark and they might well have gone home to whatever inn they were staying at, but I couldn't risk driving. It would be a two-hour hike to the Jordans' place, based on my calculations. I'd get there just after midnight, which would be as good a time as any to try to find Simon's bedroom and drag him out of there at gunpoint.

I wasn't going to hurt him. I'd promised myself that, and I was going to keep that promise. Maybe our girl was dead. It cut me in half to admit that was a possibility, but she'd been missing for a week now, and I couldn't keep pretending that she was okay. So I tried to accept the possibility that she was gone. I knew that Lee was convinced that Simon had killed her. And Julie Bradley was a good, smart kid. Julie thought that Simon was hitting Nina, and I believed her, and if he was capable of raising his hand to Nina then I had to believe that he could kill her. But the idea was like a sharp knife to the gut. If Simon had killed her, then I'd missed it. All the times Simon came by to pick her up. All the times I'd waved them off with a smile, like a fucking *fool*. There must have been signs, that's all, and I'd missed them all.

I wanted to believe he hadn't done it, because I am weak, and I didn't want to accept that it was my fault that my girl was dead. But I couldn't fool myself any longer, because I knew for sure that Simon was lying. At the search, when he'd delivered his bullshit line about breaking up with Nina and about how maybe she hadn't wanted to come home right away because she hadn't wanted to bump into him, I'd seen the lie in his eyes. And I wasn't going to allow that. Whatever it took, I was going to make him tell the truth.

I made good time. Once I was in the trees I fell into a steady jog. I'd hiked most of these trails at one time or another, with Leanne and Rufus. The ground got a little tougher when I got closer to the Jordans'. The trail turned off to the north and I had to hike cross-country. I followed a deer track, but the land dropped away into a deep gully with a fast-flowing stream. It took me some time to find a safe crossing point, and climbing up the other side was hard going in the dark. Even with the headlamp, it was a challenge to make sure that I didn't lose my footing and plunge backward to the rocks below. So my progress was slower. At some point it started to snow, but it weren't much, just a little light flurry that dusted the trees. Things got easier on the other side. There was a game trail that was going the right general direction and I followed that, and then had only a short hike through light country until I reached the back of the Jordans' house. By then I was tired. I took some time to eat a protein bar and put on another layer and my wool hat. I would cool down fast once I stopped moving.

I reached the tree line behind the Jordan house. I found a position I liked, with a real clear view of the house, and I took out my binoculars. In the trees I could watch the house and wait for my moment. They had those huge windows, and I could see right inside. It was coming up on 1:00 A.M.—the hike had taken longer than I'd expected. Everyone should be fast asleep by now, but I would wait and watch and be sure, and then I would make my move. I'd overheard Nina talking to a friend once, about how Simon's room opened directly out onto the pool patio. I let my binoculars play over the back of the house and found a set of double doors right by the pool. That must be his room. Would he lock his doors at night, or leave them open? If they were open I could get inside and have my gun to his head before he could so much as twitch.

They were making it easy for me. That enormous house, with so many windows, and all the drapes and blinds wide open. There were lights on inside, not full-on bright, and not in every room, but enough so I could see inside. I focused on what looked like the main living area, a large room with floor-to-ceiling windows. I zoomed in with the binoculars and saw a figure lying on the couch. It was too dark in the room to see features clearly, but I thought that figure was probably Jamie Jordan. There was a bottle of wine on the coffee table in front of her. I thought about her hard face, about the way she'd treated my wife, and looked away.

I scanned the second floor of the house. There were drapes closed on only one set of windows. My best guess was that that was the master bedroom. Rory might be asleep there. My binoculars wandered back to Jamie. If only the light was a little stronger. I wanted to be a hundred percent sure that it was her.

I was so focused on Jamie that I very nearly missed the moment when Simon Jordan crept out of the house. I swung the binoculars away just in time to catch him as he closed the door to his bedroom and walked away across the patio. He was dressed for the weather, and he had a full backpack on his back. He moved quickly through his parents' yard. He was coming toward me. If he kept on walking and didn't change his course, he would pass within ten yards of my hiding spot. His sudden appearance threw me. I crouched low and moved back deeper into the trees. I hid in the undergrowth and watched as he walked right by me and kept moving, toward the mountain. His face was pale in the moonlight. He looked real young, and desperate and determined.

He was running away. It was the only thing that made sense. I could stop him. I had the gun. I could grab him right now, put the gun to his forehead, and scare him into telling me the truth. But I did nothing. Suddenly everything seemed too real. Seeing Simon's face, I felt like a crazy man. What was I doing, hiding in the woods with a gun in my pocket? That made me some kind of guy. I thought about the man who'd been hanging around at Grace's school and felt a little sick. Except that . . . Nina was gone. That was a fact. And Simon was running away. Really, truly running away, and I was letting him do it. Christ almighty.

I set off after him, but I couldn't see him and I couldn't hear him. I had waited too long. My headlamp was in my pack, and I couldn't risk taking it out and switching it on. The clouds had broken up a little and there was some moonlight, but not enough, and I stumbled over the ground but kept on moving, as quickly as I could, and I listened hard. Simon was young and fit and he hadn't just jogged cross-country for the better part of three hours. He moved much faster than I did. I would lose him. He would hike to a car he'd stashed somewhere and then escape forever, taking whatever answers he had with him. Where could he go from here? Not north and not east. I knew enough of the country to know that it was real hard going from where we were, and that there was no quick and easy way through. The trail we were on was dropping away to the west. If we kept following it, where would we end up? He must have a car stashed somewhere, waiting for him. That was the only thing that made sense.

I started to run. I had to catch him before he got to the trailhead. But I was making way too much noise. He would surely hear me coming. At every corner I expected to see him waiting with a tree branch in hand, but before I knew it I burst through the cover of the trees, into a clearing and then onto a dirt road. I was at a trailhead. There was a signpost on the opposite side of the road, marking the beginning of a marked trail. I whipped my head around, looking in all directions for Simon. There were no cars parked anywhere, and I hadn't heard an engine. I would have heard one, even from a mile back, on this cold, quiet night. I fumbled for my headlamp, put it on my head, and turned it on. There were footprints in the snow. Mine, coming from the shelter of the trees, but another pair too, leading across the road, past the wooden sign that marked the entrance to the marked trail. HEDGEHOG BROOK TRAIL, the sign said. I knew it. It was a steep, three-hour hike to the summit from here. I followed the footprints, moving more slowly and more carefully than before. I could hear running water. The brook, just ahead. Had he crossed it? The footprints sure made it seem that way.

Once he crossed the water, if he continued on the trail, it would be all uphill from there. And there was nothing but wilderness after this point. My boots were waterproof, my pants were not. It didn't matter. The footsteps led the way, and I followed, stepping down into the water, which soaked my pants and got into my boots. It was real cold, not deep winter cold, but close. I moved quickly, climbed out the other side, and set off again, this time uphill. I thought about switching my headlamp off but decided not to. I was taking a risk. Simon might see the light and realize that someone was following him, but hiking without the light on this trail was too dangerous—it was too steep and the trail floor was a mass of slippery tree roots.

The moon was hidden behind heavy cloud, and it was very dark. All the time I climbed, I thought about where Simon might be going and why. Hedgehog Brook Trail connected with the Long Trail, which you could follow all the way to Canada, if you wanted. From here it was a hundred miles to the border, at least a week's hike. More, probably, even for an experienced hiker like Simon. Was he carrying a week's worth of food in his backpack? He could be. But why would he do it? There were easier ways to run away, surely, than hiking out, but maybe that was why he'd chosen it. It wasn't the obvious way to go.

I stopped worrying about where he was going and started thinking about where he might stop. It was obvious now that he was far ahead of me. I could still see footprints in the new snow, but I hadn't heard a sound. I needed him to stop. He might be well supplied, but I wasn't. I could hike a full night without rest or food, probably, but what would that get me? The sun would come up and I would be somewhere deep in the backcountry, maybe lost, and with no supplies.

I reached the top of the trail. There was a scramble over exposed granite. The snow was heavier up here, and there were clear signs of Simon's passing. I stood at the summit for a moment. The clouds parted and the stars came out. The wind was lifting little drifts of snow, and the cold bit at my cheeks. It was completely silent. I turned to look back at the valley. There were lights down there, a sprinkling of them, houses dotted among the trees, but up on the mountain, I was in a different world. The Long Trail led north and south from where I was standing, but Simon's footprints led south. Which didn't make sense if he was trying to get to Canada. I set off after him. For five minutes I followed the trail south, and then I smelled wood-smoke. I stopped walking, my head up, trying to figure out where it was coming from. And then I remembered—there was a hiker's hut on this route. Actually, more than a hut, a cabin. Most of the hiker's huts on the Long Trail were three-sided log lean-tos. You could set up your tarp and a sleeping bag inside and they would keep most of the rain off, and sometimes there was a pit toilet, but that was about all the comfort on offer. The cabin up ahead was different. I'd never had reason to stop and use it, but I'd seen it a couple times. It was fully enclosed, with a tin roof, a glass window, and a small wood-burning stove. There were even jerry cans of water that the rangers tried to keep topped up. It was a good place to overnight on the trail or to warm up for a few hours.

I switched off my headlamp and slowed down as I approached the cabin. It was in a small clearing. The door was shut, there was a glow from the window, and smoke came from the metal chimney. I crouched down and debated whether I should go straight for the door or risk looking in the window first. I chose the window, crept forward, and looked inside. The cabin was exactly how I remembered it. The bare timber floor, the little stove, a timber bed frame. Simon was there. He was hunched over the stove, feeding wood into the flames, his back to the window. He'd already rolled out his sleeping bag on the bed frame. He was heating water in a small pot on the stove.

I dropped back into a crouch, unzipped my pocket, and took out the gun. I was afraid. That I would fuck it up. Chicken out. Let Leanne down. Let Nina down. Let Grace down. This was a perfect chance, the only one I was going to get. Simon knew the truth, and I wanted it. It was up to me to take it from him.

CHAPTER THIRTY-ONE

Andy

I didn't wait. Waiting would only give me time to talk myself out of what needed to be done. I went straight to the door and wrenched it open, then took two quick steps inside, my gun raised and pointed at him. Simon was crouching in front of the fire. He turned around fast at the noise and froze when he saw the gun. The stove was still open, and he still had firewood in one hand.

"Close it," I said. I motioned with the gun. "And move back." There was steam coming from the pot on the stove. I didn't want him to throw it at me. I kept my distance, but he didn't move. "Close it," I said again.

He put the firewood on the floor, slowly closed the stove, and started to stand.

"No. Stay where you are."

He'd taken off his hat and left it on his pack, and he still had the mark from the wool on his forehead. His hair was standing up in all directions. It made him look younger. He did what I said. He sat on the ground and scooted back away from the stove.

"Mr. Fraser," he said. He looked nervous, but not scared. Memories came into my mind, one on top of the other on top of the other. Memories of Nina growing up, and Simon right there beside her. For every picture we had in our home of Nina at school plays, at dances and graduations, the Jordans would have one just the same. Simon was part of us. He was part of our community, part of what made us what we were. That was all true. But . . . he was also the guy who'd met Grace in the woods. And I believed Julie about the bruises. I really did.

"You got a gun with you, Simon?"

He shook his head.

"Don't you lie to me."

"I guess . . . there's a knife in my backpack. But it's not a weapon. It's just for . . . you know, stuff."

"Stand up. Lift up your jacket and shirt and turn around." He did what I asked, but he moved slowly, like he was seventy years old, instead of twenty. There was no gun. And his pants were too fitted to be hiding much of anything. "Sit down," I said. "We're going to talk." I put my pack down, slid out my water bottle, and took a long drink, but I never took my eyes off him, and I didn't lower my gun. He sat back down again on the floor, too carefully, and cross-legged, like he was about to start a yoga class. Other than his hat and gloves, he was still wearing all of his layers.

"I want you to tell me exactly what happened between you and Nina on Friday night in Stowe. Every single thing. Everything you said, everything she said."

"But . . . my parents already told you. I told them, and they told you. I swear, I told them everything I know."

"Don't you lie to me."

"I'm just as worried about her as everyone else. More, probably." He leaned forward. He was pale, and his eyes were wide and honest. They met mine without flinching. "I loved Nina. You know I did. Do. I always have. Just because we had a stupid fight, that doesn't matter. That was only, like, five minutes. So we lost our tempers. That doesn't change anything about how much we love each other."

I looked at him and said nothing. He seemed to think he was getting through to me.

"I dream about her, all the time. When I'm sleeping, when I'm awake. I dream that this has all just been a nightmare, and that when

I wake up, she'll be there, beside me, and our lives will just go on the way they were supposed to." It was word for word what he'd said in the television interview. I don't think he realized. Or maybe he did, and he didn't care.

"I'm sure you do." I said it quietly. Gently, almost. As if we were friends, sitting in a diner somewhere having coffee and talking about the girl who got away. Simon's face crumpled, as if he wanted to cry. Though there were no tears. His eyes were dry.

"Just tell me," I said. "I already know most of it. There's no point in lying. You can't help yourself that way."

Simon shook his head.

"I don't know what you think happened, but I've told you the truth. Nina and I had a stupid fight. She'd been drinking. Only a few glasses of wine, but you know what she's like. She doesn't drink much, and she can't hold it very well. She gets emotional. I decided that I should leave to give her some space to calm down. So that she could see things straight. That's it."

"I thought you said you broke up."

"We did. I mean . . . yeah, we did, but I don't think either of us really meant it."

"So. You walked away to give her some space. And what do you think happened after that?"

He looked away from me, looked down. "I don't like to think about it. And I could be wrong."

"Just say it."

He looked back at me, his eyes still wide, still full of that false sincerity, and I felt a black wave of dislike start low and crash all over me. I didn't know this kid. Sure, I'd seen him a hundred times at the school or at kids' sports when they were all little, and when Nina grew up and they started dating, I'd seen him around our house, but I'd never truly *looked* at him. I'd never felt the need to. Because I'd known him his whole life. I thought that made him safe. I thought he was a nice boy who was in love with my daughter. He had some growing up to do, for sure, and maybe he was a little spoiled, but at his heart, a good kid. I'd been so far from the truth. I was looking at a shell of a person. He understood people well enough that he could play the part, when he needed to, but that's all it was. A role. A thin layer of decency wrapped around what? Wrapped around a fucking animal.

"I think someone took her," Simon said, in a choked half whisper. "Maybe she left a window open. Or maybe I . . . maybe I didn't lock the door when I left. Oh God. That must have been it. I was upset. I wasn't thinking. And someone came and broke in. Maybe to rob the place. You know people do that. They case vacation homes, make sure they're empty, and then they come back at night and break in and take what they can. I mean, someone could have been there earlier in the day. Nina and I were out all day, hiking. They might have thought the house was empty. And then they come back and find Nina alone." He was speaking faster, getting more enthusiastic about his story.

"And then what?"

"I . . . I guess, they kidnap her? Take her somewhere."

"So you think she's still alive?"

I saw the knowledge in his eyes. There was a *no*, sitting right there and looking at me. His head even started to move into a shake before he stopped it. It was the smallest twitch, but I saw it.

"I think yes. I think . . . I hope so. Even though whoever took her . . . I mean . . . But I want her to be alive. I want her to survive and come back to us."

I leaned forward.

"You're lying, Simon. You killed Nina that night. You hid her body in the woods. That's why that dog went crazy. And somehow you went back and moved her, when you found out we were coming. I don't know how you did that, maybe the police are close to finding out. Something's spooked you, hasn't it? Which is why you're running away."

He was breathing hard, his face reddening. His hands, which were on his knees, clenched tight.

"I'm not running away."

"No? You're just . . . meeting a friend?" I glanced around the hut and widened my hands in a questioning gesture.

"I just . . . I needed to get away. My lawyer . . ."

"Your lawyer what?"

"Nothing." He shook his head. "None of your business."

The problem was that he wasn't afraid of me. He saw me as Nina's dad. The smiling guy who'd picked them up from parties before they were old enough to drive themselves. The guy who made pancakes on Sunday and threw extra bacon in the pan when Simon showed up uninvited.

I stood up and hit him as hard as I could across the forehead with the butt of the gun. He gave a grunt of pain. A cut opened up on his forehead and blood spilled down into his right eye. He pressed his hands to it, and I stepped back again, keeping some distance between us.

"Tell me what happened."

"You hit me." He held his hands away from his face, looked at the blood, and then stared at me.

"Yes," I said. My voice was steady. "And I'll kill you, Simon. I'll shoot you and leave your body here for the next hiker to find." I didn't mean it. It was just talk, but I had to find a way to make him afraid. I kept talking, my voice low and steady. "Who knows, maybe I'll kill myself. I don't have a whole lot to live for right now. I don't know if you've heard, but my life is a shit show. People think I'm a pedophile. I'm losing my business. My family is broken. If I kill you, I could maybe take your gear and hike to Canada and build a new life, right? That's an option. You only have one chance here. If you tell me the whole truth, if I believe you when you're done, then I will let you live."

"You're crazy," he said. "You've lost your mind."

I nodded. "You might be right about that. But it shouldn't matter to you if I'm sane or insane. All you need to know is that there is only one way that you are going to walk off this mountain. You're going to tell me what happened to Nina. You're going to tell me where her body is buried. I'll record your confession on my phone, and I'll send it to the police, and maybe you'll go to prison for a long time. But you'll live. I guess you have to decide if you want to die, here, tonight, or not. That's up to you."

"I didn't kill Nina," he said. "I didn't kill her. Okay? But if I had, and I told you, you'd kill me for sure."

"You're still lying." I stepped back and sat on the bed frame. My legs were tired. Some of the energy was leaching out of my body. I felt like I knew where this was going to end up. He would never admit that he'd killed her. I didn't want to let him go. He was a cancer. Malignant.

"I'm not lying. I didn't touch her, okay?"

"Tell me the truth, everything that happened, and I'll let you walk away. I came here for the truth, for me and for my wife. If she knows what happened, she has a chance of healing. Especially if she knows you're going to prison. Prison won't be fun, even though your dad will probably pull some strings and get you into a country club. But you'll get out, eventually. Have some kind of life. That's better than me shooting you right here in this shitty little hut. And who knows? Maybe your lawyer will get you off. A confession to me with a gun on you is probably not admissible evidence. So those are your choices. Die now. Right now. Or tell me the truth, and maybe get away with it. Choose."

I saw him think about it. I watched him consider, then decide against, telling me the truth, and the knowledge that Nina was dead truly sank in, settling on me like a stone.

"Oh, Simon," I said.

He heard it in my voice and he saw it in my eyes. I think he knew what I was going to do before I did. I stood up and raised the gun.

"She provoked me! She fucking knew what she was doing. All I ever wanted to do was love her. What's wrong with that? Nothing. Why couldn't she just leave things as they were?"

I did not lower the gun.

"She was sleeping with other men," Simon said, frantically. "Lots of other men. Imagine if that was your wife? What would you do? And it was an *accident!*"

"Nina was the best thing that ever happened to you," I said. I eased back the safety. "It wasn't an accident. You didn't get carried away. The only thing she ever did *wrong* was not want to be with you anymore. And you fucking killed her for it."

I took slow and careful aim. I pulled the trigger.

CHAPTER THIRTY-TWO

Jamie

I fell asleep on the couch on Friday night and woke up alone, in the dark. I had a sickening headache and a disgusting, sour taste in my mouth. I went to the kitchen and filled a glass of water at the sink. I drank it all, but the water sat uncomfortably in my stomach. The house was very quiet. The kitchen clock said it was 5:00 A.M., and it was still dark outside. It was cold in the kitchen. Rory must have come in late. Had he thought about waking me or had he just gone straight to bed? I told myself it didn't matter one way or the other. I thought maybe I was hungry. The fridge had cold chicken and fruit and yogurt and salad. All I wanted was a slice of warm chocolate cake, but I didn't keep anything like that in the house. I ate a grape and closed the door. I moved through the house like a ghost, floating from room to room. There were so many, and so many of them unused. Why did we have this huge house, for two of us and one child who was about to leave?

I made my way downstairs to Simon's room. The door was firmly closed. I leaned my forehead against the wood and I closed my eyes. I wanted to go in, to sit on the bed and put my hand on his cheek, to smooth his hair back from his forehead. I wanted to wave a magic wand and for him to be a little boy again, so that I could start from the beginning and get everything right this time. Be a better mother. I opened the door. His room was dark, but I could make out the shadow of his bed, his bedside tables, his footlocker. The bed was empty.

"Simon?" I whispered his name into the darkness. I cleared my throat and tried again, louder. "Simon?" I reached for the light switch and turned it on. The room was empty. The bed was unmade. I went to the bathroom and turned on the light there. Empty. I'd just been through the entire house, but I went through it again, getting more and more frantic until I was running from room to room. I started calling his name, louder and louder, until I was shouting. Rory emerged from our bedroom, half-asleep and irritable.

"For Christ's sake, Jamie."

"Simon's gone. He's missing."

"He's not gone."

I ran back down the stairs to the basement. I checked the laundry room, the games room, and the gym. Nothing. I went back upstairs. Rory was still standing there.

"Did you check for his car?" Even half asleep he was sharper than I was.

"No."

We went to the garage together. Simon's Jeep was still there. My stomach turned over. I had a sudden, horrific image of Simon's body, hanging in the darkness from one of the trees in our backyard, picked up by our expensive, specially designed outdoor lights. I turned back and ran toward the living room. Rory grabbed me and tried to hold me. I pushed him away, slapping at him to free myself. I staggered as I wrenched myself away from him and fell to my knees, then pushed myself up from the floor and ran again. The lights were on in the living room. I'd turned them on myself. I couldn't see outside properly. I ran to the sliding doors, opened them, and went outside. The wind whipped at my hair and the grass was wet underfoot. The trees were lit up and swaying in the wind. I ran again, searching and searching. My mind played tricks on me. Every shadow looked like my boy, swinging from a noose. Snow drifted through the floodlights. Simon wasn't there. There was no one there.

Rory was watching me from the open door. I went toward him but stood so that there was distance between us.

"I thought he'd killed himself."

"Simon wouldn't do that," Rory said. He was wearing pajamas. V-neck button-down pajamas. Old-man pajamas. "Simon wouldn't do that," he said again. "He's not the type." There was something ugly in his voice.

Rory held his hand out to me. A peace offering. I looked at his hand.

"What does that mean?" I asked.

He shook his head. I wanted to talk to him about the knowledge that he and I shared, but it was too dangerous. We could be overheard, couldn't we? It wasn't beyond the bounds of possibility that our house had been bugged. I took his hand and I hugged him. I rested my head on his chest, and then I whispered—

"I know."

His body stiffened. I knew I should stop, that I should leave it there, but I couldn't.

"He said you knew. That you've known."

"Yes." He said it reluctantly.

I lowered my voice until it was less than a whisper. Until it was a breath. "Did you help him in some way? You did, didn't you. Why?"

I looked up into his face, and he looked down into mine.

"Because I love him. And because I love you."

He was telling the truth. I could see it in his eyes. How had I failed to see it before? Maybe it hadn't been there. Maybe it had taken this, this *horror*, to make him realize what he felt for us. It was too late. The part of me that might have been able to respond to him, to give something back to him, that part was broken. I stepped back.

"What are we going to do?" I asked.

"Everything. Whatever it takes."

"First we need to find him. And then we need to take him away from here. To New York. Or Hawaii. Somewhere he didn't spend a lot of time with her. Somewhere where he won't have to think about things every day." Did I know, even then, that escape was a fantasy?

"Yes. That sounds good."

"Rory?"

"Yes, Jamie."

"He's never going to forgive himself, you know."

"Well. We'll have to help him with that too."

CHAPTER THIRTY-THREE

Leanne

woke up alone, in the dark. It took me a moment to orient myself, and to understand what had woken me. My phone was on my bedside table. I felt drunk and stupid. I listened to the ringing for a while and then I picked the phone up and looked at the screen. The number was local, but it wasn't one I recognized. I thought about not answering, but I pressed the green button.

"Hello?"

Someone gasped for breath on the other end of the line. "I messed up, Lee. I'm sorry, baby. I messed up so bad."

It took me a minute to understand who it was.

"Andy."

"Yeah. Yeah, it's me."

I blinked slowly, then I pushed back the blankets and got out of bed. I walked over to the windows and looked outside. It was snowing. Everything was quiet.

"Where are you?" I asked.

"At the Barretts' house. The old one near Lover's Lane."

"I don't understand."

"I shot him, Lee. I killed Simon Jordan. I didn't plan to, but I did."

My grip tightened on the phone. The world came into focus quickly. "Tell me what happened." Andy's voice, which had seemed like it was coming from very far away, was suddenly very loud.

"He killed Nina. He killed our girl. And I couldn't let him walk away."

I closed my eyes. I kept the phone pressed to my ear with my left hand, and my right hand cradled my own right cheek, as if I could hold myself together that way. Andy was still talking.

"I'm going to have to leave you and Grace. I'm going to be in prison for a very long time. I'm not going to be there for you. Fuck, Lee. I screwed up so bad."

I'd known Nina was gone, but it was different hearing it from Andy. It was like I had one small little ember of hope, still burning somewhere deep inside, and with his words that hope went out. I opened my eyes. I expected a flood of grief to come, but it didn't. Everything was too urgent. My gaze fell on the coffee table and I saw Andy's phone sitting there, the screen dark.

"Has anyone seen you?"

"There's no one here. The house is empty."

"And . . . how did you . . . did you drive? Did the press see you leave here?" I went back to the window, moved the drapes, and peered outside. I couldn't see any lights at the end of the driveway. Surely they would all have left, found somewhere warm to spend the night?

"I hiked to the Jordans' place. Simon was running away. I followed him up the trail. Then I carried him back down. It took me . . . Jesus . . . I don't know how long. But no one saw me."

Relief washed over me. "Okay. Then you listen to me, Andy. No one is ever going to know about this except you and me. What time is it?" I pulled the phone away from my ear just long enough to check. It was already after 7:00 A.M. How had I slept so long? "No one knows you left the house. Your phone is here. You've been here with me all night, okay? I'm going to get you and take you home, and you're going to shower and we'll burn your clothes in the big barrel and we'll never talk about this again, okay?"

"It won't work." He was calmer now. Less frenetic. "I carried Simon down the mountain. I dumped his bag in the woods. I washed away the blood from the hut floor, but it's not enough. I thought about dropping his body in a crevasse, like I did with his bags, but dogs would find him. I've been carrying him, and his blood . . . it's all over me. By now my DNA must be all over him. The sun will be up soon enough. There's no way I can get home without someone seeing me. And when they find his body they'll test everything. I'm going to be the obvious suspect. We both are. They'll ask us both for a DNA test. You know they will. The best we can hope is that you stay out of it. I shouldn't have even called you. I just wanted you to know. To hear it from me." He spoke with an it's-all-over tone. Like everything was past and decided. Like he was slipping away from me.

"No!" It was almost a shout. "No, Andy. You listen to me, okay? You are not leaving me, and you are not leaving Grace. Not without a fight. Not without a fight every goddamn step of the way, okay?"

"I don't know what—"

I cut across him. "We just need to think. We need to take a minute and think." We were quiet for a while. Time went by. My thoughts were slippery. They slid by too fast for me to make sense of them. I clenched my eyes shut again and forced myself to concentrate.

"Okay, this is what we're going to do. You're going to stay exactly where you are. Except . . . no. I want you to search the Barretts' house for plastic garbage bags. You need to wrap Simon's body, and you need to clean up any mess you've made there. You don't want anyone to know that you've been in the house. When you've done that, stay hidden until I get there."

"No, Lee. If you come here then you're a part of this, right? We can't both go to prison. We have to think about Grace."

"No one's going to prison, Andy. Simon killed our daughter. He's not going to destroy our family entirely. We're not going to let that happen. Mehuron's opens in less than an hour. I'm going to go there first and pick up some groceries and make sure I'm seen. And on the way back I'm going to come to you. Just do everything I asked you to, and be ready." I ended the call. I didn't want Andy to argue with me, and the call had already gone on too long. If anyone looked at my call records, would a phone call from a private house in Waitsfield be suspicious? I'd have to come up with some sort of explanation for it, if I was ever asked. You don't speak for five minutes to a wrong number.

I put my phone in my pocket and picked Andy's up. I took it up to our bedroom and sat on our bed. I couldn't leave yet. The supermarket wouldn't open for another forty minutes. I plugged Andy's phone in at his bedside table, turned on the lamp, and woke his screen. I entered his password—he uses the same one for everything—and started going through his email. He had two text messages from Craig; encouraging words and photos of Grace. I texted Craig back, saying thanks and telling him that we'd be over to see Grace later in the day. Then I went through Andy's work emails. There were three more job cancellations, and an invoice from a supplier. I wrote an email from Andy to the cancellations, just a simple "no problem, I understand, and if your circumstances change please get in touch." I sent the invoice from Andy's email to my email address, because that's what he would usually do. I pay his invoices and I do his books. After that I spent twenty minutes scrolling through YouTube clips of sports, and various landscaping gurus showing their latest work—basically whatever the algorithm served up. Then I put Andy's phone down and turned on our TV. I didn't know if police could tell if something had played on your TV screen or not, but I figured it was possible, at least, with smart TVs. I found a game and let it play. I changed my clothes, washed my face, and went back downstairs, where I left my own phone on the kitchen table.

I took my car. Andy's truck would have been better, but I never drove it, and I had to do everything the way I usually would. Before I left the house I took an old tarp from the barn and laid it out in my trunk. There was one car at the gate, and by the time I was leaving, a second had arrived. I drove to Mehuron's and saw through my rearview mirror that one of the cars—a red Jeep Renegade—was trailing me. They made no attempt to hide the fact that they were following me. They drove so close behind me that I could make out the features of the man in the driver's seat. He was in his forties, a little overweight, and wearing a hat and a scraggly beard and a bright orange jacket. I drove on like I didn't see him, but when I got to the parking lot at Mehuron's I took a spot on the far left of the building. I kept everything slow and casual when I got out of the car. When I went into the store, I got a cart and started down the first aisle. There were people there who knew me. Sarah Butler from the post office and Billy Ware who teaches at the school. Billy came over to say hello. He squeezed my hand and said how sorry he was. Sarah went red and muttered something under her breath, then ran away down the aisle. I guess she's more of a Facebook user than Billy, or maybe she's just more gullible. I loaded up the cart with all sorts of stuff. A carton of sparkling water. Three big boxes of cereal. I added three kinds of jam and a cantaloupe. I could see Orange Jacket lurking out of the corner of my eye, but I never looked directly at him. I filled up my cart quickly and then I left it in one place, as if it was too awkward to move. I walked down the aisle, trying hard to keep my body language casual, browsing as if I had all the time in the world. I picked up two cans of chickpeas and jar of pesto. I wandered back to my cart and piled the cans and jar on top of the other food. Then I wandered away again. I picked up a jar of capers, got to the end of the aisle, and kept going. As soon as I was around the corner I started jogging. I pushed through the plastic curtain that separated the supermarket from the storage warehouse at the back, and then I started running. At the back of the warehouse I nearly ran into Paul Thomas, who was signing for a delivery. I knew Paul. He'd worked for Mehuron's for ten years.

"Sorry," I gasped.

"No trouble, Leanne," he said. He looked at me curiously but passed no other comment as I walked quickly around him and outside. I ran around the side of the building, climbed into my car, and drove away. There was no sign of Orange Jacket. I drove fast, took a turn, then another and another, and then I pulled in at the side of the road to make sure that I really had lost him. A minute passed. I drove on in the direction of Lover's Lane. I knew the house, kind of. It was an old one, owned by an older couple who were having trouble maintaining it. They'd hired Andy once to do some yard work, but that was years ago now. It was still snowing, and the snow was already inches thick on the roadway, but my car had snow tires and I was used to the conditions. The Barretts' house was set back off the road, at the end of a winding driveway. I let out a long breath once I made it around the first corner of that drive and my car was hidden from the road by the trees. The house was as I remembered it. It was a hundred-year-old farmhouse, with stone chimneys at either end. The garden was overgrown and tangled and the paint on the walls was peeling a little. In the gloom of the day the place looked unloved. How long had it been since the Barretts had visited? How long until they came again?

I got out of the car and walked around to the back. Andy was there, standing under the covered porch. He looked like a stranger. Older, exhausted, broken. There was a smear of mud on his face, or maybe . . . it was dark. Maybe it was dried blood. He saw me coming and he didn't move. There was no relief in his eyes. All I saw there was dread and despair.

I went to him and threw my arms around him. He didn't move. I wrapped my arms around him tighter still, pulling him down to me, pressing my warm cheek to his cold one.

"I love you. I love you, okay? We're going to get through this."

It took time, a full minute, maybe, before something released in him and he sagged out of his rigid stance, his arms coming around me and finally hugging me back. I held on for as long as I could. When we let go, we both turned to look at the plastic-wrapped body that lay on the stone floor of the porch behind him. I shuddered. The reality of it was a mind fuck. Andy had found painter's tape and plastic bags from somewhere, and he'd done a good job wrapping Simon's body. It made it easier, that I wouldn't have to see Simon's face, or his clothes even. I told myself that what was lying in front of me was just a package. Just a package to be disposed of.

"Are there any cameras?" I asked. "Security cameras, I mean?"

"I've been all around and I didn't see any. None inside either."

"How did you get inside? Did you break a window?"

Andy shook his head. "They used to leave a spare key in the hollow of a tree at the back of the property. It was still there when I checked. I put it back."

"Okay. And you wiped the key down?"

"Yes."

"Right. Good." I went to pick up one end of Simon's body—what seemed to be his feet—but Andy held out a hand to stop me.

"No."

"You're exhausted. I can help."

"No," he said, almost fiercely. "I don't want you touching him."

I didn't argue, I just stood back and waited and watched while Andy heaved the body into his arms. He struggled, clumsy with tiredness, but I didn't try to help again. I opened the trunk of my car and Andy put the body inside. He had to bend the legs to fit them in. They bent easily. I felt queasy. Was it too soon for rigor mortis? It must be. A thought struck me.

"Are you sure he's dead?" I asked.

Andy didn't look at me. He stared into the trunk at the plastic-wrapped body. "I'm sure."

I nodded. I reached inside and tucked the tarp I'd brought around the body, then I took Andy's hand and squeezed it.

"Baby, you're going to have to get in there."

His hand jerked out of mine. He looked down at me like he didn't know who I was.

"It's the only way I can get us back to the house without you being seen. If you lie down in the back, the journalists at our house might see you. And everyone has to think that you were home all night. That we were both home all night. Everything relies on that."

"What about the back seat, under a blanket or something?"

"I don't have one, and even if I did it would be too risky."

"What about . . ." He gestured toward Simon's body. "We need to bury him. Did you bring shovels?"

I shook my head. "We're taking him home."

"What?"

"We have to get home right now. Do you understand? We don't have time to go somewhere for an hour to dig a hole and . . . whatever. We need to get you home right now, and you need to make some phone calls from the house or walk around outside where the press can see you, or both. And I need to make some calls of my own. Okay? Look, I have a plan, but I don't have time to explain. Please get in. Please, Andy."

He turned and looked back at the body. The trunk of my car was big enough for both of them, but only just. Andy clenched his fists, then did it. He climbed inside. He had to almost tuck himself around Simon's body to make himself fit.

When I hesitated, he said, "Close it, Lee. Right now. And get us home. I can't do this for very long."

I did what he said. I closed the trunk, got in the car, and drove away. Before I got to the end of the driveway I stopped the car, turned the engine off, and opened the window. I listened hard, made sure that I couldn't hear any other engines approaching, then I turned the key in the ignition and drove again, fast this time, but not too fast. The snow was falling heavily, and snow tires can only do so much. If I ran the car off the road, we could not recover from that. But I made no mistakes. I drove the car, fast but carefully, home. When I approached the driveway there were only two cars parked there, and there was no sign of the red jeep. I did not slow as I passed them.

I drove the car into our barn and closed and bolted the barn doors before I hurried to the trunk and opened it. Andy scrambled out, half falling and frantic. I reached for him.

"Was there enough air? Could you breathe?"

He was gasping. He clenched his eyes shut and opened them again, twice, three times, like he was trying to clear his vision. It was a minute before he could speak.

"There was enough air," he said. "It was just, being in there . . . with him. Fuck." I hugged him, and this time he was the one to push me away. He held me at arm's length. "What's the plan, Lee? What are we going to do with him?"

I moved around him and closed the trunk. "The first thing we're going to do is go inside. You're going to take off those clothes and put them in a plastic bag. You're going to shower and change and then you're going to make those phone calls or video calls. I don't care who you call, just make it as normal as you can, okay? I'm going to make breakfast and we're going to follow as normal a routine as possible for the next hour. And then . . . then we'll deal with him."

Andy did what I asked. He called two suppliers and put a pause on some orders he'd already placed for jobs that had just been cancelled. He sent another text message to Craig. I plugged my phone in to charge and replied to a text message that Julie Bradley had sent me, asking how I was. I called Matthew Wright. He didn't answer the phone, so I left a message. I got some messages from journalists, which I ignored. And an hour after we came home we went back out to the barn, and we buried Simon. First we crowbarred up the bricks that formed the barn floor and stacked them neatly to one side. There was a thick layer of fine stone and sand underneath, and clay underneath that, but Andy's mini excavator was parked in the barn, and we used it to dig a grave that was eight feet deep. Andy slid the body into it, but before he let the body go he cut long holes in the plastic bags, either side.

"Should we use quicklime, or something?" I asked. I had some idea that lime did something to remains to make them decompose quicker.

"I don't have any," Andy said. "I use ready-mixed concrete. Also, it wouldn't help. It would just dry out the corpse and preserve it. We want decomposition. We won't need to worry about the smell. Not when we're burying this deep."

He got back into the excavator and started pushing dirt into the hole. I went to the barn window, feeling shaken. I checked to make sure that no one was coming. The press had so far shown us the courtesy of not coming onto our property, but that could always change. And Matthew Wright could choose to stop by. There was no one there. We were lucky that Andy had everything we needed to relay the floor—bags of sand and stone dust. We got to work. By lunchtime Andy was brushing dirt across the bricks, to make them look like they'd never been moved. We stood back, dirty and tired. The barn looked like it always had.

We went inside and got into the shower together. We held on to each other as if we'd been parted for years. We got clean and got dressed. I was the first one downstairs. I called the supermarket, apologized for abandoning my cart that morning, and explained that there'd been a journalist following me and I had panicked. The store said they could deliver my shopping later in the day, and I accepted their kind offer. Then I made coffee. Andy came in. His eyes were old and haunted.

"I'm so sorry," he said.

I shook my head. "No. We're not doing this." I took his hand. "We're never going to talk about it again. Do you understand me? Last night never happened."

His eyes searched mine.

"We went to bed at ten o'clock. You didn't sleep well. Nightmares. In the morning you slept in. By the time you woke up I'd already gone downstairs. You stayed in bed. You looked at your phone, sent some emails, and watched basketball on ESPN. You heard me leave for the supermarket and you got out of bed when you heard me come back. We had a late breakfast together. That's what happened, Andy."

He poured two cups of coffee.

"That's what happened," he said. He didn't look like himself, not yet, but he would, given enough time. "I need to go and dig a drainage trench, or something. Someone might have heard the excavator. We should have an obvious explanation for that." It was good that he was thinking that way. Thinking ahead. He held my gaze. "And tomorrow we're going to get Grace back. I don't care about journalists or principals or anyone else. We're going to fight for this family. And we're staying together."

"Yes."

He turned and pulled my chair closer to his, close enough that he could put his hands to my face and rest his forehead against mine. Then he just stayed there, holding on.

"I love you," I said.

"We can do this," he said.

"Yes."

CHAPTER THIRTY-FOUR

Matthew

O n Saturday morning Matthew drove to headquarters. The place was mostly empty. Weekends were always quieter. Sarah Jane was there. She didn't seem surprised to see him. "Anything on the phone data?"

She shook her head. "I spoke to a guy who told me we've been moved onto a priority list, and we should get something next week, possibly the week after. The only way we'd get it faster would be if we could prove that there was imminent danger to life. They tell me a missing girl is not enough."

"Fuck 'em," he said. "We're going to get this bastard without their help." His buddy the prosecutor had agreed that Rita Gallo's statement was enough to justify a search of the Jordans' Waitsfield home. They'd decided to wait to submit the warrant application until the morning, as the judge on call over the weekend was a little more police friendly. But Matthew expected to have that warrant on his desk by 10:00 A.M. at the latest, and then, then they would see.

"The Jordans have agreed to hand over the GPS data on their cars," Sarah Jane said. "Their lawyer called and said if we wanted to send over a technician to download the data, that wouldn't be an issue."

Matthew made a face. "If they're handing over the data, then there's nothing there that will help us."

"I figured," Sarah Jane said. "But I checked. They actually have four vehicles. Rory Jordan drives a BMW X7, and Jamie has an X5. Simon drives the Jeep Wrangler. But there's a fourth vehicle, registered in Rory's name—a fifteen-year-old Dodge Ram. I'm guessing that doesn't have GPS. I bet they hand over the data to the BMWs and the Jeep. And I bet that'll be squeaky clean. But if Simon went back to Stowe to move her, he would have taken the Dodge Ram. He's not stupid."

Matthew nodded. It made sense.

"The only thing is, I'm pretty sure he didn't. Move her, that is." Sarah Jane gestured for Matthew to come closer. She turned her computer screen so that he could see it. "On Tuesday night, Simon Jordan was online. He posted a live video clip of himself playing a video game. He responded to comments as they came in, so I don't think it could have been a recording. When he ended the live stream he stayed in the comments, and he also watched and commented on other posts. He was pretty visible."

Matthew watched as Sarah Jane pulled up video clip after video clip. To him the content seemed inane. Pointless. Simon didn't mention Nina or the fact that she was missing. He talked about the game he was playing and bitched about his course load at Northwestern. He seemed a little agitated, a little wound up, but you could watch the video and assume that this was a normal college kid who had nothing extraordinary going on in his life. His online activity slowed and stopped at around 2:00 A.M.

"If people arrived first at the house at six A.M. and he went offline at two A.M., that leaves him four hours. He could drive to Stowe and back in less than two. Do we think he could have moved the body in that time?"

Sarah Jane was nodding. "I've been thinking about that. And I think he absolutely could have, but he would have had limited time to take her somewhere else, right? So it might make it easier for us to figure out where he brought her to."

Matthew was still looking at the computer screen. Sarah Jane had stopped the video, and Simon's face was frozen in a kind of smirking grin. Matthew gestured at the screen. "If Simon was doing all this to try to generate some kind of digital alibi, it wasn't very effective. He left himself a window of four hours, which means he's not in the clear.

"Let's say it takes him fifty minutes to drive to Stowe. An hour to get to her, dig her body up, fill in the hole and disguise the area, and get her to his car. He's got two hours and ten minutes left, including the hour it would take to drive home. I think he must have chosen a location somewhere between Stowe and Waitsfield. Somewhere he knows well. Ideally there'd be a building, right? So he doesn't have to dig again. Worst-case scenario for him, somewhere he could stash her body quickly for a few days until he can find a permanent way to dispose of it."

Sarah Jane looked grim. "That makes sense. I'll start looking for possible locations."

"It might be worth looking back over his social media feed. Look for local climbing or hiking routes he's been on in the last year. See if you can find any derelict buildings nearby. Or weekend homes, I guess, might be an option. Though that would be higher risk."

It would be like finding a needle in a haystack, but without a body this case was going to be all but impossible to solve.

"I feel like I'm going to end up with a pretty long list," said Sarah Jane.

"Yes. But let's get out and drive the routes away from the Stowe house today, and look for cameras. A lot of weekend homes have cameras on their gates now, or on their front door. If we're lucky enough to nail Simon's car on camera a few times, maybe we can start narrowing things down. I know it's a lot of work, Sarah Jane, and the chances of a result are slim, but cases have been broken on smaller chances."

Sarah Jane's back straightened. "Absolutely." She put her hands on her keyboard, hesitated, then said, "My friends call me SJ. You could, if you like. Not that we're friends." She flushed and kept her eyes on her screen.

"SJ," Matthew said. "That works."

Back at his desk he picked up the phone and dialed Arnie Waugh's number. He was confident that Waugh would answer, Saturday or not, and he wasn't disappointed.

"Mr. Waugh—"

"Call me Arnie, please."

"Sure," Matthew said, having no intention of it. "I'm following up on my call from yesterday, about Simon's phone. If he's willing to release it to us I can send someone to pick it up in the next half an hour. We're happy to provide him with a replacement if he needs one."

"I'm afraid we're not going to be able to facilitate you there."

"Mr. Waugh, I hope you told your client that this is a pointless delay. We'll get this data one way or the other. Probably as early as next week."

"Fact is, Detective, there's a little bit of a problem with the phone."

"A problem."

"I called my client last night. He explained—and he was very embarrassed, I'd just like to make that clear—he explained that his mother borrowed his phone, to take a photo I believe, and then she dropped it in a lake. Entirely by accident, of course."

Matthew looked across the squad room to Sarah Jane. He wanted to lock eyes with someone, to communicate the magnitude of the bullshit he was hearing, but Sarah Jane—SJ—had her head bent over her work.

"Which lake?" Matthew asked.

"I'm sorry?"

"Which lake, Mr. Waugh?"

"I believe it was a small lake on their own property. It really was an innocent mishap."

"Right. So your client will consent to us searching for the phone?"

"I'm sorry?"

"Divers. We can send in divers, with specialist equipment. A small body of water like that, it shouldn't be too much of a challenge to retrieve the phone. We can get a warrant, or you can get your client's parents' consent. What's it going to be?"

Arnie Waugh sighed. "Oh, I don't think we're going to be consenting to much of anything, Detective Wright. But I wish you luck with your endeavors."

Matthew ended the call and went to Sarah Jane's desk to fill her in. Her phone was on her desk, screen up and awake. Her screen saver was a photograph of her with her family. They were standing on a jetty in a row of four, with arms linked and grins for the camera. There was Sarah Jane, an older couple who were almost certainly her parents, and a man in his mid-twenties. That must be her brother who had died. He had dark hair cut very short, and a beard. And a face that looked similar to the face that looked back at Matthew every time he looked in the mirror. Oh. Okay. He looked like her brother. Was that the reason for her slight awkwardness around him?

She realized he was there, and he'd been silent too long. Matthew cleared his throat and filled her in on his conversation with Waugh.

"We'll get a warrant and get divers out," Matthew said. "That lake is more of a pond. I saw it. It can't be deeper than fifteen or twenty feet."

"I read about a case where they got data from a phone that someone had dropped in a toilet," Sarah Jane said, as her hands flew across her keyboard. "But the pond would be deeper. When did she drop it? Yesterday? How long is too long?"

Matthew frowned. "I don't know. But I'll talk to Foley. See what he says." He retreated to his own desk and made the call. It was lunchtime on a Saturday. There was every possibility that he wouldn't answer. Christopher Foley was head of forensics, and a man who liked to keep a strict boundary between his home and work lives. He'd told Matthew that unless he was on call, his cell phone was turned off and tucked away in a drawer in his kitchen.

The phone answered on the fifth ring.

"Yeah?"

"I wasn't sure you'd pick up. Thought the phone would be off."

"I forgot," Christopher said.

"Okay to run something by you?"

"Not a problem."

Matthew told him about the phone and the pond. "Might be in there twenty-four hours, maybe a little longer. At its deepest my best guess is it might be twenty feet. At its widest point I think maybe five hundred yards. I guess what I want to know is what the chances are that we find it, and if we do, whether or not we'll get anything from it."

"It shouldn't be a problem to find it. The boys will go in with metal detectors. If we know the general area it went in, that will make it go easier, but even without that information, that sort of area, we should be able to track it down."

"And the data?"

"What kind of phone was it?"

"I don't know, but given the kid, I'd say it was something new. Latest model iPhone or Samsung."

Christopher's tone was that of someone trying to work out a math problem. "Some of those phones have tested in lab conditions as waterproof for at least half an hour at ten or fifteen feet. Now, in this situation it's been in there longer, and very possibly deeper. So let's assume that water got through the case. Still not the end of the world. We can take it apart, dry it out. If it's an Android we can hack it. If it's an iPhone, hacking will be harder, but we should be able to get some information. Most of what's on an iPhone is encrypted, but not all."

"So you think it's worth it?"

"I do."

"I'm going to get the warrant."

"I'll line up the divers."

CHAPTER THIRTY-FIVE

Jamie

I went to Simon's room and started going through his things. It didn't take long to confirm that his jacket and boots were missing, and some of his clothes. I went to the mudroom and laundry and ultimately the garage, and they weren't there either. We keep our hiking packs in the garage, hanging from hooks. My day pack was there, but Simon's big backpack was gone.

I went to Rory's study and knocked. He was on a call, but he ended it when he saw my face.

"What's wrong?" he said.

I told him about the missing clothes and bag, and his face fell.

"I just, I don't know where he's going. The weather's so bad, and it's only going to get worse. He's hardly going to camp out. Where's he going to stay? Did he have money? Did he take cash?"

"I don't think so," Rory said. "Not much. I changed the code on the safe."

"Why did you do that?" I asked. What a stupid thing to do. And what a stupid time to do it.

Rory shook his head but didn't answer me. "This was such a mistake. If he gets caught . . . they'll charge him for sure and we won't be able to get him bail."

I sat in the chair opposite the desk. "Do you think he's going to

Canada? If he's hiking, maybe he's planning on taking the Long Trail north."

"Maybe. Probably." Rory straightened up. He reached out and took my hand.

"But will he be safe? The weather . . . No one hikes north at this time of year."

"Simon knows what he's doing in the backcountry. If his plan is to go north, I'm sure he'll get there. When he feels safe, I'm sure he'll call us."

I didn't say anything for a moment. I just sat there and thought things through. "Maybe it is a good thing," I said in the end. "In Canada he *will* be safe, right? And no one can accuse us of hiding him if we didn't even know that he was leaving."

"It makes him look guilty. It makes it harder to defend him. And Canada has an extradition treaty with the US. If he's charged here, they'll be able to arrest him there and bring him back. So unless he has a plan to move on from Canada . . . did he take his passport?"

I looked at Rory's desk. "They're in there. Top drawer."

Rory pulled out the drawer. Two passports inside, not three.

"Maybe we should try to get ahead of things. Do you think we could rent a place for him, and get money to him, but through . . . I don't know, a corporation or something? Some way that can't be traced back to us?"

Rory thought about it. "We could try, but anything we do to try to cover our tracks just makes us look guilty too. Right now he hasn't been charged. Probably the best thing we can do is act like everything's normal."

"We could say that we wanted Simon to get away from the press and all the attention. He's always wanted to hike the Long Trail. Now is the perfect time. He's not at school. He needs to get away from people."

"Except that we can't tell anyone where we think he is, or they'll just set out after him and pick him up before he reaches the border."

"Then we'll just fudge it for a few days. We won't say anything about Simon going for now. We'll wait. How long do you think it will take him to cross?" I started to feel hopeful.

"It's about eighty miles from here. I think . . . Simon's pretty fit. Five days, maybe. He might be able to do it in four if he pushes really hard."

"Okay." I tried to make my voice sound confident. "Then we just have to avoid talking to the police for five or six days. If they want to see Simon, we say he's come down with something. Covid, maybe. And then when the time is up we can say he's hiking to Canada for a break, and they can search for him all they like at that point. By then he should have been in touch, so we'll have worked out a plan. Really, Rory, I think he didn't tell us because he wanted to protect us. That's not a bad thing."

"I'm sure you're right," Rory said. It was a platitude. It was obvious from his tone that he was thinking about something else entirely.

"I'll leave you to it then." But I didn't leave. I sat there and looked at him. "He said it was an accident."

Rory flinched, but we seemed to have abandoned all attempts to be careful about what we said, and I needed to talk about it.

"Do you believe him?" I asked.

It was a long moment before Rory spoke. But he looked me right in the eye when he did. "Yes. I believe him."

He was lying he was lying he was lying and I could see it as clear as day. Had I always been able to read him so clearly? Pain settled in my heart like a shard of thick glass.

"Okay then."

I left his office and wandered the house. There was nowhere I could go and no one I could call. I had nothing to do. I hadn't listed any clothes online in a week and hadn't responded to any messages about older listings. I couldn't bring myself to care about it. Probably I was done with that now, for good. I would have to find a different way to earn money. I went back to the laundry room. The laundry baskets were full. I tried to remember the last time Rita had been to the house. A week? She hadn't called or messaged to say there was a problem. I guess that meant she didn't want to work for us anymore. I loaded the washing machine and switched it on, then had to fight the urge to sit on the floor and wait for it to finish. I wandered the house. I missed Simon. The missing was a physical ache, deep inside me. *I loved him I loved him I loved him.*

But I knew what he was.

What did that make me?

When Simon was a child, when he was eleven or twelve and he first started going on sleepovers at friends' houses, I'd hated it. His absence left a void in the house. And other parents were so *casual*. I would drop him to the door of whichever friend had invited him and Simon would disappear into the house immediately. I might get a half smile thrown over his shoulder if I was lucky. I would stand at the door and make polite chitchat for the expected minute or two. I would plaster a smile on my face and make and respond to little jokes about how great it was to be able to offload him for a night. *Adult time . . . ha huh huh huh.* And all the time I had to fight the ridiculous urge to tell them that I hated letting him go, that he was so much more precious than they knew, and to urge them to be careful.

I still don't know if other parents feel that way. They don't seem to, but then most parents put on a front about their kids. There are clear social rules. If your kid is a straight-A student, you can acknowledge that, but only if you follow up with a comment about how completely inept they are at softball. If they're a star athlete you have to say something about how the flip side of them being so single minded is all those nightmare 6:00 A.M. starts to get them to training. Basically, the rule is that you have to talk about your kid as if he's something between a mild and a serious inconvenience to the life you actually want to live. What you are not allowed to say is that they are the light and purpose you live for. Not, at least, unless you lose them. Then you can say anything you want. You can tell the truth.

What are the social rules when your child is a murderer?

At five o'clock I started drinking. At nine Rory came to find me and we went to bed. We didn't talk, but there was a tenderness between us that hadn't been there before. We were still in bed on Sunday morning when Arnie Waugh called. Rory put his phone on speaker.

"I just got a call from police," Arnie said. "They framed it as a courtesy call. They have a warrant to search for Simon's phone. They're sending divers to search the lake, apparently. They're probably already there. I'm pretty sure they waited to call me until after their people had gone out to the property."

"Which property?" Rory looked confused.

"Your property. The house at Stowe," Arnie said.

Rory turned to look at me. He seemed to be struggling to understand.

"Thanks, Arnie," I said. "I guess it doesn't make much difference, right? From what Simon tells me, pretty much everything on his phone they could get from the cloud eventually?"

"That's right. I guess they've decided they don't want to wait for that data to come through."

Rory was still staring at me.

"And there's no point in us trying to do anything to stop them, I guess?" I said.

"Nothing you can do, at this point. Better to cooperate. It will back up your story that you dropped it accidentally."

"Which I did."

"Of course."

Arnie rang off.

"Jamie . . ." Rory said. His face was stricken. He said my name again, like I'd done something horrifying. "Jamie."

I tried to explain about the phone. It seemed to take him a long time to understand. Then he picked up his phone and called Arnie back. He paced the room, his right hand on his head, gripping his hair, his left pressing the phone to his ear.

"I don't care what you have to do. You need to stop that search."

There was silence while Arnie responded. I found Rory's shirt and put it on. I got out of bed.

"Baby?" I said. Rory ignored me.

"I don't fucking care! Call a judge. Send someone out there. Send some men. Do *something* to earn your fucking money. And call me back."

Rory hung up. He went to our dressing room and pulled out jeans and a T-shirt.

"What's going on?" I said. But he didn't answer. He left the room, and I heard his feet on the stairs. I scrambled into underwear and jeans, picked up my sneakers, and ran after him. By the time I got downstairs he was opening the door into the garage. He'd put on his boots and grabbed his jacket.

"Rory," I said. He didn't even pause, just pressed the button to open the garage door and climbed into the driver's seat. I ran. There was just enough time for me to get into the passenger seat. He pulled out and drove insanely fast in the direction of Stowe.

"Tell me, Rory. Please, please, tell me what's going on."

He shook his head. "I can't. I would if I could, but I can't."

I stopped talking. I gripped the car door and the side of my seat and held on tight as Rory took corners like a NASCAR driver. When we got to Stowe I half expected to find police tape or an officer at the gates, something or someone to prevent us entering, but it wasn't like that. We were able to drive right up to the house. There were three other vehicles ahead of us—a single white van, a police car, and one other car. Three people stood on the jetty. One of them was Matthew Wright, the other two were police officers in uniform. Our little boat was out in the middle of the lake. There was a woman in it. She was wearing a wet suit and she was leaning over to look down into the water.

Rory got out of the car and ran toward the jetty. I followed, shivering. I didn't have a jacket. I wasn't even wearing a bra. I folded my arms across my chest. Rory waved wildly.

"Get back!" he shouted. "Get away from there."

Matthew Wright came to meet him. The two younger officers followed in Wright's wake, but he waved them backward. He walked right up to Rory until Rory had to stumble to a halt to avoid running into him.

"You can't be here," Rory said. He was breathing hard. "We haven't given our consent. Our attorney will be here any minute."

"We have a warrant, Mr. Jordan. I'd be happy to show it to you."

"I don't care about your goddamn warrant. You should have called us first. You have seriously overstepped here, Wright. Get your people out of the water and off my property, or there will be hell to pay. You hear me? That's my boat out there. Does your warrant allow you to seize my property?"

Wright didn't flinch. His face was like stone. There was no power in Rory's voice, only panic. A shiver went down my back. This wasn't about the phone. Wright's eyes met mine. I think he saw my fear. His eyes narrowed and he turned back to Rory. He opened his mouth to speak, but he was interrupted by a shout from behind him. A man in a diver's hood and mask had emerged from the water beside the boat. He shouted again, something I couldn't quite catch, but the woman in the boat obviously heard it, and her body language changed completely. She stiffened and whipped her head around to look back toward us. She stood up and the boat rocked under her feet before she steadied herself. I thought she would shout to Wright, or gesture to him to return to the jetty. Instead, she just stood there and stared at us. When Wright turned back to look at us, he seemed to have grown taller.

"Why don't you wait right here, Mr. and Mrs. Jordan? Like you said, your attorney will be here any minute." He didn't wait for us to respond. He walked back to the jetty and exchanged a few short words with one of the uniformed officers, who came to stand alongside us. We weren't under arrest. We could have left, maybe, just gotten in our car and driven away. Maybe even all the way to Canada. But we didn't. We stood there that morning and watched as Nina Fraser's body was raised up from the water. Rory was shaking. I reached out and took his hand in mine. He looked at me like he was seeing me for the first time. He took off his jacket and gave it to me. I leaned against him, and he put his arm around me.

"You put her there, didn't you?" I said, quietly, so that I couldn't be heard by the police officer. "You helped him. You tried to hide her. Why?"

He was quiet for so long that I didn't think he was going to answer. And then he said, "I wanted it not to be true. I wanted it all to go away."

I closed my eyes against the pain.

"I love you," I said.

"I'm sorry," he said.

CHAPTER THIRTY-SIX

Leanne

At 3:30 P.M. on Sunday, one week to the day after I went looking for Andy in the barn to tell him how pissed I was that Nina hadn't returned my calls, Matthew Wright came to the inn. I was the one who opened the door to him. A lot of time has passed now, and I remember everything that happened next in a series of images, almost like stills from a movie. The colors are so bright, the details so minute and exact. I remember that Matthew looked exhausted. He had the beginnings of a scruffy beard. The shoulders of his jacket were damp with snowmelt.

"Can I come in? We need to talk."

I knew right away that they'd found her. The distant look was gone. For the first time since I met him, he'd abandoned his professional distance, and there was real compassion in his eyes. I gestured to him to follow, and I led the way into the house. I kept my eyes down, and I noticed dust on the top of the baseboards. I hadn't been keeping up with the cleaning. Grace and Andy were in the living room. Grace was doing the math homework her teacher had assigned for her, and Andy was trying, and failing, to help her with it. Before I left the room to answer the door, they'd been laughing. When I came back with Matthew on my heels, the laughter stopped.

"Um . . . it might be best if I speak to you alone, for now," Matthew said.

"No," I said. "Whatever you have to tell us, Grace is going to have to hear too. Better we hear together."

There was no way to protect Grace from it. Everything would be public knowledge sooner or later. We knew now how it worked. Everything would be dissected and analyzed and discussed like it was entertainment. I sat on the couch so that Grace was between me and Andy. I took her hand. After a minute, Matthew sat in the armchair opposite us. He was awkward. The self-possession he'd had at every other meeting seemed to have deserted him. He sat with his feet apart, and he leaned forward, resting his forearms on his thighs. He took off his gloves, and the skin on his hands was red. He must have been out in the cold for a long time.

"I'm so sorry to tell you this. Nina is dead. We found her body earlier today."

Despite everything, the words hurt. My skin prickled with sudden heat, and my vision darkened at the edges. Grace squeezed my hand hard, and that brought me back. The fire was going and the room was warm, but I remember that her hand felt cold to the touch.

"Where?" asked Andy.

"Her body had been wrapped and weighed down, and placed in the pond at the Jordans' house in Stowe."

Grace was sitting between us, and Andy and I weren't touching, but I still believe that I felt the shudder that went through his body in that moment.

"Simon killed her," I said.

"We think so, but we have more work to do. I . . . I understand that this may be very difficult, but in the interests of building the strongest possible case, it would help us enormously if you didn't comment publicly for now."

"You don't need to worry about that," Andy said. "We won't be talking publicly about Nina or any of this ever again."

Grace was holding my hand so tight. She wasn't crying. None of us were crying.

"We want her back," I said.

Matthew bowed his head. "Yes. Of course. That may take a little time. There are procedures . . . I can tell you more about that when you're ready. And then she will be returned to you."

I wept at that. The words hurt so much. Returned to me. I'd dreamed of that, of having my girl handed back to me. My girl. Not her body. Not just her cold remains. But our Nina was gone forever.

"I'm so sorry," Matthew said. I thought he would leave then, but he didn't. He waited. A minute passed before he spoke again. "There's something else I need to tell you. I need you to hear it from me." He couldn't look me in the eye. "We went to the Jordans' house to speak to Simon. Simon's car was there, but he wasn't. We've tried to find him, but so far we haven't succeeded. We're not sure exactly how long he's been gone."

Matthew looked at us expectantly. My thoughts were heavy and slow, but I forced my brain to cooperate. How should we react? With anger? Outrage? I couldn't muster either, not even an artificial version.

"Did his parents help him to run away?" I asked, in the end.

"We don't know. It's a possibility. Look, again, I know how hard this is, but I need to ask you to trust us. We will do our jobs. We will find out the truth, and we will make sure that those who are guilty are punished."

Andy and I looked at each other. Grace's head was pressed into my shoulder.

"Nina's gone," Andy said, in a voice that rasped with tension and unshed tears. "That's the only thing that matters. After her funeral we'll be going away for a while. We don't want to talk to the press or anyone else. When the dust has settled, we'll come home again." His eyes met mine and I nodded.

So that's what we did. We got Nina's body back one week after she was found. We held a funeral for her, and too many people came. Her friends and ours, and family, but far too many strangers. The service was private, but at the cemetery the vultures came, standing a little distance away, watching us in our grief and taking pictures like we were a pageant put on for their amusement. The next day we left Waitsfield. We went to New York City. Andy's theory was that we needed to keep busy. A beach vacation wouldn't be good for us. We'd have too much time to sit around and think about everything. So we went to the city and we packed every day with things to do and places to go. For the first time in my life I didn't worry about money. We had savings, and while we didn't know exactly what the future held, the money didn't seem worth worrying about. We rented an AirBnB for three weeks and tried very hard to forget. Not Nina. But everything else.

We couldn't escape things completely, of course. We heard about it when Rory Jordan was arrested and charged as an accessory to Nina's murder. It turned out that Nina had been moved from that shallow grave in the woods to the lake, and the only person who could have done that was Rory. He's still denying it, but everyone says the case against him is very strong. Simon killed her. The police are sure of that. She had bruises on her body, old and new, and a fractured jaw. She also had a fractured skull. The police think that Simon might have punched her, hard enough that she fell back and hit her head on the fireplace in the living room of that house. There's some forensic evidence to support the theory, as I understand it, but I haven't asked too many questions. I know enough. Too much, really.

They haven't been able to ask Simon, because they haven't been able to find him. There's a warrant out for his arrest, and sometimes there are "sightings." Matthew Wright calls us every now and again, to reassure us that he's doing everything he can to find Simon. We listen quietly each time, thank him, and hang up. We never talk about what really happened.

We came home to Waitsfield on December 1. We would have sold the inn and moved away, if we could have, but we can never do that now. We'll live here for the rest of our lives. We've decided to keep the inn closed until January, when we're going to relaunch it under a new name, with a new website. We will reinvent ourselves and leave all the mess that was attached to the Black Friar behind. Andy's business is picking up. He got some phone calls and emails after Rory was arrested. There were one or two apologies, but mostly those people who hired him back seemed to want to pretend that nothing had happened. Andy let it go. It was hard for him, but he had no choice. We'd come close to ruin, and he was too grateful to have an income to want to punish people who'd believed the worst about him.

So life began to settle into a kind of normalcy. We missed Nina every day, but we were together, and we were rebuilding.

On December 20, Jamie Jordan came to our home. Andy answered the door, but Jamie asked for me. She looked the same as she always did, almost. She was dressed in a pair of soft brown leather trousers and a black sweater with a black wool jacket and hat. Her hair was still blond and perfect, and her eye makeup had been expertly applied. But she didn't look well. Her lips were so dry they were cracked and bloody. Her nail polish was chipped, and she had dark circles under her eyes that no amount of makeup could hide.

"I'm sorry," she said. "I'm sure you don't want to see me. I didn't come here to upset you, or Andy. Or Grace, of course."

I held the door so that it was mostly closed. I didn't want her looking past me into the house. I didn't want her near my family.

"Why did you come here?"

"I . . . look, I'm sorry. I know sorry is not enough, I know it doesn't help, but I'm so sorry about Nina. I understand the pain you're going through."

I didn't say anything. I didn't have any words.

"I came because . . ." She let her voice trail off. She seemed lost, as if whatever energy had driven her to come to our door had deserted her.

"You should go home now, Jamie," I said. "I don't think we should see each other." I started to close the door.

"Wait," she said. She took a step forward and raised her hand, as if she was going to try to force the issue by holding the door open, then she let her hand fall to her side. "Simon's missing. Everyone thinks he ran away. I thought that too, in the beginning. But it's been a month, and he hasn't touched his bank account. He doesn't have any cash. He hasn't tried to call me or his father. And the police have searched the Long Trail. They even used a helicopter with a body heat camera. They checked security footage at the bus stations. They interviewed all of his friends. There's been no sign of him." She spoke in urgent, abrupt fits and starts, falling into silences where her nerve failed her.

Her eyes were tight on mine.

"So?"

"So I don't think he ran away. I think . . . I think maybe something happened to him."

My face was stone. I stared her down.

"I keep thinking about what I would have done if I thought your child had killed mine and was going to get away with it. I couldn't live with it, I don't think." Her eyes were tight on mine. "I think maybe I would have . . . done something." She let her voice trail away again.

"What are you trying to say, Jamie?"

"Just this." Her eyes filled with tears. She tried to blink them back and failed. She wiped them away with the back of her hand. "If you know anything, if you think that something happened to Simon, please, please tell me. I don't mean that you have to say anything out loud. I'm not trying to make trouble for you or your family." She took a step closer to me. She reached out and gripped my wrist. "But you understand better than anyone what it is to lose a child and not to know. You understand that it's impossible to live with the not knowing. So please. I'm begging you, woman to woman. Mother to mother. If you think that Simon is dead, I'm asking you to nod your head. Just nod your head. I'll walk away, and you'll never hear from me again. But you'll know that you've helped me. You'll have given me some peace."

I saw the pain in her face, in the set of her body, in her eyes. It was eating her alive, in the same way that it had consumed me. She was right. We understood each other. I wanted to take away some small part of her pain. That was a human instinct. I thought about Andy. I thought about Grace. I thought about Nina.

"I can't help you," I said.

And I shut the door.

ACKNOWLEDGMENTS

The first person I want to thank is my agent, Shane Salerno, who is unfailingly ambitious for my writing, who pushes me to stretch, and believes in me when my own belief falters. Thank you, Shane. For that, and for the jokes, which are very nearly as important. And thank you to Ryan C. Coleman, and everyone at the Story Factory, for all that they do to support my books.

I'd like to thank my editors, Anna Valdinger and Emily Krump, for their generosity in bringing their finely honed story instincts to bear on this book, for helping me to get to where I wanted to go with it, and for their enthusiasm for the project. I'm very grateful.

I'd like to thank the entire team at HarperCollins for all that they do, and in particular Kimberley Allsopp, Theresa Anns, Danielle Bartlett, Michelle Bansen, Kate Butler, Lily Capewell, Christopher Connolly, Jim Demetriou, Erin Dunk, Lauren Esser, Jacqui Furlong, Karen-Maree Griffiths, Jennifer Hart, Kaitlin Harri, Tessa James, Susie Jarrett, Bethany Johnsrud, Andy LeCount, Anthony Little, Ashley Mihlebach, Carla Parker, Kelly Roberts, Marie Rossi, Kelly Rudolph, Liate Stehlik, Tina Szanto, Alice Wood, MaryBeth Thomas, Thomas Wilson, and everyone else on the sales and marketing and design teams who do so much work to get our books into the hands of readers.

I'd like to thank the booksellers and librarians who are so open-hearted that they continue to fall in love with books and stories, and who share that love by curating their shelves. Every bookshop and library is a new window into new worlds, for those of us who love words and stories and want, desperately, to visit them.

I'd like to thank Kenny and Freya and Oisín. Freya and Ois, for, among so many other things, understanding my intense need for *chat* after a day spent alone and in my own head. And Kenny, for doing his best to nod seriously and sympathetically when I tell him, on alternate days, that it's all going brilliantly and I love it and I love writing and everything about it; and also that it's the worst disaster and I'm deep in a hole with no way out and surely, *surely*, the answer is to get a real job again. Thank you for holding my hand through the wobbly moments.

I'd like to thank Peter Mandych, from Country Mile Vermont, who acted as my guide to all things Vermont. Peter brought my lazy legs most of the way up the Hedgehog Brook Trail, and drove me around and answered my endless questions. Thank you, Peter, for your patience and all your help, and apologies for the wild liberties I have at times taken, in service of the story.

Thanks to my sister, Fíona, who flew from Dublin to Vermont and hung out with me for my week of research. Fí, it was a lot of fun. (Next time I'm thinking closer to home—I have plans, let's talk).

And I'd like to thank you, reader. My theory is that the people who read all the way to the end of the acknowledgements either loved or hated the book. Either way, they have too much emotion left to just close the cover when they get to the end of the story. If my theory is correct, I really hope for you that it's the former. Either way, thanks for taking the time to read my book. Thanks for taking the chance.

If you'd like to stay in touch with me, I write a quarterly email to my readers. Generally, I write to complain (in exaggerated terms) about whatever writing challenge is bothering me that day, to share some photos from a book tour or writing life, or to tell you about a new book I'm writing/releasing. If you think you'd like to hear from me, you can sign up for my emails here:

dervlamctiernan.com/newsletter/

Would you like to hear directly from Dervla? Sign up at the link below to receive a quarterly email from Dervla with book news, giveaways, and inside jokes.*

Subscribers to Dervla's emails also get access to a private page on her website, with cut scenes from published books and excerpts from works in progress.

Newsletter sign up:
dervlamctiernan.com/newsletter/

Connect with Dervla:
dervlamctiernan.com
@dervlamctiernan
@DervlaMcTiernan
@DervlaMcTiernan

---

*Quality of jokes not guaranteed.

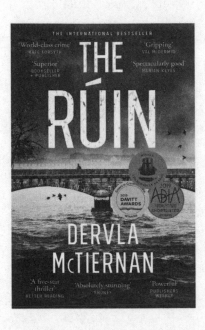

Galway 1993: Young Garda Cormac Reilly is called to a scene he will never forget. Two silent, neglected children – fifteen-year-old Maude and five-year-old Jack – are waiting for him at a crumbling country house. Upstairs, their mother lies dead.

Twenty years later, a body surfaces in the icy black waters of the River Corrib. At first it looks like an open-and-shut case, but then doubt is cast on the investigation's findings – and the integrity of the police. Cormac is thrown back into the cold case that has haunted him his entire career – what links the two deaths, two decades apart? As he navigates his way through police politics and the ghosts of the past, Detective Reilly uncovers shocking secrets and finds himself questioning who among his colleagues he can trust.

What really did happen in that house where he first met Maude and Jack? *The Rúin* draws us deep into the dark heart of Ireland and asks who will protect you when the authorities can't – or won't.

'Corruption, clandestine cover-ups and criminal conspiracy ... as moving as it is fast-paced' Val McDermid

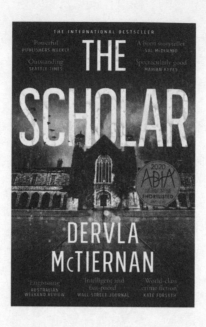

When Dr Emma Sweeney stumbles across the victim of a hit and run outside Galway University late one evening, she calls her partner, Detective Cormac Reilly, bringing him first to the scene of a murder that would otherwise never have been assigned to him. A security card in the dead woman's pocket identifies her as Carline Darcy, a gifted student and heir apparent to Irish pharmaceutical giant Darcy Therapeutics. The multi-billion-dollar company has a finger in every pie, from sponsoring university research facilities to funding political parties to philanthropy – it has funded Emma's own ground-breaking research. The enquiry into Carline's death promises to be high profile and high pressure.

As Cormac investigates, evidence mounts that the death is linked to a Darcy laboratory and, increasingly, to Emma herself. Cormac is sure she couldn't be involved, but could his loyalty to Emma have led him to overlook evidence? Has it made him a liability?

'Atmospheric and beautifully paced, with nuanced characters and a gripping plot – *The Scholar* has it all' Chris Hammer

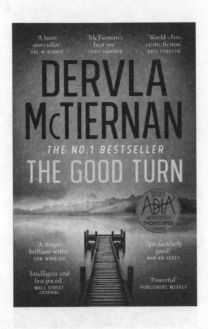

Police corruption, an investigation that ends in tragedy and the mystery of a little girl's silence – three unconnected events that will prove to be linked by one small town.

While Detective Cormac Reilly faces enemies at work and trouble in his personal life, Garda Peter Fisher is relocated out of Galway with the threat of prosecution hanging over his head. But even that is not as terrible as having to work for his overbearing father, the local copper for the pretty seaside town of Roundstone.

For some, like Anna and her young daughter, Tilly, Roundstone is a refuge from trauma. But even this village on the edge of the sea isn't far enough to escape from the shadows of evil men.

'A haunting mystery that will have you turning pages late into the night. This is *Gone Girl*-level good writing' Janet Evanovich

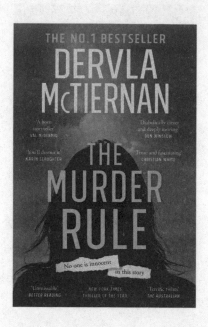

New York Times Thriller of the Year

First rule: make them like you.
Second rule: make them need you.
Third rule: make them pay.

They think I'm a young, idealistic law student, that I'm passionate about reforming a corrupt and brutal system.

They think I'm working hard to impress them.

They think I'm here to save an innocent man from death row.

They're wrong.

I'm going to bury him.

'You'll devour it' Karin Slaughter

'Tense and fascinating' Christian White

'Terrific twists' *The Australian*